For my granddaughter Brinley,

May her path as a young woman in today's world be far easier than it was for the women who preceded her.

Also by Lynda Drews

Run at Destruction: A True Fatal Love Triangle

Circle of Innocence: A Door County Mystery

Acknowledgements

Desperate Parallels is a work of fiction inspired by my IBM global executive career. While working in America and Japan, I learned first-hand the issues women faced, and continue to face, in the corporate business world.

I would like to express my thanks to Darlene Blecha and her book club for providing valuable critiques of *Desperate Parallels* during its infancy. In addition, I want to thank Kozuko Stone for validating the Japanese culture and customs' research I portray in these pages.

Note: For consistency, all Japanese names are given in English order with given name first and family name second.

-1-

Sunday October 24, 2010
Tokyo and New York

Asami Fujioka's French-manicured fingernails had been her dinner, a wretched substitute for sushi. She bolted off the train at Shimokitazawa on the lookout for her best friend. Curry-scented wind gusts threw dirt in her eyes and tangled her henna streaked hair. Under the inky sky, the distant music clubs' pounding beats matched those inside her chest.

It was her *hāfu*—half Japanese/half American—daughter's twenty-first birthday. She and Hana were to have met at Inokashira Park for Asami's power walk, one of her best coping measures, then to have followed that with Hana's birthday dinner at Sushi Dai. The restaurant's wait time would've been long. Asami had planned to suffer it graciously.

Hana, however, had never shown up.

Asami scurried down the stairs in three inch heels, her Burberry jacket billowing out, her shoulder bag swinging erratically.

Jiro Kishima waved, a cigarette elegantly held in his fingertips. As an award winning film director and actor, his strikingly "pretty" features always drew glances from women who didn't know he was gay and from men who did. They'd met in primary school where neither had fit in.

Asami hopped off the last step and crushed his free hand with hers. "Oh Jiro-kun, thank you for coming. I know you've got a flight at daybreak."

"My dear, take a deep breath. I have plenty of time. You said you haven't been able to reach Hana, but she sent you a text?"

"Yes. It arrived three nights ago while I was sleeping. Here, I'll read it to you." She pulled out her cell. "*Off to Fuji Five Lakes Region to hike and think. See you on Sunday at 4.*"

Asami's eyes jerked up. "That was nearly five hours ago! Over the weekend, I tried Hana's cell a number of times, but she never answered. Until today, I wasn't really worried. Beneath those hiking trails are magnetic deposits, often making cell phones useless."

Jiro soothed, "I'm certain there's a logical explanation. After all, it *is* Hana's birthday. Before meeting you, she might've been celebrating with friends. Maybe she got caught up in all the excitement, not to mention the saké." He smiled, raising his brows.

"I thought of that." Asami's fingers latched on to her jacket zipper, sliding it up and down, up and down. "But I've already contacted Hana's best girlfriends and they haven't heard from her. I've also checked the news. No train or bus incidents have been reported, so then I considered a hiking accident. I even called the closest hospital to the Five Lakes Region, but she wasn't admitted."

Asami clutched Jiro's arm. "What—what if Hana didn't go hiking? She keeps her gear in her apartment. I couldn't go in alone, you know, just—just in case. Hana said she needed to think. What does that mean?"

"My dear, it does no good to speculate."

How could she not? When heavy issues clouded a young person's mind, suicide, so often, was the solution. Yet Asami had no reason to believe Hana would do such a thing.

Jiro linked his arm into hers. "I'm sure Hana's fine. I bet she simply returned to her apartment, exhausted from her trip, and dozed off. Come, we'll go check."

Down the narrow street he directed Asami leading her into the bohemian stomping grounds for Tokyo's young and earthy crowd. In addition to enticing hipsters into quirky cafés and funky late night shops, the flashing marquees made Jiro's silver ponytail glimmer.

The red paper lantern of Kimura's Izakaya, a Japanese pub and eatery, came into view. Sandwiched between it and a small Shinto shrine was Hana's apartment entrance.

Asami rushed into the dimly lit vestibule and sped up the stairs, Jiro behind her. Toward Hana's second floor door she hustled, rapped loudly, then placed her ear to the door.

A faint mewing sound was her only response.

"Oh Jiro-kun... Hana's not here, unless..."

There was no way she would utter the unspeakable.

A dose of hives exploded on her neck.

* * *

Mom's sagely advice, "Worry gives small things big shadows," chided Etta Martin's thoughts. She pressed her palm to the cab's smudgy window, her fingers splayed peacock-plumage style. Slices and slivers of Manhattan peeked through. Coffee churned in her stomach. The stench from her half eaten breakfast burrito, still in her carry on, made it worse.

Decked out in what her daughter had dubbed "mom's cowboy tuxedo," jeans and a jean jacket—totally uncool for hip New York—Etta leaned over the seat. "Is that your daughter?" Taped to the taxi's dashboard was a photo of a young woman attired in a cap and purple gown.

The female cabbie glanced back and smiled. "Yes, she just graduated from NYU."

"You must be proud. Mine attended Northwestern. I'm here to visit her, but she better call soon. She's to tell me where you're to drop me off."

"No worries."

Etta only wished that was true. The prior evening, she'd left messages for both Chloe and her boyfriend, Henri. They were to have confirmed whether Etta should go directly to the Bliss Café or to first make a stop at their Greenwich Village apartment. Etta's Chicago flight had touched down at 9:02 a.m. There'd been no voice messages or texts so she'd tried Chloe again. When her recorded message had clicked in, that specific "small thing" had sprouted roots and had been gaining ground ever since.

In the rearview mirror, the cabbie's eyes intersected with Etta's. "So what's on your agenda?"

"Central Park, the 9/11 site, and tickets to *Jersey Boys*, but girl-talk is the main event. My daughter and her boyfriend just moved in together. It'll be good to see if that arrangement is working out as well as she claims." Etta gazed out the window as her cab joined dozens of others spilling off the Williamsburg Bridge into Manhattan's Lower East Side. Why could she voice her concerns to a friendly stranger but not to her thirty-two-year-old daughter?

When Henri had moved in with Chloe it had been a big step for her daughter—a big one for Etta as well. She continued to feel as if she had chronic heartburn and nothing would relieve it. Her fear that Henri might hurt Chloe, as Paul had, was getting in the way. *Shit!* or *Merde!* as Henri would say. It was a despicable thing for a mother to admit, but jealousy could also be a factor. Chloe and her charming French Canadian were living the life Etta had yearned for but had only briefly tasted.

The taxi drove past the shoddy brick storefront of Stan's Mattress Outlet and it triggered a viable thought. Perhaps Chloe and Henri were making up for lost time and they'd muted their cells.

That made perfect sense!

Chloe had just returned from a Japanese business trip. Etta and her daughter both worked for Tripoint Technology, Chloe in New York and Etta in Chicago. Chloe had called as soon as she'd landed in Tokyo, already missing Henri.

Etta had given her a pep talk. "Honey, hang in there. Remember, this is a career stepping stone for you, just as it was for me. What's more, you'll get to spend time with Hana and her mom. How lucky is that?" Dear, crazy Asami. For twenty-six years, Etta had considered their friendship to be a sweet responsibility.

Chloe, however, was an extra-sweet responsibility—one with confetti sprinkles and bitter chocolate shavings on top. Even if Chloe had muted her cell, before doing so, she should've texted Etta their Sunday plans. Her daughter knew how Etta worried.

She also knew her prior actions were the reason why.

Up ahead, Etta could spot the Bliss Café's yellow awning. She had to make a decision. It was senseless to secure a table and hope Chloe and Henri would show. She leaned across the seat to give the cabbie Chloe's address, just as her cell rang, the name "Henri Broussard" on the display.

Relief surged through Etta, renewed excitement on its heels. "Hi there!" she said, opting for a perky greeting rather than a reprimand. "I'm—"

"Listen Etta…" A tremor filled Henri's voice.

Her stomach lurched. "Is—is something wrong? Are you with Chloe?"

"No. I'm in the hall outside our apartment. She's inside and the door's dead-bolted. I didn't call you last night because—well, because we'd had an argument—"

Her body curled forward. *Dear God!* Could history be repeating itself?

"—but Etta, believe me, it wasn't that bad. I'd taken a gig after I promised I wouldn't."

Her torso straightened up. Henri was right! Of course, he was right!

"She texted me," he continued. "She said I should sleep at a friend's. This morning, I knew you were coming. I wanted to patch things up. But, mon Dieu! She won't answer her cell or our door!"

Etta gripped her knee, her knuckles white. "Henri, you must call the police!"

* * *

Outside her daughter's apartment, Asami paced on the dimly lit tiled floor, her heels clicking in rhythm to her breathing's rapid tempo. Jiro had offered to go in first. If Hana was inside, she had to be okay. Asami couldn't think about the alternative. Instead, she concentrated on not scratching her neck with her fingernail nubs, although it felt as if a colony of fire ants had nested.

Her eyes strayed to the adjoining apartment. Weeks earlier, she'd voiced her concern over Hana's building's lack of security. "Mama, don't stress." Hana had kissed Asami's cheek. "This neighborhood's safe. Remember, Lucas will also look out for me."

Asami had huffed, "You mean that New York hippie? The one who lives next door? The one who'd had his fill of Sapporos and was feeling no pain? How can *he* be of any help?" From the glow in her daughter's eyes, it had dawned on Asami, Hana's relationship with Lucas McKenzie, employed by the Japan Exchange and Teaching Program, had moved beyond the acquaintance stage.

Asami knocked on Lucas's door. Frustrated when he didn't answer, she lifted her fist to try again just as her daughter's door clicked open.

"Listen..." Jiro strode toward her. "Our Hana's not here."

She stumbled against him.

"Come in and see if anything's out of order."

The compact space was infused with the grassy tatami floor covering scent, and a timer-controlled lamp was on. Hana's white calico scampered under the couch as Asami kicked off her heels.

"Poor guy." Jiro bent down and tried to coax Satu out. "Before we leave, I'll check on his food and water."

Behind a shoji screen was her daughter's sleeping space. Bright festival posters were mounted above the red lacquered chest of drawers. The futon bed was neatly made with a white duvet. Asami got down on her hands and knees to check under the bed, her hair sweeping the floor. "Hana's hiking boots are gone," she reported. "So is her backpack where she stores her tent and sleeping bag."

To get her petite frame off the floor, she didn't use the bed for support.

Asami checked Hana's three lower chest drawers. "She keeps her hiking clothes in here and they're missing." She pulled open the top drawer and drummed her fingertips on its handle. "Hana keeps her checkbook, passport, and extra cash in here, but the drawer's empty. Why would she have taken her passport on a hiking trip?"

Jiro frowned. "That does seem odd. Check the bathroom."

Within the miniscule space, Asami touched a hanging towel by the empty shower. Both were dry. Hana's travel toiletry pouch wasn't in the cabinet. She stepped out. "It looks as if Hana did pack for a hike, but why hasn't she returned?"

Worry lines formed above Jiro's high bridge nose, his positivity fading. "Maybe we *should* talk to the police."

Asami couldn't help herself. She scratched her neck.

At ground level, Jiro attempted to wave down a cab while Asami paced and continued to scratch. She peered through Kimura's window and halted. "I should've known Hana's neighbor would be here." Her daughter's shaggy blond-headed friend was seated at the bar, a pint of beer in hand.

"You go talk to him. I forgot about Satu's food and water. Can you give me the key?"

She handed it to Jiro. "I'm glad you remembered."

Asami entered Kimura's, its grilled meat scent making her stomach turn. Customers dined at low tables. Traditional Japanese music played. She placed her shoes in the cupboard and approached Lucas calling out his name. He was dressed in a roomy fisherman sweater, the sort you wanted to live in on cool fall days.

He turned and blinked, a twine beaded choker around his neck. "Fujioka-san, what a surprise." He sat next to a Japanese man, a purple birthmark on his right cheek.

"Sorry to bother you, Lucas-san." Her fingers located her jacket zipper. "I'm looking for Hana. Have you seen her?"

He shook his head. "Early Friday, I found a note she'd slipped under my door. She asked me to check on Satu while she went hiking, but I thought she would've returned by now."

Asami digested his words. "How about Thursday night? Did you talk to Hana then?"

A heavy weight of sadness settled on his face, quashing his handsome features. "No—no, I didn't."

Asami gripped his arm. "What aren't you telling me?"

He gazed into his beer. "It's nothing I should tell a mama."

"Please?"

He sighed. "At about 2:00 a.m., through our adjoining wall, I heard a male voice."

Asami's hand flew to her chest. Who could that have been? Hana had recently broken up with her university boyfriend, and she was not the sort who'd pick up a random guy at a bar and bring him home to her bed. Plus, as Asami had suspected, Hana and Lucas seemed to be more than friends.

Asami desperately needed *her* friend. She gazed out the window, into the darkness, her eyes searching for Jiro as the izakaya's red paper lantern whipped frantically.

* * *

The elevator doors rattled open and Etta surged out. *Chloe's fine, of course she's fine!*

The first door to the right was her daughter's apartment. Two NYPD officers had already arrived, badges secured to their navy blue caps. Beside them was Henri, his face eggshell white. "Mon Dieu, Etta!" He raked his hands through his dark curls. "She's still not responding."

Etta pushed forward. "Chloe!" She banged on the door. "Sweetheart! It's Mom. *Please* let me in." She pressed her ear to it, praying Chloe would answer.

The black officer stepped forward. "Ms. Martin, we've tried to kick in your daughter's door, but the two dead bolts won't budge. The outside fire escape passes by the apartment's windows. You stay here with Officer Kamata. Mr. Broussard and I'll attempt to break in there."

Etta continued to pound as the elevator doors closed. Chloe *had* to answer.

"Ms. Martin?" Officer Kamata's half-moon eyes scrutinized her. "Why don't you tell me about your daughter? Is she, you know, emotionally stable?"

Her hands dropped to her sides. Her shoulders slumped. She focused on the hallway floor. Strands of hair, more silver than sandy, slipped out from under her headband obstructing her view.

Was the carpet green or red? Her colorblind eyes couldn't tell. She should've asked Chloe.

"Ms. Martin? I asked about your daughter."

"I know..." She peered up, putting on a brave face. "Chloe's been doing well—extremely well." That *was* the truth. "It's been years since she suffered from clinical depression."

He frowned. "Was that triggered by anything specific?"

Through starts and stops, Etta told him about Chloe's senior year in high school. How her daughter had discovered her steady boyfriend, Paul, had been sleeping with Chloe's best girlfriend. How, subsequently, Chloe had attempted suicide. "But my daughter's psychiatrist really helped. And meeting Henri definitely helped. He said they'd argued, but it was a minor spat—very minor." She had to convince herself that was true—it *had* to be true.

His feet shifted. "You said her past suicide attempt was over a boyfriend?"

"Yes! Weren't you listening? It's not the same. Paul cheated on Chloe. It's not the same!"

Kamata placed a consolatory hand on her upper arm.

She shrugged it off as the sound of breaking glass seeped through the door. *Oh God! Chloe has to be fine!* Etta slapped her forehead. *Of course! Sleeping pills!* Chloe used them on overseas business flights. It made perfect sense! After her argument with Henri, she'd taken one to fall asleep. In a minute, Chloe would be opening the door, dressed in her jammies, her eyelids heavy, a sheepish grin on her face. "Mom," she'd say, "I didn't mean to worry you."

Etta leaned against the door and tried to relax. Footsteps resonated inside. Male voices bantered back and forth. Then a piercing cry.

"No!" she moaned as the doleful sound continued.

The deadbolts clicked, first one, then the other.

The lock on the door handle turned.

Etta shoved past the officer. "Sweetheart, I'm here!" Her loafers scooted across the living room floor, her body propelled toward the sobbing.

Hunched over in the bathroom doorway was Henri. She gazed beyond him, into the shadows—*the big shadows.*

Inside the clawfoot tub, her child's hair floated like seaweed, her long eyelashes rested on her freckled cheeks, her kneecaps, like two islands, were exposed in the water—the ugly water—the color of the hallway carpet.

"No!" Etta screamed. "No!"

She turned on Henri, her arms flailing, her vision blurring, she beat on him until everything went dark.

-2-

1974 - Chicago

Chatter and tobacco smoke filled the Delta Zeta House's common area. About a dozen "sisters," most with a cup of java and cigarette in hand, lounged on a pair of Chippendale couches upholstered in a Killarney rose and twisted vine print. If the lights had gone out, Etta could still have located Moni Spencer by sniffing out her oddly comforting scent of cannabis and new age herbs. The two had pledged together. Ever since, Moni had been fused to Etta's hip, a sister Etta had never had. At Northwestern University, it had felt like the right thing to do, to be part of a close-knit group of girls as Etta had been in her small hometown of Carter, Illinois.

Etta posed in her best grown-up attire: a maroon vest, paisley blouse, mini-skirt, and the maroon tights she'd switched into. "Is this better?"

Moni snorted. "Like, yeah! Your kelly green tights would've knocked the interviewer's socks right off. Now, honey, off you go." She flipped her hand. "I refuse to wish you luck. Tripoint will be lucky to have you!"

Etta grinned. She was headed for an interview with Tripoint Technology, an up-and-coming firm founded in 1969 by three Harvard graduates: Tom Pollard, Dick Bengston, and Harry Davison.

Tripoint's charter was to focus on the retail industry and their innovative point-of-sale programmable software, to replace hard-coded cash register instructions, had taken off.

The front desk pledge waved wildly at Etta. "Your dad's on line one. He insists on talking to you."

Shit! That could only mean trouble. Etta traipsed over to the phone alcove, passing the TV airing the *Today Show.* Barbara Walters was discussing Nixon's Watergate tapes. Etta, apparently, wasn't the only one in hot water.

She lifted the receiver and said, "Hi, Dad," keeping her tone neutral, not succumbing to "the child being reprimanded mode," even when his greeting of "Henrietta, what are you thinking!" exploded in her ear. "Your mother just told me you're interviewing with a new-fangled technology firm. You'll be eaten up. There are no women in that field. You know I've arranged a Carter High teaching job for you. That's where you belong."

Etta could visualize Dad's mouth, the spittle in the corners, as if he was giving a voracious sermon from his Methodist pulpit. Every garden had some weeds. Dad was her thistle. He called her Miss Contrary—and not affectionately. When he'd take on a righteous stand, she'd assume the opposite position just to piss him off. The Methodist Church had ordained women since the late fifties, yet he still believed no woman could do what a man could do.

"Well, Dad, Mom and her friends think it's a wonderful idea."

"What does your mother and those women libbers know!"

She hated how he degraded Mom. But it was as if her mother had resigned herself to a double life, one under Dad's dark cloud, one with her nurturing female friends where she'd pretend her life was perfect.

If Mom was beside her, Etta knew she'd be whispering in her ear, "Sweetheart, don't listen to him. You can be whatever you want to be."

1980 - Tokyo

Inside the noisy *Todai*—Tokyo University—auditorium, Asami's feet tapped in time to the hit song "Hana" playing inside her head. It was the Okinawan version of the John Lennon song "Imagine." Beside her sat Jiro. As expected, her flamboyant best friend was breaking the university's unpublished rules. He was the only male sitting in the female section.

His eyes twinkled. "We look like Ueno Zoo penguins, but your perfume definitely smells better."

She laughed covering red lips with her hand. Around them were carbon copies of themselves, all in black recruit suits and white shirts or blouses. Approximately two hundred male and fifty female students were starting their final university year and launching into the twelve-month recruiting process known as *aotagai*—buying rice before it's harvested—Japan's custom since the postwar years to produce a steady employment stream.

Asami was amazed she'd reached that milestone. As a child, she'd been an embarrassment, constantly interrupting her classmates, elbowing her way into trouble, breaking time-honored social norms. She couldn't be an obedient daughter like her female peers. She'd been evaluated at age nine and diagnosed with Hyperkinetic Reaction of Childhood, recently renamed: Attention Deficit Hyperactivity Disorder. She'd struggled without any sort of medication until seventh grade when an American doctor had joined their neighborhood clinic. He'd prescribed a stimulant for Asami, a life-changing event, and her humiliated parents had taken great care to hide that fact.

She glanced across the aisle and her feet sped up. Seated there was Masato Ito. In addition to his rat-like facial features, her arrogant classmate had an uncanny knack for sniffing out another's weakness. She whispered to Jiro, "Did you notice who's been listening to us?"

Jiro's eyes followed hers and he frowned. "Masato's not worth the tissue I flush down the toilet. You and I are far better candidates than he will ever be."

Asami wanted to believe Jiro's words were true. At least, Masato didn't know her older brother, Arata, also had issues. He suffered from M.S.

The siblings had been born on the ninth in two different months. The number nine had the same pronunciation as "agony." Mama often moaned, "That's what my children have caused me." As the best of the worst, like a trained monkey on a leash, Papa had reluctantly taught Asami the ins-and-outs of their family's souvenir business.

Jiro had been the only one who had truly believed in her.

Asami gazed up at him, her hero, her ninja, the one who'd persistently fought for her well-being, the one who'd helped her with her studies, her time management, her never ending ruminating that things weren't perfect. Because of him, she'd graduated near the top of her senior high class. Instead of finding a good husband, as Mama had hoped, one who could handle Asami's "personality flaws" and help out with the family business—Jiro had convinced her to apply to Todai and they'd both been accepted. Due to her acquired retail skills, she'd chosen a business major while Jiro had selected fine arts with a film emphasis.

Asami's eyes focused on the section to be filled by company speakers and reality set in. "Jiro-kun, most respected firms will certainly prefer a woman like Izumi, with a two-year Home Economics degree, who was snapped up by Canon."

"My dear, a so called 'marriage degree' certainly wouldn't have been a fit for you. As much as I love you, unlike our friend, you'd fail as an office lady trying to prioritize which was more important: the copy machine, the tea area, or the phones."

Asami laughed. "At least, more women are beginning to think like me. Last weekend, I moved off the Ginza sidewalk for the Pink Helmet Brigade campaigning for equal pay, birth control, and divorce rights. Think of it Jiro-kun. You and I are sitting here on the cusp of change, about to part the grass."

1974 - Chicago

Still attempting to erase Dad's bad karma, Etta stood outside room 208 within Northwestern's Community Center. She adjusted a thin headband in her long sandy hair, pleased it was reasonably straight. It should be after sleeping on orange juice container curlers all night.

It was time to show Dad he was wrong! She firmed up her shoulders. "Be proud of your height," Mom would say. "Don't slouch like you're a sad sack." Etta smiled at the thought and decisively knocked on the door.

A voice boomed, "Come in."

Startled by the tone, she guardedly did. A man was standing beside a table, his features nearly a mirror image of Robert Redford's: the same sun streaked hair, craggy chin, and roguish lips. She'd recently seen *The Way We Were.* Rather than getting a rush of movie star ecstasy, Etta's internal warning system had switched on. Intimidation vibes radiated from the man's steely gray eyes—similar to Dad's. About ten years her senior and dressed in a pin-striped suit, he took two steps toward her revealing his masterful swagger. His hand reached for hers. "You must be Henrietta Martin?"

She kept her voice steady as she said, "Yes," and firmly shook his hand. "But, please, call me Etta."

He took in her nearly six feet of height, just a bit shorter than he. "I'm Thomas Pollard. Please take a seat."

Etta was taken aback. Why would Tripoint's CEO be interviewing her? That flustered her. So did her mini-skirt as she settled onto a chair across from him and attempted to wiggle the skirt down. At least her legs weren't green!

Etta had to regroup, to escape the flighty state he'd placed her in. "I've heard good things about your company, Mr. Pollard. Sam Madrid, a former Northwestern teaching assistant of mine, works for Tripoint in New York City."

At Sam's mention, renewed bravado had swelled into Etta.

Sam believed in her.

Tom Pollard would too.

His eyes fixed on her, a half-smile on his lips. "So you know Sam Madrid?"

She met his gaze. "Yes. He told me you also have offices in Chicago and Los Angeles."

"That's right. So tell me Etta Martin, why do you want to work for Tripoint?"

She sat up straight. Normally she was humble, but it wasn't the time to be so. "I assume you've reviewed my resume?" She'd noticed it on the table in front of him. "In addition to double majoring in business and computer science, I've had experience with your software at the Evanston Marshall Field's where I work part time."

His finger slid down the page. "I saw that."

"I can also bring to Tripoint something ninety-five percent of your employees can't."

His brow furrowed. "What's that?"

"Women's intuition."

He scoffed.

"I'm serious. I was one of five hundred participants in a Northwestern graduate study. It tested facial cue recognition. The study discovered women test far better than men."

"Hmm..." He leaned back in his chair. "So how might you use that?"

She could tell she'd piqued his interest and was excited to share. "Let's say a major retailer was making a purchase decision on your software. A male Marketing Rep might think the deal was solid. A woman Rep might see the slight tick in the CFO's cheek and realize there could be issues. Women's intuition can be a key component in negotiating a deal."

He crossed his arms, inspecting her.

"In your New York office, Sam told me there are only a handful of women and most of them are secretaries."

He laughed. "So you're prepared to go head-to-head with a man in the business world?"

She felt his leg bump hers then casually move away. He couldn't rattle her. She pictured Mom whispering in her ear as she said, "Most definitely."

1980 - Tokyo

The Todai auditorium quieted as the company speakers filed in. Asami turned to Jiro. "Notice..." she kept her voice low, "there's only one female speaker."

"Do you know her?"

"That's Mrs. Kichida, a vice president from Yamada Department Stores. I've seen her photo in the press. Few women have achieved her status."

The dean took the stage. Speakers from the Bank of Tokyo, Mitsubishi, and Kadokawa Pictures followed. All the while, Asami's fingers fidgeted with her blouse buttons. That motion kept her focused until Mrs. Kichida stepped up to the stage, her hair dull gray, her eyes bright. She gripped the podium and leaned toward Asami's section. "When I was hired by Yamada, women's labor standards only allowed me to work two hours of overtime per day or six hours per week—sadly—the same as now. I was forced to clock out, but I continued to work for free, to prove I was as productive as the males I worked beside."

Mrs. Kichida's gumption instilled a sense of pride in Asami. Most companies didn't feel a woman could provide lifelong service. She'd broken that mold.

"'New Women,' born and educated after World War II, make up one quarter of Japan's population." Mrs. Kichida's eyes engaged with the male section. "You, young men, should now realize the women in this auditorium are worthy competitors. But, regrettably, most companies are still run by old men—"

Asami gasped, amazed at Mrs. Kichida's daring.

"—those who hold no concept of equality with their wives. Why would the workplace be any different?"

Asami stole a glance across the aisle. Unlike Jiro, chuckling beside her, Asami's arrogant classmate looked disgusted. A superior air oozed from Masato's pores.

"You should all know," Mrs. Kichida continued, "Japan's plan for women's equality has been launched. But it may be ahead of its time. Many Japanese women are not ready for it." She zoned in on Asami's section. "In your interviews, young ladies, prove that you are."

Asami turned to Jiro. "I want more than anything to accomplish what she has!"

"My dear, then go do it! In addition to having a business degree, think of all the retail experience you'll bring to the table from working in your family's business."

Jiro was right! Asami looked sideways at Masato. His haughty eyes stared down his nose at her. His lips curled into a nasty smile as if itching to say, "Don't be swayed by your friend's sugar-coated words. You'll never succeed."

She raised her chin. Her enthusiasm couldn't be curbed, her hope for the future. In the years to come, she could picture herself walking in Mrs. Kichida's shoes, giving inspiration to other young women as Mrs. Kichida had given to her.

-3-

Sunday - New York

A sense of doom seeped into Etta's barely conscious thoughts. A silky softness brushed against her cheek. It had to be her chenille throw! Relief gushed through Etta. The misery she'd seen in Chloe's bathroom was only a horrendous dream. She'd fallen asleep on her Evanston condo couch. Yet the cushions were too saggy for leather. A memory tugged at Etta. Chloe opening Etta's Christmas gift, a chenille throw that matched hers.

Etta's eyelids burst open. She stared up at the high ceiling, its white crown molding, its ornate lighting fixture. *Oh God!* She wasn't in her condo. Her hand touched a wet cloth stretched across her forehead. Around her were muffled voices. She sat up and the cloth fell to her lap. The officers from her nightmare were across the room.

Etta moaned.

But then a spark of hope surfaced. A flicker of Chloe's light. Surely her child could be alive! Her suicide an attempt like before.

Etta clamored to her feet. "Where's my daughter? You took her to the hospital, didn't you?"

The Asian officer approached. "I'm sorry, Ms. Martin. She had no pulse."

"You're wrong!" She pushed past him to reach the black officer. He was blocking the bathroom entrance, a rolling stretcher beside him. "I must see my daughter!"

"I'm sorry, I can't let you in. The paramedics are with her now." But as he'd said that, Etta had managed to catch a glimpse of her child, still in that dreadful water, her daughter's eyes closed as if she was simply sleeping. *Oh God!* Why couldn't that be so? Etta started to pant. She spun around, her lips, hands, and feet tingling, her agony finding its source. Hunched over in a chair was Henri, his chin on his chest, his eyes closed.

Etta jabbed a shaky finger his way. "That bastard's to blame! He murdered my daughter! She's dead because of him. She's—"

"Ms. Martin..." The black officer placed a hand on her elbow. "Let's get you a glass of water." He judiciously directed her toward the kitchen where Etta collapsed onto a pressed back chair. Fruit flies hovered above a bowl of ripe bananas centered on the oak table, their sickly sweet scent filling the room.

The officer handed her the water and glanced out into the front room. "Detective Harper just arrived. She'll check on your daughter then she'll want to talk to you."

Etta sat there all alone, the horrific reality sinking in. Tears trickled down her cheeks. She tried not to picture her child in that wretched bathroom, but it was impossible. *God!* If she'd only protected Chloe for a bit longer—just a bit longer—she never would've met Henri...

In the aftermath of Chloe's high school suicide attempt, in addition to a caring psychiatrist, her daughter's counselor had taken her under his wing. Northwestern had already accepted Chloe, so he'd personally made sure she'd completed her final term's requirements. For her daughter's university freshman year, Etta had persuaded Chloe it'd be emotionally best for her to commute from home. That living arrangement, and her daughter's weekly psychiatric sessions, had continued even after Chloe had secured her MBA, and she'd landed a job at Tripoint's Chicago office. "Like mother, like daughter," Chloe had often said as she and Etta had climbed off the "L" at Clark and Lake, their morning coffee in hand, the lilt in her daughter's voice sometimes off.

Etta knew Chloe had deserved a life of her own, one away from her mom's watchful eyes. So when her daughter had gotten a much deserved promotion to Tripoint's New York headquarters, Etta had convinced herself she'd been ready to let Chloe go.

Etta swayed in the chair, her blurry eyes gazing at the subway tile backsplash, the potted herbs on the windowsill. Eleven months ago, a few inches from where she sat, sunlight had been playing across Chloe's freckled cheeks, her daughter's ballet years evident as her feet had assumed the third position, one foot gracefully angled in front of the other. She'd squeezed Etta's hands, a tentative smile on her lips. "Mom, I think it's time for me to test the water." Of course, Chloe had been referring to Henri.

The two had met at the Bryant Hotel where her daughter had insisted they stay while hunting for her apartment. That choice, more like a hostel than a hotel, had been prompted by Moni, still a constant in their lives. Rather than staying at a boring New York luxury hotel, Etta's sorority sister had convinced Chloe she needed to experience the Village's bohemian lifestyle. The room had been the size of a walk-in-closet with two bunks secured to one wall. They'd flipped for the bottom and Etta had lost.

In hotel-provided white terry cloth robes and paper slippers, she and Chloe had been giggling as they'd shuffled into the unisex bathroom down the hall. A gangly young man, in matching intimate attire, had been hogging the sink to shave his angular face, his dark curls untidy. Below arched eyebrows, his hazel eyes, as quick as a cat's, had located her daughter's. Through lips covered in shaving cream, he'd mouthed, "*Bonjour*," not even noticing Etta had been there. The bathroom's harsh lighting had seemed to soften when Chloe had responded with an endearingly bashful smile.

That young man had been Henri Broussard, and his authentically uttered greeting had sealed Chloe's heart—and now her fate.

A sob caught in Etta's throat. Henri's actions *had* to be the reason behind Chloe's rash act. She closed her eyes and rocked. *I should've known better. I should've listened closer to Chloe. She should've continued her therapy. I never should've outlived my child. I—*

"Ms. Martin?"

Etta squinted up at a tall latte-colored woman in a navy pants suit, her dark hair cut in a pixie style, and a gap between her front teeth.

"I'm Detective Harper. May—may I join you?" Her brown eyes, too big for her face, seemed anxious as she took a seat at the table, a notebook and pen in hand. "First," she said, "I want to offer you my condolences."

Etta nodded, just barely.

"Can—can you recall when you last talked to your daughter?"

Etta had to pull herself together, to think. "Last Sunday. Chloe called from Tokyo. She works—" her body wilted, "worked for Tripoint Technology. She was there for business."

"How did she sound?"

Heat spurted into Etta's cheeks. "Fine. Except for missing that damn bastard in the other room! Henri must've been cheating on Chloe and she found out."

Skin bunched around the detective's eyes and mouth, but she didn't comment. "One of the officers told me your daughter had attempted suicide before? Is that right?"

Etta hung her head. "Yes. It was the same as here. In a bathtub. And she took pills." From the front room, she could hear rattles and squeaks. Her head jerked up. It had to be her daughter's gurney. "Where—where is Chloe being taken?"

"To the Manhattan medical examiner's office. An autopsy will be performed later today."

Etta stifled a sob. "We should be at breakfast right now. We should be—"

"Ms. Martin, please, you need to concentrate."

Etta's body deflated. The detective was right.

"Can you give me the names of anyone your daughter might've talked to this week?"

She forced herself to focus. "In—in Tokyo, Chloe was spending time with Asami and Hana Fujioka. The two are family friends and also work colleagues."

Etta placed her elbows on the table, her face in her hands. Poor Hana. She'd be inconsolable. Chloe was nearly a dozen years older, yet they'd called themselves "international besties."

"Ms. Martin?" The detective's voice drew her back. "Is there anyone else?"

"Yes, Sam—Sam Madrid, Tripoint's Chief Operating Officer. He's Chloe's mentor. The two were in Tokyo together."

Like Hana, Sam would be heartbroken. He'd cared for Chloe as her daughter had cared for him. Shortly before Chloe's New York move, Etta had marshaled her courage and had given him a call. No matter what had transpired between them, she'd appreciated how he'd helped advance her career. She'd cautiously asked if he'd consider mentoring her daughter as well.

Sam hadn't even hesitated. "I'd love to, Etta. It's the least I can do." His words had turned her legs into jelly, the grape kind Mom had served with waffles that had jiggled with anticipated sweetness on the knife. Sam, the man she still loved, had reentered her life, albeit as a friend.

Etta was strong, but that friend's support was what she desperately needed.

Monday - Tokyo

Clad in Hana's nightshirt, Asami pressed her cheek against her daughter's pillowcase, bathed in her child's scents of chamomile soap and rosemary shampoo.

Hours earlier, she and Jiro had taken a cab to the Setagaya Police Station. "Your daughter's an adult," the duty sergeant had said. "It's not illegal for her to go missing. You can file a report, but why not wait until morning? Most likely, she'll return by then."

Asami and Jiro had discussed the pros and cons. Hana had asked Lucas to watch Satu. She'd also taken her passport. But who could the male in her apartment be?

Jiro had asked, "What about Felipe Rodriguez? The guy Hana was dating while at university, the one from Seville Spain?"

"I considered him, but Hana told me she was breaking off their relationship."

"Well, maybe she didn't. Maybe he accompanied her to the Five Lakes Region. Or maybe Hana changed their hiking destination all together. You know how spontaneous she is. After sending you the text, she and Felipe could've used their passports to fly to someplace like Hong Kong or Taiwan for a three-day adventure. Maybe their return flight was delayed and Hana's plans to meet you at Inokashira Park slipped her mind."

Each of Jiro's conjectures, although doubtful, could be true, so Asami had decided to wait. She couldn't mortify Hana by unduly reacting.

But if her daughter didn't return by morning, Asami would be waiting alone. Jiro's favorite aunt had died. He couldn't cancel his flight to the Shiretoko Peninsula to attend her funeral and cremation.

Asami checked her cell's bright display. It was nearly 4:30 a.m. Maybe she'd made the wrong decision.

Hana's kitty was curled up beside her. To subdue her overactive brain, Asami concentrated on Satu's soft breathing, yet thoughts of Hana couldn't help but slip in.

Luckily her daughter hadn't inherited her ADHD gene, although Hana had been burdened by other stigmas. In her primary school, she'd been the only child without two parents and a *gaijin*—foreigner—as well. She'd often been bullied and shunned. Asami had suffered beside Hana, knowing that same feeling of rejection.

In Japan, the nail that sticks out gets hammered down.

Her daughter, however, had been far stronger and wiser than Asami could've imagined. "Mama, don't worry," Hana had often said, placing her small hands on Asami's cheeks, using the consoling words Asami should've been giving her daughter. "Who needs those friends when I have you?"

But at the present moment, how could Asami not worry? She checked her cell again. Satu's breathing wasn't doing the trick. Asami crawled out of bed and knelt on the floor. She rolled her torso forward, arms extended, and slowly inhaled and exhaled, holding the "child's pose," imagining her child beside her.

If Hana wasn't with Felipe, could she still be out in the Five Lakes Region contemplating some problem in her life? Could she possibly be pregnant?

Asami shivered.

She knew what *that* felt like.

Or could Hana be dealing with some job related problem? She'd recently been hired by Tripoint Technology's Tokyo branch where Asami also worked.

It was ironic. At university, instead of being badgered, Hana had been envied. Most of the so-called glamorous Japanese jobs, like newscaster or model, were secured by hāfu women like Hana. She probably would've landed one because of her beauty, confidence, and excellent bilingual skills. Blended with Asami's features—dark straight hair and full lower lip—Hana was willowy tall like her papa with his handsome cheekbones and double-lidded eyes.

Due to Asami's constant prodding, however, Hana had followed in her mama's footsteps. Could Hana's current situation be linked to that decision, possibly remorse on her part? Had she confided her concerns to Sumie, her recruit class friend? Or had she talked to Chloe Martin before she'd flown back to New York? As of yet, neither young woman had responded to the messages Asami had left on their work extensions. Both might also know how Asami could reach Felipe.

She stood and turned on the nightstand light, just as her cell rang. At seeing the name "Etta Martin" on the display, she was confused.

"Oh Asami..." her friend's distressed voice filled her ear, "I apologize for calling you at this hour."

"Etta-san, you didn't wake me. I only hoped you were Hana. She should've returned from a hiking trip nearly twelve hours ago."

"Hana's missing?"

Asami sank down on the bed. "Yes, and your daughter might've been one of the last to see her. That's why I left her a—"

"Chloe's dead..."

Asami recoiled at Etta's words.

"My baby took her life."

"How—how can that be? I saw her last Sunday. She joined Hana and me for a bite to eat. Chloe looked wonderful—so full of life—a role model for Hana. Why would she have done such a thing?"

Asami listened in horror as Etta condemned Henri for her daughter's impulsive act. What would Etta do? Asami's eyes clouded. Other than Etta's Tripoint job, Chloe was her friend's life.

Asami had met mama and daughter when Chloe had been nine. That year in Japan, Asami had coveted their intimacy. The two had often shared a secret smile and grabbed the other's hand, a synchronized movement neither realized they were performing. As Chloe had matured, she'd emulated Etta's thoughtfulness. The previous Sunday, Asami had watched Chloe help a young mama carry a stroller up a flight of stairs. At Kimura's, Etta's daughter had talked about Henri, what a good man he was. In her absence, he was picking up groceries for their wheelchair-bound neighbor, something Chloe usually did. And after the meal, Chloe had pulled Mr. Kimura aside to tell him about the fine service their waitress had provided.

Yet Chloe's suicide was the ultimate in thoughtlessness. How could she have hurt her mama so?

Asami pulled Hana's pillow into her lap, her fingers racing back and forth along the stitched edge. "Etta-san, I'm trying to wrap my mind around your tragic words."

"I know... But, Asami, you must tell me about Hana. You said she's missing?"

"Yes. I last heard from her at around 2:00 a.m. on Friday. Her text said she was going hiking and needed to think. Our daughters could've been together on Thursday night, shortly before Hana sent me that text."

A sickening wave of fear welled up in Asami's belly. "Oh Etta-san, could something have happened to our daughters that night? Something so horrific they made a pact to end their lives? Could Hana have committed suicide like Chloe? Is that why she hasn't returned?"

It wasn't as if Asami hadn't considered that dreadful idea.

"Listen! You must be positive. Hana is alive! I'm certain Chloe's death has nothing to do with Hana's disappearance."

Asami sagged forward, ashamed. Etta needed far more solace than she, yet it was Etta who was boosting her up as she'd always done. Asami clutched her cell and whispered, "My culture's based on actions rather than words. I can't make you a soothing cup of tea or hold you in my arms. I ache for you and your terrible loss. But even though you're suffering, somehow, you always know the right words to say to me... I wish I had some for you."

-4-

1974 – Chicago

Etta gazed up at the Art Deco high rise on West Wacker, the home to Tripoint's Chicago branch. She'd been offered a Technical Rep position with its amazing annual salary of $11,600! Enough to buy three Ford Mustangs right out of the showroom.

Mom had whispered over the phone, "Don't tell Dad I told you, but he's only making a bit more than you."

Dad's hurtful words still rattled around in Etta's head. "They're paying a woman that! Henrietta, let's just see how long you last." He continued to blame President Kennedy for signing the Equal Pay Act.

Head held high, Etta stepped into the mosaic-tiled lobby, ready to prove she was worth every cent and more.

Two guys about Etta's age chatted beside the elevator. Both were dressed in conservative dark suits, wing-tipped shoes, and carried leather briefcases. One was the wolfish type, cocksure with calculating eyes. The curly-haired guy seemed to have a puppy's persona, his grin radiating happiness and good will.

Etta's only exposure to the proper work attire had been gleaned from the *Charlie* perfume "New Professional Women" ads and the *Mary Tyler Moore Show*. Its main character, an unmarried career woman, had been a recent television breakthrough.

For Etta's first day of work, she'd wanted to do things right. Mom, living in the Carter sticks, certainly couldn't give her advice, so Etta had asked a Marshall Field's co-worker. "Well," Judy had said, "society women, teachers, secretaries, and nurses have shopped here, but I've never assisted a woman with a profession like yours." In the women's department, she'd showed Etta a black trouser suit with a bomber jacket. Then what she'd assured Etta was a pretty red suit, its skirt pleated and its jacket sporting an over-sized top-stitched collar.

Etta entered the elevator in the latter and pressed the tenth floor button. She felt like Little Red Riding Hood, a target for the wolf beside her.

His crafty eyes inspected her. "It appears as if we're all headed up to the same floor."

She stared back, concentrating hard so her cheeks wouldn't match her attire.

The doors dinged open and the wolf's hand motioned out. "Ladies first."

She fought back the urge to roll her eyes. Mom and her friends had discussed that exact phrase. Sybil had posed, "Is it being sexist? When I hold the door for a guy I don't say, 'Gentlemen first' or for people my parents' age, 'Elderly first' or for those with walkers, 'Slow pokes first.' Why do men point out my gender?"

Mom and her friends had agreed, if you had to differentiate, the comment was sexist.

Etta shook her head. She had bigger fish to fry.

Seated at the reception desk was a young female, her eyes darkly lined and her wavy black hair parted in the center.

As the wolf's eyes swallowed her up, he apparently forgot his manners and spoke up first, "I'm Pete Brownell and," he jerked his head toward the other guy, "this is Neil Thompson. We were told to ask for the branch manager, George Buckley."

"I bet you're two of the new hires."

Pete nodded as Etta interjected, "So am I."

The surprised receptionist gave her an approving smile as Etta introduced herself.

"I'll let George know the three of you are here."

Pete's shifty eyes analyzed Etta in a new light.

The door opened and a man with a comb-over and thick sideburns walked out. His age was in Dad's realm. As introductions were made, George's warm smile relaxed Etta.

He led them into a hazy bullpen area. Each cubicle held a dark-suited man. Nearly all were puffing on cigarettes, pipes, or cigars. No females were visible until they reached two desks stationed by the private offices. As the women seated there beamed up at George, he said, "These two lovely ladies' secretarial services are invaluable to our staff."

Sam had said Tripoint's New York headquarters was slim on female professionals. At first glance, Etta believed she might be the only one in the Chicago branch. She notched up her chin, ready for that challenge.

They all took seats in George's office, Neil to Etta's right, Pete to her left.

Pete's hands relaxed around the wooden chair arms, an entitled look on his face.

George leaned forward and crossed his arms on his desk. "I want to welcome you three into the Tripoint Technology family. A fourth Technical Rep will be joining us tomorrow. Next week, you'll all be flying into New York City for a month of training."

Etta's heart quickened. Maybe she'd get to see Sam!

"You'll also be doing Fifth Avenue fieldwork, shopping the stores while analyzing their checkout procedures. Etta, though, may have a leg up on you two gentlemen." George smiled at her. "She's worked with our point-of-sale software at the Evanston Marshall Field's."

Pete raised one brow. "Let's see who has a leg up once we complete our training."

George laughed. "I like your spirit. But remember, teamwork's important."

Neil nudged Etta. "I'll take any help I can get."

She gave her ally an appreciative nod. Etta so wanted to give the wolf a kick in the shins. Instead, she slid her armchair a bit closer to his, intentionally pinching his fingers, and she was awarded with a yelp. Apologizing profusely, Etta feigned distress while inwardly grinning. She knew she had her work cut out for her. In addition to Tripoint's training regimen, she'd be dealing with the egotistical jerk to her left, his attitude disgustingly similar to Dad's.

Of course, she'd had years of practice handling him.

1981 - Tokyo

Asami whirled through the Yamada flagship store's revolving door and stepped into a kaleidoscope of color: white gardenias, orange tiger lilies, blue hyacinth, and all hues of roses. Infused with the floral department's aromatic scent, Asami fixed her eyes on the distant elevator bank so as not to get distracted. Two weeks before graduation, she'd been thrilled to receive a job offer from Yamada Department Stores. That had been especially exciting knowing her male classmates had been given a three month running start.

Jiro had accepted a position at Kadokawa Pictures—what he'd considered to be his dream job.

Asami scurried past the cosmetic, accessory, and shoe department clerks, mainly women under thirty. Each bowed to her, exhibiting the subservient behavior consistent with their inferior status to Yamada "guests." According to Asami's hiring handbook, company regulations only governed women employees' dress codes. Each young lady looked similar to her: hair style less than shoulder length, to enable a proper bow; dark suit; conservative makeup; skin-colored stockings; and dark shoes, their heels under two inches.

Asami was eager to meet her recruit class, yet also apprehensive. Jiro had always kept her on track, given her pep talks, convinced her she didn't need to be perfect when perfection wasn't possible.

She'd be tackling her new job all on her own.

Asami reached the elevator bank. Two fashionably dressed women exited as she stepped on. Asami politely asked the female operator to press the button for the corporate floor. In a moment, she'd be entering Mrs. Kichida's domain, ready to make her own waves.

The doors opened and Asami saw a familiar face. She bowed to Miss Sando, the rosy-cheeked HR woman who'd been present during Asami's Todai interview.

Miss Sando smiled and returned the bow. "Welcome, Fujioka-san. Please join the other recruits." She motioned toward a doorway.

Asami entered the conference room and her stomach cramped as if she'd just gobbled down a massive bowl of rice noodles. One of those seated around the rectangular table was Masato Ito, her arrogant university classmate. How could that be? How could he have secured a job at Yamada as well? In the Todai auditorium, she knew he'd been listening to her conversation with Jiro when she'd expressed her desire to work for Yamada. Had he actually gone after the same job just to spite her, to intimidate her, to prove he'd be far superior in their new professions?

Asami's eyes rapidly scanned the other recruits—all males. Two seats remained. Rather than awkwardly skirting around the table, she took the seat beside Masato.

He immediately scooted away as if she had body odor.

Asami attempted to ignore his insult. They were on equal ground. All Japanese recruits were hired as core employees. Nevertheless, his attitude distressed her. She felt unsettled, off kilter.

The impressive HR deputy director, from Asami's interview, entered the room. "Welcome recruits," Mr. Shibata said. "Yamada's president and the corporate employees want to welcome you. Following your initiation ceremony, you'll return here and I'll outline your training schedule."

Twinges of excitement tempered Asami's nervousness. With the others, she rose and followed him out. About three hundred seated employees got to their feet. In Japan, a company's corporate staff was arranged in order of rank. Directly in front of Asami was a row of women. Like her friend, Izumi, Asami assumed they were office ladies. Directly behind them were five additional women. Asami clasped and unclasped her hands while she and the other recruits trailed behind Mr. Shibata. Only dark-suited men filled the remaining office space.

Mrs. Kichida should be there, yet Asami didn't see her.

They reached the rear executive section. Behind a podium, a stately gentleman stood. "Welcome recruits," he spoke into a microphone. "I'm Mr. Yamada, president of Yamada Department Stores." A pitch pipe sounded and the employees' voices broke into the company song. Speeches were made and executive introductions followed. Asami tried to focus, but her mind was consumed by the fact that Mrs. Kichida was not among them.

Asami and the other recruits headed back toward the conference room. Before she could enter, Miss Sando stopped her. "Fujioka-san, please follow me."

Asami's forehead creased. "Mr. Shibata said he'd be discussing our training."

Masato paused to listen.

"He'll talk to the male recruits. I'll talk to you."

Masato gave Asami a snide look and pulled the door shut, as if to keep the riff raff out.

Nothing was as she'd expected! It was as if a typhoon had hit, drowning her spirit. Tail between her legs, she followed Miss Sando into an adjoining room and dropped onto a chair.

The woman's kind eyes connected with hers. "I can see your disappointment. But don't despair. I'll keep you busy until the male recruits return from their two months of training."

"Two months! What will they be doing without me?"

"They'll be at an offsite retreat for intensive team-building. Their regimen includes physical endurance tests, not fit for a woman. Once they return, you'll rejoin them for two weeks of job-related training."

It was even worse than Asami had imagined. Her feet tapped. Once her recruit class returned, why would they accept her back into their fold? In her interview, Mr. Shibata had said, "Each recruit's goal is to be promoted, but if the star is not one's self, the hope is one's team members will make it to the top." Why would anyone in her recruit class encourage her to succeed, especially Masato? It appeared as if Yamada was only investing in its male recruits. She was a challenge, a necessary evil. She'd probably filled an employment quota. Her fingers fidgeted madly on her blouse buttons. Had she been tricked? She'd gone to the best university. She'd competed with her male classmates. She'd been awarded a Yamada position, believing she was an equal.

Evidently, she was not.

Asami forced her feet and hands to quiet. "At Todai, Mrs. Kichida spoke to the students. Ever since, I've felt empowered. I believed Yamada was different. That she'd paved the way for women like me."

Miss Sando's face saddened. "Mrs. Kichida was a great vice president who received much respect. Unfortunately, she left the company due to health issues."

Asami's hands flew to her cheeks.

"Listen Fujioka-san, I will help you in any way I can, but the rest will be up to you."

Asami gave her a dismal nod.

At least, she knew where she stood.

-5-

Sunday - New York

Etta gazed out at the Hudson River scalloping a blue seam between the New York and New Jersey shores. She'd decided to stay at the Bryant Hotel because of Chloe. It was a Greenwich Village location where Etta could picture her daughter, the two of them squeezed together, both of them peering out through the tiny window's vertical blinds while Chloe raved, "Where else can you get a New York room, with this view, for this price?"

Etta turned away. Her daughter was dead. Asami's was missing. Neither incident made sense. In addition to dealing with her own grief, she was suffering for her friend. It was as if a swarm of garden chiggers had massively bitten the skin beneath her clothes when she'd already been crying.

Etta sank onto the lower bunk. She felt so alone. She'd called Moni, her constant rock ever since Mom's passing. It had followed Dad's by two years. Moni had repeatedly said, "Honey, I'm catching a flight. I know you're strong but not that strong." Etta had insisted she stay put. That Sam would help her through the next few days.

Etta reclined against two pillows and hoped that was true. He hadn't answered his cell when she'd tried to reach him.

Over the past year, the career mentoring Sam had provided Chloe had far exceeded the norm. He'd even co-hosted a recent cocktail party at her apartment. Because of Sam's COO status, key Tripoint executives had attended including Tripoint's CEO, his wife, and their son. As the Pollards' only heir, TJ was being groomed to replace his dad.

Chloe had appreciated Sam's help. She'd often said, "Mom, I can bounce anything off him. He would've made a great dad!"

Etta had struggled with her daughter's words. Had she been selfish? Not including Chloe's father in her life?

Obviously, that was water over the dam.

* * *

In jogging attire, Etta entered the nearby subway station. Posted on the wall were color-coded MTA routes, difficult for her to decipher. The last time she'd visited Chloe the two had used that station to reach Central Park. Both had felt running relieved work stress. What about the gut-wrenching trauma from losing a child? If Etta got mugged, she wouldn't even care.

She stopped a woman who pointed her in the right direction. Etta slipped a metro card into the proper turnstile and descended the stairs. On the dank smelling platform, a public address system blared competing with the trains' rush and roar. Etta stood among New York's melting pot: a Chasidic Jewish man with long side curls; an African American, his pants hung low; and a dark-suited Asian man.

Out of the corner of her eye, Etta noticed the Asian man's deformed left little finger. A recent *60 Minutes* episode had featured Japan's top yakuza crime bosses. Earlier in their careers, those featured had all performed self-mutilations, on that same finger, to ask for atonement after displeasing the bosses they'd eventually replaced. Could the man beside her be a yakuza gangster? It was possible. According to the broadcast, Japan's organized crime syndicate had joined forces with the American Mafia in such cities as Honolulu, Las Vegas, and New York City to channel Japanese tourists to illicit casinos and illegal sex businesses.

Etta boarded the train and distanced herself from that man, yet recognized she needed her own atonement—something to curb her guilt. Throughout the many stops, perched on a fiberglass seat, she racked her brain. Had Chloe provided her any sort of hint about Henri's infidelity? Prior to Chloe's initial suicide attempt, there'd been numerous signs, those which Etta had regretfully ignored: Mariah Carey's *Always Be My Baby* repeatedly playing from inside Chloe's Evanston bedroom, her lack of appetite, her refusal to attend school, her lack of hygiene.

Etta sat back. Since Chloe's New York move, nothing remotely similar came to mind. The triggering incident had to have occurred right after Chloe returned from Japan.

Asami's panicky words about a potential suicide pact niggled at Etta as well.

She got off at the Seventy-Second Street stop and entered Central Park. The scent of decomposing autumn foliage normally conjured up nostalgic memories of Northwestern football games, Halloween trick-or-treating with Etta's little Princess Leia, and jostling in the leaves with Chloe. But Etta's life had tragically changed. That scent would forever evoke painful memories of her daughter's senseless death, of loss and decay.

Etta started off at a sluggish pace. Surrounded by traffic noise and Canadian geese's honking, she followed West Drive. On prior runs, her daughter had pointed out eclectic New York locals, unusual flora, and favorite concession stands. They'd jogged side-by-side, their voices filled with endorphin induced laughter, Chloe's gait shortened to match Etta's aging pace. In the near dusk, she only noticed the park's ugliness: the homeless man sleeping on a bench, the goose poop on the path, the trash can's rotting garbage spilling over.

To Etta's left was the Hayden Planetarium, the home to the Rose Center for Earth and Space. Chloe had reveled in that exhibit, their universe's history, the galaxies, the stars, the planets.

A knot in her throat, Etta looked up to the heavens. Her daughter was part of that history.

Etta arrived at the Jacqueline Kennedy Onassis Reservoir, her legs heavy like her heart. She joined other joggers and walkers, some pushing strollers, all of them circling the mile and a half soft cinder track. She could picture Dustin Hoffman in the classic movie *Marathon Man*. Instead of being chased by bad guys, Etta was being stalked by memories. She kept glancing to her left, praying Chloe would appear.

Her cell's ringing startled her, dragging Etta from her thoughts. She fumbled for it and felt a pinch of relief. The name "Sam Madrid" was on the display. Over the past twenty years, she'd only seen him at Tripoint's annual achievement events, yet she could easily summon him up: his kind eyes, those which always looked for the best in an individual, sometimes to a fault; his warm and easy smile, which continued to do crazy things to her insides; and his strong arms, those she so needed to enfold her, to absorb even an iota of her pain.

She cried into her cell, "Oh Sam!"

"Etta? Is something wrong?"

"I'm here in Manhattan. Can we meet somewhere to talk?"

"I'm sorry. That's not going to work."

She was crestfallen.

"I'm on Heathrow's runway, heading for Berlin, but I'll be back on Tuesday morning. Are you with Chloe? She was so looking forward to your visit."

Etta slumped against the fence. "Chloe—" her voice broke, "Chloe's dead."

There was a stunned silence. "Did you say dead?"

She whimpered, "Yes... Suicide."

She heard him gasp. In the background, a female was reprimanding him. "Christ, Etta! I don't want to hang up, but I must. I promise. I'll call as soon as I land."

Etta slid down along the fence, her butt hitting the ground.

A young man stopped and squatted. "Ma'am? Are you okay?"

"I'll never be okay!"

She buried her face in her hands.

Monday - Tokyo

In the early morning light, Asami rode in a taxi's backseat. Chloe's shocking suicide news was still doing laps inside her head. She selected Jiro's number, the second call she'd made to him since they'd parted ways. He was about to board his flight. "How tragic," his voice caught. "How could Chloe have done that to her mama? But, my dear, Hana's situation is nothing like Chloe's. You know Etta's daughter attempted suicide before. You must stay calm, stay focused. Have you taken your meds?"

"Yes," she lied.

Her prescription had actually run out the prior day. Her monthly med-check appointment was in a few hours. But securing her new allotment seemed far less important than locating her daughter.

The cab pulled up in front of the Setagaya Police Station's aqua-colored marquee. Asami was attempting to be strong, yet in that spot in her heart, the one all mamas shared, she knew something was wrong—terribly wrong.

Hana hadn't been with her university boyfriend. Asami had called one of Hana's girlfriends and she'd answered, her voice groggy with sleep. She'd confirmed Hana had broken off her relationship with Felipe. She'd even checked Facebook for Asami. The night Hana had sent her the text, Felipe had posted a photo from a Seville soccer match. He'd been in the stands, a new girl on his arm.

Asami entered the seven-story police station and spoke to the woman behind the reception window.

"Detective Mori should be able to assist you," she said. "Please make yourself a cup of tea and take a seat."

Two couches flanked a table holding a thermos and a tea set. An elderly man, badly in need of a bath, and crying softly, sat on the closest couch. Asami couldn't do as she'd been instructed. Instead, she paced. Most Japanese had an ingrained respect for authority. Burglary was the most common felony. The worst threats to citizens were flashers and drunks. Women still walked dark Tokyo streets alone without fear of being attacked. Because of all that, Asami couldn't understand what might've happened to Hana.

A diminutive man stepped into the reception area, a sharp look in his intelligent eyes. Sergeant Mori introduced himself. "Your daughter, I take it, has not returned?"

"No." She bowed, her fingers finding her jacket zipper.

The detective also dipped his balding head. "Please follow me."

She entered the surprisingly fragrant bullpen area. Nearly every desk contained a vase of fresh cut flowers or a potted bonsai tree. The Tokyo prefecture employed about forty thousand officers. They defended their citizens. Citizens did not defend themselves. Only the police could carry handguns. Enforcement was so strict it was said the yakuza considered one weapon to be as valuable as ten gangsters.

Tokyo's vast police resource *should* be able to locate Hana.

Mori whisked Asami into a quiet room. Other than an Imperial Palace photo, the compact space was devoid of trimmings.

She took a seat at a table so as not to look at it.

Mori sat down and opened his notebook. "I've read the duty sergeant's report. From my experience, missing person cases are rarely the result of foul play."

Asami's feet tapped.

"Maybe your daughter simply extended her hiking trip and neglected to tell you?"

"I'm certain Hana would've called by now."

"Well then..." He looked down at the report. "I see you've only contacted Yamanashi Red Cross Hospital. Is that correct?"

"Yes."

"I'll check with the Tokyo hospitals and the relevant coroners' offices as well."

Asami winced at hearing the latter.

"Do you know your daughter's blood type?"

"Type—type B." According to Japanese popular belief, blood type determined one's personality. Hana should be active, passionate, strong, and spontaneous. Those traits fit her child like a snug pair of jeans. But, on occasion, Hana's spontaneity had gotten her into trouble. She'd act before considering the consequences. That thought plagued Asami as did the detective's question. He'd only need to know Hana's blood type to help identify her body.

From her shoulder bag, Asami removed a framed photo. She'd located it inside Hana's apartment. Her daughter and Hana's friend Lucas were pictured, both dressed in hiking gear. "I believe that's what my daughter packed to wear: that yellow cap, those khaki shorts, the orange jacket, the hiking boots, and the blue backpack. All were missing from her apartment."

"Do you recognize the male in the photo?"

"Hana's New York friend, Lucas McKenzie. He lives next door to her. At about the same time as I received her text, Lucas said he heard a male voice in her apartment. I thought it might've been a former boyfriend's, but it wasn't."

Mori tented his fingers. "Could this McKenzie fellow be involved?"

Asami was taken aback. Lucas had seemed as concerned about Hana as she. Prior to leaving her daughter's apartment, Asami had talked to him. He'd been up all night, working his social media contacts, posting Hana's photo and pertinent facts, reaching out to friends for information. She told Mori all that and added, "Lucas can't be involved."

He didn't seem convinced. "Does your daughter carry identification?"

"A driver's license for her moped. I checked. It's still locked behind her apartment building. She also has a passport, but it was missing from the drawer she keeps it in."

His brows lifted. "Could she have left the country?"

"I considered that. I thought she and her former boyfriend might've flown someplace for the weekend. But if Hana did she wasn't with him. She just returned from a work-related month of training in New York City. Because of that, I don't think she would've taken any additional time off from work."

"I see. Nevertheless, I'll contact Japan Customs to see if she used her passport. Would your daughter have talked to any work colleagues?"

"Possibly? Her recruit class friend returned my call. We're to meet in about an hour. There's also an American colleague and family friend, Chloe Martin. She—she was in Japan last week. Now she's dead."

He stiffened.

She told him about Etta's disturbing call.

His forehead creased. "What about family members? Your husband? Hana's siblings?"

That question had had to come up. It always did. "Hana has no siblings and there's never been a father involved."

His face shifted into that familiar disapproving look. "I must ask." He crossed his arms. "Has your daughter had any trouble with the yakuza?"

Asami's feet stopped.

He hastily added, "It's something we ask when anyone goes missing."

Asami couldn't believe Hana had been mixed up with anyone in Japan's organized crime syndicate—or with any of their shady endeavors—and she said so.

Yet, his question had disturbed her.

If her personal history was any sort of barometer, she couldn't reject that possibility.

-6-

1974 - New York

Etta emerged from a Midtown Manhattan subway station. The street traffic was stalled and a chorus of horns filled the air. Beside her was Donna Fitzpatrick, the Tripoint Chicago branch's fourth new Technical Rep. Perfumed by exhaust fumes, they trekked back to the Cambria Hotel near Grand Central Terminal, their home away from home for their month of training.

Donna gave Etta a dazzling smile. "Did you see Pete's face when our instructor announced you'd aced our first test? At least one of us gals did better than him."

"I admit it felt great. It also feels great to have a female colleague I can confide in and celebrate with." Etta nudged Donna. "Next time, it'll be your turn."

"Don't bet on it! I'm not as bright as you. But I have other assets that might help." Donna arched her brows and like a feisty mare shook her long chestnut mane of hair.

Etta grinned. "That could be the case. I saw the stares we got in the Chicago bullpen. Here I was, tall and athletic. There you were, short and sexy with a pouty mouth, nearly making me take pause. The office guys were confused by me. You, they wanted to seduce."

Donna giggled, not taking offense. From the get-go, Etta had realized her new colleague was uninhibited and wild, something

Donna was proud of. Male attention stuck to her like Krazy Glue. She made the guys in their class laugh, sing, and salivate—something Etta would love to emulate but never could.

They entered the Cambria lobby and took the elevator to their fifth floor domain. As the only two females in their training class, they'd been assigned to the same hotel room. They changed into lounging attire and each settled onto their respective twin bed. The nightstand between them held a bottle of red wine. Donna uncorked it and filled two water glasses handing one to Etta. "You already told me you don't have a serious boyfriend. Did you in high school or college?"

"Well, at Carter High, there were only about thirty guys to pick from. Those who weren't taken were too short, too boring, or not interested in me." Etta smiled sheepishly. "I craved that magical *Love Story* connection like Jennifer Cavalleri had for Oliver Barrett."

Donna snorted. "Who didn't? So did you find the perfect guy at Northwestern?"

"I thought I had." Etta twisted a strand of hair around her finger. "In my freshman year, one of my teaching assistants was a grad student named Sam Madrid."

"That name sounds familiar."

"Yeah. He now works for Tripoint, right here in New York. Back then, I'd watch him glide across the auditorium stage in my Fundamentals of Computer Science class. He looked like one of those Norwegian speed skaters, his long dark hair, already sprinkled with silver, flowing behind him in something like a speedboat wake.

"Wow!" Donna fanned her face with her hand.

Etta laughed. "He did the same to me. But there were loads of students in my class. I didn't think he'd even noticed me. Then, about two months into the course, I got a test back. He'd written on top, *Please see me.*"

Donna's eyes glowed. "I bet you were excited. Nervous too?"

"I was, but I'd done well on that test. So I didn't think I was in trouble. Instead, I felt sort of special, being singled out. Sam watched me as I hiked down the stairs. He was leaning on the podium in a skinny-rib turtleneck and low-riding jeans showing off his very fine body." Etta flushed at the thought. "And he smelled wonderful like lemon slices dipped in cinnamon and cloves."

She'd never forgotten that day. Her heart had similarly been galloping as she'd stood eye-to-eye with Sam.

"So, Etta, what did he say?"

"That I had a knack for Computer Science. I usually downplay a compliment, so I went on and on about the front row socks-and-sandal guys. I insisted I was not in their league."

Donna rolled off the bed. "I bet he didn't agree." She located a bag of chips.

"You're right. He said I was on even par—or better. He wanted me to consider going into the field and becoming a woman pioneer," Etta smiled, "like you."

"And you did because of him?" Donna held out the bag.

Etta reached inside for a handful. "Yes. But also to spite my chauvinistic dad. Sam was so different—a real mentor. He believed women should have an equal place in the business world."

Donna topped off Etta's glass. "So did he ask you out?"

"No..." Etta sighed then munched on a chip. "It was just my luck. I'd fallen for a guy who was engaged to a NYU medical student. Sam was also in his MBA's final months and he'd already landed his Tripoint job."

Donna settled back on the bed. "Did you stay in contact with him?"

"Yeah, I was thrilled when he'd call me from New York. Somehow, he'd gotten my sorority house's phone number. He'd ask about my studies and give me encouragement. He hadn't married yet, so I held onto hope, rejecting other guys who didn't stack up."

"So tell me. Were you still a virgin?"

"Hey, I need more chips if you want those details."

Donna readily passed the bag.

"Okay..." Etta reached in for another fistful. "I was, but not for long." Recalling that painful segment of her life, she grimaced. "Two months prior to graduation, I received Sam's wedding invitation."

"Geez! I'm sorry."

"Yeah, it was rough. I slugged around campus in a funk. I couldn't watch Sam walk down the aisle with Ms. Soon-To-Be-Doctor when I wished I was her, so I sent my regrets along with a fondue set. Then I slept with Davy Duncan, a Northwestern basketball center. I'd been casually dating him and he met my requirements. He was as socially inept as me, six inches taller, and I could drop him right after we'd done the deed."

"He sounds like most of the guys I've slept with!"

Etta giggled.

Donna joined in then leaned on her elbow. "So what are you going to do? You and Sam both work for Tripoint, and we're training in the city where he lives. Does he know how you felt about him and, I assume, still do?"

"I'm certain he never knew. But knowing I might see him has made me anxious. I asked one of our instructors about him. For the month of October, Sam's traveling overseas, researching whether Tripoint should expand globally."

"Shit!" Donna sat up. "I wanted to meet your Oliver Barrett!"

"Well, I'm relieved. It'll give me more time to show Sam his belief in me was founded. It may sound silly, but I need to succeed at Tripoint for both of us."

1974 - New York

Etta was swept up into the evening sky's glitz high above Times Square. The spectacularly lit Canadian Club, Coca Cola, and Sony advertisements contended with the *Gypsy*, *Fame*, and *Cat on a Hot Tin Roof* Broadway billboards. The street level marquees, dodgy second cousins, twice removed, were promoting burlesque shows, peep houses, and pawn shops. A raggedy saxophone busker competed with traffic noise. Hotdog, sauerkraut, and pretzel scents drifted up from push carts seeing better days. At night, the Square was considered to be a dangerous place unless traveling in a pack. For that reason, Etta and Donna were cocooned within their training class's group of guys, all on a hike to the Paradise Disco.

Donna, as usual, was the highlight of the group. She prattled away, Pete hanging on every word. Etta's eyes kept flicking over to Randy, a tall blond from the L.A. office, both witty and smart. He looked as if a surfboard should be under his arm rather than a briefcase.

The Paradise Disco had to appear seedy in the daylight. But at that witching hour, as Etta and the others piled in, it transformed into a magical hookup place.

"Come on." Donna pulled Etta up to the bar. The two gulped down their first drinks as the DJ started to spin "The Bump." Donna squealed with delight and dragged Etta onto the dance floor. While the music pounded in Etta's ears, she and Donna banged hips on every other beat. Flushed from the ritual, Etta glanced at Randy. She felt certain his eyes had connected with hers. "Can't Get Enough of You Babe" began to pour from the speakers and he approached.

Etta's heart pummeled her chest. She'd been right!

"Hey, I've been watching you two boogying. Mind if I cut in?" He slid his arm around Donna.

Crushed like a cigarette butt, Etta plodded back to the bar. To torture herself further, she watched Donna's gyrating body under the flashing strobe lights, not a thread of air between her crotch and Randy's.

"What's going on?"

She turned.

"Why's a foxy lady like you so forlorn?" The questions had come from the bartender, a twinkle in his Asian shaped eyes, their color a surprising blue, "Haruki" on his name badge. Based on his physique, he was probably into martial arts like Bruce Lee.

Etta slid onto a barstool, attempting to smile. "Make me a screwdriver and I'll tell you why."

He whipped up the orange concoction. It was her second one of the evening. In addition to easily guzzling it down, without tasting the alcohol, it had a less revolting hue than a Bloody Mary.

"You're part of the Tripoint Technology group, aren't you?"

She tipped her head. "How did you know?"

"I talked to the guy out dancing with the girl you were with. If you want my opinion, he picked the wrong one."

She sighed. "You probably tell that to all the rejected females who line the bar." Her head swiveled back toward Donna. She was still hanging onto Randy. He obviously didn't mind. His hands had been given free rein to knead her buttocks. Totally depressed, Etta's gaze returned to the bartender. "Well, Haruki, nobody seems to have the same opinion as you. But it's probably my fault." Etta drained her glass and pushed it forward for another. "I keep wishing I was with a guy I can't have."

"Isn't that the way it always goes?"

In a flash, a fresh drink appeared.

She gave him a crooked smile and toasted. "So, have other Tripoint employees come here?"

"It seems as if each trainee group shows up. The tradition started because of my brother."

"He works for Tripoint?"

"Yeah. Sam Madrid. You know him?"

Etta was blown over. Thankfully, she hadn't mentioned his name in her confession. "You're actually Sam's brother?"

"I am, obviously adopted, the 'black sheep' of the family. Sam's the 'golden son.'"

She grinned up at him. "Well you're a charming 'black sheep,' if you want my opinion." She was definitely getting soused. But what the hell! Why not?

He grinned back. "Sam keeps encouraging me to finish college and do more with my life. He brought that first Tripoint group here probably hoping they'd rub off on me. Obviously, his efforts have failed."

"I wouldn't say that." Etta swayed to the music, her inhibitions taking flight. "So tell me, Mr. Haruki Madrid..." She propped her head on her hand. "Does your brother come here with his wife?"

He snorted. "This place is beneath Cindy. For that matter, so am I. But," he shrugged, "it's no big deal. She's a tight-assed snooty bitch. Nothing like you."

Etta was stunned yet immensely pleased.

"Cindy's all work and no play—makes Sam a frustrated boy."

It was as if Etta had been skimming along the water on her cousin's Hobie-Cat, and the wind over Lake Galena had suddenly changed. If Sam was unhappily married, there could still be hope for her.

The music changed to Kool and the Gang's "Jungle Boogie."

Haruki smiled. "It's been nice shooting the breeze, but duty calls." He and the other bartenders hoisted themselves up onto the polished oak bar. A clapping and hooting frenzy followed as they each removed their shirts in a synchronized fashion.

Bursting with renewed optimism, Etta's voice joined in. On every stanza of "Get down, get down," her eyes tracked Haruki's madly moving hips. Etta, however, was picturing his brother, Sam's limber body doing wicked damage in her bed. She gulped down her third screwdriver's remains, teeth crunching the ice.

Haruki's eyes met hers and she blushed, as if caught in the act.

1984 - Tokyo

Yamada Department Stores had been in the news but not for the right reasons. Rumors were running rampant about an affair between its married chairman and his young mistress. That issue compounded Asami's depression as she applied fresh lipstick in the ladies room scented by potpourri. She'd worked at Yamada for three years and she felt as if she'd already hit the "glass ceiling." Once Mrs. Kichida had retired, Yamada had returned to feudal times. Her recruit class had never accepted her. Masato Ito, her arrogant university classmate, had also been promoted.

The bathroom door opened and an office lady entered. "Fujioka-san, I'm so glad I found you! But you must hurry. The meeting's to begin in fifteen minutes."

"Don't worry. I'll be there." Two years earlier, Jiro had encouraged Asami to take advanced English night classes at the Berlitz School of Languages. He'd even offered to help pay for the expensive tuition. "I understand your challenges at Yamada. This may be your only option to set yourself apart."

The classes and coursework had been difficult. Asami had regulated her medication dosage to stay on task, often suffering from restless nights.

But Jiro had been right.

She'd recently been called into meetings to translate. But with that job came the detested tea serving task.

Asami entered the conference room. Until everyone arrived, she stood with the sun from the windows warming her back. A blank wall was in front of her. It would help reduce distractions. To combat the negative press, Yamada was focusing on ways to improve its image. Replacing its antiquated cash registers would be one. Masato had disgustingly been chosen to assist a deputy director with that new initiative. The two were the last to enter with a distinguished man she'd been told was from a U.S. firm, and all three took seats at the teak conference table.

Asami poured coffee and tea, gritting her teeth as she served Masato. To his right was the American, about ten years her senior. While at Todai, she'd fantasized about meeting her "White Western Male" who'd be far different than the Japanese guys in her classes. She'd romanticized about his *yasashisa*—sensitivity—and dreamt how he might become her *koibito*—boyfriend—and mentor, to help her navigate the "outside" world.

Asami poured the American gentleman's coffee. Her heart clenched as he smiled up at her. She checked his left hand. It was indented where a wedding band had apparently been.

The business card ritual came next. Each Yamada attendee handed one to the man introduced as Sam Madrid. He turned to Asami. "Do you have a card as well?"

She translated.

Masato looked shocked. "She's not important to our meeting's content."

Humiliated, she relayed his words. Masato was treating her as if she was simply garnish for raw fish.

Sam snuck a compassionate look her way.

Throughout his presentation, she purposely improved his words with courteous Japanese verbiage. Tripoint Technology's software was one of the three that could run on the IBM point-of-sale terminals Yamada had already selected.

The meeting had ended well.

Asami was collecting the dirty tea and coffee cups when Sam returned to the room. "I want to thank you for your assistance. May I now ask your name?"

She bowed. "Asami Fujioka. It was my pleasure."

"Well Asami, would you care to have dinner with me? I'd love to get your viewpoint on Tripoint's software fit for Yamada as well."

She felt flattered. "Have you invited the others?"

"No," he chuckled. "You're the only one who seems to understand what I'm saying!"

She lowered her eyes and smiled. *Why not!*

At the Hayashi restaurant, a former saké brewery, Asami and Sam were seated at a low dining table. She tried not to giggle as he organized his long legs in the hollowed-out floor space. A desirable Japanese boyfriend was called "three-K"— *kōshinchō* (tall), *kōgakureki* (well educated), and *kōshunū* (high salary). Sam certainly met the standard. Plus, he seemed to be very kind and considerate—attributes Asami rarely saw in a Japanese man other than Jiro.

Once settled, Sam was direct. "You seem to be a very bright woman. Why weren't you a major player in today's meeting?"

She explained Japan's working woman's situation, her feet lightly tapping. How male politicians continued to resist passing any kind of equal-opportunity laws. How they argued they'd be the result of Western intervention and would destroy Japan's time-honored customs. "But the United Nations' *Decade for Women* initiative will end next year. Japan will lose face if we don't show some progress." She sighed. "I feel as if I'm wrestling a one-man sumo, receiving little support from my Yamada co-workers and management."

Their *shabu shabu* arrived, a Japanese hot pot for two. She showed Sam how to dip thinly sliced beef, mushrooms, and tofu into the hot broth centered on the table. As they ate, she also provided him tips on how, with a few culturally specific modifications, Tripoint's software could rise to the top in Yamada's selection process.

At meal's end, Sam thanked her for her excellent input then gave her a thoughtful smile. "You remind me a bit of my brother, Haruki."

Her forehead creased. "That's an odd name for an American."

"He's my adopted brother. Our dad was stationed in Tokyo in the years following Japan's surrender. That's when Haruki was adopted. He was born to a Japanese woman and, most likely, an American GI."

She caught her lower lip between her teeth, her eyes finding his. "I've heard of those children. The ones nobody wanted."

Sam shifted in his seat. "Well, my brother's always felt like an outsider in our family. That he's inferior to me." He shook his head. "But that's definitely not the case. Ever since Haruki dropped out of NYU, he's been drifting, working at bars, not knowing where he fits in, wanting to discover where he came from." A thought seemed to come to Sam. "My request may be way out of line, but would you know anyone who could help him track down his birth mother, assuming she's still alive?"

Asami empathized with Sam's brother, much like her own, who continued to struggle with M.S. Both believed they were inferior to others. She hesitated. "Why—why don't you let me try?"

"Really? You'd do that?" Sam grabbed her hand, an extremely intimate gesture in Japan.

She nodded and felt a surge of exhilaration.

Could she be looking at her "White Western Male"? The cure to her stalemated life?

1984 - Tokyo

The Japanese countryside's rice fields, red-roofed villas, and rural towns flashed by amid the train's rhythmic click and clack. Asami smoothed out her yellow sheath dress, the one she'd specifically picked out for Sam. She'd been attempting to hide her disappointment. Across from her sat only his brother, Haruki Madrid.

She'd traded letters with Sam to arrange the two men's logistics. Much to her delight, Sam's written words had strayed off-topic. They'd become more personal, enhancing her crush. Sam had planned to combine his business trip with Haruki's. At the last minute, Yamada had moved Tripoint's meeting out two weeks. It hadn't made sense to adjust Sam's brother's plans as well, and to pay two hefty change fees, so Haruki had arrived alone.

Asami analyzed him, her fingers fiddling with a silver charm bracelet. They were headed toward a small seaside town, forty-five miles south of Tokyo, where St. Catherine's Home for Children was located. Franciscan nuns had established the orphanage in 1948. According to Sam, that same year, an eight-week-old Haruki had been adopted from that Home.

For the umpteenth time, Haruki said, "I hope it's not a problem that Sam didn't accompany me."

Asami forced a smile. "I told you not to worry."

About a half foot shorter than his brother and a few inches taller than Asami, Haruki was dressed in a black leather jacket, gray T-shirt, and jeans. He looked a bit dangerous with his olive skin, moussed dark hair, thin mustache and goatee. She could tell he was attracted to her. His eyes, a startling blue, kept lingering. She knew she was being a snob as she rated him against Sam. Haruki wasn't tall, he wasn't well educated, and he didn't make a high salary.

Yet, in his own way, he was appealing.

He removed a well-worn photo from his jacket pocket and handed it to her. "St. Catherine's provided this to my parents."

Pictured was a middle-aged Caucasian priest. He stood beside a gaunt Japanese woman, a baby in her arms. A boy, not more than three, was at her side.

He pointed at the baby. "My parents said that's me. On my adoption papers, my name was listed as Haruki Endo."

Asami was elated. "Sam didn't mention your family name was Endo. That should help. What about the others in the photo? Do you know their names?"

"No, but I've speculated about the woman and the child for years. Maybe she's my mother and he's my natural brother."

Asami gave him an encouraging look. "Someone at St. Catherine's might recognize the priest and you'll get your answers."

He shrugged as if it was no big deal.

Asami knew it was. "Sam said your adoptive papa worked at a Navy Medical Hospital in Japan?"

Haruki's brows had furrowed at Sam's mention. "Yes. My adoptive mom joined my dad for his five year service stint. Three years in, they adopted me. Soon after, she discovered she was pregnant with Sam." He looked down. "I've always wondered whether they would've gone through with my adoption if they'd known."

Asami didn't know what to say. Had his parents favored their natural son over Haruki? She'd been a difficult child, but her issues had been far easier to handle than those of her sickly brother. Did he harbor feelings similar to Haruki's? It made her take pause.

St. Catherine's Home for Children was located near the train station in a white stucco villa with an ocean view. The grounds and gardens, where uniformed children played, looked more like a vacation retreat than an orphanage. Asami and Haruki entered the

Home's lobby filled with plants and sunlight. A young Japanese woman was watering the greenery. She stopped and bowed. "May I help you?"

Asami dipped her head. "We're here to see Sister Joan." They followed the girl to an office where a nun in full habit, and not of Japanese descent, sat behind a desk. A vase held fresh-cut yellow peonies with a clean, slightly citrus scent. A benevolent smile appeared on the nun's face landscaped with deep wrinkles.

Asami bowed. In English, she introduced Haruki and herself.

Sister Joan said, "Welcome," taking the language cue. "Please take a seat. It's rewarding to see a child we helped." She gazed affectionately at Haruki. "I was here from the start and probably held you in my arms." She pointed to a framed wall photo where about fifty bi-racial toddlers and babies were pictured. "These were our first children. You may be among them."

Haruki studied the photo. "Did you maintain records of their birth parents?"

"Regrettably, very few."

"My last name was Endo. That should help, shouldn't it?"

She sighed. "I'm afraid not. Those children, without birth records, were all given that family name."

His face remained stoic, as if that disappointing information hadn't fazed him.

Asami knew better, so did her feet as they tapped.

"So many, like you, have come here to ask that same question," Sister Joan continued. "Those years following Japan's surrender, and America's occupation, were a confusing time. By 1952, nearly ten-thousand babies had been born to U.S. servicemen and Japanese women. Many were either abandoned by their mothers or brought to an orphanage similar to ours. Most of those women were living in poverty, trying to raise a baby on their own. On top of that, because their children were half-Japanese with different skin and eye color—"

"Like mine?"

"Yes." Her voice was soft. "Like yours. Both mother and child were discriminated against."

Haruki's lips tightened. "I figured as much." He handed his dog-eared photo to her. "Do you recognize this priest? My parents said this was taken in 1948."

She seemed surprised. "Why that's Father Antonio from the Tokyo diocese. He often delivered children to the Home. Unfortunately, he's passed away."

A groundswell of frustration surged through Asami. "What about the woman?"

"I'm sorry, I don't know her, but I'm quite certain the boy is Kato. He's a hard child to forget." Sister Joan hobbled over to the wall photo and pointed. "That's him next to his best friend, Hiro. Like you, they were both given the Endo family name. The two boys were quite a pair, always into mischief." From a bookcase, Sister Joan pulled out a ledger. Its binding showed extensive wear. "Now that I know you and Kato arrived together, I might be able to tell whether you two are related."

Cautious optimism trickled through Asami. She gazed at Haruki. He couldn't hide the hope glimmering in his eyes.

The nun opened the book to the beginning, ran her finger down the yellowed page, and stopped. "Your name *is* next to Kato's. The intake person noted you two were brothers."

Haruki's voice exploded, "I was right!"

Asami was buoyed up as well. "Tell me, Sister, do you have Kato's adoption records?"

"I'm sorry, I don't." She resettled in her chair. "Neither he nor his friend were ever placed."

The wind seemed to peter out from under Haruki's high flying kite. "So what happened to them?"

"When they turned eighteen, they both left for Tokyo to find work. I'm afraid, on more than one occasion, one or the other got into trouble with the authorities. I'd personally travel into the city to bail them out." A despondent look crossed the sister's face. "Your brother blamed me for not preparing them for the real world, and he was probably right."

Asami wasn't ready to give up. "Kato could still live in Tokyo, couldn't he?"

Sister Joan hesitated. "Possibly? I lost contact with both boys nearly two decades ago. Because of that, I was afraid they'd become involved with the yakuza."

Haruki frowned. "That's Japan's organized crime syndicate, isn't it?"

Asami touched his arm. "Yes."

"So what does that actually mean?"

"Well, for centuries, the yakuza's been part of Japan's fabric. Initially, their operations centered on gambling and stolen goods, but they've expanded into such things as drugs, prostitution, and protection rackets."

"So my brother could be a criminal?"

"Maybe? But the yakuza's also involved in legitimate ventures." Asami's feet quieted. "It does make sense that Kato and Hiro could be members. They would've become adopted sons to the *oyabun*—father figure—of one of the gang's clans. In exchange for their service, they would've been offered lifetime protection, work, and advice."

Renewed hope expanded across Haruki's face. "I must locate Kato! He might also have information about our mother."

Asami took a deep breath. "If he is indeed a yakuza member, I may have a way."

-7-

Monday - New York

Twenty-four hours had passed since Etta's plane had landed in New York City. She and her daughter should've been seated in Chloe's kitchen enjoying a third cup of coffee amid avid conversation. Instead, Etta was slumped over in one of the GV Coffee Shop's battered booths across from Detective Harper.

Etta pushed aside her chipped mug of untouched coffee. Outside, it was appropriately raining cats and dogs. Etta felt like a miserable version of both. Her raincoat was soaked. Her hair secured by a headband was damp and stringy, its herbal scent providing a false sense of normalcy. Her wet loafers were sticking to the drab floor tiles scuffed by people like her who'd found it difficult to pick up their feet as they'd shuffled in, filled with emptiness, feeling far drabber, scuffed, and beaten than the restaurant.

Etta told Harper she'd been playing phone tag with Sam. She also mentioned Hana's disappearance.

"Really?" Harper stirred on the booth seat. "That's distressing for her mother. But—but I can't see how that situation has any bearing on your daughter's." She took a deep breath, as if to calm her nerves, and placed a report titled *Martin, Chloe - Preliminary Postmortem Pathology* on the scratched melamine table. "I know how difficult this will be." She reached across the table to touch Etta's hand. "I'm a mother too."

That kind gesture made Etta feel even worse. She felt so weary, so wasted, as if nothing mattered, and she tore her hand away. "Let's just get this over with."

Harper nodded. "I understand." She turned the report to its first page. "Your daughter died on Saturday evening between seven and eleven o'clock."

"Oh God!" Etta placed her head in her hands. "I first tried Chloe's cell at about eight. I should've tried earlier. Maybe she would've answered. Maybe she'd still be alive. Maybe—"

"Ms. Martin, you can't blame yourself."

"That's fine for you to say! What about that bastard, Henri? Wasn't he still with Chloe during a portion of that time?"

"The Rusty Nail manager confirmed Mr. Broussard arrived at the bar at about six forty-five and he didn't leave until after midnight."

Etta rubbed her forehead. A pounding headache added to her agony. "When Chloe attempted suicide before, her doctor told me it had been a cry for help. If she'd really wanted to kill herself, she would've taken more pills—she would've made more cuts." Etta shook her head. "Chloe had years of psychiatric help. Her therapist told me a person who attempts suicide may do it again. That's why I was so protective. But when Chloe moved to New York, she said she'd had enough therapy. She'd found Henri. She'd moved on with her life. She'd claimed she hadn't had any suicidal thoughts for years," Etta's voice cracked, "and—and I believed her!"

"Ms. Martin, you did your best. Some things are simply out of your control."

Etta knew she was right, but that didn't help. "Tell me. Did my daughter suffer?"

Harper gazed down at the report as if it could provide that answer. "I don't think she suffered much. Her cause of death was cardiac arrest due to rapid blood loss. She cut both lengthwise and across her wrists. Her heart would've stopped soon after."

Etta closed her eyes, attempting to block out that image of her daughter, but it was useless. "What—what did she use?"

"Mr. Broussard's straight razor."

Etta trembled, a gag reaction in her throat. When Henri's eyes had first located Chloe's, within the Bryant Hotel's bathroom mirror, that same razor had been skimming across his cheeks.

How she hated that man.

"Ms. Martin, she also took sleeping pills."

"God! It's just like before! How many did she take?"

"Only a few more than the recommended dosage, but something else showed up in your daughter's autopsy." The detective hesitated. "There was some bruising around her wrists, as if she'd been held or restrained."

Etta gripped her mug, her thoughts racing. "Henri told me they'd had an argument."

"Yes. He said he might've grabbed one of Chloe's wrists but not firm enough to have caused a bruise."

"Do you believe him?"

"I'm not sure. Either way, that action didn't cause your daughter's death, though their fight could've been its mitigating circumstance."

"So you're convinced my daughter committed suicide?"

"Yes. There's no other explanation. The front door was dead bolted and all the apartment windows were locked from inside. That's why the officer and Mr. Broussard had to break in. Then there's also your daughter's cell." From inside her satchel, Harper located an evidence bag and removed the device.

"Where did you find it?"

"On the bathroom floor. Only your daughter's prints were on it." The detective powered it on. No password was required and the wallpaper photo appeared. Chloe's arms were wrapped around Henri, their foreheads touching, an intimate moment some friend had captured.

The detective selected the Message App with a stylus and a new message appeared, addressed to "Mom." It hadn't been sent.

Etta moaned. *I'm sorry...* was burned onto the display.

Why hadn't Chloe reached out to her? They could've talked things through. What could've been so terrible that she'd allowed Etta to fly into New York and find her that way? Yet, in her daughter's high school senior year, Chloe had allowed Etta to do the same.

She covered her face with her hands.

What had caused her daughter such pain she believed death was her only option?

Monday - Tokyo

Asami bulldozed her way off the train at *Chuo*—Tokyo's Central Ward—where Tripoint's Japanese branch was located. It was as if her lack of sleep had filled her engine with extra adrenaline. She was also going without meds. She'd decided to skip her appointment. Asami couldn't spare one second of time when her daughter's life could be on the line.

Her first destination was Hamarikyu Gardens, a public park originally built by seventeenth-century shoguns for their sole enjoyment. The park's tea house would provide more privacy for Asami's talk with Hana's recruit class friend. Depressing thoughts about Etta's loss, however, kept swirling inside Asami's head. For the moment, she pushed those aside. She had to focus on Hana.

En route to the park, Asami neared the Tsukiji fish market and caught a whiff of its pungent scent. About two months earlier, she and Hana had picked up sushi bento boxes from a neighboring stand. They'd eaten lunch together beside the Gardens' quaint Inabu Shinto Shrine. The majority of Japan's population did not identify with one specific religion. Traditional rituals from many were imbedded within their culture. If Asami's mama had still been alive, she would've been offering up prayers to family spirits to gain help and guidance. That wasn't going to cut it for Asami. Taking action in the physical world was what was needed.

The live tuna auctions were over and fishmongers were filleting the day's catch. Out of the corner of Asami's eye, she noticed a Japanese man standing beside a booth.

She squinted. Was that possibly a purple birthmark on his right cheek? Or was that simply a shadow from the booth's awning? Then her eyes darted down to his hands. His left little finger was stubby, a sure sign he was affiliated with the yakuza or had been. Asami's hands fiddled with her jacket zipper. Could he be the same man from the previous evening? The one at Kimura's? The one seated on the bar stool next to Hana's friend Lucas?

Asami shook off those disconcerting thoughts and hustled through the park gate. Surrounded by ginkgo and maple trees, all dressed in autumn colors, she threaded along the path. Asami reached a tidal pond, where red-crowned cranes perched on boulders, and she crossed a cedar bridge. Outside the glass-enclosed teahouse was Sumie Ono, seated on a bench, her long dark hair and slash of bangs gleaming in the sun.

Like Hana, Sumie was a beauty—fine skin and perfect white teeth. Both young women took care of themselves, eating healthy foods and exercising regularly. Both were clever.

Japanese women struggled in their workplace. Should they use "women's language," considered to be self-effacing and deferential, when their jobs called for sureness and expertise? To create harmony, most Japanese females were non-confrontational. That did not define Hana or Sumie or, for that matter, Asami.

Although it had taken her close to a decade before she'd felt as confident in her work environment as her daughter already did. None of them would succeed at a *gaishikei*—foreign capital company—if they didn't share their insights and opinions. But they walked a fine line. They couldn't appear "uppity." Their suggestions had to be offered with modesty and quiet strength.

Asami used that strength to hold back tears as she reached Hana's recruit class friend attired in a black suit, a shoulder-strap briefcase by her side.

Sumie stood and bowed. "Fujioka-san, I know you want information about Hana, but I may not be very helpful. I haven't talked to her since Thursday."

Asami returned the bow. "My dear, anything will help. First, let's get a sweet and some tea." They each ordered inside and returned to the bench. Once seated, Asami's feet tapped. "Last week, I was in Fukuoka with clients." She placed the small wreath-shaped cake beside her and took a sip of green tea. "My last communication with Hana was a text she sent me at about 2:00 a.m. on Friday. She said she was going hiking in the Fuji Five Lakes Region and she needed to think."

Sumie's brows lifted while she nibbled on the cake.

"You said you last saw Hana on Thursday?"

"Yes. We both participated in Tripoint's new point-of-sale release training. A woman colleague from New York conducted it."

"Was she Chloe Martin?"

Sumie nodded. "Hana seemed to know her quite well. It was Miss Martin's last night in Tokyo so she asked Hana and me to join her at the British Pub for a drink. I had other plans, but Hana agreed to go."

Asami sat back. Her daughter had indeed been with Etta's on Thursday night. "Was there anyone else who might've joined them?"

"Well, there was another American, a high level executive. I should remember his name. Oh wait." She extracted Tripoint's annual report from her briefcase. "He's pictured in here." Adjacent to the three founders' inside cover photo was the next executive tier. Sumie pointed at Sam Madrid. "He's the one who presented the sales strategy with Miss Martin."

Asami flushed, her mind jumping to a memory. Any mention or sight of Sam still had that effect on her. The annual report had been released prior to his COO promotion. Both he and the CEO's son would be featured on the inside cover at the next printing. Could Sam have been the male in Hana's room? Asami couldn't imagine why he would've been there, but she couldn't rule him out.

She refocused on Sumie. "Did Hana mention her hiking plans to you?"

Small frown lines appeared between Sumie's dark eyes. "No. I was surprised when she didn't come into work on Friday. We were to install the new software release on our lab system."

Asami's hand crumbled her uneaten sweet. Hana would not have missed that learning opportunity without good reason.

Who could the male, inside her daughter's apartment, have been? And what had Hana needed to think about? Maybe Etta's daughter would've known both answers.

Could Chloe's suicide be linked to Hana's disappearance? The prior Sunday, at Kimura's, Chloe's eyes had sparkled when she'd talked about Henri Broussard. If he'd cheated on her, she would've been devastated, but suicide?

Jiro had reminded Asami, Chloe *had* attempted that impulsive act before. But she'd been a teenager, driven by irrational emotions. On Sunday, Asami had seen the exceptionally balanced and beautiful woman Chloe had become—so like her mama. How could Chloe have taken her life knowing the pain she would've caused Etta... dear Etta?

An oriental turtle dove landed on the bench. The bird's "her-her-oo-oo" call normally soothed Asami. She thought of Chloe. She thought of her own daughter—wise beyond her years—who'd been handed the unfair role of parenting her own mama.

Asami couldn't lose Hana.

Monday - New York

The weather had cleared. Sunlight streamed through two of Chloe's apartment living room windows. The third was patched with cardboard and duct tape. Natural light was one of the things Etta's daughter had craved most. Chloe had often curled up in her butterfly patterned chair, by their Evanston condo window, her eyes closed, her fingers extended as if to suck in the heat. She'd said it had recharged her—helped her power through the day. "Each has so much potential, Mom, you only have to uncover it."

Etta couldn't fathom that possibility.

To pack up a few keepsakes, she dragged in two cardboard boxes while averting her eyes from the closed bathroom door.

What a miserable job.

Etta had managed to call her Chicago assistant and Tripoint's New York HR manager. She'd told both women about Chloe's passing. The latter's response had disturbed her. "Oh Etta, how tragic! On Friday, your daughter had made an appointment to see me. It was scheduled for nine this morning. Now I understand why she didn't show up."

Etta continued to speculate about that meeting. What had Chloe planned to discuss with HR? In addition to Henri's probable infidelity, could her daughter have been struggling over some work related issues? In combination, had those pushed her over the brink? Had she succumbed to feelings of hopelessness as she had years earlier?

A guitar and a banjo rested in stands along the window wall. The third stand was empty. It had to be the home for the stringed instrument Henri had used at the Rusty Nail.

She couldn't talk to him. She blamed him. Chloe's wrists had been bruised. He'd been rough with her. Had he been that way in the past?

A black leather chair held Chloe's "Home Sweet Home" cross-stitched pillow, the one her daughter had made when she'd been about ten. In recent years, she'd used it to prop up her laptop while multitasking: answering emails, web surfing, fine tuning a spreadsheet, and watching TV.

Etta picked up the pillow and smothered her nose in her daughter's scent. My poor child...

Asami had to be feeling similar emotions. She'd promised to call when she had any news about Hana.

The bookcase was filled with framed photos. One included a boy with caramel-colored skin and Asian eyes—probably Deon—the seventeen-year-old her daughter and Henri had been mentoring in the Tripoint for Kids program. It was a lifeline for at-risk teens—a way for them to escape from their never-ending cycle of poverty, drugs, and crime.

Chloe, ironically, had needed that lifeline more than Deon.

Etta located her daughter's Tripoint entry badge attached to a key ring holding two keys. One would open Chloe's desk, the other her credenza. Cleaning out Chloe's work possessions would be another painful chore. Chloe's laptop was a Tripoint asset Etta would also need to return.

She searched the living room and kitchen for it, then stepped over the bedroom threshold and froze. Chloe had been meticulous when handling her belongings, but her clothes and shoes were strewn about. The closet door was also open revealing Chloe's remaining shoes scattered left and right. That especially bothered

Etta. In Chloe's Evanston closet, her shoes had been perfectly aligned heel to toe. They could've been used in a Macy's display.

It was hard to believe her daughter had left her room in such disarray when she'd had plans to take her own life.

Etta sank down on the bed. Had Henri gone through Chloe's things and thrown them about? What about her daughter's laptop? Etta's gaze scavenged the bedroom. It was nowhere in sight.

Ignoring Henri was no longer an option.

It was Monday, a work day. Could he be teaching?

Henri and his mom had moved from Montreal to upstate New York in the eighties. He'd attended Skidmore College and, until the prior year, had been teaching his native language at a Saratoga Springs grade school. When Chloe had met him, he'd been hired to teach French at Public School 41. Located in the Village's heart, it was one of the top K-5 schools in New York City.

Etta called Henri's cell. On the fourth ring, he picked up. "Oh Etta! I'm so glad you called!" Young voices were in the background.

"You're actually teaching today?"

"Yes, I—I didn't know what else to do. But can you hold for a minute? I can't talk in my classroom." He muffled the phone.

Her loathing for Henri bubbled up inside. Chloe was dead because of him. She stared out the window. Perched on the sill was a wren, its tiny beak pecking away at some sort of insect.

Shit! Just another fatality in the lousy scheme of life.

Henri came back on. "I'm out in the hall. But listen..." There was a hitch in his voice. "I can't—I just can't understand why Chloe killed herself. I know she attempted suicide before, but that was ages ago. Sure, we had our minor arguments, like the one on Saturday, but I saw no signs of depression. Chloe was really happy. We truly loved each other. She was *mon coeur*—my heart. We were talking about a permanent life together. We were—"

Etta harshly broke in, "You were cheating on Chloe, weren't you?"

"Mon Dieu! Why would you think that? She was everything to me. You must believe that!"

"Why else would she have done what she did?"

"I only wish I knew."

Etta didn't know what to think. "I'm inside your apartment's bedroom. Did you mess up Chloe's clothes and shoes?"

"No? I haven't been back there yet. It—it's too painful..."

Nothing was making sense. "What about Chloe's laptop. Did the police take it?"

"I don't know... Merde! I don't know anything! Maybe they took it. Or maybe it's locked to her work desk or inside it. She went into Tripoint's office on Friday after she landed. Sometimes she doesn't lug it home. Oh Etta... I can't—I can't believe she's dead."

Etta's desolate eyes drifted back to the wren.

"I know, Henri, I know..."

Monday - Tokyo

Many top firms were housed in Tokyo's Central Ward. Tripoint and its subsidiary, Pollard Property Group, better known as PPG, were among them. Asami gripped the handrail inside her building's elevator. The British Pub wouldn't open for another hour. Without her meds she felt naked, stripped of her protective armor, unable to subdue her overactive brain. She was also dressed in her quilted jacket and yesterday's clothes: designer jeans, form fitting red cowl neck sweater, and three inch heels—far from proper work attire. Plus her fingernails were a mess.

Asami stepped off onto the eighteenth floor and used her badge to enter the sales bullpen area. Unlike traditional Japanese firms, Tripoint's Tokyo office resembled its American counterparts. She drew anxious glances from colleagues as she rushed past them. She'd alerted her assistant about Hana's disappearance. Yoshi had promised to circulate that news throughout the office and gather any leads.

Three years earlier, Asami had been promoted to the Tokyo branch management position. To achieve that status had amazed her far more than Jiro. "My dear, that's wonderful!" He'd crushed her into a hug. "Both your Tripoint experience and your bilingual skills far outweigh any other candidate's in your office. Your excessive energy and hyper-focus on the big issues are also assets. They set you apart from the docile Japanese women you work beside."

But she'd also believed Sam Madrid, Tripoint's VP of Operations at that time, might've put in a good word for her. Prior to the official announcement, she'd received his personal note of congratulations.

Asami knew most Japanese women, lucky enough to break through the "glass ceiling," were still hidden behind "shoji screens." It was as if their companies didn't want to admit their female employees had achieved a leadership position. Most often, they were only visible to colleagues, not clients. But working for a gaishikei was different. As a Tripoint woman executive, Asami and her male peers were treated as equals. She was expected to take a leadership role at client meetings. She felt proud of her accomplishment. It was what she'd dreamed about back at Todai when Mrs. Kichida had first taken the stage.

Asami reached her assistant and Yoshi bowed, her youthful face creased with worry lines. "Fujioka-san, how are you doing?"

Asami bowed. "Not so good. Please, come into my office so we can talk." Sunlight reflected off the surrounding skyscrapers and filled Asami's office with warmth. She took a seat at her desk and peered up at Yoshi. "Do you have any information about Hana?"

"Only the message she left for the receptionist last Friday. I'll queue it up for you." Yoshi leaned over, punched an access code into Asami's desk phone, and passed the receiver to her.

Hana's message had been recorded at 2:12 a.m. on Friday morning, shortly after she'd sent Asami the text. The message said, "This is Hana Fujioka. I'll—I'll be taking a few days of vacation." Asami could hear a muffled deep voice saying, "Hang up." That was what Hana did.

Asami clutched the receiver. Her daughter *had* been with a male at around 2 a.m. just as Hana's friend Lucas had said. Both Hana and the man had spoken in Japanese. Could the male have been Lucas? She couldn't tell. But she could definitely rule out Sam Madrid. He didn't speak any Japanese.

Asami replayed the message three more times and listened to the intonation in her daughter's voice. Hana had seemed frightened.

Shaken, Asami replaced the receiver in its cradle and looked up. "You know I was out of town last week. Did you happen to see Hana leave the office on Thursday?"

"I didn't, but Mr. Pollard might have. He's still in his office packing up a few things."

The CEO's son, TJ Pollard, had arrived in Tokyo two years earlier to manage the Asia Pacific Region. He'd spent most of that time traveling between Tripoint's Chinese, South Korean, and Australian branches, meeting with clients and Tripoint colleagues. But his primary office was located two doors down from Asami's.

The previous week, his assignment had ended.

Asami took a fortifying breath and strode out of her office. She knocked on TJ's door and walked in. The sight of him always unsettled her. Unlike most American men in their forties, TJ didn't carry any extra weight around his belly and he often bragged about his personal fitness. Even at Asami's stressful time, his eyes couldn't help but sweep her body, and the glint in them was not condemnation for her casual attire, just the opposite.

TJ patted his coiffed silver hair into place as he stood. "Asami! I heard your daughter is missing!" His voice seemed overly effusive as if he was stoked on too much caffeine. "I'm so sorry. Tell me, do you have any leads?"

She shook her head. Prior to TJ's Tokyo arrival, he'd been married and divorced three times. Most Japanese women considered him to be a definite "three-K." TJ had hosted a number of Tripoint staff parties at his luxurious apartment and the young female employees had vied for his attention.

That had worried Asami knowing her own history with him.

"Did you see my daughter leave the office last Thursday? It would've been soon after the point-of-sale new release training."

TJ nodded. "Sam Madrid and Chloe Martin were here from the states. They stopped into my office with Hana. All three were going out for drinks. Maybe to the British Pub?"

"Did you go as well?"

"No. I had a client dinner engagement." Color had crept up TJ's neck. "Did someone say I was there?"

She stared at him. "No?"

He shuffled some papers on his desk and checked his watch. "I'm sorry. I have to finish up. My flight leaves in five hours, but I'll be back at our New York headquarters on Tuesday. If there's anything else I can do, please don't hesitate to call."

Asami's hand slipped under her hair, her fingernail nubs cruising over the nape of her neck.

TJ was normally a cocky gaijin. His helpful demeanor had seemed as far out of character as the distance to New York and back.

-8-

1974 - New York

The 6:00 a.m. alarm went off and Etta groaned, her head pounding from the Paradise Club's prior night's libations. However, Sam's brother's information, about Sam's marital situation, was somewhat of a soothing balm. Through crusty eye-slits, she viewed her roommate's languid shape curled up on top of the adjacent twin bed, her makeup smeared, her dress in shambles, her chunky heeled shoes still strapped to her ankles.

Even though Donna had stumbled in at about 4 a.m., she sprung off the bed all bright and bubbly like the gin fizz she'd chugged down the previous evening.

Donna stretched her arms toward the ceiling. "That was some night! I call firsts in the shower." Through the bathroom wall, her off-pitch voice belted out "You and Me against the World" sounding nothing like Helen Reddy's.

Etta dragged herself out of bed. *What a girl!* Donna never had trouble getting the guys or gearing up for the day.

But that evening, after their training session, Etta and Donna both had to gear up. The Chicago hires had been invited to dinner at the home of Tripoint's CEO and his wife, Sylvia Pollard.

Donna asked, "Do you know the inside scoop on the Pollards?" Her fingers rippled through her hanging clothes, located inside their hotel room's closet, as she tried to decide what to wear. Unlike Etta, Donna came from money.

"No, tell me." Etta gazed at her two suits, her interview attire, and five blouse changes. She had slim pickings to choose from.

"My dad met Sylvia's on a Montana hunting trip. Her parents own acreage in the Adirondacks. That's where Sylvia's dad taught her to hunt deer, coyote and even bear."

"Wow! Do you know how she met Tom?"

"She was at Radcliffe when he was at Harvard. But they were the reverse of *Love Story.* She comes from old money while Tom was on a scholarship."

Etta's shoulders slumped. "Great! Tonight, I bet she'll be dressed to the hilt."

Donna pulled out two dresses and held one up to Etta. "Hey, why don't you wear this? I haven't shortened it yet." It was a black and white geometric wrap dress with a plunging neckline and, if one weren't careful, an upper thigh reveal.

Etta sucked in a quick breath. "Are you sure?"

"Absolutely!"

She slipped inside it, the jersey fabric clinging to her skin. She felt so feminine, so sensual, very different than her traditional self.

Donna nodded her approval. "We gals have to stick together."

A limo arrived for the Chicago contingency. The guys sat on one side, she and Donna on the other.

Pete's eyes normally focused on Donna. Instead, they were peeling Etta like the banana she'd had for breakfast. It was just like Pete to be so vulgar, yet Etta was secretly pleased to have evoked that sort of reaction from him. Neil wasn't as gauche. "Boy, Etta!" He gave her his affable grin. "You look amazing!"

They arrived at the Dakota Apartments near Central Park West. Etta was impressed. John Lennon and Yoko Ono had been featured in the newly launched *People Magazine*. They also resided at the Dakota.

The limo entered the arched main entrance, large enough for horse-drawn carriages from yesteryears. The doorman alerted Tom Pollard and, moments later, the dashing man from Etta's interview stepped off the elevator in an elegant suit. He said, "I'm glad the four of you could make it," but his gaze met only Etta's. He placed his left hand on the small of Donna's back and his right hand on Etta's. Its warmth penetrated the fabric of her dress making her uncomfortable.

Donna's response was just the opposite. She leaned into him, as if she were drunk, and gushed, "I can't wait to see your apartment!"

Neil said, "Same here," as he buttoned his navy sport coat and straightened his tie.

Pete simply looked ticked at Donna's reaction.

Tom escorted them up to his third floor apartment. Its beautiful drawing room, filled with antique furniture and oriental rugs, smelled like Chanel N°5. That scent invariably brought Etta's mom's presence into the room. It continued to be her only splurge.

Standing by the expansive windows were three women and a boy about eight, a devilish grin on his face. Etta knew his type from her babysitting years—the kind who'd blamed his innocent siblings for his bad behavior. Beside the boy were two men Etta recognized from office photos: Tripoint's CFO and COO, Harry Davison and Dick Bengston.

Tom made the introductions. They included his wife and their son, TJ.

Etta had certainly been wrong about Sylvia Pollard's attire. Stuffed into a tan skirt and matching blouse, Tom's wife had a genuine smile. She was the one wearing Chanel N°5. Along with a muscular build, she was sporting a Dorothy Hamill wedge-cut. Etta could picture a shotgun in Sylvia's hands. Conversely, the wives of Harry and Dick were fashionably dressed and seemed snobbish.

Sylvia whispered in her son's ear.

He smirked at Etta, held out his small hand, and said, "I'm pleased to meet you."

Etta shook it, surprised by his grip and appraising stare. *Like father, like son.*

Sylvia excused herself to get the "miniature Tom" ready for bed. Once the two had departed, Tom senior's eyes drilled into Etta. His cigarette in hand, he cocked his head when he exhaled, the smoke rising and hovering against the coffered ceiling. He was a handsome and powerful man, but as Mom would say, "Until you cut through the crust, you can't tell much about a chicken potpie." Etta might get that chance at dinner.

The dining table seating was assigned. Tom was to Etta's right, his wife across from him. As Etta had feared, unless she held her skirt's front closure together, her right thigh would show.

Dick raised his water glass. "Here's to Tom, Sylvia and the new Chicago hires. It isn't every day we get to dine in such a historic landmark and one designed by the same firm as the Plaza Hotel."

Tom smiled and lifted his glass.

Etta did the same and the jersey fabric slipped off her lap.

Tom's thigh touched her exposed one.

Shit! She jumped and shifted away. From the corner of her eye, she checked his reaction.

There was none.

Sylvia addressed the new hires. "Have any of you been inside the Plaza?"

Etta was the only one who hadn't.

Sylvia beamed at her. "You must see it. The lobby is magnificent and so is the Oak Room, although its bar was formerly a male-only domain."

Seated beside Sylvia, Harry scowled. "It should've remained that way, but that damn Betty Friedan took care of that!"

In mock sympathy, Sylvia cooed, "Poor, Harry," and patted his hand.

Etta's ears had perked up. "Isn't Betty Friedan that feminist fighter?" Mom and her friends had mentioned Betty's name.

Sylvia nodded. "About five years ago, to protest the Oak Bar's gender-exclusive policy, she sat down to eat. But rather than being served, the waiter removed her table."

Etta's eyes opened wide. "Betty had guts."

A victory smile spread across Sylvia's lips. "She sure did."

Etta admired Tom's wife. Sylvia was an anomaly: a liberal, gun carrying, feminist. She reminded Etta of Mom, also a sharpshooter, but with a pellet gun, which came in handy for driving rabbits away from their backyard vegetable garden.

It was an exciting time, albeit a bit dangerous, Etta looked to her right, to be an assertive and smart female. Like Betty Friedan, Etta's plan was to leave her own mark.

1974 - New York

A taxi dropped Etta off in front of the Plaza Hotel where the final scene to *The Way We Were* had been filmed. She was thrilled to be meeting the other Robert Redford and his wife inside.

That morning, Etta's instructor had handed her a note: *Please join Sylvia and me at 7:00 p.m. for dinner at the Plaza Hotel. Regards, Tom Pollard.*

Etta had felt special—singled out—just as she'd felt at Northwestern when Sam had asked her to come down to the podium. Sure, Donna had charmed all the guys in their training class, but Etta had caught both the CEO's and his wife's attention.

Etta entered the magnificent Beaux Arts lobby in a new black dress and ankle strapped platform pumps, a black velvet headband in her long sandy hair. It would've been tacky if she'd worn Donna's dress again. To treat herself, Etta had used her first paycheck at Macy's.

Tom was standing by the front desk, an appreciative look on his face.

"Hello, Mr. Pollard," Etta said, her eyes searching for his wife.

Tom noticed. "I'm sorry. Sylvia's not here. Our son had a fever and she didn't want to leave him with a sitter."

Etta's ebullience faded. She recalled the dinner at Tom's home, his thigh touching hers.

"Since it'll be just the two of us, why don't we eat in the Oak Bar?" He placed his hand on the small of Etta's back and turned her in that direction. "And please, call me Tom."

As a teenager, Etta had waited tables at the Carter Café, a local greasy spoon. Her pay, plus tips, had been far better than babysitting. In turn, she'd had to put up with the owner, Big Bob. Eons before, he'd been the high school star quarterback. Many a girl had fought to get into his Pinto's back seat. Even though he'd become fat and sloppy, he'd still believed he was "God's gift to women." He'd often touched Etta on her back or her behind or brushed against her breasts.

The Women's Christian Temperance Union was headquartered near Northwestern's campus. Etta had leafed through an early nineteen hundreds' guidebook. Female workers had been advised on how to handle unwanted workplace advances. If all else failed, quitting had been the recommended solution.

Nothing had changed.

That was why Etta had quit her job, after confronting Big Bob, so he couldn't enjoy firing her and tarnishing her work record.

She eyed Tom as they entered the Oak Bar and convinced herself his actions were innocent. This was her opportunity, her one-on-one time to show him he'd made the right decision by hiring her.

The Oak Bar's dark paneled walls, gilded coffered ceiling, and mahogany bar exuded New York City. A man in white tails was playing the grand piano. Black jacketed waiters scurried around with drinks on silver trays.

Etta inhaled the glamor.

Once she and Tom were seated, he asked, "Would you like a drink?"

No alcohol had been served at his dinner party. Would he think she was a lush if she said yes? Or should she decline with the risk he'd believe she was a prude? If Donna had been present, Etta would've followed her lead. When the waiter appeared, Tom made the decision for her. "We'd like two vodka martinis."

The waiter departed and Tom lit a cigarette. "I understand your training is going well."

She was pleased he'd inquired about her. Though, as customary, she had to downplay his compliment. "My tests and mock sales calls have gone well, but I've also relied on my classmates for assistance."

He skewed his head. "In what way?"

"For instance, on the point-of-sale terminals, I can't tell whether the LED lights are the desired green or instead red, signaling an issue."

He seemed surprised.

Etta shrugged. "Every LED electrical device is an annoyance for me." She explained how she was colorblind; how she rarely ate chicken or pork because she couldn't tell whether the entrée was fully cooked; how her skin had to glow before she could determine whether she was sunburned; how on golf courses—yes she liked to golf—she couldn't tell whether the Porta Potties were vacant or occupied.

Tom laughed at each scenario and Etta relaxed. She knew airline pilots, police officers, and electrical engineers required good-to-perfect color vision. She didn't carry any of those titles.

The waiter returned with two chilled martinis. Those turned into four along with salads and lobster corn bisque. The martinis loosened Etta up and her conversation flowed. Amid work talk and current events, her banter verged on flirtatious. That had been the norm at Northwestern, what girls had been expected to do with guys their own age. But the man across from her was ten years her senior and Tripoint's CEO.

Tom signaled to the waiter, and he left with Tom's credit card. At that moment, Tom's eyes seemed to change, appraising Etta before he spoke. "Tripoint maintains a Plaza meeting suite. I'd like to show it to you."

Etta's radar had gone up. It was time to politely bow out. "I appreciate the meal, but—"

"I insist. In the future, you may be able to use the suite with your clients. It'll give you a better idea."

What could she do? Tom was the most powerful man at Tripoint and he'd insisted.

They took the elevator up to the fourth floor. Each hallway door had a name. Tom used a key to open the Manhattan Suite and he ushered Etta in. Her eyes quickly scanned the furnishings: a large conference table, upholstered chairs, flipchart stands, *and* a large couch. *Shit!* She'd placed herself in a precarious situation.

Tom smiled. "Nice facility, isn't it?" He began to prepare drinks at a wet bar.

Etta looked at her watch and angled toward the door. "I'm sorry. It's getting late and I have a test on retail concepts tomorrow."

He returned to her side. “Come on.” His voice was hot in her ear. “One more drink.” He shoved it into her hand.

She felt that warm palm on her back directing her toward the couch. “No, Tom, I think I’ve had enough. But thanks for dinner. I need to go.”

The evening’s magic had burst like a balloon caught in a bramble bush. At Tripoint, Etta wanted to use her brains to get ahead, not her body. She wanted to win respect for her business abilities, not favors for her extracurricular activities.

Anger worked behind Tom’s cheeks. “Don’t be a tease. When you entered this suite you knew what you were getting into.”

Etta wanted her job but not that way. As if nothing improper had been said, she set down her drink and forced a bright smile. “Thanks again, but I’m leaving.”

His steely eyes filled with rage.

In sheer panic, Etta abruptly left the suite.

The door slammed shut behind her and she shuddered.

My God! What did I do? What did *I do?*

1984 - Tokyo

The Roppongi entertainment district’s neon lights dissolved behind Asami as she stepped into the Kingo Club’s marble-floored reception area. To her left was Sam’s brother, Haruki. Worried for her safety, Jiro had also insisted on accompanying them. “That club has known yakuza connections,” he’d said. “It also targets customers with heavy expense accounts and those looking for cocaine.”

Asami felt she might regret her decision, but she’d still talked to her papa. Small business owners often paid the yakuza for protection. Her parents believed the organization’s credible threat of violence deterred shoplifting and robberies at their souvenir shop. The yakuza member Asami's father paid had located Haruki's natural brother, but only after Haruki's New York bank had wired the gangster three hundred American dollars. Kato worked for the Wada-kai, Japan's fourth largest yakuza organization, with roughly ten thousand members divided into two-hundred and ninety clans. Apparently, he'd made a name for himself.

Adjacent to the coat check counter, a pair of opaque paper sliding panels provided access to the club's inner sanctum. The *fusuma* were painted with a misty landscape of ancient cherry trees and lush peonies, symbols of spring, wealth, honor and the omen of good fortune.

Asami twisted a charm back and forth on her bracelet. She hoped the latter would hold true for Haruki.

She nudged him. "Aren't you excited to meet your brother?"

He shrugged.

His nonchalance was an act, one to hide his fear of being accepted. He'd told Asami as much. Based on his "no big deal" attitude, she'd felt honored when he'd revealed that personal fact.

Haruki touched her hand, to stop its fidgeting, and Jiro lifted one eyebrow.

Over the prior two days, Haruki had done the same numerous times, even when her hand had been at rest. She'd tried to convince herself that human contact was helping him handle his emotional quest. Yet she felt guilty. It was probably more than that to him.

Haruki stepped toward the fusuma panels. "Asami, it doesn't seem right. You should be accompanying me inside. You arranged this entire meeting."

Jiro placed his arm around Asami's shoulders. "Don't worry. I'll take good care of her."

Haruki grudgingly nodded, slid the panels apart, and entered the male-only hostess club. Like so many others, the Kingo Club had evolved from a former *geisha* lodging house to provide total relaxation for the overworked "salaryman."

Before the panels closed, Asami caught a glimpse of the Chanel-shift-clad women, both Asian and Caucasian, lined up by the entrance. A silver haired woman sat at an antique desk. She seemed to be in charge, most likely the club's mama-san.

If Haruki had not been meeting Kato, he would've been paying about five thousand yen per hour for *nomihoudai*—all-you-can-drink—cheap whiskey and gin, and for companionship. One of the hostesses, by the door, would've taken him to his designated table to talk, to light his cigarette, to place ice in his drink, and to boost his ego telling him, "You're quite the man." Her goal would've been to make him happy, to make him want to stay and pay for additional time. No sex would've been involved—at least not on the premises.

Jiro helped Asami out of her coat. He handed it, along with his, to the woman behind the counter. She flapped her eyelashes at Jiro, a common occurrence. At that year's Japan Academy Prize Ceremony, he'd won awards for *The Shogun Tradition* in two film categories: best supporting actor and assistant director.

Asami and Jiro settled onto one of the two plush burgundy couches to wait. Her eyes were drawn to a gigantic music video screen on the opposite wall. The singing sensation Sieko was flipping her dark hair and romping around to her number one hit "Dancing Shoes."

The catchy lyrics hit home: *"Do you wanna dance... I'm a shy girl in a man's world... Dancing shoes stepped right up and said... You're the one..."*

Asami linked her arm into Jiro's. "When I'm around most men, I'm often as shy as a borrowed cat. But Sam Madrid has been helping me find my voice."

Jiro smiled. "It appears as if his brother has as well?"

"No... I'm not interested in Haruki. I'm just being kind."

"Okay? So when Haruki's brother returns for the Yamada meeting, are you going to tell him, *'You're the one'*?"

She laughed and leaned against her friend.

Men entered and exited the club, many eyeballing both of them. Eventually, the sliding panels opened and Haruki emerged. Following him was a man in a suit, his starched white shirt unbuttoned at the neck to expose elaborate tattoos. He had to be Kato. The two men looked so much alike in stature, in skin tone, in the slight curl to their hair, and their eyes, especially their eyes. But, as the two men approached, rather than seeing the warmth always evident in Haruki's, Kato's icy blue ones pierced into hers.

Haruki's open admiration, when he introduced Kato, disturbed Asami. She remained seated, frozen among the couch cushions while Jiro stood.

Kato bowed deeply, his shrewd face aimed directly at Asami. In perfect English he said, "Thank you for delivering my brother to me."

Asami clasped her hands, nearly crushing the bones. What had she done! How could she have handed Haruki over to a man stationed high up inside Japan's criminal world? Behind Kato's impeccable English, she could hear his warning, "Haruki is indeed my blood. Any claims to him must first go through me."

A waiter emerged from the club. He placed four cups and a white ceramic flask on a glass table situated between the two facing couches. Kato motioned. "Let's sit and talk."

Haruki settled to Asami's left and Jiro to her right. Kato sat across from them and, using both hands, he poured saké from the flask into three cups.

Asami averted her eyes from his disfigured little finger. Attempting to hide her apprehension, she turned toward Haruki and with inbred etiquette said, "It's your duty to pour your brother's cup."

Haruki's eyes lit up and he performed the ritual.

Kato gave him an approving nod and lifted his cup.

Although it pained Asami to do so, she followed suit, as did Haruki and Jiro.

Kato touched his cup to theirs. "Kanpai! A toast to my newfound brother and our mama."

Asami twisted toward Haruki. "Is she alive?"

His facial features dropped. "Kato, tell them what you told me."

He set down his cup and leaned in as if relishing the opportunity to do so. "Soon after Haruki's birth, our mama died from TB and malnutrition."

Asami's fingers located her charm bracelet. "I'm so sorry. How do you know?"

"I talked to another woman who worked with her. Both were prostitutes for the Japanese Government."

Asami shrank into the couch cushions. "What do you mean?"

"I'm certain you've read about those months after our country's surrender. How our government believed the American troops would rape our women as we did to our defeated enemies?"

Jiro grimaced. "You must be referring to the Chinese." Most Japanese wanted that embarrassing subject swept under the tatami. In 1937, the Japanese Imperial Army had marched into China's capital city of Nanking, gang-raped more than twenty-thousand females, then bayoneted them to death.

Kato nodded, his eyes bright, as he continued to savor the conversation. "Nearly fifty-five thousand Japanese women volunteered to become 'comfort women' for the American GIs, our mama included."

Haruki looked down at his hands. "It had to be our mother's only option, otherwise she might not have survived as long as she did."

Kato eyed Asami. "She worked in a brothel with about thirty other women. The one I talked to said they charged eight American cents for a fuck and a bottle of beer."

Asami cringed at his course words.

"Our mama had a special GI," Kato sneered, "a New Jersey wop transplanted from Sicily. Now seeing my brother, he probably fathered both of us, then left her with two bastards."

The club's panels slid open and an unusually tall mixed-race Asian man stepped out, a jagged scar beneath his left eye. Kato nodded toward him, then addressed Haruki. "I must leave with my friend who just happens to share a similar history to ours."

Asami glanced at the man's left hand, the little finger a match to Kato's. He had to be Hiro Endo, Kato's orphanage friend, and in the yakuza as well. Sister Joan had been right.

Kato stood and bowed toward his brother. "I will stay in touch." He gave Asami a discerning last look and departed as did Jiro to retrieve their coats.

For Haruki's sake, Asami had to shake off her unease. "It's tragic your birth mama suffered so. But by placing you at St. Catherine's, she gave you a second chance. That shows how much she loved you." Without thinking about the ramifications, she pulled Haruki into a comforting hug, his scratchy cheek pressed to hers. It was something she never would've done to a Japanese man other than Jiro, or to a close male relative. But Haruki was an American, and that's what Americans did.

She realized her mistake when she pulled away and looked into his eyes. His tough guy persona had totally vanished.

He grabbed her hands. "You've changed my life, Asami. I know you were disappointed when I arrived without Sam, but you must admit, we've formed our own connection."

She couldn't be callous. She couldn't tell Haruki her feelings for him were far different than those she had for his American brother.

Instead, she gave him a playful shove. "Hey, I care about *both* you and Sam. Now, I'll see whether Kato—" she inadvertently shivered "—gets added to the mix."

1984 - Tokyo

Asami was elated as she and Sam Madrid climbed off the Subaru Line shuttle at around 5:00 p.m. Dressed in layered clothing, hats, and well-stocked backpacks, they joined throngs of Japanese tour groups spilling off chartered buses at the Yoshida Trail fifth station—the halfway point from the dormant volcano's base.

Yamada had selected Tripoint's software for their forty stores. After the meeting, Sam had stopped Asami in the hall, grinning like a little boy. "I'll be forever grateful to you. Without your strategy tips, translation assistance, and the spin you put on it, I'd never have won the deal."

She'd soaked in his glowing compliments as he'd continued, "This weekend, is there any chance you could accompany me on a trek up to Mount Fuji's summit to see the sunrise? In your letters, you mentioned you liked to hike and I came prepared with the proper gear. If you're busy, or not interested, I would definitely understand. But if you could make it, that would be the perfect way to celebrate Tripoint's first win in Japan."

Of course, Asami had said yes. As teens, she and Jiro had annually hiked Fuji-san together. The strenuous exercise and breathtaking views had always brought out the best in her. She'd never imagined she'd get to experience that amazing climb with Sam.

Asami breathed in the conifer-scented mountain air as they started up the red soil trail marbled with rocks and pebbles.

Sam nudged her. "You're certain I'll have no trouble hiking at this altitude?"

"Not if you maintain a comfortable pace to first acclimate yourself. But just in case," she patted her backpack, "I've brought along an oxygen bottle." She didn't mention it was item number ten on her hiking checklist. Without it, she definitely would've forgotten something.

"You're such a smart woman!"

"Ha!"

"I'm serious. First you helped me secure the Yamada win, but more importantly, you managed to change my brother's life, something I've been attempting to do for years. I nearly fell over when he returned to New York. In addition to hearing about his newfound brother, Haruki told me he'd decided to complete his NYU business degree—that you'd encouraged him."

A satisfying feeling, like sipping on a cozy cup of tea, spread through Asami's body. "That's wonderful!"

"It is. I'm hoping Haruki's relationship with his natural brother will be the same. He said Kato was a yakuza member. Is that as bad as say being in the American Mafia?"

"Well, it depends on whom you ask." Asami kept her eyes focused on the ground, to watch her footing, as she tried to explain the love-hate relationship Japan had with its outlaws. "Much of our country still views the yakuza as folk heroes."

"Like the Western's Robin Hood?" Sam grabbed a water bottle from his backpack.

"Yes. After WWII, one of our political parties even engaged the yakuza to help break up trade unions and left-wing demonstrations. Those ties have not faded."

"I've got to say, your words have eased my mind." He took a couple of swallows.

Asami frowned. "Maybe they shouldn't have. Are you going to meet Kato before you fly back?"

"Yes." Sam slipped the bottle back into a side pouch. "Should I have reservations?"

"Well... he seemed very smooth, very polished, and he spoke excellent English—not what I'd expected. He's probably valuable in the white-collar businesses the Wada-kai front. But I warned Haruki to be cautious. You should be too. Behind Kato's gracious exterior, he seemed to be cold and calculating, not warm and sensitive like your brother."

Sam laughed. "So Haruki's warm and sensitive?"

Asami blushed. "Yes. Just like you." Her eyes met his and a rush of pleasure caught in her throat. To subdue it, she paused to admire the view. "Below us is the Fuji Five Lakes Region. It's a great hiking spot and beside it," she pointed, "is Aokigahara Forest. Inside it are some interesting ice caves."

"I've heard of that forest. Doesn't it rank only second behind the Golden Gate Bridge as the most popular place for suicides?"

"I'm afraid so. The trend started when the *Black Sea of Trees* was published about twenty-five years ago. In that novel, two lovers commit suicide inside that forest. Since then, hundreds of troubled individuals have followed suit." Asami shook her head. "Our culture's always glorified the act of taking one's life." Her fingers had found her jacket zipper. "It's so sad. A university friend of mine recently took hers. Among other things, I know she'd been depressed about her manager's sexist behavior and her career outlook."

Worry lines appeared between Sam's brows. "I know you've been frustrated at Yamada, so I want you to know something. I'm not making promises, but I've recommended to your company's executives, you be placed on the Tripoint software implementation team."

She gave an unladylike squeal. Sam had spoken up for her! Basically staking his reputation on her!

He laughed. "Next year, let's hope you'll be climbing up more than Mount Fuji."

Standing on an incline, slightly above Sam, the words to "Dancing Shoes" frolicked inside her head: *I'm a shy girl in a man's world... Dancing shoes stepped right up and said... You're the one...* Before Asami could change her mind, she leaned over and kissed Sam's cheek.

Startled, he turned his head at the same time and their lips brushed.

She jerked away and he grinned.

Asami wanted to dance!

Sam believed in her.

She'd kissed him and he wasn't upset. It was just the opposite. Grinning back, she motioned with her hand. "Come on. I'll race you to the next station."

He smiled. "You're on. But I may need a whiff of oxygen once I beat you..."

Fatigued and chilled, yet still egging each other on, they reached the eighth station. Inside a warm mountain hut, they purchased two bento boxes, ate, then dozed before their final assent.

The trail was as crowded as a Tokyo train station at rush hour. Headlamps secured, they blindly followed the hikers ahead of them.

Exhausted, yet euphoric, Asami and Sam reached the Fuji-san Shrine at about 4:00 a.m., its yellow torri gate marking their finish line achievement.

Sam pulled her into a hug. "I'm so glad I got to experience this with you."

She whispered, "Me too..."

A brilliant light broke through the clouds and a red hue filled the atmosphere. Asami and Sam joined the clapping, cheering, and shouting of "*Banzai! Banzai!*—Hurrah! Hurrah!"

Like a triumphant prize fighter, Sam grabbed Asami's hand and held it skyward.

An energy surrounded her, a mystical aura. She felt revitalized as if nothing could stop her.

It was all because of Sam.

-9-

Monday - Tokyo

The British Pub was situated between a strip club and a karaoke box. Within the Roppongi entertainment district those "water businesses" tempted expatriates and tourists alike. Sometimes their income flowed strong, more often weak, even those with yakuza connections. Asami entered the pub's cavern-like atmosphere and paused to let her eyes adjust to the dim lighting as "Abbey Road" played through the speakers. The only patrons were two balding Western men shoveling fish and chips into their mouths. She approached the large wraparound bar and slid onto a wooden stool. Against a mirror backdrop, liquor bottles, glasses, and condiments were displayed on oak shelves.

A Pub employee would hopefully remember Hana, but it was a long shot. The bar was a nighttime hangout for foreigners who worked at a gaishikei like Tripoint, P&G, or IBM. Barely legal Japanese women, on their hunt for their "White Western Male," were also regulars. Hana would've blended into that crowd.

From behind the bar, a young Caucasian woman's sleepy eyes met Asami's, "Millie" on her nameplate, a blond braid wrapped around her head, and the bodice of her British Redcoat jacket cut low. She asked in stilted Japanese, "Would you like a drink or a lunch menu?"

Asami answered in English, "I'll take a Coke."

Millie beamed, evidently pleased to hear her native tongue. She poured the soda into a glass and placed it on a napkin within Asami's reach.

Her fingers immediately gravitated to the beverage's red swizzle stick as she gazed up at Millie. "Did you work here last Thursday night?"

Millie gave her a questioning look. "Sure did, pet."

What luck! Asami pulled out her cell and located a photo. It pictured Hana and Chloe at Kimura's, and it had been taken on the last day Asami had seen her daughter and Etta's. "Did you notice these two women?" She turned her phone toward Millie and held her breath.

She leaned in and studied the photo. "Most females who frequent this place are Japanese so this one," she pointed at Chloe, "I definitely remember."

Asami couldn't believe her good fortune! She breathed out, "What about the other woman?"

"I'm quite certain she arrived with that American woman and also with a distinguished man about sixty—a Yank as well."

That had to be Sam. From her handbag, Asami removed Tripoint's annual report. Sumie had told her to keep it. "Is this him?"

Millie squinted at Sam's photo. "I believe so. The three were sitting at the bar when two mixed-race Japanese men joined them. In this pub, Asian males are rare, unless they're bartenders, so they also stuck out. I was surprised to overhear the Yank introducing one as his brother."

That had to be Haruki. Ever since Sam's brother had graduated from NYU, he'd worked for PPG's Tokyo branch. Asami asked, "What about the other man?"

"That Yank's brother was the one who introduced the third man to the women in your photo. He said he was his biological brother."

Asami's swizzle stick snapped.

"But I've got to say, the third guy was rather seedy." Millie's gaze swept the bar. "You know the type with fancy tattoos and a stubby little finger—"

Asami's eyes caught her image in the bar mirror, the color leeching from her cheeks.

"—the sort fan magazines and video games like to glamorize. The sort that—" Millie's eyes landed back on Asami. "Pet, are you okay?"

Her kindness constricted Asami's throat. "I'm far from okay. You know the American woman in the photo? Two days after you saw her, she committed suicide and—"

"Bloody Hell!"

Asami nodded. "That's how I feel, especially about my daughter. She's the other woman in the photo. Soon after she left this bar, she went missing."

Millie's sleepy eyes had awakened. "Do you think the men we discussed are involved in both situations?"

"I don't know. But if it hadn't been for me, that yakuza gangster would not have been included in that group." She told Millie about the mid-eighties, how she'd met Kato Endo inside the Kingo Club. "Does it still exist?"

"Yes. It's owned by the Wada-kai. Some of the top DPJ politicians hang out there."

Millie patted Asami's hand. "Why don't you text me that photo. Your daughter and her friend were still here when I left at 9 p.m. I'll talk to the bartenders who replaced me. And don't worry about the Coke. It's on me."

Asami expressed her gratitude and texted Millie the photo, then headed out. Had the male voice in Hana's apartment belonged to

Sam's brother, Haruki, or to Haruki's gangster brother, Kato? Both men spoke Japanese, as did Hana's friend Lucas. Could one of them be responsible for her daughter's disappearance? But if so, why? And what about Chloe's tragic suicide? Could it be connected to Hana's situation?

But the key question remained. Where was her daughter?

Asami pushed open the pub's front door and shaded her eyes. Directly across the busy street, a Japanese man quickly turned away.

Asami's neck prickled.

She was certain.

A purple birthmark had been on his right cheek.

Monday - New York

Jammed into Chloe's front room closet was a Chicago Cubbies carry bag still stained with small chocolate fingerprints. A pop up tent would be inside. Etta's version of "roughing it" had been camping out with her daughter in front of their Evanston condo's fireplace. They'd toasted marshmallows for s'mores and sung campfire songs.

Chloe had planned to carry on that same tradition with her own child.

It was heartbreaking.

Her daughter had barely begun to live...

The door handle rattled and a muffled, "Etta?" followed.

She peered through the peephole into Henri's miserable eyes, raccoon rings around them. Etta unbolted both locks and dropped her arms limply to her sides. She couldn't reach out to Henri. He could still be the enemy. Instead, she said, "Come look."

He followed her and stepped inside the bedroom, confusion marring his face. "Etta, you're right. Chloe would not have left the room like this, especially her shoes. To me, it looks as if they might've been pushed aside to get at something."

The closet was tightly packed with Chloe's clothes. Rather than removing them, Henri got down on his hands and knees and dipped his head beneath them. "Hey!" His voice burst out. "There's some sort of panel on the back wall."

Etta tugged on his herringbone sport coat. "Let me see."

He scooted back out and she crawled in, her knees cracking in the process. Chloe's citrus floral scent enveloped Etta. It was as if her daughter was beside her, and maybe she was. Maybe she was guiding Etta toward some insight into that dreadful night. Etta shoved that thought and a bit of clothing off to one side, the latter giving her a sliver of light. On the white plaster wall, a gray drywall panel, about three-foot square, was exposed. Etta slid her fingernails between it and the metal frame that secured it, attempting to pry it open. She broke two fingernails in the process.

Etta shimmied out, her hands covered in plaster dust. Perplexed, she wiped them on her jeans. "Look Henri. You have the same stuff on your knees."

He gazed down, surprised. "That panel must've been recently installed. But how can that be? Chloe and I would've known if any construction work had been done."

In Etta's head, a light clicked on. "Maybe we should be tackling this from the opposite side. Isn't the elevator shaft behind the closet?"

"Yes. And now that I think about it, on Saturday, the elevator next to our apartment was out of order."

Etta's hands started to tingle. "Can you be more specific?"

Henri's brow furrowed as he dusted off his pants. "It was working at around noon when Chloe and I left for a Tripoint for Kids' event. But when we returned, it was shut down."

"How about when you left for the Rusty Nail?"

"It was still out of order."

Etta absorbed that fact. "From inside the elevator, could someone have gained access to install that closet panel?"

"Merde!" Henri darted out of the room and Etta followed. "This building was constructed in the forties." He opened the apartment's front door and stepped out into the hallway. "Back then, the doorman told me the elevators often got stuck. Between them were access panels creating a pathway to remove passengers." His finger jabbed the "down" button located between the two elevators. "Maybe those panels are still there—as well as the ones on the opposite walls."

The doors to the elevator adjacent to Chloe and Henri's apartment opened. Etta's gaze traveled down its left wall. Below the handrail, a panel was secured by screws and the paint around them was chipped.

She stood there stunned. New scenarios, leading up to her daughter's death, attacked her.

Henri's grim voice commanded, "Etta, you stay here." He flipped the switch to hold the elevator and he disappeared.

Etta could hardly breathe. Was she stepping out of her daughter's suicide shadow into a far more ominous situation?

From behind the panel, she heard pounding. In disbelief, she pounded back. It was hard to comprehend. Chloe's death might not be a suicide.

Henri returned. He looked like a man twice his age. "What if that panel was installed on Saturday afternoon? What if someone used it to crawl into our apartment that night? That could explain why Chloe's shoes were knocked all about." His body faltered against the elevator. "And if that's so, could that sick person have murdered Chloe, our Chloe?" Tears filled his eyes. "But why Etta? Why?"

She didn't have an answer. The shocking situational turn was too much to grasp.

Henri reengaged the elevator switch and pressed the lobby button. "We need to talk to Baxter." At ground level, the doors opened and Etta lurched out. On the front stoop, they located the doorman. Baxter's bushy white eyebrows were a stark contrast to his dark face. "Mr. Broussard," he tipped his cap, "I'm so sorry to hear about Miss Martin. She was a fine lady."

"She certainly was, but I need some information. Can you tell me about last weekend's elevator maintenance? It's important."

Baxter's hand rubbed his chin's white stubble. "Important you say? Well, as I recall, the Otis guy showed up soon after I arrived for my noon shift."

Etta gripped Henri's arm. "That's right after you and Chloe left for the Tripoint event."

A kind of hopelessness filled Henri's face. "Was it scheduled maintenance?"

"No. Emergency service. A building on Tenth had an electrical issue and a woman was injured. All the elevators with that same model number had to be checked out."

"How long was he here?" The wind was whipping Henri's curls into his eyes. He didn't seem to notice.

"A few hours. Then he left to get some parts. He returned, I'd say, around seven."

Henri stumbled back. "Mon Dieu! That's right after I left for the Rusty Nail."

Etta squeezed his arm. "Listen Henri, this is not your fault." She refocused on the doorman. "Do you know when the guy left?"

"No. He was still here when my shift ended, but it'll be in the service log."

Etta shadowed Baxter back into the lobby. Behind his station, he located a binder and, inside it, the specific notation. "Jack Bando's the guy's name and he signed out at 11:17 p.m."

Etta clutched the doorman's station. All the times fit Henri's gruesome theory. Her eyes frantically searched the lobby and they located what she'd hoped to find.

A security camera was aimed at the elevator bank.

Monday - Tokyo

Asami rushed onto the train as fast as her heels would carry her. Her jaunt from the British Pub had been filled with excessive worry. She'd constantly looked over her shoulder to see whether that purple-birthmarked man had been following her. She didn't think he had, yet it was difficult to decipher. If he kept his face turned, he'd look like most Japanese "salarymen" and she'd never be able to pick him out. Too bad it wasn't rush hour. She could've easily lost herself in the throngs of people being politely but firmly pushed into cars by white-gloved attendants to utilize every bit of space.

Asami caught her breath, suddenly realizing how stupid she'd been. Rather than high-tailing it to the station, she should've chased after that man and confronted him. That would've been the smart thing to do. Why hadn't she been thinking straight? But if she was truthful, without someone like Jiro beside her, she probably wouldn't have found the courage to follow through.

Asami's train car contained about a dozen passengers. Among them were three female teens, all standing due to their stiff petticoats peeking out from under their Victorian doll costumes. Japan had a number of subcultures that rejected traditional female stereotypes. These young women, weighted down with curly pink wigs and ribbon-tied bonnets, were obviously "lolitas."

Asami settled onto a bench seat behind the three, her view of the remaining car's occupants obstructed. Conversely, other than the teens, no one would be able to catch a glimpse of her.

She located Sergeant Mori's card and called his cell. As she did, she rubbed her eyes and nose, both under attack from the teens' flowery scents. Asami wanted to tell the detective about the purple-birthmarked man, but first things first. Any news about Hana was more important.

"Fujioka-san," Mori said, "I talked to the coroner's office in the Five Lakes Region and those in Tokyo. One unidentified woman from the Roppongi district was brought in, and—"

"She can't be Hana! Not Hana!"

"My apologies. You're right. She's not your daughter. The blood type was not a match."

If the detective had been sitting beside her, Asami would've strangled him for distressing her so. Instead, she took a calming breath and told him how her daughter and Etta's had been at the British Pub—in that same district—with Sam Madrid, his adopted brother, Haruki, and Haruki's natural brother, Kato Endo. "In the mid-eighties, when I met Kato, he was a member of the Wada-kai yakuza gang."

"So the yakuza *may* be involved?"

"Yes." She'd noted a concerned tone in his voice. "Are you familiar with the Wada-kai?"

"I am. It operates a number of businesses in the Roppongi district—both legitimate and shady. Its arms also stretch overseas. I don't know Kato, but if he was once a yakuza, to wash his feet and go straight would not have been easy. I'll check to see whether he has a record and I'll call you back."

"Wait! I must tell you about a man who could be following me..." But Asami realized Mori had already hung up, and she'd been speaking to herself.

The train rumbled to a stop, announcements were made, and the lolitas stayed put. As the train began to move, Asami's cell rang and she quickly answered it. Rather than hearing the detective's voice a female's said, "This is Kiko from the British Pub. Millie asked me to call you. She showed me your photo."

"Please, tell me, do you remember my daughter and her friend?"

"Yes."

"Really! What about the three men they were with?"

"I saw them as well. The entire group left the pub together at about ten p.m."

Asami's feet tapped. "Do you have any idea where they were going?"

"No, but my shift ended at 1:00 a.m. I was waiting for the Shibuya train and saw your daughter and her friend again. I'm afraid to say, they both seemed upset."

Asami's stomach pitched.

"Your daughter's hair and clothes were wet and it hadn't been raining."

Asami gasped. "Did—did they both get on the train?"

"No. Only your daughter."

Asami's shaky finger pressed END. Straightaway, she called Sergeant Mori and repeated the bartender's disturbing information.

"Hmm... So Hana's hair was wet?" He hesitated. "Most of the foreign embassies are situated within the Roppongi district. Some have courtyard fountains. The up-scale hotels also have pools. Maybe your daughter was at one of those locations and she either fell into the water or was pushed."

Asami raked her fingers through her hair. "Maybe? Or maybe something far worse happened to Hana."

"Well knowing she was with a Wada-kai gangster does concern me. Kato Endo has served time for both organized gambling and drug trafficking. Most recently, he's been involved in a number of corporate extortion schemes."

"What does that mean?"

"In the Wada-kai, he holds the title of 'shareholder meeting man.' His job is to look for dirt on executives from high-profile companies, things like secret mistresses, underage schoolgirl fetishes, tax evasion, and the list goes on. If he finds something, he purchases a few shares of the company's stock. That allows him to attend its shareholders' meeting. But before doing so, he contacts those company executives who have something to hide. He threatens them, promising to disclose harmful information at the meeting unless he's compensated."

Asami snagged her bottom lip with her teeth, contemplating his words. "I'm quite certain the retail companies I work with would fear embarrassment far more than physical threats. My guess is they often pay. But how could Kato's corporate schemes have anything to do with my daughter's disappearance?"

"I don't know, but now that a yakuza connection has been established, I assure you, your daughter's situation will get more attention. We'll try to locate Kato and bring him in for questioning."

The announcements blared again as the train reduced its speed for another stop. Asami checked the station name on the outside wall as Mori continued, "I'll also check your daughter's credit cards for any recent activity and secure her cell phone records. I'll contact Tripoint's COO and his PPG brother as well. But I'm not discounting your daughter's neighbor either."

"Did you talk to him?"

"Yes. He told me about that male voice in your daughter's apartment. He did seem sincere about locating Hana and assisting you in your search, but he could be covering up for his own actions."

The train's momentum rapidly increased, the lolitas hanging onto the overhead clutch handles while Asami considered Mori's words. She didn't believe Lucas was involved, yet, at Kimura's, he *had* been sitting next to the purple-birthmarked man. She finally told the detective about him. "Maybe I'm overreacting, but there's a chance he's been following me."

"You must keep a sharp eye out. If you fear for your safety, please call me day or night."

Asami's eyes closed. Her own fear paled in comparison to the dread she felt for Hana, that abominable anxiety swallowing up Asami's insides and causing constant havoc to her thoughts. She took a deep breath, willing her child to be alive.

Monday - New York

Fried food scents hovered inside the GV Coffee Shop. Etta sat in the same booth, a mug clutched in her hands, and the taste of retribution in her mouth. She couldn't control her raw breathing. She felt certain her daughter had been murdered.

Ever since Henri had reluctantly returned to school, the last moments of her child's life had been torturing Etta—the fear Chloe would've suffered.

Her daughter had refused to play night games as a child, to watch slasher flicks as a teen, to jog alone in the dark as an adult. It had all started when a playmate had hidden inside Chloe's shadowy bedroom and jumped out from a closet.

Chloe's murderer could've done the same.

Etta shuddered, slopping coffee onto the table. She thanked God her daughter had either voluntarily swallowed sleeping pills, soon after Henri's Rusty Nail departure, or she'd been forced to take them once her assailant had arrived. At least her child's trauma had ended sooner. In Chloe's drowsy state, her assailant would've stripped her or instructed her to do so. Maybe, in her daughter's final surge of clarity, she'd tossed her belongings on the floor to leave a message—one only Etta and Henri would've understood.

Henri hadn't caused the bruises on Chloe's wrists. They had to be the assailant's doing when he'd dragged her daughter into the bathroom, placed her in the tub, and sliced her slender arms.

Tears ran down Etta's cheeks and fell into her coffee. While Chloe died, while her baby died, that monster had probably used gloves and a stylus to type that cruel *I'm sorry* message into her daughter's cell.

Etta hung her head, drained. Who could've murdered her child? It made no sense! Nothing made sense. Yet she knew she had to pull herself together. Once Detective Harper arrived, Etta had to convince her Chloe's death might not be a suicide.

A discarded *New York Times* sat on the adjacent window ledge. To distract her morose thoughts, Etta picked up the folded over business section and an article caught her attention.

> *Only three days remain until Tripoint Technology, the privately owned three billion dollar retail software company, goes public. Tripoint's CEO, Thomas Pollard, is reportedly planning to sell twenty percent of the company. With this move, Tripoint's cash could balloon to six-hundred million or more. The company's COO, Sam Madrid, stated, "Tripoint has been buying complimentary software companies and a sudden cash infusion would allow us to pick up speed." Sources confirm this infusion would also help the struggling Pollard Property Group (PPG), a subsidiary of Tripoint Technology. Ultimately, whether the company continues to flourish isn't about whether or not it goes public. It's about Thomas Pollard and his son TJ Pollard, Tripoint's heir apparent. How good are they as leaders? That's what the world will be watching.*

Etta sat back. For months, she'd known Tripoint's initial public stock offering was going to happen. The IPO had been a key element within her company's strategic growth plan. Tripoint was banking on its success, and rightly so. Over the prior three decades, its innovative retail software had consistently gained market share, especially in the department store and specialty segments. In addition, Sylvia and Tom Pollard were well known philanthropists, investing substantial sums into socially conscious endeavors like Tripoint for Kids.

But Tom senior's press coverage hadn't always been complimentary. Each time Etta had read about his alleged involvement with a Los Angeles movie actress or a London fashion model, she'd thought about his wife. Etta had always admired Sylvia Pollard's outspoken demeanor—as powerful as Tom's in many ways. It was hard to understand why Sylvia had continued to stand by him.

"Ms. Martin?"

Startled, Etta peered up at the detective and blurted out, "Listen! Chloe's death might not be a suicide."

Harper frowned. "We've been through this."

"But I have new information."

The detective sighed, "Go ahead." She slid into the booth, but it seemed as if she was only staying to appease her. For that reason, Etta carefully articulated what she'd discovered: Chloe's shoes, the closet and elevator aligned panels, the Otis maintenance man, his possible connection to Chloe's death, and the potential lobby video footage. Etta held her breath, her eyes glued to Harper.

The detective was silent for a long time, the muscles around her eyes twitching. She finally nodded. "Although it's farfetched, it's a theory." She opened her satchel and removed Chloe's case file and a pen. "Tell me again, what's the Otis guy's name? I'll check him out."

"Jack Bando. But you don't need to. I already have."

A tendon stood out on Harper's neck, visibly pulsating. "Ms. Martin! You can't be doing that. I need to follow up—especially if your daughter's death could be foul play."

The reprimand riled Etta. "I refuse to sit on the sidelines. If your child was possibly murdered, you'd be acting as I am. I did call the local Otis office. No employee by that name works for them, and no maintenance was ordered for Chloe's building on Saturday." Etta leveled her eyes on Harper. "See! I could be right! There's a good chance Chloe's death is not a suicide."

Harper's eyebrows drew closer together. "Then tell me, who would want to murder your daughter? What could be the possible motive?"

Etta's body deflated. She wanted those answers as well.

A disturbing thought suddenly popped into her head: any new Tripoint scandal could definitely hurt its IPO.

Maybe she did have an answer.

Etta thrust her finger at the newspaper. "Read this Tripoint article." As the detective did, Etta watched Harper's tongue nervously flicking across the gap between her front teeth. When the detective looked up, Etta was prepared to make her case. "This morning, Tripoint's HR manager informed me that Chloe had called her office on Friday and my daughter had wanted to meet that day. But the manager hadn't been available, so their appointment had been scheduled for first thing this morning which, of course, Chloe never made."

Harper looked rattled. "Do you know what she planned to discuss?"

"No. But I can speculate. Maybe something happened in Japan, something that could compromise Tripoint's IPO. Something bad enough to have created the need to silence Chloe before she talked."

Etta stared at Harper. "I know my daughter. To prepare for that HR meeting, she would've made some notes. Probably on her laptop, but I couldn't locate it. Did you take it?"

"No, only her cell. Could she have left it at work?"

"Possibly? I'll check." Etta leaned in aggressively. "Of course, that's if I have your permission."

"Ms. Martin, you need to understand, I still believe your daughter committed suicide. But I'll give you the benefit of the doubt. Go ahead and check. I'll have our techs go back over the apartment and— "

"What about the lobby camera footage?"

"Hold on... I was getting to that. I'll secure it, if it exists, and I'll have you and Mr. Broussard view it. Maybe one of you will recognize the maintenance man."

"Let's say he's connected to Tripoint. Chloe's mentor, Sam Madrid, should also view it. He's due back tomorrow, and— "

"No!" The detective shook her head hard. "He was mentioned in that article. You said he was also in Japan. It would be best if all Tripoint employees continued to believe Chloe's death was a suicide. Do you understand?"

Etta's face tightened. "I do." Ever since her arrival in New York, she'd been spinning herself into a cocoon of remorse and pain. But in the last few hours, she'd transformed into a vengeful mother. She felt certain her child's life had been taken by another's hand.

Etta would never give up until that bastard paid!

-10-

1974 - New York & Chicago

Inside the Metropolitan Museum of Art's Great Hall, Etta sagged against a limestone column, her eyes searching for her sorority sister. Three days had passed since Etta's abysmal encounter with Tripoint's CEO. She'd started to believe that incident had been her fault. If she hadn't gone up to Tripoint's Plaza Hotel suite, it never would've happened.

Over the crowd noise, she heard, "Hey Etta!" and she pasted on a smile. She had to shake off her gloom.

Moni rushed toward her in bell bottom jeans, faux fur jacket, and a floppy hat.

Until her arms tired, Etta hugged her pledge sister, her nose nestled into Moni's comforting scent. "My God, it's so good to see you!"

She grinned. "Ditto!" Instead of joining the workforce, Moni had been attending Cornell University for her Master of Fine Arts degree. The university was located in Ithaca, a four-hour bus ride from Manhattan. Although Etta wasn't up for sightseeing, their plans had been made two weeks before.

They purchased tickets and Moni checked the museum map. "Let's start on the second level. I've always wanted to see the nineteenth century European gallery." Moni chatted nonstop until they reached those exhibits. As they meandered through the Rodin, Dresser, Monet and Degas paintings, Etta hardly noticed the exquisite art. Her dilemma was consuming her thoughts.

"Oh look!" Moni pointed at an oil of a young woman attired in a floor-length business dress, a boutonniere pinned to her chest, and a hatbox in her left hand. "I've seen reproductions of this." She stepped up and read the caption out loud: "Renoir painted this Parisian milliner focusing on the young salesgirl's charms." Moni beamed at Etta. "Hey, you're the twentieth century version."

It was fruitless. Etta's pent up tears could no longer be kept at bay. "Oh Moni..." She collapsed on a cement bench, self-conscious as others looked on.

Her friend sat down beside her. "Honey, what's wrong?"

"I—I need your opinion on something."

Through granny glasses, Moni's concerned eyes peered at Etta. "So what's going on?"

"I don't know what to do." Amid constant sniffles, Etta's Plaza Hotel disaster dribbled out.

"That bastard!" Moni snarled and gave Etta a tissue. "But you're definitely not alone. One of my Cornell professors asked me to participate in a female discussion group. We described our work experiences and noticed a pattern."

Etta dabbed at the corners of her eyes. "Like what?"

"Every one of us had either quit due to our male boss's behavior or we'd been fired for the way we'd responded to it."

"That sounds like my Carter Café situation."

"It does."

"So, Moni, what can be done?"

"Well, there are brave women trying to change our laws. A recent legal case was discussed. A female employee claimed, because she'd rejected her boss's sexual advances, he'd retaliated against her."

Etta cringed. "I hope that doesn't happen to me. Did the court rule in her favor?"

Moni looked disgusted. "No. It was decided there was no sexual discrimination involved. That her supervisor had merely found her attractive and he'd felt rejected."

Etta's shoulders slumped. "That's just great..."

"Do you remember when I quit my college job at Finley's Bookstore?"

"Yeah. You said you didn't like the hours."

"Well, that's true, but I also didn't like the owner. He asked me out to lunch and, afterward, instead of driving me back to campus, he turned down a beach access road. When he asked me to jerk him off—"

"My God!"

"I know. Anyway, I couldn't get out of his car fast enough. Of course, I didn't go back to work. Later, I discovered he'd done similar things to other female employees. It was stupid. We all felt guilty. We thought we should've known better than to have had lunch with him and put ourselves in that position."

"That sounds just like me."

"It does, doesn't it? But even though you went up to that Plaza Hotel suite, Tom Pollard shouldn't have said that to you."

They both stared at the painting.

"Etta, it's so hard for us as women. Most often, we work for men who hold our careers in their hands. If you reported Tom, it would be your word against his."

"How shitty is that? And who would I report him to anyway? He's the CEO of the company."

* * *

Etta returned to Chicago proud of her accomplishments and relieved to be eight hundred miles away from Tom Pollard. Out of the fourteen new hires, she'd placed in the top three. The other two were guys from Los Angeles, one of them Randy, oh well. Etta was pumped, ready to apply her honed skills, although she felt sorry for Donna. She'd finished last in their class.

The four new Chicago Technical Reps had their own pod of desks near George Buckley's office. The first day back, Etta kept waiting to be recognized, but Pete was called into George's office first. Moments later, he returned to their pod gloating. "I was paired up with Brian Foster, you know, one of the office's most successful Marketing Reps." Pete grabbed his briefcase and sashayed out.

Next was Neil. He emerged from George's office beside another Marketing Rep. Neil snuck a peek Etta's way. She could tell he was embarrassed.

Etta sat with Donna, both of them twiddling their thumbs, not sure what they should do. Etta couldn't comprehend why she hadn't been called in first.

George's secretary eventually approached.

This is it! Etta smiled and pushed back her chair.

The secretary's eyes passed over her and settled on Donna. "George would like to see you."

Etta felt like Agnes Howard, a grade school classmate, who'd always been picked last for dodgeball. She couldn't understand George's thought process, especially when Donna left with yet another Marketing Rep. Mortified, Etta sat there all alone, waiting... and waiting.... Guys would pass and glance her way. Nobody stopped to talk. She finally mustered up enough courage to knock on George's door.

He looked terribly uncomfortable and waved her in.

"Please, George, tell me what's going on? Why haven't I been assigned a Marketing Rep like the others? I did far better than any of them in training."

He squirmed in his chair. "That isn't necessarily so."

"What do you mean?"

"I understand you had difficulty with the point-of-sale terminals. You couldn't tell whether they were functioning correctly."

Etta was astonished. She couldn't believe her fellow trainees would've told George about her colorblindness—that it was actually an issue. It would never impact a sale. Sure, when she was troubleshooting a terminal problem, she might have to ask someone about the LED color, but that would be rare—the exception.

Then it dawned on her. *My God!* Her shunning was Tom Pollard's doing—his retaliation. Tripoint's CEO was blackballing her—trying to force her out.

1975 - Chicago

Baker's Tavern was packed with a young professional after-work crowd. Bee Gees' "Jive Talkin'" was playing through the jukebox speakers. Perched on bar stools, Etta and Donna ordered drinks. It wasn't surprising her colleague had picked that smoky Rush Street location. Most people who frequented it were looking for love—at least for one night.

Etta raised her voice over the din. "Our branch manager is such a coward. He keeps assigning me tasks his secretary should be handling. I've organized every office meeting, reserved umpteen hotel conference rooms for marketing events, and collated hundreds of client binders. He doesn't know what to do with me."

Etta's office trauma had been going on for three months. She'd told Donna about George's colorblind lame excuse for her office shunning, but she'd omitted her Plaza Hotel encounter with Tripoint's CEO. She suspected Donna had had a similar one—with far different results. Etta kept waiting for Tom Pollard to visit the Chicago office. She'd decided to confront him, even if that meant losing her job.

Donna had been sipping on a Tequila Sunrise, nodding along. "Your colorblind issue makes no sense." Ironically, she was giving Etta a pep talk. "But maybe things will change. Our branch is growing so fast. George told me, only the Marketing Reps will be reporting to him. The Technical Reps will have their own manager."

Etta felt a sudden surge of hope.

* * *

As expected, George had asked Etta to handle the new manager announcement meeting's logistics. Early that morning, Etta arrived in her red suit, her shoes polished, her long sandy hair perfectly straight and neatly pulled back with a thin headband. She hoped to make a good first impression on her new manager. Etta set up the meeting essentials: chairs, foil projector, and screen. She believed she was the only one on the floor until she saw a light in the office adjacent to George's, one that had never been occupied.

She approached it and sucked in her breath.

Sam Madrid stared out at her.

He smiled and stood, his fingers motioning her in. "Etta, it's so wonderful to see you! You look amazing, so grown up.

Her heart was bursting through her blouse. "Well so do you!" As Mom would say, "He looked finer than frog hair." His suit, the color of his warm gray eyes, was tailored to fit his slim build. His beautiful dark hair was still fashionably long and shimmering with heavier streaks of silver. He was perfect, so Sam.

Instead of shaking her hand, he pulled her into a hug.

Pressed against his chest, she breathed in his wonderful scent, her knees turning to oatmeal. Heat bubbled inside her, exploding on every contact point.

Regrettably, he pulled away.

"So Sam," she managed to say, "why—why are you here?"

"I'm your new manager."

Had she heard right? Would she actually be reporting to Sam? The one who'd encouraged her to succeed, to take risks, to show those university socks-and-sandal guys she was as good as them or better! A swell of exhilaration rushed into her, intoxicating her. Could she be getting a second chance?

Sam sat down behind his desk. "After today's announcement meeting, I'm planning to individually talk to each of my new team members. But since you're already here, why don't you take a seat and I'll start with you? Can you tell me what you've been working on?"

Her cheeks burned as she slid onto a chair across from him. "I—I have to admit... very little." She couldn't bring up her encounter with Tom, so she hit her colorblind issue head on.

His face grew taunt as he listened. "At Northwestern, I knew you were colorblind. Remember? I was using red and green ink to mark papers. You politely asked me to change one of the colors to black."

Of course, she remembered. She could recall every moment she'd interacted with Sam.

"Your colorblindness should have no bearing on your job. If it had, I wouldn't have encouraged you to enter this field. I don't know how this happened, and I don't really care. Before the day is over, I promise, I'll rectify the situation." He shook his head. "It's unbelievable that Tripoint's been wasting such talent!"

Etta nearly skipped out of Sam's office. She felt as light and carefree as she had in her youth when she'd survived a bout of Dad's ridicule and she'd gained the upper hand.

Sam was her manager!

He still believed in her!

It was the best day of her life.

1986 - Tokyo

Soft petals landed on Asami's cheeks and she breathed in their fragrant scent. It was *Hanami* season, the Japanese traditional custom of enjoying the fleeting beauty of the cherry blossoms. On Inokashira Park's scenic pond, under a pink and white canopy of ancient trees, she and ten-year-old Chloe Martin manned oars. It was the perfect activity to keep Asami's hands busy. As their rowboat glided by oodles of others, she smiled affectionately at Chloe's mama who sat facing them in the bow.

Etta smiled back, her cheeks freckled from the afternoon sun.

Chloe pointed. "Look!" Behind them was a mob of ducks, trailing their boat.

Asami ruffled Chloe's flaxen curls. "What do you expect little one? You keep tossing them corn."

Etta dipped her hand into the water and laughed. "What a beautiful day to end our stay in Japan."

Asami looked down. It was tough for her to admit that was so. Over the past two years, Etta had become her mentor and dear friend. She'd co-managed Yamada's point-of-sale software project with none other than Asami's nemesis, Masato Ito. Although Asami was certain Masato never would've selected her for the team, Sam Madrid's recommendation had carried weight.

Asami had assumed she'd get to interact with Sam during the project. Disappointingly, that had not been the case. Once he'd won

Yamada's business, he'd only returned for a few high level status meetings where Asami had translated. After them, she'd barely had the chance to converse with him before Etta had whisked him away for confidential strategy talks.

Asami dragged her oar to avoid another boat. "Oh Etta-san, I don't know what I'm going to do without you. Throughout the project, I'd offer my ideas and Masato would dismiss them. Somehow, you found a way to incorporate them, making him believe they were his."

Etta snorted. "He certainly is a piece of work. I'll never forget Masato's standard line to me." She placed her hands on her hips and using her best Japanese accent said, "Women can't boss men."

They all giggled.

Asami and Etta had been doing what her friend called "the woman's dance." Outwardly, there could be no misstep. Neither could inadvertently crush their partner's toes for fear of retribution or ridicule. Both had to let him lead while they followed. Yet, inwardly, they were both determined to change the "dance"—taking measured steps—eyes always focused above his shoulder.

"Asami, we must pick our battles. But you are well positioned. English is your weapon, your means to express your opinions to those Westerners like me. Yamada will see your value. Just wait and see."

They returned to the dock and Chloe dashed off to find a picnic spot. Etta's arm linked into hers and they followed, Asami's short legs taking two steps to Etta's one.

Etta tilted her head toward Asami. "I'll never forget our late night chats. So like those I have with my sorority sister back in the states. But I blame you for getting me hooked on Sapporo and edamame. Quite a change from my U.S. vices of potato chips and wine."

Asami smiled then looked away, fearful she might cry. "Oh Etta-san, I did love our chats, sprawling out on your apartment floor while Chloe slept, hearing about your seventies' work experiences, similar to my current ones."

"Yes." Etta hesitated. "But there's one I've only mentioned to Moni—that's until now." Her arm slipped back to her side. "It—it was in my first month at Tripoint."

As Etta talked about her Plaza Hotel incident, Asami was dismayed. Yet she also felt honored that Etta had put her into the same friend category as her sorority sister. That Etta felt Asami would keep her secret as Moni had.

Asami reached for her friend's hand. "You had no recourse, did you? The U.S. was like Japan still is, with no sexual harassment laws in place?"

"Yes, that's true. But in Japan, sexual harassment seems far worse—flagrantly accepted. At last Friday's after-work get-together, did you notice how Masato forced two of the office ladies to sing karaoke duets with him? On the stage, his hands were all over their bodies."

Asami frowned. "I did notice. And yesterday, inside Yamada's ladies room, I heard the same women bragging about his sleazy attention. Most Japanese men are nothing like the majority of your American ones, though Tripoint's CEO sounds like one of the exceptions."

Etta nudged her. "Hey, your friend Jiro is Japanese, and he's certainly nothing like Masato. It was so sweet of him to take Chloe on a Sanrio anime studios' tour."

Asami smiled. "Jiro *is* special. As children, he and I would read the seductive Western fairy tales together like *Sleeping Beauty*, *Snow White*, and *Cinderella*."

"Doesn't Japan have its own?" Etta stepped aside to let an elderly couple totter by, a leashed dachshund in tow.

"Yes, but they're moralistic, not centered on love and romance. Jiro and I would fantasize about our future. How he'd carry me off on his steed. How we'd live happily ever after. But as we matured, both of us knew that wasn't in the tea leaves."

"That must've been difficult."

"It was. He tried to compensate by setting me up with guys he knew. But nobody stacked up to him. In fact, those blind dates cemented my belief that I didn't want to settle for a short, clumsy, and arrogant Japanese man."

"Like Masato?" Etta rolled her eyes. "Who hoots and hollers as soon as one drop of saké hits his lips."

Caught up in a fit of laughter, the two drew smiles from those approaching. When both settled down, Etta turned serious. "I thought I would find my prince early on, but there have been lots of bumps along the way."

Asami gazed at her friend. Obviously, there was a hidden meaning in her words. Asami had wondered about Chloe's papa. Etta had told her Chloe had been the result of a short-lived marriage with a guy she'd met at Northwestern. Apparently, he hadn't wanted children and they'd divorced before Chloe had been born.

Perhaps Etta still hung onto that devastating outcome.

But before her friend left Japan, Asami had to ask her a question, one which had been consuming her for two years. "I've been wondering about Sam Madrid. When he attends Yamada meetings, I—I've noticed he doesn't wear a wedding band. Is he seeing anyone? You know, romantically?"

Etta looked startled. "You should ask *him* that question."

A flush of heat rushed into Asami's cheeks.

Up ahead, Chloe waved and pointed.

As if to apologize for her curtness, Etta tightly wrapped her arm back into Asami's and the awkward moment passed.

Amid a multitude of revelers, Asami helped Chloe spread out a picnic mat and the three sat down. Etta opened a cooler and removed onigiri rice balls, Japanese fried chicken, two Sapporos, and a Pepsi for Chloe. Asami popped the tops and handed out the cans.

The three clicked them together and Chloe's eyes suddenly sprouted tears.

Asami said, "Oh little one, come here." She drew Chloe close. On the opposite side, Etta scooted in and did the same.

Asami felt a strong emotional pull—a three-way connection.

It couldn't help but last.

In a black cowboy hat, an Asian street musician strolled over, his gravelly voice and steel guitar serenading the picnickers with "House of the Rising Sun."

Chloe slipped out of the embrace and scrambled to her feet. Face pensive, she swayed to the music, her curls floating in the breeze.

Asami shifted toward Etta, filling Chloe's void, her arm resettling around Etta's shoulders. Asami felt the warmth of her friend—her "sister." By meeting Etta, the sun had certainly risen in Asami's challenging world.

Chloe patted her mama's head. "Can I give him a tip?"

The spell broken, Asami dropped her arm and cocked her head toward the musician. "Notice, he has no tip jar or open guitar case? He's doing this for his own pleasure."

Etta seemed surprised. "Tomorrow is Yamada's point-of-sale recognition meeting. You have received personal pleasure by knowing you've done your best work. But, periodically, our egos need to be fed." Etta gave her a crafty look.

The Reverdin blue butterflies, of Asami's youth, fluttered inside her stomach. Her fingers tapped her knees. Etta seemed to be hinting, Asami might finally receive the honor she was due.

1986 - Tokyo

Asami climbed onto Yamada's elevator, a sunny feeling in her soul.

The female operator, about Asami's age, bowed. "Fujioka-san, you must be headed up to the twelfth floor. Am I right?"

"You are."

The operator pushed that floor's button then shyly held out her left hand. "Look!" On it was an engagement ring.

"Congratulations!" Asami smiled and admired the setting. Both Asami's Mama and Auntie Emi would certainly have approved if the ring had instead been on Asami's finger. They'd reminded her, on more than one occasion, women were like traditional Japanese Christmas cakes, primarily purchased on December 24th or 25th. However, if they couldn't be unloaded before the New Year, they'd rarely find a buyer.

Asami stepped off the elevator. A Japanese husband was the furthest thing from her mind. Sam Madrid was another story and within a few minutes she'd catch a glimpse of him. Etta had said he'd be attending Yamada's point-of-sale recognition meeting. Still burning inside Asami, like a pilot light, was that memory of their Mount Fuji climb. Over the past two years, she felt she'd done right by him. That he would be proud of her work, as Etta had been.

That was terribly important to Asami.

During the five years she'd worked for Yamada, three other senior degree women had been hired. Only one remained. The others had become disillusioned and had quit to complete their MBA abroad. One was at London's Brunel University, the other at NYU's Stern School of Business. The latter had told Asami, "The U.S. will give me a second chance."

Asami was anticipating her second chance—and right in her homeland.

The large meeting room could seat nearly one hundred employees. Yamada's president sat in the front row flanked by the point-of-sale project leads: Etta and Masato. Sam was to Etta's right. An expansive smile spread across his face at seeing Asami, and he waved.

A rush of pleasure warmed her cheeks. She recalled that same hand in hers, reaching for the sky, celebrating their Fuji-san climb.

Another celebration would hopefully be in order.

Asami located her teammates in the second and third rows and she slid in beside Funato. Like Masato, he'd been one of Asami's recruit class members. But unlike her, Funato idolized her nemesis. She still recalled her university interview and Mr. Shibata's words: "Each recruit hopes to be promoted, but if the star is not one's self then the hope is one's team members will make it to the top."

That was a noble sentiment. It probably held true for Funato. Not for Asami. She'd prefer personal recognition.

Yamada's president positioned himself behind the podium. His own interpreter would be translating. To listen in English, Etta and Sam had slipped on headsets plugged into the floor panel's audio jacks.

President Yamada said, "Yamada Department Stores are positioned for the twenty-first century. This is due to the diligent team who worked round-the-clock to make our point-of-sale rollout an immense success. We want to thank our American friends for their support, Miss Martin and Mr. Madrid." He bowed.

Sam and Etta stood and returned the bows.

"But today," Mr. Yamada continued as Etta and Sam sat down, "is the time to honor our own employees." He opened a notebook. "Please proceed to the front when your name is called."

Asami's heart raced so fast she feared its movement might pop a button right off her blouse, as first one, then a second, then a third teammate's name was called. Each walked up to Mr. Yamada where they bowed, then formed a line to his left.

"I've saved these important names for last."

Asami sat on the edge of her seat, her feet tapping the floor, as Funato's name was called. *Please, please,* Asami clasped her hands together, *please let him announce me!*

"And the final name," Mr. Yamada said, "is Masato Ito."

Tears of humiliation burned in Asami's eyes. How could Mr. Yamada be like her grandpapa? When she'd been twelve, she'd spent hours arranging new nick-knacks on the shelves of her family's souvenir shop, so pleased with her work. But instead of praise, he'd spit out, "You've done it all wrong!" and he'd swept his arm across her handiwork.

"Without Masato's leadership," Mr. Yamada continued, "and creative ideas— "

My ideas! she wanted to shout. *My ideas!*

"—our point-of-sale project may never have come to fruition."

Funato slid past Asami and joined Masato in the front. Her nemesis's rat-like eyes gleamed at her. What hope did she have for a rewarding future at Yamada?

Her disgrace was his doing.

The attendees clapped three times—the traditional custom to conclude a business meeting—and Asami dashed out. The only safe haven was the ladies room where Masato couldn't delight in her shame. Within the white-tiled retreat, she entered the first stall and let her tears come.

That morning, she'd elbowed her way into a train packed like sushi, her nose pushed into a man's smelly armpit. She'd felt a hand squeeze one of her breasts. She'd wanted to grab the disgusting groper's hand and hold it up while shouting "pervert, pervert" to shame him. But she'd been wrapped up in her earlier excitement, anticipating the meeting, and she'd let it go. That groper was like most men at Yamada: they didn't respect her—and they never would—simply because she was a woman.

She heard a creak, followed by footsteps, and a knock on the bathroom stall's door. "Asami? Are you in there?"

It was Etta's voice.

On toilet tissue, Asami blew her nose, wiped her eyes, and emerged, her head held high.

Etta's eyes were on fire. "Neither Sam nor I saw this coming. It's an outrage! I nominated you for recognition. I felt certain you'd receive it, as well as a promotion. Your executives obviously got feedback from another party, one whom they trust far more than a Western woman."

Asami touched her friend's hand. "This is not your fault. It was their ill-advised error and now their loss. I'm resigning. I've saved a good bit of money. I'll get a U.S. study visa and secure my MBA. Your country rewards women for creativity and personal expression. That's where I belong."

Etta pressed her palm to Asami's cheek. "Honey, I'm so proud of you!"

Although Asami's words had been brave, she was trembling inside. She stepped toward the bank of sinks, turned on a faucet, and washed her hands of Yamada, over and over, until her knuckles were raw.

-11-

Monday - New York

The Greenwich Village Starbucks should have made Etta feel safe: the coffee aroma, the friendly barista, the mellow music, and the middle-aged couple, their fingers entwined. But how could she feel safe? How could anyone feel safe when their life could be stolen in short order *and* for no logical reason?

On the lookout for Henri, Etta sat on a stool along the window wall sipping on a pumpkin spice latte. She felt certain Chloe's death was a homicide. But that meant the Otis guy had been privy to inside knowledge about her daughter's and Henri's personal lives. He had to have known he'd have uninterrupted time to install the closet panel and to murder her daughter.

But who could he be? And what information had Chloe known that had been detrimental enough to have destroyed her life?

A cool draft of air made her turn and she watched Henri approach. Her feelings for him had turned a full circle. Rather than loathing she felt empathy. They'd both lost Chloe and neither could fathom why.

"Oh Etta, I could see you through the window." Henri's hazel eyes were misted over and his dark curls untidy, just as they'd been when her daughter had first met him. "For a second, I thought you were Chloe. She looked so much like you." He hung his head. "What a beautiful woman she would've become."

A lump had formed in Etta's throat and she squeezed Henri's arm. "All I can say is when my daughter chose you, she picked a good man. Now go order a beverage and we'll talk."

"I'm all coffeed out." He slid onto the adjacent stool. "Tell me, did you talk to Detective Harper?"

"Yes, and she's reopened Chloe's case."

"Mon Dieu..." He shook his head. "It's hard to believe her death could actually be a homicide."

"I know, but I might've uncovered a motive." She told him about Tripoint's impending IPO and Chloe's scheduled HR meeting. "I also talked to our New York administration manager to see if Chloe had left her laptop at work."

"Did she?"

"If she did, it's not there now. It wasn't cable-locked to her desktop. The manager also used a master key to open her desk and credenza. The laptop wasn't in either. I'm thinking the Otis guy took it."

"Merde!" Henri stuffed his neck scarf into his sport coat pocket. "What's going on? What was Chloe mixed up in?"

"I wish I knew." She gazed into his troubled eyes. "Did Chloe say anything about her Tokyo trip? Anything about Hana?"

"She said the training sessions went well. She didn't mention Hana, but she did bring up Sam Madrid. Chloe seemed upset that he hadn't flown back with her. She'd wanted to get his advice on something, but she didn't elaborate."

"Really? Do you know why Sam wasn't on her flight?"

"No, and she didn't know either."

"Shit!" Etta twisted a strand of hair around her finger. "It's frustrating not to talk to Sam. Other than that initial short call, we haven't connected, not that we haven't tried. He'd tell me why he didn't fly back with Chloe. That line of inquiry is legitimate even if I'm to pretend her death is still a suicide." She explained the detective's request.

"Doesn't it seem crazy that someone from Tripoint could've murdered Chloe?"

"It does, so let's consider other options."

"Well..." Henri seemed reluctant. "There's a seventeen-year-old in Tripoint for Kids."

"Do you mean Deon—the teen you and Chloe were mentoring?"

"Yes. Prior to joining TFK, he'd had some run-ins with the police. But he's been thriving, that was until this month."

"What do you mean?"

"You know Chloe's been traveling, conducting training sessions in other branches, not just the one in Tokyo. Because of that, Deon started to act out, blaming her for not helping him get prepared for last Saturday's event."

"What kind of event?"

"It took place inside a local shopping mall. About thirty TFK teens were provided center court space to setup a retail shop using donated merchandise, loaner hardware, and Tripoint software. Local retailers judged and prize money was given out."

"So was Deon there?"

"He was supposed to be, but he never showed up. That upset Chloe. One of the teens gave her a note from him. It said she'd be sorry for encouraging him to participate. That the program had been a waste of his time. That he should've listened to his uncle."

The sweet coffee taste had turned sour in Etta's mouth. "What do you know about Deon's uncle?"

"I've never met him, but Chloe felt he was a bad influence. He's the younger brother of Deon's mom. I understand he's served time for both burglary and drugs. When Deon was picked up for his B&E offense, he was with his uncle."

"What about Deon's dad?"

"He passed away when he was small and his uncle stepped in. But he hasn't been the sort of role model Deon needed. Nevertheless, the two have always been close."

"Did Deon know about Chloe's earlier suicide attempt?" Etta inched closer to the window counter so a woman with a stroller could squeeze by.

Henri nodded. "It wasn't something she necessarily hid. Talking about her depression, and how she'd addressed it, helped her establish rapport with some of the troubled kids—Deon included."

"He knew both of you would've been at Saturday's event, leaving the apartment empty. What about that night? Would he have known Chloe could've been alone?"

"I've mentioned my Rusty Nail gigs to him."

Etta leaned on her elbow and stared out at the traffic. "I can't picture him posing as an Otis repairman and orchestrating Chloe's death, just because he was pissed off at her. Can you?"

Henri frowned. "When you say it that way, it does sound farfetched."

"Chloe's death has to be connected to someone else—someone who knew your apartment was located next to the elevator." Etta hesitated. "What about the guests at that cocktail party, the one Sam helped Chloe host at your apartment."

"About fifty people attended. That's when the wife of Tripoint's CEO asked Chloe if she'd help her co-chair last Saturday's event."

Etta raised her brows. "Chloe seems to have been traveling in some pretty important circles."

"She said she owed much of that to Sam. But, Etta, something else has been bothering me. You know how Chloe wanted me to cut back on my Rusty Nail gigs?"

She nodded.

"Last Saturday, I'd asked Hank Perry, another musician friend, to fill in for me."

"On the night Chloe died?"

"Yes. We'd just gotten home from the TFK event when some guy called me. He said Hank couldn't make it. I felt I had no option. I had to fulfill my earlier obligation. I tried to explain that to Chloe." Henri's tortured eyes found hers. "Those were the last words we exchanged. But here's the odd part. When I got to the bar, Hank was there."

She shifted on her stool. "So who called you?"

"I don't know. Nobody owned up to making the call. I almost left, but Hank persuaded me to stay. If I hadn't—Chloe might still be alive."

She squeezed his arm. "Or you might be dead as well. Tell me, do you still have that phone number?"

"I think so."

She drummed her fingers on the counter until he located it. "Go ahead Henri, place that call."

He looked worried. "Maybe Detective Harper should."

Etta recalled the detective's warning, but she didn't care. "If you won't, I will." She put out her hand.

He sighed. "No, I'll do it."

Etta watched as Henri selected the number then held the cell against his ear. "What's happening?"

"It's ringing and ringing." He seemed startled. "Who's this?"

Etta held her breath.

"Okay, thanks." Henri pressed END, a hangdog expression on his face. "It's a dead end. The call was made from the ancient payphone inside the Rusty Nail."

Etta's determined gaze met his. "Think positive. Maybe someone saw the guy who made it."

Monday - Tokyo

Asami raced across Kimura's threshold. Bobbling back and forth, she removed her shoes then shoved them into the cupboard. The piped-in traditional music wasn't calming her nerves. She'd just talked to Etta.

If Chloe could've been murdered could Hana have been too?

Is that why her daughter hadn't returned?

In a tie-dyed long-sleeve T-shirt, Hana's teacher friend sat at a low dining table below the brightly lit menu board, his shaggy head bent over a laptop. Lucas had texted Asami to meet him there. She had only slight qualms in doing so, even though, the prior evening, he'd been sitting next to the purple-birthmarked man. Based on Lucas's family background, Asami doubted her daughter's friend would hang out with that sort of guy, one who was most likely a yakuza gangster.

Hana had said Lucas's mama, who'd actually been a Grateful Dead groupie, had met his mixed-race-Japanese papa at one of their concerts. They'd both been attending Berkley and, three months later, had married. After graduation, his papa had secured an Asian Studies teaching position at NYU where he was currently tenured. Lucas seemed to be a blended version of his parents' personalities. Hana had said she'd been drawn to him for that reason.

Asami's eyes scanned the restaurant's patrons, hoping to locate that purple-birthmarked man, but he was nowhere in sight. That was unfortunate. With Lucas nearby, she would've confronted him.

Asami reached Lucas's table, slid onto the chair across from him, and immediately told him about her cell conversation with Etta.

"Fujioka-san, that's heavy stuff. Your American friend's theory about her daughter's death sounds so bizarre. Her possible murderer crawling out of a closet panel?"

"I don't know what to think. Maybe Etta simply wants to believe that scenario rather than the alternative. But what if she's right?"

Asami's fingers fiddled with the table setting's chopsticks while she told Lucas about Thursday evening, how Etta's daughter and hers had been together at the British Pub until 10:00 p.m. and at the Roppongi train station at 1:00 a.m. "It's frustrating not to know what happened between those two sightings, why Hana's clothes and hair were wet."

Lucas nodded, consternation lining his face.

"Etta thinks Chloe was murdered because she was going to reveal some information—something that could hurt Tripoint's initial public stock offering."

His head jerked up. "When does that occur?"

"In three days."

"So you think Chloe's death could be connected to Hana's disappearance?"

"Possibly? Oh Luca-san, could Hana be dead as well?"

He placed his hand over hers. "You can't think those thoughts. Although we don't know what happened to Hana during that three hour segment, I might have some information about her whereabouts once she got off the Roppongi train. But first things first. You haven't eaten all day have you?"

She pulled her hand away. "I'm not hungry."

"Fujioka-san, you must eat." He waved a waiter over and ordered for the two of them. Once that was done, he turned his laptop toward her. "Look at this."

Asami gazed at the photo. Against a sea of trees, a Japanese man was dressed in hiking clothes. She looked up. "Do you know him?"

"No. But a Facebook friend of mine does."

"Why is he important?"

"Look over his shoulder, at the roped off trail, the one leading into that dense forest section."

A bright yellow canvas cap, fringed with long dark hair, jumped out, as did an orange jacket, a blue backpack, and a pair of khaki shorts. The hiker's back was to the camera, but the build was tall and slim.

Asami gasped, "That has to be Hana!"

"Yes. I just talked to the guy who posted the photo. This was taken at around 10 a.m. on Saturday."

The waiter placed two beers on the table.

Lucas nodded his thanks and continued, "Notice the man beside Hana?" He pointed. "The one with the Asian build who's pulling the large roller bag?"

Asami squinted. "That certainly is not standard camping equipment. Tell me, where was this taken?"

Lucas hesitated, his eyes not meeting hers.

She tipped her head. "Lucas-san?"

He sighed. "At Aokigahara's entrance."

Asami swayed in her chair.

The waiter placed two plates of skewered grilled chicken on the table.

She pushed hers away.

Asami had grown up near that forest. It attracted three types of visitors: trekkers interested in the caves, the curious who hoped to catch a glimpse of a suicide victim, and those sad souls who didn't plan on returning home.

Asami tried to control her breathing. Maybe Etta was wrong about Chloe's death. Could it still be a suicide? Could their daughters have indeed made a pact?

Asami grabbed Lucas's arm. "Hana's text said she needed to think. Did she mention any recent worries to you?"

"No. But ever since her New York training she's been a bit off. You must've noticed."

His words were alarming. "I—I've been traveling. But her New York instructors told me she'd done extremely well. The last time I saw Hana, the two of us and Chloe Martin had lunch right here. Hana's training never came up."

Asami's mind was churning. Could something have happened to Hana in New York? Asami thought back to the eighties, to her Tripoint training completion party. That night's memories still made Asami queasy. Nevertheless, she believed Tripoint had given her the career opportunities she never would've had at a Japanese firm. That was what she'd told Hana. That was why she'd pushed her daughter toward a Tripoint job.

Had that been a deadly mistake?

Monday - New York

Damn! Etta collapsed onto her hotel room's lower bunk. She'd been in the bathroom and had missed another call from Sam. She tried him back, but her call went into his recorded message.

Next to her hotel was a deli. She'd refused Henri's dinner invitation, yet she could only subsist on adrenalin and caffeine for so long. She slipped on her raincoat just as her cell rang.

It had to be Sam.

When Etta answered, she was startled to hear a female voice say, "Etta? This is Sylvia Pollard."

She sank back down. Etta hadn't talked to the wife of Tripoint's CEO since the company's February achievement event. Given Etta's initial problem with Tom Pollard, others might find it surprising that she and Sylvia had always sought each other out. But from that first dinner, at the Pollards' Dakota apartment, a bond of mutual respect had been formed.

"My dear," Sylvia said. "I'm so sorry for your loss. Sam Madrid just called, right before his flight took off. He said you two have been playing phone tag. He wanted me to check on you."

At Sam's kind gesture, Etta's eyes pooled.

"Have you had supper?"

"No, but don't—don't worry about me."

"Nonsense. You need to eat. I'll send a car. Tom's traveling so it'll be just the two of us."

* * *

Etta entered the opulent wood-paneled Dakota lobby. Sylvia Pollard was waiting dressed casually in jeans and a cabled sweater. Although her hair had turned silver, the wedge cut had never changed. "I'm so glad you came." Sylvia pulled Etta into a hug.

Mom's Chanel N°5's soothing scent triggered another avalanche of emotion, as did Sylvia's soft hand patting, and her voice cooing, "There, there."

Etta finally pulled away and found a tissue to blow her nose.

They walked over to an elevator, about the same vintage as the one in Chloe's building. The doors opened and the two stepped over the bronze Otis insignia.

As Sylvia pressed the third floor button, Etta's eyes gravitated to the area below the handrails—and she flinched.

The lower elevator panels on both side walls were identical to those in Chloe's building.

That couldn't mean anything, could it? Hundreds of New York elevators would be the same. Chloe's doorman had known about the Otis panels in her daughter's building. That escape feature had to be common knowledge to so many others.

On the third floor, she and Sylvia stepped off. The Pollards' apartment was the second door to the right. Her friend used her key and they entered a small foyer. Ahead was the drawing room Etta remembered. To her left was a wide archway. She followed Sylvia in that direction and they arrived in the kitchen.

Her friend motioned toward a stool beside a granite island. "Please sit. Would you prefer red or white wine?"

"Red, please." Etta slid onto a stool.

Sylvia uncorked a bottle and poured two glasses, placing one in front of Etta. "I can tell your daughter's death is taking a toll on you." On the adjacent kitchen counter, she picked up tongs to toss the salad. "Etta, what can I do?"

"What can anyone do? For thirty-two years, I've protected Chloe, encouraged her and, of course, desperately loved her. I feel so lost. So abandoned." Etta stared into her friend's sympathetic eyes. Etta so wanted to reveal Chloe's death could be a homicide, but she couldn't.

"Oh Etta, I don't know what to say."

"I know. I'm used to solving work-related problems. But there's no way to fix this, to bring my daughter back."

Sylvia placed two salads on the island's placemats. "I can't imagine what you're going through." She perched on the adjacent stool. "If I lost TJ, I don't know what I'd do. This past year, I got to know Chloe. She was a special young woman: smart, caring, funny, a wonderful asset and spokesperson for the Tripoint for Kids program." She hesitated. "I don't mean to pry, but was Chloe suffering from depression? Sam said she committed suicide."

Etta wasn't sure what to say. She decided to tell a few white lies coupled with the truth. "Chloe *had* attempted suicide in the past."

Sylvia's shocked expression seemed authentic.

"Both Henri and I blame ourselves for her death. We believe we should've noticed some sort of change in Chloe's demeanor. Tell me, did she mention any concerns to you? Henri said you two had co-chaired last weekend's TFK event."

"If I think back to Saturday, Chloe did seem preoccupied. But that unfortunate note, from the teen she was mentoring, was the only issue she brought up." Sylvia looked uncomfortable. "Deon's mom would be distressed if she knew."

Etta's fork stopped in mid-air. "You know Deon's mom?"

She nodded. "For years, Lorna has cleaned our apartment and Sam's. When Deon got into his earlier trouble, his mom confided that to Sam and he told Chloe."

"So my daughter's the one who reached out to Deon?"

"Yes." As Sylvia refilled their wine glasses, Etta contemplated her friend's words. One fact was certain: Deon was carrying blame for her daughter's death. Either he was the Otis man or he believed his note might have instigated Chloe's suicide. Whatever the case, she had to find out.

Sylvia cocked her head toward Etta. "How long are you staying in New York?"

"I'm not sure. I have to finish packing up Chloe's apartment belongings and those from her Tripoint desk as well."

"Tom and Sam will arrive back tomorrow. I know they'll both offer you their assistance."

"They're traveling together?"

"Yes. Their schedule's been hectic. Last week, they were in Tokyo."

Etta stiffened.

"Both arrived back here on Saturday morning, and the two left again on Sunday afternoon for London and Berlin."

Etta's breathing had shallowed.

Both men had been in Tokyo the night Hana had disappeared *and* in New York the evening Chloe had died.

Tuesday – Five Lakes Region

Aokigahara Forest had taken root and flourished over Mount Fuji's last eruption in 1708. Spread across fourteen square miles, it was the home to Japanese hemlocks, hinoki cypresses, and firs. It was also the final home for many suicide victims.

In the early morning light, everything was green and mossy, ironically full of life. Asami read the large sign leading into the forest: *Your life is a precious gift from your parents. Don't keep troubled thoughts to yourself.*

That sentiment only increased Asami's fear for her daughter. Beside her was Hana's friend Lucas dressed in a Baja striped hoodie. She looked into his apprehensive eyes, her fingers finding her jacket zipper. "I'm so grateful you're here." She wiggled her toes inside a pair of Hana's workout shoes, about one size too big, but a better choice than heels.

Lucas touched her arm. "No mama should have to handle this alone."

Asami had called Sergeant Mori from Kimura's. He'd promised to have a park ranger meet Lucas and her at the forest entrance at daybreak. But transportation to get there had been an issue. It had been too late to take a train or a bus, so she'd called Jiro. Her friend had come through as she knew he would. A Kadokawa Pictures limo had picked them up and delivered them to a guesthouse in the village of Narusawa, a short distance from Aokigahara.

A park ranger in a khaki jacket and pants approached, "Abe" on his nameplate. "You must be Fujioka-san?" He bowed. "Sergeant Mori told me we'll be looking for signs of your daughter."

"Yes." She also bowed and introduced Lucas. "Is—is camping allowed in that area?" She pointed toward the unmarked forest section.

"Not after dark. But there are those determined to do so. Often they've taken on a friend's wager to spend the night. But there are others, I'm sad to say, who come here contemplating suicide." His eyes avoided hers. "On my patrols, I sometimes discover those individuals inside tents and offer my assistance. Some take it. Others ask me to leave." He hesitated. "I must warn you, on our search, we may see badly decomposed bodies."

Asami drew her jacket collar tight as if that could ward off his chilling words. Hana couldn't be inside Aokigahara. But if she was, Asami had to believe she was in her tent, still "thinking" as her text had said.

Dense trees blocked the wind as she and Lucas followed Abe onto the unofficial trail used for "body hunts." The forest was quiet, devoid of life. There were no insects, no chirping birds, not even a rustle of a chipmunk or squirrel.

Lucas asked, "Why is all the tape strung between trees?"

"It's like in *Hansel and Gretel*," Abe said. "But rather than dropping breadcrumbs, troubled individuals often wrap a specific color of masking tape around one tree, moving on to the next, then the next, to mark their path. If they are indecisive about killing themselves, and decide to return, they'll find their way out."

Asami's mother had told her frightening stories about Aokigahara. How, in ancient times, during famine periods, families had abandoned loved ones inside the forest to reduce the mouths to feed. But instead of being haunted by those abandoned souls, Asami preferred to imagine those of her departed family aiding her in Hana's search—those of her parents, who'd both passed away, and her brother, who'd died at age thirty-six from cardiomyopathy.

Hana was her only family.

Under dried leaves, solidified lava made the terrain uneven and deceptive. Lucas kept reaching out to steady her. It was unnerving to see the homemade nooses still hanging from trees and scattered on the ground. Beside some were flower bouquets, boxes of chocolates, one had a teddy bear with a photo.

Lucas whispered, "This is heavy stuff. Why would anyone choose to take their life in this place? It's so— "

"Stop!" Abe commanded.

Asami's eyes frantically searched the area, her gaze halting on a nearby tree. A corpse hung, its faceless flesh disintegrating, and she buckled over.

Lucas cried out, "Fujioka-san! Look up! It's not Hana! From the clothing, you can tell the victim's a male."

Asami felt faint. The grotesque corpse was not her daughter's! Yet she was ashamed to feel such relief. The victim's poor relatives must still be hoping for the best as she was.

Abe tried his cell without success and frowned. "When we return, I'll alert forest workers. They'll transport the body to the local police station." The corpse's discovery and recovery seemed to be Abe's everyday routine, like rescuing Hana's kitty from a ginkgo tree.

Asami forced herself to start off again, the forest thickening. In the dim light, her eyes were drawn to a tan-colored tent up ahead. "Look!" She pointed. "It could be Hana's!"

Asami threaded through the exposed network of twisted tree roots, holding onto Lucas's arm, until they reached the tent. She trembled as Abe put on gloves before lifting the front flap.

A blue backpack, a yellow canvas cap, and a book were the only things inside.

Asami fell to her knees. "This tent is Hana's, but where is she?"

Abe removed the backpack and dumped its contents out onto the forest floor. Toiletries and a rolled up sleeping bag hit the ground. In a side pocket, he located Hana's cell. He powered it on then turned the display toward Asami. According to the message icon, thirty-six new ones had arrived, probably the majority from her.

From Abe's own backpack, he removed a stylus and selected that icon. An unsent message appeared addressed to "Mama."

Gomennasai was typed on the display.

Asami's jaw quivered. What had her child done? Why was she sorry?

Abe removed the book from the tent and Asami reached for it.

He shook his head. "You don't need to see this. It's often among the abandoned belongings I find."

"You must show it to me."

He sighed and turned it toward her. *The Complete Manual of Suicide* was emblazed across the cover.

Her desperate eyes jerked up and she peered into the gloom. About a soccer field away, she could see another human shape hanging from a tree. It couldn't be Hana! Not Hana!

Abe had also noticed the body. "You said your daughter was last seen on Saturday. If this is indeed her, she will be unrecognizable. You must stay here."

Lucas echoed Abe's words as Asami scrambled to her feet. "That's not Hana! Not Hana!"

She ran, ducking under low hanging branches, not caring whether she injured an ankle or scratched her face.

"Not Hana! Not Hana!" she continued to cry until she reached the spot.

She stared up at the woman: her long dark hair, orange jacket, khaki shorts, and hiking boots. Yes, those were Hana's clothes. But the bloated green face and protruding tongue and eyes were those of an ogre—not her beautiful daughter.

From deep within Asami, an unearthly sound exploded, flooding the silent forest.

It was that of a mama, a broken mama.

One who had lost her only child.

-12-

1975 - Chicago

Etta's world had changed. In her Clark Street flat, she'd jump out of bed each morning eagerly anticipating the day. Sam had paired her up with Michael Tower, considered to be on even par with the Marketing Rep Pete had been assigned. Michael and she had already bested them, winning two major deals: one at a specialty retailer, the second at a discount chain. Donna and Neil were proud of Etta. Pete just stayed out of her way.

She couldn't believe her luck. Sam was her manager, but he was also her friend. "It's interesting to be a woman in this field," she'd told him after closing the second deal. "It's like I have to be better than a guy before the clients take me seriously. Initially, there were some raised eyebrows, some reticence to speak to me without Michael present. But once I proved I knew what I was doing, I actually won extra Brownie points."

Sam had grinned. "If I were your client, and realized you were as capable as your male counterpart, I'd certainly prefer working with you. You're much better on the eyes."

"I certainly hope so!" she'd quipped back, concentrating hard so her cheeks wouldn't match Mom's window boxes' red geraniums. Etta's rampant yearning for Sam hadn't dwindled and those kinds of comments only intensified her feelings. If the same sort of compliment had come from Tom Pollard, she would've been distressed. Coming from Sam, it felt right—what good friends might say to one another. But she vowed to keep her feelings in check. He was a married man, and although his bartender brother had hinted Sam might have some marital issues, Sam had never let on. But he also hadn't discussed his wife.

That night, they entered the elevator together. Sam seemed to work all hours of the day as did she.

Etta decided to broach the subject. "I have no one to go home to, but you have a wife. How does she like the hours you keep?"

His eyes connected with hers. "I thought you knew. As a fourth year NYU medical student, Cindy is completing her OB/GYN rotations at New York's Bellevue Hospital."

Etta's fingers fumbled on the raincoat button she was trying to secure. Sam was in Chi-town—all alone—and so was she?

"It's been difficult living apart," he continued, "but I manage to fly back to New York once a month. When Cindy finishes her rotations we're hoping she can find a Chicago position."

The elevator doors opened.

"Hey Etta, any chance you'd like to share a Gino's pizza tonight? But listen, I'd understand if that doesn't work."

She tried to control her elation. "Why—why sure, Sam, that sounds nice."

They crossed Wacker and arrived at the Wabash Avenue Bridge. Reflected in the dark Chicago River were the lights from the surrounding high rise buildings.

Sam looked up. "Chicago's a big city, but it's tiny in comparison to Manhattan."

"If you think Chicago's small, you should see Carter." Caught up in their communal closeness, Etta babbled, telling him about her hometown's dilapidated movie theater, its two greasy spoons, its one department-slash-hardware store. How her exciting weekend activities had been going to church, attending ailing parishioners' fundraisers at Rocky's Tavern, or bowling on the lanes attached to that same bar. How the population, just inching over two thousand, subsisted on non-stop gossip revolving around people who'd moved away, those who'd moved back, and those everybody wished would leave.

Sam's laughter filled the night air as they waited for the crosswalk light, vehicles speeding past. "Your life was far different than mine." He talked about Haruki, how the two brothers had been allowed to ride on the subway solo by the age of six. How, as teens, they'd browsed for hours at the Flatirons Record Store and rocked out to the latest hits squeezed inside the same soundproof listening booth. Because Sam had grown up in the Big Apple, with the craziest of the crazies, he felt comfortable in any sort of environment. "And," he hesitated, "my wife does as well."

Midstride, Etta stumbled, her euphoria dissipating. "So—so how did you two meet?"

"I've always known Cindy. Her father's my dad's best friend. They work for the same New York investment firm. Our families assumed we'd end up together. Obviously, we did." He shrugged as if that hadn't been fully his choice.

Sam's attitude gave Etta hope. She hadn't heard him express any passion when he'd talked about his wife. Once again, Etta recalled her conversation with Sam's brother. Had Haruki been right? Was Cindy, as he'd said, a tight-assed snooty bitch? Was Sam happy in his marriage? Or was he simply fulfilling his parents' expectations?

They arrived at Gino's and stepped inside, the walls covered in graffiti. James Taylor's "Fire and Rain" played from the speakers and Etta sniffed the air. "Don't you love it? I feel as if I've been transported back to Northwestern. Every Sunday night, a Spot delivery guy would show up at my sorority house with a stack of cheese pies hoping to find buyers. The scent always drove me down to the lobby."

"The Spot did have the best pizza. Too bad we didn't share one when we were both there."

The hostess intervened, thankfully giving Etta time to hide her lovelorn regret as she and Sam were seated in a back corner booth.

The waiter appeared and Sam took charge. He ordered a deep dish pizza, a beer for him, and a wine for her.

Sam gazed into her eyes, his chin resting on his hand, his elbow on the table, and his thumb spinning his wedding band. He often did the same in the office while making some sort of decision. A slow smile formed on his lips and he slid that hand under the table.

Shit! It suddenly felt awkward, as if they were on a date, like back in junior high when she'd had her first crush on a boy and he'd asked her out to a street dance. It had been a warm summer evening, the perfect setting to begin a young romance, but all night long Etta had been tongue-tied and she'd lost her opportunity. She couldn't let that happen again.

She leaned in. "I've got to say, being with you tonight certainly beats eating leftovers while watching *The Waltons* on my black and white twelve-inch TV. But, of course, that wouldn't take much."

He laughed. Her comment had definitely broken the ice. So did the beer and wine that followed. Their conversation flowed, more intimate than before. She told him about Dad's negative attitude, about Mom's nurturing one, about Moni and her hidden stash of pot. She nearly told him about her Plaza Hotel incident but stopped short. Tom Pollard couldn't destroy the night's magic.

The waiter delivered a second round of drinks with their pizza and Etta dug in, her eyes meeting Sam's.

Between them, she felt an electric charge.

Their relationship had changed.

That thrilled Etta and scared her.

1976 - Chicago

The Tripoint Chicago meeting room was decorated with streamers, balloons, and motivational signs. A boom box played a marching band rendition. Festivities were in place for Tripoint's 1976 Kickoff Meeting. Etta had been blackballed at the prior year's event, slogging around the room in self-pity mode, far different than her current state.

She filled a plate from a buffet table and squeezed into a chair between Neil and Donna. Nervous anticipation packed the room. Those lucky few would be earning an all-expense-paid trip to Tripoint's week-long Miami Beach achievement event.

Etta's stomach was doing the jitterbug for more than one reason. Tripoint's CEO would be their meeting's host. Over the past six months, Tom Pollard had made a few visits to the Chicago office. Each time, she'd been with clients and had managed to miss him. She'd originally wanted to confront him. However, once Sam had recognized her worth as an employee, she'd dropped her vendetta. Yet ever since that Plaza Hotel fiasco, she'd held her breath, those worries still biting at her heels. She continued to fear Tom would send additional punishment her way.

None had come.

Etta wanted to believe she was home free.

She nibbled on a pastrami sandwich and watched Pete slide in beside the Marketing Reps, his preferred companions. For a few months, Pete and Donna had been an item. But she'd dumped him for a United Airlines pilot. That had ticked Pete off to no end. Neil and his high school sweetheart had tied the knot. Etta was still pining for Sam.

He stood beside the conference room's foil projector, his gray eyes targeting hers.

Etta smiled at him and self-consciously looked away. She took a bite of sandwich, chewed, and swallowed just as Donna whispered, "Are you sleeping with Sam?"

Etta nearly choked.

"Pete's convinced that's the reason you've been assigned the lucrative retail accounts. He says you're Sam's favorite." She nudged Etta. "Better you than Pete! But don't worry. I have no issues. I know you've had a thing for Sam ever since your college days. And I can see why!"

Etta probably *was* Sam's favorite. But she wasn't sleeping with him. Though, after that first night at Gino's, their employee/manager relationship had crossed a dangerous line. They'd surreptitiously continued to meet in that same back booth where they would touch hands and press knees. They'd hug at departure time, their bodies glued together rather than modestly apart. Between them, there was an intense, unsatisfied sexual attraction.

Sam's wife, Cindy, had accepted an OB/GYN position in New York City. Etta had watched Sam struggle over his wife's decision. "This isn't a marriage!" he'd say, the situation grating on him.

Sam had talked to Tripoint's Chief Operating Officer to see whether he could secure an equivalent position or better in the New York branch. When Sam had told Etta, "That's not going to happen anytime soon," she'd commiserated with him, but she'd actually been elated.

Her emotional response had continued to bother her. Etta was in a never-ending tug of war with her conscience. She'd rarely seen eye-to-eye with Dad, but her religious upbringing was still ingrained. Sam was married. That fact weighed heavily on her. She didn't know what she would do if the opportunity to sleep with him would arise.

As Tom Pollard entered the room, Etta purged those heated thoughts and braced herself. She'd had one issue with Tom. She had to let it go. He was a great leader. Tripoint was growing. She loved her job. Making an issue over his past indiscretion would probably hurt Etta more than Tom—although laws were changing.

The woman professor who'd led Moni's Cornell discussion group had recently testified before New York City's Human Rights Commission. The Civil Rights Act of '64 prohibited sexual discrimination in the workplace, but not what she'd termed "sexual harassment." If proven in court, it would be considered a new form of sex discrimination, in violation of the Civil Rights Act. The key words were "if proven." It was still difficult for most women to prove their allegations.

Behind the podium, Etta watched Tom Pollard's magnetic eyes focus on his Chicago employees. His hands expansive, he said, "You should all be proud! 1975 was a banner year! Tripoint exceeded its projected revenue numbers, controlled expenses, and acquired twenty-one new accounts. We'll be opening three new branches in the next two years. Our future growth is unlimited!"

Everyone applauded and cheered.

"Now I'd like to recognize a few individuals who made a substantial difference." Envelopes from George Buckley, Sam, and the administration manager were in Tom's hand. It was like the Academy Awards. The Chicago managers had made their secret decisions. Even Tom didn't know the names hidden inside.

He first read two administrative staff names. Etta was pleased when Tripoint's front desk receptionist stood, amid hearty applause, and advanced to the front.

Next would be four Marketing Reps. Tom called one name, then a second. The third was the one Pete worked with. As Brian Foster sauntered up, Pete preened himself, anticipating his own recognition. The fourth name was Michael Tower, the Rep Etta worked with. Unlike Pete, she didn't believe she deserved a Miami slot. Not until March, after Sam had arrived in Chicago, had Etta actually performed the role she'd been hired for.

The Technical Reps would finally be announced. Before Etta had accepted her Tripoint position, there'd been nine seasoned ones in the Chicago office. Three of those men's names were called. Etta gazed over at Pete. He was on the edge of his seat, ready to fill the fourth slot. She turned back toward Tom Pollard and watched a stunned expression extend across his face. He cleared his throat, as if it pained him, and announced, "Etta—Etta Martin."

She sat there in disbelief.

Donna gave her a nudge, a big grin on her face.

Neil leaned over and whispered, "Congrats, Etta! You deserve it!"

She stood, took a deep breath, and cautiously approached Tom.

A grudging look of acceptance, with a hint of admiration, was on his face, *and* for the right reason.

She glanced at Sam. He looked far more than proud.

1987 - Chicago

Hazy peach-colored light broke across Lake Michigan's horizon and sunk into Asami's bones. In Nikes and a stylish pink workout suit, she strode beside Etta along the shoreline path snaking south toward Chicago. Waves pounded the concrete embankment, their action spraying both of them. Asami gazed up at Etta's damp face, veiled in an effervescent sheen. "I've felt so invigorated being a student again. There's a saying in Japan, once the child has awakened, you cannot put her back to sleep."

Asami had been searching for a new *ikikata*—lifestyle or way of life—when she'd left Japan. She'd found it when she'd been accepted into Northwestern's MBA program. It had been a risky decision: quitting her job, leaving her country, her family, and especially Jiro who'd always kept her on track. But in the U.S., she'd been treated with respect by her American classmates—both male and female. With Etta's help, she'd also been hired on as a Delta Zeta Sorority housemother. In addition to free room and board, Asami lived within blocks of Etta and Chloe.

Etta pulled off her gray sweatshirt and tied it around her white T-shirt's waist. "It's hard to believe you'll be graduating next month."

"I know. I envy the Japanese males in my program. Their firms funded their studies. They'll be returning to promising futures. Even if I could return to Yamada, I wouldn't. I'm also almost twenty-nine. At that age, the odds another Japanese company will hire me are slim."

"It seems criminal knowing how well you've done."

"That's made my decision easier." Asami slowed as two black labs and their attentive owner dashed across the path, and the dogs surged into the water. "I want to stay in the U.S. But to do so, I've got two options: to be sponsored by a U.S. company or to marry a U.S. citizen."

"I've told you, Tripoint's Chicago branch is hiring two interns. Those jobs can potentially grow into full-fledged positions. Why haven't you applied? You know the deadline's next Friday."

"I'm afraid those intern positions wouldn't be right for me." Asami glanced sideways at Etta. "Because, well because of Brad, although I know you've never warmed up to him."

Asami had met Brad Glidden during her first week at Northwestern. He'd taken a one year sabbatical from his Indianapolis IBM job to complete his MBA. In their Business Strategy course, they'd been paired-up on a project. He'd seen firsthand how she'd struggled with time management and obsessed over silly things. He'd helped her relax, helped her concentrate, and enabled her to excel—much like Jiro had.

Brad had also received some perks in return.

Prior to arriving in the U.S., Asami had talked to three Japanese female friends who'd studied or traveled abroad. She'd wanted advice on how to date an American without falling prey to undignified behavior. They'd told her the male "crème de la crème" resided in the upper eastern seaboard states. To meet one, Asami should attend charity events at venues like Christie's, Sotheby's, or the Guggenheim.

But she'd met Brad in America's heartland, and their relationship had moved into the bedroom that first week.

Her fear of looking undignified had flown right out the window.

Etta nudged her. "It's not that I dislike Brad. He just seems too good to be true. He's thirty. He's handsome. He's intelligent. He's never been married. Why hasn't some other woman snapped him up? Are you certain he's not gay?"

Asami gave her a perturbed look. "He's definitely not gay!" She squinted ahead at Chicago's downtown skyline, but noted that Etta was right. Brad was a definite "three-K"—tall, blond, blue-eyed, and incredibly smart. Once she'd met him, her fantasies about Sam Madrid had blown away much like wispy dandelion seeds.

Etta touched her hand. "I'm sorry if I've offended you."

Asami gave her a playful shove. "Don't worry. I'd expect as much from my wiser and *much* older American sister."

Etta jabbed her back. "Very funny. So is Brad finishing his MBA next month like you?"

"Yes, and his IBM office is hiring." Asami couldn't contain her excitement. "I've told you, I want an equal partner. One who will split traditional home duties and also be sensitive to my career needs. I think I've found him! I'm also quite certain he's on the verge of asking me something big."

Etta halted. "You mean proposing to you—like marriage?"

"Possibly?"

Etta grabbed Asami's hands and squeezed them. "You really need to think this through. I don't want you to get hurt. I know you believe Brad walks on water, but why does he disappear nearly every weekend?"

Asami yanked her hands away. "You mean like you do? I thought you and Chloe were spending that time together, but she told me she's been staying at Moni's. Your weekends can't all be work-related."

Color rose in Etta's cheeks. "Don't change the subject. So where has Brad been spending his weekends?"

"You know his mama's dealing with cancer. He goes back to Indianapolis to help her out."

Etta raised her brows. "It's admirable he's such a good son."

"Yes it is!"

Yet Asami was pricked by shards of doubt.

1987 - Chicago

The intercom in Asami's rosebud-papered bedroom buzzed. "Yes?" she said into the speaker.

"Miss Fujioka, Brad Glidden is here. He said he'd wait on the outside stoop for you."

Asami had been at the library when Brad had left her a note at the Delta Zeta house's front desk. She reread it, attempting to control her excitement: *Dear Asami, I need to discuss something important with you. I'll be back at 4:30. Love, Brad*

She pressed the note to her chest. In three inch heels, she danced around the room. She'd adopted them once she'd been freed from Yamada's conservative dress code. Her qualms had been unfounded! Etta had thought she was being foolish, placing her future in Brad's hands, but Etta had been wrong! Brad was ready to purchase his

"Christmas Cake" before the deadline passed. Or, as the Americans would say, he was ready to pop the question.

Asami combed her hair, put on fresh lipstick, and slipped on her toffee-colored sweater, Brad's favorite. He said it matched the flecks of light in her eyes. She sped down two flights of stairs and pushed open the front door. Under the porch's green awning, Brad's rugged face was as pale as the chapter house's limestone facade.

Her hands flew to her mouth. "Is something wrong? Is it your mama?"

His eyes wouldn't meet hers.

She grabbed his hands. As she did, her legs faltered. She'd touched a ring on his left hand.

Brad reached out to catch her. "I know, I should've told you. But when I met you, my marriage was shaky at best."

She staggered back. "You're married?"

"Yes, but the only good thing was Jacob, my five-year-old son. That's the reason for my weekend departures."

She couldn't comprehend.

"Honestly, my only intent was to see him. But whenever I picked him up, Patty was there. Last weekend, one thing led to another. For Jacob's sake, we—we've decided to work on our marriage."

Asami was speechless.

His pleading eyes found hers. "I want you to understand."

"Understand?" She lunged at him. "You bastard!" Her small fists beat on his chest. "How could you be like so many men in my country? Those who have mistresses on the side? You made me love you. You enticed me with an IBM job. You made me believe I was special. That we had a future together. How could you not have mentioned you were married? That you had a son?"

He placed his hands on her arms to restrain her. "Asami, please, listen."

"No!" She shoved him away and turned her back on him. Her fingers groped for the front door handle. She twisted it, and heaved her body inside, her tears exploding.

Etta had been right—so right.

How could she have been so stupid?

She'd loved and trusted Brad, yet she'd been nothing more than his concubine. He'd had his fill of her and he'd discarded her like a pair of old slippers. What was she to do?

In a few weeks, she'd complete her MBA with no legal U.S. standing. She'd succumbed to the "need to marry a white-man syndrome," and it had failed. There was no marriage proposal. Even if Brad's office had a potential job opening, she'd never pursue it. The Tripoint intern positions had also slipped away.

* * *

Three weeks passed. Two suitcases sat on Asami's bed. Her plight's weight had crushed her spirit. There'd been positions at Sears, Compaq, MCI Worldcom, Arthur Anderson, and the list went on and on, but her timing had been off. They'd been filled the same week as the Chicago Tripoint positions.

Asami had no choice. She had to return to Japan.

She unzipped a suitcase just as her room's intercom buzzed. Asami traipsed over, pushed the button, and listened, "Miss Fujioka, there's a call for you. I'll transfer it to the hall phone."

She opened the door and trudged out. The caller had to be Etta. She picked up the receiver and despairingly said, "Hello?"

"Asami? I'm so glad I caught you. This is Sam Madrid."

Asami grabbed the hallway chair, her legs wobbling like a ten-month-old child's. She hadn't talked to Sam since that humiliating Yamada meeting. She had to gather her wits—to think straight. But that was impossible. "How—how did you get this number?"

He laughed. "Etta gave it to me."

"But why are you calling?"

"She said you'd just completed your MBA. Naturally, she was raving about you. I understand you'd like to stay in the U.S."

"I would! I really would! But I don't know how."

"Maybe I can help. Tripoint's New York branch has already filled its two intern positions, but due to your Yamada experience, I'm certain I can pull some strings."

"What do you mean?"

"We have a full-fledged Technical Rep position open. I know you'd be a great fit."

She dropped onto the chair, dumbstruck.

Sam prodded, "Asami, are you there? Are you interested?"

Her head bobbed. "Absolutely!"

He laughed. "I thought you might be. My secretary will provide you the paperwork to make your position official. Oh, and as soon as you get settled in New York, let's plan on dinner, so we can catch up."

Asami floated back to her room. The turn of events was astounding—and all because of Etta, dear Etta. Rather than returning to Tokyo in defeat, Asami's *akogare*—yearnings and dreams—were miraculously being fulfilled. She was moving to New York for a fabulous job!

Asami stood beside her window and gazed out at Northwestern's campus. Brad had discarded her. So what!

Sam was back in the picture.

-13-

Tuesday - Japan

It was as if Asami was inside a Shinagawa Aquarium tank, floating underwater, peering out at the activity around her. She vaguely remembered stumbling out of the forest, Hana's friend's arm linked into hers. Every ten steps or so, she'd stopped to vomit as her daughter's bloated face had resurfaced.

Had Lucas carried her at some point?

She wasn't sure.

Everything was fuzzy... unbearable...

"Fujioka-san?" her name bubbled out of the void.

Asami's eyes tried to focus. She was in some sort of room. Desks, phones, people—so many people. A sickening pressure rose up beneath her breastbone. She leaned over, moisture dripping down her face, and she gagged up bile into a tissue.

Hana's death did not make sense.

Although her daughter had been emotionally strong, she'd had an extremely low threshold for handling any sort of pain: a skinned knee, a hangnail, a banged toe, a neck kink. Her death by hanging seemed incomprehensible. How could Hana have fashioned that noose, climbed up that tree, tied that rope to that branch, slipped the noose over her neck, and jumped into space. Asami had seen movies. Unless the victim's neck broke, the troubled person would suffer.

What was more, Hana would never have purchased that suicide book. It meant she'd been planning her death for some time.

Nothing made sense.

The bloated face flashed again in front of Asami's eyes. She cried out, her hand swiping at it, but she only grabbed air.

"Fujioka-san?"

She had to focus. Seated across from her was Sergeant Mori. "I'm so sorry for your loss." The detective's face was grim. "I just arrived to help with the search."

Asami hissed, "Listen to me! I know my daughter. I don't believe she'd take her life, but if she did, it would never be like this!"

"I agree!"

Her head swiveled. She had an ally. Beside her was Hana's friend, his grimy face streaked with dried tears. Lucas located Hana's Aokigahara Facebook photo on his cell and he showed it to Mori. "See the man next to her? The one pulling the large roller bag? I told you I heard a male voice in Hana's room. It could belong to him. I bet he was forcing her into the forest."

Asami's head pivoted back. "He's right!" She told the detective about Etta's daughter, how the American authorities had reopened her case. How her death could be a homicide. "Maybe Hana was murdered as well."

Mori tented his fingers. "I'm concerned by your words. The death of every poor soul, located in Aokigahara, has always been ruled a suicide." The detective eyed the forest ranger seated beside him. "Am I right?"

"Yes. There's never been foul play."

"But my daughter's death could be the exception, couldn't it?"

Mori shrugged. "Anything is possible."

Lucas scowled. "It's more than possible. We didn't find Hana's passport, credit cards, or money in the forest. That man in the photo probably took them."

The park ranger said, "Maybe? But more than likely, someone looted Hana's valuables before we located her body. Her cell might've been overlooked since it was in a separate backpack pocket."

Lucas was undeterred. "Let's assume you're wrong. Activity on Hana's credit cards, or her passport usage, could certainly lead us somewhere."

Mori nodded. "I was working that angle. I'll see if anything has turned up. But Fujioka-san..." His concerned gaze returned to Asami. "It still might be best for you to accept your daughter took her own life."

Asami knew what Etta was going through, both of them grieving mothers, both believing their daughters' deaths were not a suicide, both needing to convince the authorities their beliefs were founded.

But in the scheme of things, what did that matter?

Hana was dead.

Nothing could bring her back.

Her courageous child was dead—the one who'd been far stronger than her mama.

How would she survive?

Monday - New York

Etta slid out of a cab in front of the Rusty Nail, a Dylan-era bar, its knotty pine exterior papered with upcoming live music events.

Henri had called Etta while she'd been en route from the Dakota to her hotel. "There's an open jam session tonight. I'm already here. Merde! It's my only relief from the hurt. Please say you'll come."

Her sadness had drained her. She had no energy left. Sleep seemed to be a better option, but the odds were against that happening.

In the end, Etta had relented.

She stepped into the unpretentious club that smelled like stale beer. Her eyes were drawn to the payphone near the bathrooms. That had to be where the call to Henri had been made. He was up on stage with a co-ed group of six. As Etta took a seat at a table, the first bars of a DMB cover, "Crash into Me," resonated through the club.

A young waitress approached, her ponytail bouncing. "What can I get for you?"

Etta ordered the house cabernet as a heavy melancholy settled over her. That DMB song, with Henri on lead vocal, had been one of Chloe's favorites, as were so many others the group performed over the next forty minutes.

The last chords of a Lady Antebellum tune faded. Moments later, Henri joined her. Although his eyes were filled with unspeakable pain, they still made Etta feel as if she was the prettiest woman in the bar. Of course, she knew why.

"Great job, Henri." Etta tried to smile.

"Thanks. I'm glad you came. But that payphone call's been on my mind. Let's talk to Tess. She arrived while I was up on stage and she was bartending last Saturday."

Etta followed Henri until he stopped behind an empty stool. Across the bar from them was a young woman with a punk haircut and multiple ear piercings. Henri introduced Etta to her.

Tess rubbed a fist into her chest. "God, Henri! I'm so sorry. I know what Chloe meant to you and—" her dismal eyes focused on Etta, "and you're her mom! I can't imagine what you both are going through."

That suffocating feeling of loss overwhelmed Etta, once again, as Henri said, "Thanks Tess, but I need you to think back to last Saturday night. Prior to my arrival, did you notice anyone on that payphone?" He jerked his head toward it.

"Let me think." She pinched her eyes shut, slowly nodded, and reopened them. "Almost everyone has a cell. That's why I remember. The caller was a kid, about seventeen."

Etta grabbed Henri's arm. "Could that be Deon? Would he have had your cell number?"

"Yeah, I'm quite certain Chloe gave him mine and hers." He pulled out his cell and showed Tess Deon's photo. "Could this be the kid?"

She looked surprised and nodded. "That's him."

Etta's back stiffened. Deon *was* involved!

"I'd seen him before," Tess continued, "over at Washington Square Park. He's often there with an older black dude. I figured that guy might've been in the bar as well since that kid's underage."

Etta sank down on the stool. "Henri, I bet Deon was with his uncle. Maybe he put his nephew up to making that call. Maybe his uncle was the one who broke into your apartment and—"

"—and took Chloe's life." Henri's bleak eyes met hers. "But why, Etta? Why?"

Tuesday - Tokyo

Asami gulped in fresh air as unchecked tears trickled down her dirty cheeks and splattered onto her lap. It was difficult to breathe. There seemed to be a hole in her lungs where Hana's breath had been ripped out.

She'd called Jiro before leaving the Five Lakes Region and she'd told him about Hana's death. "I can't go home. Her birthday cake and white spray roses are still on my dining table."

Asami's mama had started those annual traditions with Asami and she'd carried them forward to her daughter's birthdays. Only bittersweet memories would remain: her four-year-old Hana using the back of a wooden spoon to smooth the pink frosting her mama had messed up; her daughter at ten, wrapping Asami's fingers in wet toweling after she'd carelessly stuffed the roses into a porcelain vase; and the prior year, at a mature twenty, Hana taking charge of her birthday cake, serving Jiro the largest piece.

How could Asami exist without her child?

Jiro had returned from his aunt's funeral, and he'd asked the limo driver to deliver Asami to his apartment after Lucas had been dropped off. On Jiro's balcony settee, Asami huddled beside him, his arm around her trembling body.

"Asami-chan, I don't understand. How could Hana, our Hana, the strongest young woman I've known, have taken her life?"

Asami pulled away and looked into Jiro's anguished eyes. "I don't believe she did." She told him her reasons why.

"My dear..." He shook his head. "I don't know what to say. You must come inside. You're shivering. You need to take a hot shower. You need to rest. Sergeant Mori will contact you once Hana's autopsy is complete. I'll listen for his call."

"It will be impossible to sleep. I must talk to Etta."

Jiro sighed, "I understand. Then you must take that shower." He stepped inside to give her some privacy.

Asami placed the call.

Etta answered from halfway around the world. "Tell me! Did you find Hana?"

"Yes..." In between Etta's cries of, "That can't be!" Asami relayed her horrendous news. She finally took a ragged breath. "You believe Chloe was murdered. I believe Hana was too."

"Honey! I so wish I was there for you. Do you have support?"

"Yes. What about you?"

"Henri's with me right now. Wait..." Etta muffled her cell. "He wants me to tell you about Tripoint's CEO. Last week, Tom Pollard was also in Japan. Did you know?"

Asami rubbed her forehead, unable to process anything more. "No, no I didn't."

"Oh Asami... I still can't believe our daughters are gone. How can our children have simply vanished from our lives? But—but listen to me. I know it's going to be difficult. But nobody from Tripoint can know their deaths can be anything but suicides. Do you understand?"

Asami gazed across the street into a park where an ornamental bridge spanned a small lotus pond. On a nearby bench, a mama sat clapping her hands as her little girl nimbly kicked a red rubber ball. Unable to watch, Asami turned her head away. "Yes, Etta-san, I understand."

"Good, and listen. You and I are not giving up until we find those bastards who stole our daughters' lives."

Stretching across the airwaves was their mutual grief, an intense sorrow beyond definition, one that could bury them or bring renewed purpose. Etta had always been strong. Rather than succumbing to grief, retribution would be her battle cry.

Could Asami join her?

She hung her head. No. Nothing seemed to matter. Without Hana she couldn't endure.

As Asami pressed END on her cell, she felt Jiro's gentle touch. "My dear, are you okay?"

Asami turned. She wasn't, but she nodded anyway, bits of leaves scattering from her hair. Dully, she stared into the street below. A flashy car pulled up, its license plate 44-44.

Jiro squinted in that same direction. "Why would a yakuza have parked in front of my building?"

It was common knowledge, only the yakuza would select that designer plate. Four was an unlucky number pronounced *shi*. It meant death. The vehicle's owner was publically advertising: *since I don't fear death, you should fear me*.

Asami's shoulders hunched forward, the weight of "everything" too much to bear, yet she still managed to tell Jiro about the purple birth-marked man.

"My dear, you must call Sergeant Mori!"

Resigned to that fact, she reached for her cell as the car pulled away. "Jiro-kun, what's going on? Why are Hana and Chloe dead? Why is the yakuza involved? What happened to Hana on Thursday night? Or did something bad happen earlier—something that escalated that night?"

Jiro smoothed her matted hair. "My dear, you must settle down."

"I can't. Hana's friend Lucas said she hadn't seemed herself ever since her New York training." Asami started to rock. "I should've noticed. I was a miserable mama. My issues always overrode hers."

"Don't say that! You were a wonderful mama. Hana always told me so. You know how she confided in me. My dear, come, you must take that shower." He reached for her hand.

"Not yet. Tell me. Did Hana mention her Tripoint training to you?"

An uneasy look jostled Jiro's face.

She grasped his arm. "So she did tell you something?"

His guilty eyes met hers. "Well, yes. Last week. While you were in Fukuoka. But she didn't want to worry you."

She blinked hard. "What did she say?"

He sat down beside her. "You don't need to know. It won't change anything."

"You must tell me!"

He released a heavy sigh. "Apparently, a Tripoint executive propositioned Hana with some unwanted sexual advances."

She gasped. "Did something happen to her?"

"No. She escaped from the situation."

"Did she tell you the executive's name?"

He shook his head. "But I did encourage her to report him. She said she'd consider that." Jiro's eyes were filled with remorse. "I'm sorry, I should've told you. I just hope that situation isn't connected to her death."

"Whether it is or not, it's not your fault. It's mine—all mine. I should've been there for Hana."

"Oh Asami-chan, she didn't feel that way. She just wanted an opinion from someone who didn't have ties to Tripoint."

Her feet tapped the tiled patio floor. "Maybe Sumie knows more."

Asami called Tripoint's office number and followed the prompts to connect to Hana's recruit class friend. Asami first told Sumie about her daughter's death. Amid Sumie's soft crying, per Etta's instructions, Asami carefully worded her inquiry. "I'm trying to understand why Hana took her life. During her New York training, I understand a Tripoint executive inappropriately propositioned her. Is that right?"

Sumi sniffled, "I—I wasn't to tell anyone. But now, I guess it's okay. Hana called me from the ladies room—the one inside the Plaza Hotel's lobby."

It was if Asami had stepped on an ancient pile of dog shit, the dried dung sticking between her toes. She remembered Etta's secret, the one she'd shared so many years before.

"Hana was overwrought," Sumie continued. "I took a cab to the Plaza and brought her back to our hotel."

"Was the man Thomas Pollard, Tripoint's CEO?"

"How—how did you know?"

Unbridled rage rippled from the roots of Asami's hair to the tips of her tapping toes.

Monday - New York

Etta plodded beside Henri in the dark. She clutched her raincoat to her neck to block the draft tunneling down. It was too much to comprehend. Both her daughter and Asami's were dead.

It was close to midnight, a school night. Nevertheless, she and Henri had decided to see whether Deon, the kid who'd called Henri from the Rusty Nail, might be at Washington Square Park. The ten-acre green space, nestled between NYU campus buildings, was known to attract drug dealers like Deon's uncle, trolling for business. It would've been far easier to have reached the teen on his cell, but Henri had never secured his number.

"Tell me about Deon's family," Etta said as they passed under the massive white marble arch designed with the Arc de Triumph in mind. "Is his mom black or Asian?"

"She's black. His deceased dad was part Asian. There's also a grandfather who lives with them, but Deon told me they don't get along. He expects his grandson to obey him without question, as children do to their seniors in Japan."

"Was his grandfather born there?"

"I believe so. He often works nights. That's when Deon likes to play his mom. She's the one who's lax on his curfew." Henri stuffed his hands inside his pockets. "That's why he might be here tonight."

They arrived at the park's spotlighted fountain. Dozens were seated on its raised ledge listening to a male dreadlocked folk singer playing an acoustic guitar.

Etta smelled Moni's familiar scent.

A white guy in a hoodie motioned to Henri. "Yo mister, what can I do for you?"

Henri drew closer. "We're looking for this kid." He showed him Deon's cellphone photo. "Have you seen him?"'

He looked insulted. "Hey! What's in it for me?"

Henri scowled and peeled off a twenty.

The guy slipped it into his pocket and gave Henri a wily smile. "My man, it's your lucky night! The home boy you're looking for is right over there." He jerked his head toward the southwest park corner.

Illuminated by globed streetlights, Etta and Henri hurried along the sidewalk. Beneath a leafless patch of trees, three Japanese businessmen were clustered around a man with an Afro, his back to them. Beside him was a tall teen. Relief shot through Etta. He was the one pictured in Henri's cellphone photo.

Henri charged forward. "Hey Deon!" He firmly seized the teen's arm. "I understand you called me from the Rusty Nail."

Fear rippled across Deon's face. He yanked his arm from Henri's grip and dropped some business cards in the process.

Like a pair of black crows, he and the other man took flight.

Henri sprinted off after them, yelling over his shoulder, "Come on, Etta. We can't lose them."

If she'd been wearing her Nikes, she might've kept up, at least for a block or so. In loafers, she immediately fell behind. Henri was doing far better. Up ahead, she watched him expertly dodge people until he reached a subway entrance where Deon and the other man had dashed down.

Henri did too.

Etta reached the stairs, blisters sprouting on her heels. She scurried down and arrived in the central ticketing area. Henri was nowhere in sight. Head pounding, and sweat trickling down her back, she pulled out her cell and tried his number.

He answered on the fourth ring, panting, "I—I lost them."

"Damn! All I wanted was one smidgen of good news. But you must know where Deon lives, don't you?"

"No. It's near Battery Park. That's all I know." He hung up and came into view. Spinning through the exit turnstile, he joined Etta, a defeated look on his face.

"Listen..." Etta forced a calm tone into her voice, one she did not feel, one she'd often used with Chloe to perk her daughter up. "We'll figure this out. Deon's address must be in the Tripoint for Kids' database."

Henri's face brightened a bit. "You're right."

"I'll find a way to look it up, but in the meantime, let's return to the park. Deon dropped some business cards. They could give us a lead."

Outside the station, Etta hobbled along beside Henri. They retraced their steps through University Village and arrived at the spot where Deon had been standing. It butted up to a dog run currently inhabited by a Dalmatian and its owner.

Henri located the cards, scattered in the leaves, and picked up a few, handing one to Etta. "*Hiro House,*" he read out loud, "*Tokyo Entertainment, right here in the Big Apple: Saké, Hostesses, and Other Enjoyments.*" He looked up. "I bet Deon's grandfather owns this place. His first name is Hiro."

"What's his last name?"

"Endo."

Etta stared at Henri. "Remember? I told you about that Tokyo gangster? The natural brother of Sam's brother? The one Chloe and Hana were with on Thursday night?"

He nodded.

"His name is Kato Endo. Could he and Hiro be somehow related?" Etta told Henri about the *60 Minutes'* episode that referenced the yakuza's illegal gambling and sex businesses in New York.

Henri gazed at the card. "This could be a match." He turned it over. "There's no address, just a number to text. He pulled out his cell, punched in the card's number, texted "*Hi*," and pressed send. Another text, "*Enter password*," arrived. He frowned. "Deon must give that out, once he's hooked a client, and Hiro House's address is probably texted back."

"Damn!" Etta stamped her foot, the Dalmatian barking in agreement. "Nothing's easy." Yet she realized, by discovering the Hiro House business cards, she might've connected some dots. Maybe the yakuza was involved in both Chloe and Hana's deaths.

-14-

1987 - New York

Asami waited in line outside Club Roco—a sophisticated New York City dance club. Icons like Madonna and Billy Idol were often sighted there. Dressed in designer jeans, a revealing black and white polka dot blouse, and a touch of perfume wafting up from her cleavage, she was caught up in the exhilarating vibe.

She knew she shouldn't be there. Still in the midst of her Tripoint training, she had a presentation scheduled for the next morning.

Under the club's marquee, Asami's roommate glowed. Kira had resigned from Yamada, prior to Asami, and she'd completed her MBA at NYU. Three months earlier, she'd also been hired by an American firm. The two currently shared a SoHo apartment.

Kira smiled at Asami. "I love New York's nightlife scene."

It had started when Studio 54 had opened in '77. However, due to the AIDS epidemic, attendance had been dwindling.

Kira's sister, visiting from Japan, piped in, "I love the clubs too!" She was squeezed into a tight black bodysuit, a Louis Vuitton handbag over her shoulder.

"So tell me." Kira nudged Asami, pinning her dark hair behind her ears to expose large hoop earrings. "How has the CEO's son been behaving? Is he still pursuing you?"

TJ Pollard, at twenty-four, with an MBA under his belt, had joined the Tripoint ranks at the same time as Asami. She'd never met his father, the one who'd propositioned Etta years earlier, but everyone said TJ was a younger version of his dad. "Well..." her fingers fiddled with a blouse button. "In our class today, he purposely dropped a pen by my chair so he had an excuse to bend down. As he did he whispered, 'Japanese girls take my breath away.'" She rolled her eyes. "Coming here *may* be a mistake. He's the one who told me about this club."

Kira's sister frowned. "Last night, I heard that same line inside this club. I know what I did. Asami-san, what did you do?"

She huffed. "I couldn't help but laugh."

Asami's roommate touched her arm. "Why aren't you interested in him?"

She hesitated. "He's not Sam Madrid."

A few days after Asami had arrived in New York, she'd met Sam for dinner, and her earlier obsession for him had returned in full force. Back in Japan, Etta hadn't offered any insight into whether Sam was romantically involved. He hadn't mentioned anyone at dinner, either. But when his left thumb had started to do a spinning motion on its bare ring finger, it had suddenly dawned on Asami: maybe Sam was married! Maybe he'd been keeping his distance from her for that reason.

She'd finally gotten up the nerve to ask.

He'd slid his left hand under the table. "I was, for a number of years. It didn't work out."

"I'm sorry," she'd said, yet she hadn't been. Her hopes had been resurrected. But throughout the meal, Sam's interaction with her had felt more like a big-brother-little-sister relationship than an amorous attraction. In fact, he'd kept bringing up his brother. How Haruki had graduated from NYU with an international business degree and a Japanese Language minor. How he'd landed a job at

PPG's Tokyo branch. How he'd hoped to reconnect with both Asami and his yakuza brother. "Ironically, you now work in New York and Haruki's stationed in Tokyo."

While listening to Sam's words, it had also dawned on Asami, by leading Haruki on, nearly three years ago in Japan, she'd hurt her chances with Sam.

Somehow, she'd have to rectify that situation.

Asami inched toward the club's entrance, protected by two bouncers. Through the hazy film of exhaust, tobacco, and pot fumes, she refocused on her roommate's sister. "How long did you work as an office lady in Japan?"

"For eight years. But before I quit, I managed to save a chunk of change. I also broke off my engagement to a man at my company."

"Really? I bet your parents were upset." Asami knew hers would've been.

"They were, but I told them I couldn't settle for a traditional Japanese marriage before I saw what I was missing. I was so envious of my sister. That's why I came here. And, my goodness!" She surveyed the men in line. "Everyone here is far sexier, more classy, and better looking than the puny Japanese guy I was engaged to. Plus, these gaijin are probably kinder and have larger cocks than his!"

Asami and Kira broke into giggles.

Kira's sister grinned. "Tonight I want to have sex, like last night, without any commitment."

Kiri admonished, "You don't want to be labeled a 'yellow cab'!"

The media had termed Japanese women, like Kira's sister, who'd left their dead-end office lady jobs, to seek out gaijin for short-term sexual affairs, "yellow cabs." These women, as easy to ride as taxis, often paid all the expenses for nightly romps in the bed at some swanky hotel.

Kira's sister put her hands on her hips and pushed out her meager bosom. "I don't care what I'm called. For once, I'm in the driver's seat. I'm sick of being a modest and mild mannered Japanese girl."

Asami was shocked by her flippant attitude. Moving from one partner to the next put her at risk for AIDS or some other STD. As a serious career woman, Asami certainly didn't want to be branded a "yellow cab." But once she was inside Club Roco, and men discovered she was a Japanese citizen living abroad, they might also assume she had loose sexual behavior.

Kira's sister's eyebrows went up. "Oh, oh! There's the guy I slept with last night."

Asami turned and froze. "That's TJ! The guy in my training class. The son of Tripoint's CEO!" TJ was approaching in a gray silk jacket, his feathered blond hair lacquered into place, his confident swagger attracting female attention. A firm jawline normally showed strength of character. But that didn't seem to be true in TJ's case.

Asami shook her head. "You actually slept with him?"

Before her roommate's sister could answer, he reached their side. His eyes flicked between them, then narrowed on Asami. "Fancy seeing you two together. I take it you're friends?"

Blood rushed into Asami's cheeks. "TJ, you have the wrong idea."

He gave her a smug smile. "Sure I do." And he strutted away.

A sick, more-like sleazy feeling settled into Asami's gut.

1987 - New York

Like a Japanese grass lizard, TJ Pollard flitted around in his parents' Dakota apartment refilling glasses from a champagne bottle. Although he had his own place, as the privileged son of Tripoint's

CEO, he'd been given free rein in his childhood domicile that night. Tom and Sylvia had flown into London for the opening of an art exhibition.

The sixteen Tripoint recent hires were celebrating their training graduation *and* Asami's twenty-ninth birthday. Dressed in a floral blouse, gathered skirt, her standard three inch heels, and her hair swept into a chignon, Asami felt like the eldest sibling to the three women and twelve males—all in their early to mid-twenties. But she owed one of the young women heaps of gratitude. The spritely redhead beside her had a brother with ADHD. Throughout their months of training, Darla had understood Asami's unique struggles and had provided Asami her ungrudging assistance.

TJ seemed to be the most immature of the bunch. He kept shooting lewd grins Asami's way. Ever since that night at the dance club, she'd thwarted his advances. But from the underlying tone in TJ's voice, it was evident he wasn't going to give up until he got what he wanted.

The only male Asami wanted was Sam Madrid and she'd made progress in that department. He would frequently stop at her desk to chat, to ask about her training, to see how New York was treating her, to make sure she wasn't homesick.

Yet she was a bit.

She'd used that to her advantage. She'd invited him out to a Japanese restaurant to share a meal of *shabu shabu* as they'd done in Tokyo. When he'd accepted, she'd been thrilled. All evening long, in the demure Japanese woman's style, she'd flirted with him. Once Sam's saké had kicked in, she was certain he'd begun to respond. Otherwise, why would he have kissed her cheek, later that night, when she'd slid out of their cab?

Had it simply been a friendly kiss?

She'd convinced herself it hadn't been.

She'd convinced herself he was beginning to see in her, what she'd always seen in him.

Asami's mind was jetted back to the present when Darla chimed in, "My birthday's next week so, Asami, you're an Aquarius like me!"

Asami smiled. "Yes. Your country's astrological signs seem similar to Japan's blood type personality predictions."

TJ cozied up to her. "My blood type is O. Tell me, Asami, what should my personality traits be?"

It pained her to tell TJ Type O individuals were considered to be natural leaders, self-confident, and ambitious.

He gloated as she quickly added, "But they often act before thinking things through."

He mumbled close to her ear, "That's not the case tonight," as he turned away, slopping champagne on the Oriental rug. "Don't worry." He waved his hand. "The maid will clean it up."

TJ's devil-may-care attitude irked Asami. But it had been most apparent when, unbeknownst to him, she'd watched him answer his parents' front door. A man she'd recognized from the Roco Club had been on the other side. Her roommate's sister had pointed out the Brit to her, the one who catered to the rich and famous with his exotic stash of drugs. Asami had watched TJ exchange some bills for two plastic baggies. She'd expected as much and wondered what his dad would think.

TJ carried out a tray of martinis and winked at Asami. "To honor your birthday, I've whipped up some saké cocktails. I want you to feel right at home."

Surprised at his thoughtful gesture, she watched him replace Darla's champagne glass, then hers.

Darla took a sip and gushed, "Marvelous! Come on Asami, you must try it!"

Because of her meds, Asami usually limited her alcohol consumption. But Darla was persuasive. Asami took one sip, then another, and another. A heady feeling and sense of well-being engulfed her.

She located a green velvet couch and burrowed her backside into the soft fabric. Asami felt superb—magnificent! She was embarking on the next phase of her life—the one she'd imagined at Todai—the one where she'd finally be rewarded for her job efforts, where she'd end up with Sam.

In the next few weeks, she wanted to move into the bedroom with him as she had with Brad. Once there, she was certain Sam would see she was also adept in that department.

Immersed in her euphoric state, she heard TJ announce, "The fucking neighbors are complaining. Everyone must clear out." His vulgar words had hardly disturbed Asami's dreamy state. Amid her colleagues' grumbles, she attempted to stand, but her legs felt limp like sautéed mushrooms.

The room spun and her eyelids fluttered. Oh, to curl up, to go to sleep, to dream about Sam...

Asami vaguely heard a door open and close... open and close...

The couch sagged and a voice growled, "Bitch! I told you I'd made plans."

The room was reeling.

Asami's hands felt useless, flaccid, like a beached whale's fins.

A slimy tongue parted her lips and entered her mouth, its taste sour. Damp hands slid under her skirt as Asami's perception faded to gray...

1976 - Miami Beach

Palm trees swayed and wispy clouds coated the evening sky. Scents of char-broiled red snapper and steaks saturated the balmy air.

About one hundred attendees were gathered around the Fontainebleau Hotel's pool area for Tripoint's Miami Beach Achievement Event. On the lookout for Sam and his physician wife, Etta sipped on a Pina Colada. Although she'd never met Cindy, Etta had vilified her into a person not worthy of Sam.

It would be difficult for her to keep her jealousy in check.

The CEO's wife approached. "It's wonderful to see you." Sylvia's eyes were bright as she ran a hand through her hair, its natural curl, like Etta's, misbehaving in Miami's humidity. "I'm not surprised you're one of the five women selected for this event."

The modest words Etta normally used, to downplay any sort of compliment, were on the tip of her tongue. But look where they had gotten her with Sylvia's husband. It was time for Etta to accept praise when it had been rightly deserved. "Thank you," she simply said and gave Sylvia a gracious smile. "In the years to come, let's hope the female representation nears the male's."

"That's certainly plausible, unless my husband drives them away."

Etta's muscles tensed as her gaze followed Sylvia's. Tom Pollard was leaning against the Tiki Bar, a drink in one hand, the other pressed to the Chicago receptionist's back. Sylvia couldn't know about her Plaza Hotel incident, could she? But from Sylvia's candid words, Etta realized she probably hadn't been the first woman Tom had targeted—or the last.

A disgruntled looking Sam joined the Tiki Bar group, his entrance giving Etta the opportunity to change the subject. "Sylvia, could you point out Sam Madrid's wife? I'd like to meet her."

"Poor, Sam, Cindy cancelled at the last minute due to a premature twin delivery."

Wow! It was as if Etta had won the Illinois Lottery, especially when Sam's eyes met hers. His countenance changed from a grimace to a slow, sensual smile, and Etta melted.

After dinner, most Tripoint attendees either stayed by the bar or changed into bathing attire. Etta and Sam had done the latter. Scents of orange trees and sea salt filled the cool night air. For hours, she, Sam, and three additional Chicago attendees splashed around in the pool, solving the world's problems.

Near midnight, Etta gazed up at the lanterns, hidden in the palms, their light shimmering on the pool water. Her teeth were chattering, but she didn't want the night to end.

"Well, Etta Martin..." Sam's eyebrows lifted as the last of their group headed back toward the hotel. "We're finally alone."

The underlying meaning in his words made her heart seize.

"I can tell you're chilled. Let's try the hot tub." To help her out, he grabbed her hand.

She didn't want to release it, but she did, to pick up their plastic wine cups.

They dashed across the deck and stepped in, his naked thigh pressed against hers.

Etta thrilled at the intimate touch. Yet it also evoked memories of Tom Pollard's similar body part brushing against hers, a warning sign she'd regrettably ignored. He'd been Tripoint's CEO and married; Sam was her manager, also with a wife. Etta's conscience reared its disapproving head. She knew Sam's physical contact was wrong. But far from Chicago's city lights, Etta didn't care—she craved it.

"I'm Not in Love" by 10cc played through the outdoor speakers. In her Clark Street flat, Etta often fell asleep with the radio on. The previous week, she'd awakened to that same song. The lyrics seemed to be about a married man's conflicted feelings for a woman—definitely not his wife. The song mirrored the impossible situation she and Sam were in.

He'd been listening too. As if in slow motion, his hands broke through the water and they cradled her face, his tormented eyes meeting hers. "I can't deny it—I wish I didn't love you—but I do."

She stared at Sam. Had he actually said those words?

His lips pressed against hers.

Oh God! From deep inside Etta, a moan escaped.

But that sound, that damn primal sound, seemed to startle Sam back to reality.

He pulled away, his face distraught. "I'm sorry, Etta... I shouldn't have done that. I'm your manager." He struggled to his feet. "And I didn't mean what I said."

Her cheeks flamed as if the hot tub's temperature had been cranked up to boiling. She'd been on the precipice, prepared to dive into deep water. Rather than surfacing, feeling exhilarated, she was sinking, filled with humiliation and despair.

Without a word, they both climbed out of the hot tub and wrapped hotel robes around their bodies. They entered the Fontainebleau in silence. Like strangers, they stepped into the elevator, their eyes focused forward. Etta pushed "4." Sam pushed "5." It felt like an endless trip, as if to the top of Sears Tower, until the doors finally opened and she flew out, not even saying "good night." How could she when it had transformed into a bloody mess! She located her room key. As she fumbled to open the door, a warm hand covered hers and she turned.

Sam's face was within inches of hers, his eyes a color she'd never seen before. "I lied. God help me, I do love you!" His arms embraced her.

"Oh Sam, I've loved you ever since we met at Northwestern." She held on tight, crushing him with all the desire she'd kept hidden in her heart.

It was time for her to choose their path. She pulled away and opened the door. Before either Sam or she could change their minds, Etta grabbed his hand and led him inside.

The room was dimly lit by a nightstand lamp and the bed was turned down. A foil-wrapped chocolate rested on the pillowcase—a promise of something decadent.

Their robes dropped and Sam peeled off her wet swimsuit, she his. Naked, but not self-conscious, Etta stood in front of Sam, the only man she'd loved.

He gathered her into his arms.

Like teenagers in heat, their mouths pressed together, their tongues tasting each other, their hands exploring previously forbidden areas. Etta was rather inept, having only slept with one man. She let Sam take the lead as thoughts filled her head: *He's been with the same woman for years. Is he pleasing me like he pleases her? Am I pleasing him like she pleases him?*

Etta had to erase those thoughts.

She loved Sam. He loved her.

That was all that mattered.

They fell onto the bed, her body sandwiched between the cool sheets and Sam.

His fingers stroked her hair, her face, her breasts, the inside of her thighs. "You're so beautiful."

He suddenly pulled back. "I have no protection with me." His husky voice had turned anxious. "I didn't expect this to happen. Tell me, are you safe?"

Her eyes didn't waver.

Of course she was safe.

She was with Sam.

1976 - Miami & Chicago

Stuck in the airplane's smoking section, Etta stewed in her cramped seat, the air quality nauseating her. She sat six rows behind Sam on their return flight from Miami. Her skin tone had transformed from a Midwestern pale to a tropical glowing tan. Tripoint's Miami Beach event had felt like a fabulous honeymoon. But in its aftermath, Etta was suffering from guilt.

She closed her eyes recalling their breakfast buffets, how Sam had walked by each morning and murmured, "I so want you," making her pulse quicken with that same desire. Or during their business meetings' coffee breaks, how he'd come just close enough, so she'd felt the heat from his shoulder, and she'd seen the suggestive smile on his lips. Or each evening, by the Tiki bar, while conversing with him and other colleagues, she'd imagined Sam's mouth on hers, so long and slow her cheeks had burned.

In between those meetings and activities, they'd made love seven more times: on the moonlit beach, the surf spilling over them; in the ocean, miles down from their hotel where nobody had known them; in his room and in hers. They'd been secretive—on elicit trysts—making their encounters all the more thrilling and all the more wrong.

Earlier, in the gate's waiting area, Etta had surveyed Sam from afar. He'd been spinning his wedding band, his face deep in thought. During the past week, neither she nor he had discussed his wife. Prior to Miami, Etta had felt his marriage had been troubled. When Cindy had been a conference no-show—that had seemed to be the last straw.

Etta tried to convince herself she wasn't the only guilty party. Of course, Sam was equally to blame. Then there was Cindy. If Sam's wife had been at the conference, nothing would've happened.

When Etta had stood to board, Sam had approached and whispered, "We need to talk." But they hadn't gotten the chance.

Etta squirmed in her seat and wondered whether he'd been contemplating his marriage. Had he come to the same conclusion as Etta: it hadn't been working for years; he needed to end it; he needed to choose the woman who made him happy—that being her?

In addition to those thoughts, others were fighting to replace them. Etta had awakened to abdominal cramps and noticed blood spots in her panties. That would make sense if her period was on the horizon. But it wasn't due for two weeks.

Back in college, a sorority sister of Etta's had had a one night stand with some guy she'd met inside a neon lit bar on Howard Street's Chicago side. About a week later, she'd suffered from similar symptoms to Etta's. After her sorority sister had missed two periods, Etta had accompanied her to a doctor for moral support.

Her friend had walked out of his office, a stunned look on her face, and she'd started to cry. She was pregnant. The doctor had told her, when she'd first spotted and cramped, the fertilized egg had most likely been attaching itself to her womb.

Before Miami, Etta had been on and off the pill. She'd disliked how bloated she felt. Plus, taking a daily contraception dose had seemed ridiculous when she'd yet to meet a man, other than Sam, who'd enthralled her enough to sleep with him. In Miami, she'd been in an "off" phase of the pill.

She'd never dreamed the week would lead to where it had.

Etta looked out the window as her seatmate lit up his third cigarette. She couldn't be pregnant, could she? That first hotel room encounter had been the only time they'd had unprotected sex. Yet that coupling had occurred exactly seven days earlier, like her sorority sister's timeframe. During the other instances, Etta had asked Sam to use a condom. She'd told him she'd feel safer being doubly protected, and he'd agreed.

On the three and a half hour return flight, Etta tried to nap, but those pregnancy thoughts wouldn't let up...

The plane touched down and taxied to the gate. Etta slowly disembarked. Inside O'Hare's terminal, she could see Sam.

He waved her over, his face tense—not the ardent look she'd grown accustomed to.

"First, Etta, I want you to know how amazing you are."

She clutched her carry on. His words didn't sound good.

He touched her elbow. "Let's walk."

She focused on placing one foot in front of the other, inhaling and exhaling...

"I had breakfast with Tom Pollard this morning."

"Okay?" she managed.

"He told me how pleased he was with my work. The New York branch manager is moving to London next month to open Tripoint's UK office." Sam hesitated. "Tom—Tom believes I'm the right person to take over the New York branch."

Etta stopped dead in her tracks. "So you're taking it? You're moving back to New York?"

"Think about it, Etta. In the Chicago office, George Buckley's forty-one. I'm only twenty-nine. I'd be handling the largest Tripoint branch. How could I say no?"

It felt as if the airport terminal's linoleum floor had transformed into an ice rink, her feet sliding out from under her. She grabbed onto Sam's arm for support. "But what about me?"

"You know I've been trying to move back to New York. Now I've been told I can." He shook his head. "Please, Etta, *please* understand?"

How could she when her world was collapsing.

"I really do love you." He gently touched her cheek, his face stricken. "But when I'm back in New York, I need to give my marriage a second chance."

Oh God! Sam's tender touch felt like a slap. Maybe it was what she deserved. She had to escape. She started to run. Racked by sobs, she pushed past other travelers, trying to find a safe harbor that wasn't Sam.

-15-

Tuesday - Tokyo

Neither Asami's mind nor her muscles would relax as hot water pelted her torso and face. Although the grime from Aokigahara Forest was running down Jiro's shower drain, her pain and anger remained, permanently tattooed to her body.

Her daughter was dead.

Could Tripoint's CEO be connected in some way? The night Hana had disappeared, he'd been in Tokyo. He'd also sexually harassed Hana in New York. Had some detrimental work-related actions followed—targeted specifically at her daughter?

Asami thought back to the eighties when her university friend had committed suicide, possibly due to her career outlook and her manager's sexist behavior.

Asami's adamant belief—that Hana had been murdered—waivered. Could her daughter have been driven to commit suicide like Asami's university friend?

Maybe Hana *had* purchased that suicide manual after returning from Tripoint's New York training.

Asami stumbled out of the shower and reached for a towel, barely draping her body with it. What difference did it make? Hana was dead. Nothing could bring her back. In the misted mirror, she looked at her desolate reflection. What did she have to live for?

Deep retching cries burst from her trembling body. She opened Jiro's bathroom cabinet and foraged inside for pills—any pills—something to take away her pain.

Jiro charged in, his panic-filled eyes focused on the medication containers scattered in the sink. "Asami-chan! Tell me! Did you take anything?"

She hung her head, misery sprouting from every conceivable pore. "No, but I wish I had."

He pulled her into his arms. "My dear, believe me, we'll get through this together."

* * *

It was approaching 6:30 p.m. when Asami shuffled into the Setagaya Police Station's reception area, Jiro's arm supporting her. But that wasn't the support Asami most needed, what she'd always counted on, what had gotten her through so many difficult times—the support from her daughter, her Hana, her dear child, her ship's mast standing tall on Asami's life journey, even when the gales had hit hard. To listen to her daughter's preliminary autopsy results would be agonizing, excruciating, nearly more than Asami could endure, but she had to know whether her child had suffered.

Jiro's female neighbor had loaned Asami fresh undergarments and socks, a baggy pair of jeans, and a blue fleece top. On her feet were Hana's workout shoes, smudged with grime from the forest. Asami's attire was as tasteless as one could get and she didn't care. Jiro had even brushed her teeth as if she'd been a child and the peppermint paste still coated her mouth.

Hana's friend Lucas was in the reception area dressed in a black and white Baja hoodie, his hands stuffed into the kangaroo pocket, his shaggy head drooped. After all the support he'd given Asami, Jiro had asked him to come. The three were ushered into a small room where Sergeant Mori was located. Jiro helped her settle onto a chair and he placed a water bottle in front of her. "Asami-chan, you must drink."

She shook her head. What did it matter?

The detective's eyes were overly bright. "First, Fujioka-san, I want to confirm your daughter's blood type is B, correct?"

Asami mumbled, "Yes," even finding it hard to say that small word.

"Okay... Are you ready for this?" He hesitated to make sure he had her attention. "The body we recovered from the forest is blood type A."

She cocked her head, confused. "What are you saying?"

"The deceased woman is not your daughter."

Still trapped inside her forsaken world, Asami could not comprehend.

Lucas and Jiro seemed to, and the latter shouted, "My dear! That's incredible!"

The jubilation in Jiro's voice jolted Asami's brain. "Are—are you saying my daughter's alive?"

Mori shook his head. "No. I can't tell you that. But the forest body we recovered is definitely not hers."

Jiro leaned in. "So who is the woman?"

"We've taken her prints. If she has a record we should know shortly. We—"

"Listen Fujioka-san!" Lucas excitedly broke in. "Hana must be alive! There would be no other reason for someone to have gone to such pains, to make us believe that woman was her."

Asami pressed her palm to her chest. She felt light-headed and giddy, her grief taking flight. She unscrewed the water bottle's top and took a healthy swallow. Hana had to be alive! How stupid she'd been. What if Jiro hadn't interrupted her frenzied quest in his bathroom?

It was too much to consider.

Asami threaded her fingers through her hair, her feet tapping the floor. "So tell me. Is the woman in that Aokigahara photo Hana or not?" She turned to Lucas. "Can you find it again?"

He did and held up his cell.

Mori's eyes inspected the image. "I believe that woman is Hana. You said the photo was taken on Saturday morning. The autopsied woman died prior to that time. Her body, most likely, is inside that large roller bag, the one the man beside Hana is pulling."

"So you believe my daughter removed her clothes in the forest to dress that victim?"

"It looks that way. But you have to consider this: Hana could be voluntarily involved in whatever is going on."

Asami flushed under his measured squint. "I don't believe that!"

Lucas said, "Neither do I! You thought I might've been involved, but you were wrong. You're wrong about Hana as well."

"Maybe..." Mori opened a notebook, his eyes scanning a document. "But Fujioka-san..." He looked up, his gaze meeting hers. "You told me your daughter's hair and clothes were wet. The deceased woman's cause of death was drowning. She aspirated water into her lungs. There's a good chance Hana was present when that occurred."

Asami tried to take that all in. "Even so, Hana can't be a party to that woman's death."

"That's what we must find out. The victim's lungs were filled with chlorinated fresh water. You and I discussed possible locations where your daughter might've been. Now I think the Roppongi district's swimming pools are our best bet."

Jiro interjected, "But I'm still confused. This whole forest situation doesn't make sense. Those involved would've known there'd be an autopsy, that you would discover that woman was not Hana. That—"

"Slow down..." Lucas held up his hand. "Think about this. If I hadn't uncovered that Facebook photo, that woman's body might not have been discovered for weeks."

There was a knock on the door and a man entered. He handed the detective a sheet of paper and left.

Mori started to read, nodding as if everything was making more sense. "The deceased woman is Chika Himura." He looked up. "Three years ago, she was arrested for prostitution. At that time, she was working for the Wada-kai."

Asami's feet stilled. "Kato Endo works for that yakuza gang."

Mori nodded. "And he was with your daughter at the British Pub." He hesitated. "We also know he's adept at corporate extortion schemes."

Asami sat back. "Chloe Martin's mama believes something happened in Tokyo, something that could compromise Tripoint's IPO, something bad enough to have silenced her daughter before she talked. Maybe that something was Chika's drowning."

By the set of Mori's jaw, Asami could tell the detective was considering her premise. "Listen..." he said. "As I mentioned before, there's a good chance your daughter was present when Chika drowned. For the moment, let's make three assumptions: first, that Hana isn't responsible for Chika's drowning death, but she can identify the person who is; second, Hana's American colleague, Chloe Martin, could as well; and third, the person responsible for Chika's death is a Tripoint executive highly vested in the IPO's success."

Jiro had been closely following the conversation. "So Hana and Chloe would've been major threats."

Mori nodded as he made some notes. "But let's also assume that yakuza gangster, Kato Endo, was present when Chika drowned. For a hefty fee, he could've offered to take care of both threats. But in Hana's case, maybe he concocted a more lucrative two-phased approach. Her staged suicide, using Chika's body, obviously was the first. In the forest, the man with the roller bag, most likely, took photos to prove Hana was dead, and compensation to the Wada-kai would've followed. Only then would Kato have revealed his hoax, and a second extortion payment would've been negotiated to—to finish the job." His apologetic gaze met Asami's.

She shivered. "If your assumptions are right, we must locate Hana before that second payment is made."

Jiro's warm hand grasped hers. "I agree." He turned toward the detective. "Your entire supposition revolves around Kato Endo. Have you talked to him yet?"

"No. We haven't been able to locate him, but based on the current turn of events, finding him and Hana will be my top priority."

Jiro nodded and squeezed Asami's hand. "What about the two other men from that night? Have you contacted them?"

"I talked to their assistants. Haruki Madrid's said he was to have arrived in New York on Saturday for business and he was staying at the Plaza Hotel. Once she reaches him, she'll have him give me a call. Sam Madrid is currently in the air, flying back to New York from Berlin. After he lands, his assistant will also have him contact me."

Asami checked her watch. "That should be in the next few hours. Etta Martin also plans to talk to him then. But there's a third executive who was in Tokyo, one who could be involved as well." Asami attempted to keep her anger in check as she told Mori about Tripoint's CEO—how he'd sexually harassed Hana in New York.

Lucas breathed out, "That bastard! That's probably what was bothering Hana." Enraged, his eyes focused on the detective. "What about Hana's credit cards and passport? You said you were going to check into their usage."

"There's been no activity on her credit cards, and Japan Customs has promised to contact me by day's end. If Hana used her passport, either under duress or voluntarily, and her ticket was purchased with another traveler's, the custom records will include her flying companion's name."

Cautious hope leapt through Asami. But a bucket of reality quickly doused that optimistic flame.

Time was ticking away.

Only forty-eight hours remained until the general public could purchase Tripoint's stock. If that IPO event was the impetus behind Hana's disappearance, little time remained to locate her child.

Tuesday - New York

In the pre-dawn light, Etta sat on the Bryant Hotel room's lower bunk and pressed END on her cell. She'd wanted one smidgen of good news. She'd received a boatload. Hana could still be alive!

Etta couldn't help but envy her friend. Asami's daughter had risen from her grave while Etta's lay in the New York City morgue. She'd wanted to view Chloe again, but Detective Harper had convinced her to wait until a funeral director made her daughter look more presentable—more like the Chloe she remembered—rather than the one who'd been poked and prodded by a pathologist during her autopsy.

It was difficult to think about the days to come. How she'd have to make arrangements to have Chloe's body flown back to Carter to be buried beside her grandmother—the one who'd been her daughter's cheerleader—the one who'd encouraged her to claim the things that would make her happy.

A sob caught in Etta's throat.

Chloe had done just that. She'd charged through emotional adversity and she'd emerged as a confident young woman, one who'd excelled in her personal life and short career. Most importantly, she'd found a good man who'd loved her, and Chloe had loved him back.

On the call, Asami had told Etta about the Japanese detective's assumptions. Etta sagged back against the pillows, drawing no satisfaction from knowing she'd basically been right. She'd believed something had happened in Tokyo, something that could've compromised Tripoint's IPO, something bad enough to have silenced her daughter before she talked. Well that something appeared to be that Japanese woman's drowning and, most likely, by a Tripoint executive's hand.

Could that executive be Tripoint's CEO? When Asami had told her that Tom Pollard had recently propositioned Hana during her New York training, Etta had been needled with guilt. Could her non-action, back in the seventies, have jeopardized Asami's daughter's life? And what about her child's? In Tokyo, could Tom have acted in a similarly inappropriate sexual manner? Could that have possibly been the driving force behind that woman's drowning?

Those thoughts would only eat Etta up if she let them.

When she'd told Asami about the Hiro house business cards, Deon had dropped in the park, Asami's excited voice had broken in, "Oh, Etta-san! Haruki's yakuza brother had a best friend at the orphanage. I'm certain his name was Hiro—Hiro Endo. And in the eighties, as adults, both men were in the Wada-kai."

A chill still hung in Etta's room from that revelation. She reached for her bathrobe and slipped it on. She'd wondered whether the yakuza could be involved in Chloe's and Hana's deaths. Could Deon's grandfather be Kato Endo's yakuza friend? It seemed farfetched. But just assuming that was so, could the two men have partnered up to orchestrate their daughters' staged suicides? Asami had mentioned a potential yakuza extortion scheme tied to that Japanese woman's drowning and Tripoint's IPO.

But why was Hana possibly alive and her Chloe dead?

Etta stepped out into the hallway and headed toward the bathroom. Hopefully Sam would provide her some answers.

If only he and Chloe had flown back from Tokyo together. Henri had said her daughter had wanted Sam's advice on some matter. It probably had concerned that woman's drowning. But since Chloe had never gotten the opportunity to talk to Sam, it appeared as if she'd scheduled that HR meeting instead.

Etta pushed open the bathroom door. If only she could locate Chloe's laptop. On her return flight from Tokyo, Etta could picture her daughter sitting in business class, her laptop open, her fingers speeding across the keys, authoring notes for that HR meeting—important notes—ones that could provide Etta some answers.

A thought suddenly sparked.

Yes, Chloe's laptop was missing. But there could be another way to retrieve her daughter's work.

* * *

Tripoint's Headquarters were located in the Manhattan Financial District. Etta entered its lobby at 6:17 a.m. Her first Tripoint ally, puppy-dog Neil, was waiting for her.

Over Etta's career, she'd nurtured friendships with numerous colleagues. Some had advanced to high places, Neil being one. As Tripoint's Director of Technical Support, he managed a staff of about fifty people who manned phones and provided clients second level technical support, twenty-four-seven.

Like Etta, it appeared as if Neil had hastily dressed. Both were attired in jeans. Even though he'd gained weight and lost most of his hair, his sweet persona hadn't changed.

He offered his heartfelt condolences and gave Etta a big squeeze.

She kissed his cheek. "Thanks, I sure needed that." Etta pulled away, blinking fast to hold back tears. "Please tell me, were you able to recreate Chloe's laptop on a loaner?"

All Tripoint employees shared the same password protected private network. Each evening, at 11 p.m., if an employee's laptop was logged onto the network a backup image would automatically be created on Tripoint's central servers.

"Yes, Etta, Saturday's backup was loaded, but—"

"That's wonderful!"

"Not so fast." He steered her into the elevator, pushed the fifth floor button, and the doors closed. "Your daughter's information is still password protected."

"There *must* be a way around that!"

"There is. I've started the process."

The elevator doors opened and Etta stepped out. "I know it's against security regulations, but I store my password on a notepad inside my Chicago desk. Chloe might've done the same. I have her desk key so I'll check."

Etta followed Neil to a cubicle where a horn-rimmed-glassed technician was seated.

He looked up. "The laptop is all set to go." He handed it to Etta.

She patted his shoulder. "I'm so grateful."

Etta took the elevator down to the sales and marketing floor, the reconstructed laptop under her arm. Due to the early hour, the reception area was unstaffed. Chloe's badge still provided access to the dimly lit bullpen area. At least one Tripoint go-getter should be at their desk to direct Etta to Chloe's.

A brightly lit office caught Etta's attention. She approached it and stopped short.

TJ Pollard was inside.

Etta had last seen him at February's achievement event where his father had announced his plans to retire. By year-end, TJ would be assuming Tripoint's CEO position. TJ had paraded around in Miami, enjoying the limelight. Although he had excellent business acumen, beneath his Armani suits and tight facelifts, Etta believed he had a sleazy underside.

TJ looked up, startled to see her. "I'm so sorry." He stood as she entered. "My mother told me about your daughter's death. Is there anything I can do?"

Etta stared at him. "Possibly?" She'd take him up on his offer and put him on the spot. "Chloe was in Tokyo last week and I know you were too. On Thursday night, I understand you didn't accompany her, Sam Madrid, or Hana Fujioka to the British Pub. Am I right?"

It appeared as if her question had caught him off guard.

"That—that's right. I had a dinner engagement."

As Mom would've said, TJ seemed as jumpy as a cockroach in a frying pan. "Is there any chance you joined them after they left the Pub?"

His eyes wouldn't meet hers. "I have to admit, I hardly recall that night."

"Really? Why's that?"

"Well, following dinner, the client took me to a karaoke bar. I—I'm afraid, I drank far too much."

Etta refused to give up. "So TJ, did you, or did you not see my daughter, Sam, or Hana?"

His ears had turned Etta's shade of red. "As far as I can remember, I didn't see any of them."

What kind of answer was that? She had to let it go and hope to God Sam would fill in the blanks. Etta forced a sympathetic smile. "Hey, I know the feeling."

A look of relief ousted TJ's agitated demeanor.

Etta gazed back at the bullpen. "Can you point me toward Chloe's desk? I'd like to retrieve her personal belongings."

"I'm sorry. I was already on my Asia Pacific assignment when your daughter started here. But the admin manager will know." As if to get back in her good graces, he quickly selected a number from his cell, talked briefly, and hung up. "Follow me."

Etta did so, passing three rows of cubicles to reach the window desks.

TJ counted down and pointed to the fourth one. "That should be Chloe's."

Etta pulled out her daughter's keys, walked to that specific desk and successfully unlocked it. She turned back to TJ. "Thanks for your help. I'll take it from here."

"Are you certain?" He hovered, noting the laptop under Etta's arm.

"Yes." Her voice was firm. She waited until he entered his office, then she placed the laptop on Chloe's desk and sat down. The four-foot high dividers hid her from TJ's view.

She hunted through the top drawer's notepads and post-it notes. Nothing appeared to contain a password. She opened the side drawer. Under a miniature *Kit-Kat* bag was a lined yellow sheet. Three combinations of letters, numbers and special characters had been crossed out. One remained.

That had to be it.

Etta booted up the laptop. She typed the combination into the password prompt, held her breath, and pressed enter.

She was in!

It seemed to take forever until the desktop icons responded to the mouse. Etta double-clicked on the documents folder. Within it were five additional folders. She opened each and her eyes quickly scanned their contents.

Shit! The most recent documents had been saved on Wednesday night or, converted to Tokyo time, Thursday morning. They all looked like training session documents.

Dejected, Etta sank back against Chloe's chair.

Yet it didn't make sense.

Her daughter would've created or refined some sort of work on her thirteen hour return flight.

Could an incriminating document have been deleted? Etta clicked on the trash icon. Normally hundreds of discarded files should've appeared, but in Chloe's case, there were none.

Years earlier, Etta had been a Technical Rep. She'd never lost her problem determination skills. Yes, Chloe's laptop contained her most recent backup, but that was the wrong one. Tripoint's central servers retained daily backups for three months.

Etta picked up her cell and called Neil again.

Tuesday - Tokyo

Hounded by strip club and other seedy promoters, Asami hurried along the Roppongi district sidewalk with Jiro, a cigarette pinched between his fingertips. While Hana's friend Lucas was working his social media contacts, she and Jiro were headed toward the district's police station.

On the train ride, Asami had been at her drama queen's best, unable to keep her emotional teeter totter in check. "Hana must be alive," she'd say then shake her head. "But what if she's dead?" Back and forth she'd gone, not knowing which to believe. Jiro normally would've been calming her, but he'd been silent, pensive, further unnerving her.

They passed a noisy karaoke club as Jiro finally said, "I'm sorry. I know I've been quiet, but I've been considering whether I should tell you something."

Asami abruptly stopped. "What is it? You can't leave me hanging like this."

He sighed. "I don't want to get your hopes up. But if the Wada-kai is still holding Hana, I believe she's safe—at least for the moment."

Under the flashing marquees, Asami gazed up at Jiro, his face a changing mask of colors and patterns. "Why do you say that?"

"Remember, in the nineties, when I directed the *Yakuza Diaries*?"

"Yes?" Jiro's three-film trilogy had followed the shifting powers within Tokyo's yakuza gangs. They'd won critical acclaim, even being compared to Francis Ford Coppola's *Godfather* series.

"To better prepare for the films," he continued, "I contacted Haruki's yakuza brother."

"Really? Why didn't you tell me?"

"I couldn't. After I fed Kato's ego, as well as his pockets, he only agreed to talk to me if I didn't divulge he was my source. But Hana's current situation changes that agreement. I'll tell you what he told me, but we must keep walking."

Jiro first relayed how Kato had provided him inside information about the infighting within the Tokyo clans. "But, Asami-chan, think about this. Over the years, yakuza violence, directed at someone like you or me, has been rare, hasn't it?"

She nodded, her forehead creased. "So what are you getting at?"

"Kato told me the reason. It's based on one of the yakuza's ancient creeds: to never harm *katagi no shu*."

"The citizens under the sun?"

Jiro nodded. "Kato said this creed is as old as the yakuza itself, of never hurting the common people. The Wada-kai prides itself on honoring the old traditions. Of course, that doesn't rule out extortion or blackmail, which could still ruin a person's life. But that creed is why I believe Hana's alive."

His calm assurance flowed into Asami. They walked the final two blocks and she marched to a new internal rhythm: *Hana's alive, my child* is *alive.*

Yet, Etta's daughter was dead.

Was it because she'd returned to the U.S.? Was it because someone other than Kato had arranged her death to make it look like a suicide? Could that be Kato's childhood cohort and fellow yakuza member, Hiro Endo? Etta had mentioned his name on the phone. It seemed unlikely he could be the same man, but if he was, shouldn't Hiro have followed the same Wada-kai creed?

Maybe Jiro's belief about her daughter was wrong.

No! Asami snuffed out that thought as they reached the police station.

Jiro did the same to his cigarette in the outside container.

At the reception desk, he asked for Sergeant Hondo, the detective Sergeant Mori had engaged to aid in Hana's disappearance case. A man dressed impeccably in a designer suit entered. He favored one of the detectives in the *Tokyo Dogs* television drama. Hana had told Asami to watch that show since the two detectives were so "hot"! Along with Hondo's lanky build, perfect complexion, and spikey hair, a twist of concern touched his full lips. A lump lodged in Asami's throat. She so missed her daughter, the look of complicity the two would've shared.

Bows and introductions were made. Asami noticed Jiro's eyes also admiring the handsome detective.

Hondo seemed equally interested, but his professional manner returned when he addressed Asami. "I understand you're trying to locate your daughter. Let's talk inside."

Once they were seated at a small conference table, Sergeant Hondo said, "Detective Mori told me your daughter was at the British Pub last Thursday night with a Wada-kai member."

"Yes." Asami's feet tapped. "Back in the eighties, when I first met Kato Endo inside the Kingo Club, he seemed to be a very cold and determined man."

"He still is, and he's still associated with that hostess club. His black Mercedes is often parked outside."

Jiro's eyebrows lifted. "Could its license plate numbers be all fours?"

Hondo nodded.

Startled, Jiro explained how he and Asami had seen that same vehicle parked outside his apartment.

Asami added, "I'm also quite certain a yakuza, with a purple birthmark on his right cheek, has been following me."

The detective frowned. "I've seen that gangster around. He also works for the Wada-kai. In addition to locating Kato, I'll round him up for questioning."

Asami attempted to remain calm as Jiro told Hondo about his discussion with Kato, back in the nineties, and the yakuza creed. "Does the Wada-kai still operate in that fashion?"

"In concept. But, I'm afraid, there are always exceptions."

Asami's optimism faded.

Hondo removed a mugshot from a notebook. "Detective Mori said you located this woman in Aokigahara Forest." He placed Chika Himura's photo in front of her.

Asami grimly nodded and picked it up. "Did you know her?"

"Yes. During my first year on the job, Chika was a hostess at the Kingo Club. She was also engaged in pillow business with her clientele. As I'm sure you know, Japan law defines prostitution as intercourse with an unspecified person in exchange for payment. She often got around that by claiming her clients knew her."

Jiro's gaze met the detective's. "But she slipped up?"

Hondo nodded. "Since serving time, she's been working for the Erotica Massage Parlor, one of the Wada-kai health shops located here in the district. In addition to massages, their services include non-penetrating legal sexual acts. Last Thursday night, Chika was providing off-premise delivery services to two different clients."

Asami placed the photo back on the table. "Do you have their names?"

"Only the first client, but I've already ruled him out. I talked to the woman responsible for Chika's bookings. She told me Chika had met that first 'date' at the Casablanca Love Hotel. Afterward, Chika had reported in at about nine p.m. She'd said another client engagement had been directly scheduled for her by a high-ranking Wada-kai member, but no other details were provided." Hondo opened a map. "Since we know she drowned, it could've been at one of the Roppongi hotels with an indoor pool. I've marked them on the map. Another detective and I will be canvassing those hotels tonight."

Jiro shook his head. "We must accompany you. For five days, Hana's been missing. Any insight we can immediately provide might save her life."

Hondo hesitated.

"Detective?" Suggestive undertones saturated Jiro's voice. "I know my request isn't your norm, but if you'd honor it, I'd be indebted to you." Jiro slid his hand across the table, his perfectly tapered nails just inches from Hondo's, and the two men's eyes reconnected.

Asami waited with baited breath.

Yet she knew Hondo's response would be yes.

Tuesday - New York

Etta's cab pulled up in front of Chloe's apartment building. Less than forty-eight hours had passed since her daughter's body had been discovered, a horror film that had no end. It should've been Etta's final day in New York City. Two *Jersey Boys* tickets were waiting inside the August Wilson Theater for that night's performance. Neither would be claimed.

Etta had planned to wait at Tripoint for the laptop to be reloaded with Chloe's Friday night backup, assuming it had occurred. But Detective Harper had called her cell. She'd been able to secure Saturday's video footage from Chloe's apartment building's lobby. "Ms. Martin, we also completed the second sweep of the apartment. Other than that closet panel, we didn't find any suspicious evidence. But I talked to the building manager. She hadn't authorized any sort of work within your daughter's apartment, so I'm not ruling out homicide. However, I'm afraid our plan to keep Chloe's ongoing investigation a secret may have been compromised. Your daughter's building is managed by Pollard Property Group."

Although it had pleased Etta that the detective had seemed more open-minded about Chloe's cause of death, Etta had initially been taken aback by the PPG comment. On second thought, it had made sense. When she'd helped Chloe locate her apartment, Tripoint's HR department had provided a recommended list. The PPG managed buildings would've been placed at the top.

Etta stepped out of the cab onto the tree lined street. Wind gusts rattled the mostly bare and boney branches and kicked up fallen leaves. On the ride over, Etta's mind had been whirling, much like the taxi's pine scented air freshener hanging from its rearview mirror. Etta had wondered how someone would've known about the panel in Chloe's building's elevator and its proximity to her daughter's closet.

PPG would maintain blueprints for all the buildings they managed. Any number of people could've gotten their hands on them. Sam's brother, Haruki, also worked for that property group. According to Asami, he'd flown into New York for business on the day Chloe had died. Etta had called the Plaza Hotel where he was to have stayed. The front desk clerk had told her he'd never checked in.

That only added to Etta's confusion.

Asami's daughter was missing. Could Haruki be too?

Etta approached the building doorman bundled up in a long gray coat and plaid muffler.

"Good morning, Ms. Martin." He tipped his cap. "Detective Harper and Mr. Broussard are waiting for you in the business office." Baxter opened the front door for her. "Turn right at the elevator bank and it will be the first door on your left."

She nodded her thanks and followed his instructions. Stepping out from the office was a brunette woman, around forty, a beauty mark slightly above her lip giving her a Cindy Crawford sort of look. She wore a professional black suit and introduced herself as Paula Draper, the building manager. "Ms. Martin, I'm sorry for your loss. I told the detective inside, I'll be in the adjacent office. If there's anything else I can do, please let me know."

"Thank you." Etta stared at the woman's sincere face. She worked for PPG. Could she also be involved? For the moment, Etta couldn't worry about that.

She entered the small windowless office. Henri and Harper were seated by a desk, a PC monitor on top. Frozen on the display, in grainy black and white shades, was an image of the lobby she'd just walked through.

Henri handed Etta a cup of coffee. "I made a pot upstairs."

At the kind gesture, she squeezed his arm and pulled up a third chair. "First, I have some amazing news." Etta explained how the forest body, thought to be Hana's, was that of a Wada-kai health shop worker. "The Japanese authorities believe Hana's staged suicide could be part of a yakuza extortion scheme, possibly tied to Tripoint's IPO."

Harper's tongue had been nervously flicking across her front teeth while Henri's eyes had widened. "Mon Dieu! So Hana could still be alive?"

Etta nodded as Harper remained silent. But when Etta also revealed her theory concerning Chloe's laptop, the detective finally spoke up. "Ms. Martin, I told you before! You must keep me in the loop. That goes for last night's fiasco as well. Mr. Broussard told me about Deon Endo. That he believes he's the person who called him from the Rusty Nail. If you'd called me prior to entering Washington Square Park, I would've requested officer assistance. Deon might not have escaped."

"You're right," Etta admitted. "But what's done is done. It's fruitless to argue the point." She handed Harper a slip of paper, hoping to mollify her. "Tripoint's tech support director accessed the Tripoint for Kids database for me. That's Deon's address and home phone number."

Harper stiffened at Etta's words. "You didn't go there, did you?"

"No. I did call though, but when the answering machine picked up, I didn't leave a message."

The detective gave her a curt nod. "I'll stop there."

Etta could tell she was rubbing the detective the wrong way. She couldn't help it. She was used to taking charge. How could she not be proactive when the challenge at hand concerned her daughter?

Their exchange had seemed to make Henri uncomfortable. As if trying to reduce the friction, he added, "I gave Detective Harper one of Deon's business cards."

Harper took a calming breath. "Ms. Martin, I'm sorry if I've been sharp with you. It wasn't very professional. I realize Chloe's tragedy is difficult for both of you."

Etta stared into the detective's large eyes. Harper was trying to make amends. It would only help Chloe's situation if Etta did the same. She touched the detective's arm. "I appreciate your words."

She nodded. "And rest assured, I'll talk to our vice department. Hiro House may already be in their line of sight. Now, let's look at this video. I've already run through it a couple of times. I'm afraid it might not be very helpful. You'll see from the Otis man's actions he probably knew he was being recorded."

She clicked the "Play" icon. The footage resumed, its bottom left corner timestamped at 1:02 p.m. on the day Chloe had died. An average weight guy, dressed in a dark jumpsuit and an Otis hardhat, walked into the lobby. His head was lowered, his face totally hidden from view. In his right hand was a toolbox. A thin carton, about three feet square, was under his left arm. At the doorman station, he set down the toolbox and used his gloved right hand to sign in.

Harper stopped the video. "The two doormen said the guy pictured here is about six feet tall. A dark mustache and beard covered his lower face. Of course, both could've been fake. He also wore dark sunglasses. Because of all that, neither doorman could even tell his race. I know it's not much to go on."

"Shit!" Etta massaged her temples. "You're right. But I bet the carton contains the drywall panel installed in Chloe's closet."

Henri squinted at the man. "There's no way to tell whether he's Deon, his uncle, or someone else entirely."

"Well, at the very end of the video there's something that might help." Harper first fast-forwarded to 3:26 p.m. where the same guy, still with his head lowered, stepped off the elevator carrying the flattened down carton and toolbox.

At 7:07 p.m., he returned with only the toolbox. As before, his face never came into view. Finally, he climbed off the elevator at 11:16 p.m., his head dipped low.

Etta watched as the Otis guy placed the toolbox on the floor. There was no laptop.

It had to have been stolen from Chloe's Tripoint desk.

In the man's back pocket, Etta could see gloves sticking out. It appeared as if he'd forgotten to put them back on before he used his own pen to sign the service log.

Etta's eyes zoomed in on his hands, either dark-skinned or very tan, and she gasped.

The man's left thumb was performing a spinning motion on that hand's bare ring finger as Sam always had.

-16-

1976 - Chicago

Etta guzzled down another glass of wine like it was oxygen. Within her dark front room, her lava lamp's incandescent glow provided the only light. Her bleary eyes followed its irregular blobs, their rise and fall, as if the lamp was also hemorrhaging. At the airport, Sam's words had wounded her beyond repair. For two days she'd been holed up in her flat, not eating, not sleeping, not bathing. She'd only left once to buy three bottles of red wine. Etta lifted her arm and sniffed. *My God!* She hadn't smelled that ripe since she and Moni had backpacked out west. That summer, following their university graduation, the natural scent had suited her.

How pitiful she'd become.

Before Miami, Etta's apartment had filled her with delight: the paisley shaded lamps she'd scavenged from a thrift store; her bed's patchwork quilt hand-stitched by Grandmother Gracie; the decoupage family photo collage Mom had lovingly made. Etta's flat had been her first independent living adventure. In the dim light, she looked at the shabby space and her makeshift attempts to make it a home. She'd failed, just as she'd failed in both her personal and work life—all because she'd slept with Sam.

For nearly two years, Etta had been proud of her progress, proud of how she'd managed the challenges thrown her way (especially those from Dad and Tripoint's CEO), and proud that her co-workers believed she'd been doing an excellent job.

But my God! She had nothing to be proud of. In a purple stained bathrobe, she huddled on the couch, blaming Sam for making her love him, blaming him for enticing her to consummate that love, yet ashamed to know she had.

But it had been love—she was certain of that—not simply sex. What had previously felt magical, like a week in Shangri-La, albeit a guilt ridden week, now felt dirty and dank, like a tavern's back alley.

She reached for the last bottle of wine and winced as her unsteady hand brushed against her breasts. Fermenting grapes, flavored with fear, gurgled up from her belly. Her sorority sister had complained about her breasts, how tender they'd become before she'd known she was pregnant. Etta refused to believe she could be. Instead, her breast tenderness had to be another reason to condemn Sam. During those seven days in Miami, he'd given them a workout.

Etta burst into tears, surprised she had any left.

When she hadn't shown up for work on Monday, Sam had called and left a message on her answering machine. He'd tried four more times, his voice increasingly measured with worry and guilt. That had provided her some solace. She wanted to believe Sam hadn't intentionally used her before tossing her away.

The phone rang again and she let the answering machine pick up. "Please, Etta!" Sam's distraught voice sprang from the speaker. "I know you're there. Please, pick up! We need to talk."

Shit! She knew that was true. She tipped the bottle into her glass. Not a single drop came out. *What the hell!* Her pity party had come to an end.

* * *

The next morning, Etta painstakingly cleaned herself up. Head held high, she marched into Sam's office dressed in her Little Red Riding Hood suit.

New crease lines encompassed Sam's gray eyes. It served him right. Her silent treatment had taken a toll on him.

At seeing her, a look of guarded relief crossed his face.

Etta's voice was unbelievably steady as she said, "I know you're moving to New York." She'd practiced those same words in front of her bathroom mirror, nearly a dozen times, until she could control her voice's quaver. "Just tell me, are you still moving in with your wife?"

"Yes, but—"

Etta held up her hand. It was killing her, but it was the pact she'd made with herself. "Then Sam, there's nothing more to discuss." She opened the door and strode out. She refused to grovel as she'd done at the airport. But how could she forget Sam, knowing what every inch of him looked like—knowing he knew the same about her. Knowing she loved him. And, she believed, he had to love her too.

Etta kept up an amazing front over the next two weeks. It was the only way she could control her chronic depression *and* pregnancy fear. The latter was boiling up inside her, just below the surface, like the Yellowstone hot springs she'd seen on her graduation trip—ready to launch relief or despair.

The critical week arrived when Etta's period should've started. Every chance she'd get she'd enter the bathroom, praying her purse's tampon would be put to good use. Perched on the toilet seat, noting only negative results, she'd wring her hands, recalling her sorority sister's similar emotions.

That nerve-racking routine went on for an additional week.

Etta's sorority sister had talked to a pre-med student to see whether there were any options, other than visiting a doctor, to determine whether she was pregnant. He'd told her about a new method to rapidly detect a pregnancy, but the first in-home test wouldn't be available until about 1977.

That was one year away.

Etta called a drugstore. The pre-med student had been correct.

She had no alternative.

She had to see a doctor.

1976 - Chicago

A Northwestern University medical clinic was within walking distance to Tripoint's Chicago branch. Not making eye contact, Etta handed the receptionist two things: her completed medical history and a jar containing a urine sample.

"Please have a seat Mrs.," the woman looked at Etta's medical history and gave a slight frown, "Miss Martin." She motioned toward the waiting room bathed in soft lights. "You'll be called into a consultation room as soon as our in-house lab has your pregnancy results."

Etta blinked hard. It was both alarming and embarrassing to hear the "P" word spoken out loud. She slinked toward a padded chair and sat down. Across from her, a woman moaned and rubbed her massive belly. Etta stared in fascinated dread. She'd never seen a female who might be in labor. The man seated next to the woman looked frantic as he cooed, "Honey, just breathe."

To Etta's left was another soon-to-be-mother, her face either a shade of green or red. "Jeez!" she said. "I hate the morning sickness. Then there's the gas, the heartburn, the hemorrhoids. This whole pregnancy thing isn't my cup of tea or, in my case, coffee," she groaned. "I sure miss my coffee!"

Agitated, Etta continued to take in the expectant mothers' tableau, wondering whether her life was about to change.

Her name was finally called and she followed the nurse into an examination room. Above the sterilized instruments, a poster was displayed, a woman's abdomen cut away to expose internal organs and a baby nestled inside. The nurse recorded Etta's height and weight, then velcroed a blood pressure cuff around her upper arm.

Etta was certain her numbers were going through the building's roof and heading for the aircrafts making their O'Hare and Midway approaches.

There was a knock on the door and a male physician entered. "Miss Martin, I'm Dr. Bowen and I've got your results."

She gulped. "Tell me. Am I pregnant?"

* * *

Outside the clinic, Etta leaned against its portico, her eyes closed. The "P" word and all its ramifications were swimming behind her lids, plunging their heads into the pool of mistakes she'd made. A new life was growing inside her. She was carrying Sam's child.

Amid Michigan Avenue's heavy pedestrian traffic she traipsed. What should she do?

Her pregnant sorority sister had struggled with that same question. When they'd been sophomores, only four states had allowed unrestricted abortions within a pregnancy's first twenty-four weeks. Illinois had not been among them. After much soul-searching, her sorority sister had made her decision and a local doctor had performed the illegal backroom procedure.

Laws had changed. In 1973, the U.S. Supreme Court had ruled in Roe v. Wade: no state could restrict a woman's right to an abortion during her first three months of pregnancy.

Could Etta abort?

As a Methodist minister's daughter, she knew the church's stance. It believed in the sanctity of an unborn life. But it also understood tragic life-events, like rape, might justify abortion. Etta shook her head. Her situation certainly didn't match that definition.

A few yards ahead, a woman was pushing a stroller and holding a toddler's hand. The curly-headed child was dragging a cloth doll behind her and it slipped from her grip.

Etta called out, "Wait!" and she gathered it up.

The little girl turned, her trusting eyes zoning in on Etta.

"Did you lose your baby?" Etta crouched down low and smiled. Scents of Brown sugar and warm milk filled her nose as the child's pudgy hand touched hers.

The mother tousled her daughter's hair. "Chloe, please tell the nice lady 'thank you.'"

Her shy voice mimicked her mother's.

Etta knew at that moment: *I can't lose my baby.*

It was part of her. Part of Sam.

Etta reached the Michigan Avenue Bridge, and she touched her belly, her mind jumbled with a concoction of wonder and fear. What would Dad say? She couldn't tell him who'd fathered her baby. She could already hear his rant. "Henrietta, it's just like I told you. That's what happens when you take a job where you don't belong. I bet you slept with every Tom, Dick, and Harry, just to get ahead! See where it got you?"

No matter what Dad had to say, she'd work through it. But what did she really know about raising a child *and* as a single mom? Sure she'd babysat, but her goal had been to get her charges quickly into bed so she could do homework, chat on the phone, or watch TV. It would be hard to be tied down at age twenty-three, to find reputable sitters, to hurry home at 5:00 p.m. while colleagues were going out for after-work drinks.

That was *if* she had the same colleagues.

Off to her right, Etta could see Tripoint's Art Deco high rise. How could she continue to work there once her pregnancy became evident?

She'd recently read about another company's unwed pregnant employee. The woman had challenged her termination and had won in the U.S. Court of Appeals. Etta didn't believe she'd be fired. But could she handle being unmarried and pregnant in her male-dominated office? The constant whispers would be intolerable.

And what would her clients think?

Etta made a right turn onto Wacker Drive which paralleled the Chicago River. St. Patrick's Day was on the horizon. Prior to the parade, authorized boats would be spreading orange dye into the river to turn its hue into what she'd been told was a deep emerald green. Moni had secured an English Literature teaching position at Northwestern. Ever since Miami, Etta had made excuses for not meeting her friend for a drink. The previous evening, Moni had called and said, "Listen, I won't take no for an answer. We're celebrating St. Patty's together."

Etta had finally caved in.

It was just as well.

She had to talk to someone.

1988 - New York

A gentle kiss touched Asami's forehead. In the darkness, there were footsteps, a click, then quiet once more. She drifted off again, into a dreamless sleep...

A muffled siren startled her awake, the sounds of the city, New York City. Her eyes fluttered open and sparse light filled the room. A soft pillow supported her head and a warm quilt covered her body. She was achy, uncomfortable. Her blouse and skirt were bunched up, her pantyhose no longer pinching at the waist. Her mouth felt icky, dry, her head pounding.

She tried to get her bearings. She—she'd been at a party... TJ's party? Was she still there? His lecherous grin resurfaced and an ominous chill rippled down her spine.

She crawled off the couch and grabbed its arm for support. She had to find some pain killers. The doorway ahead could be a bathroom. She took one wobbly step, then another, and crossed the threshold. Her bare feet touched a tile floor. Head woozy, she blindly fumbled for a wall switch. The bright lights made her cringe. It was indeed a bathroom. She closed the door and locked it, then pried open a medicine cabinet. The first shelf contained a deodorant stick, a razor, a prescription bottle. She picked it up, squinted at the owner's name, and dropped the container into the sink.

She was in Sam Madrid's home?

How could that be?

Had he been at the party?

She had no recollection, but somehow she'd ended up inside his apartment.

She had to clear her mind. Asami placed the prescription bottle back into the cabinet and located some pain killers. Using her palm to cup the faucet water, she took three. To her right was a shower. Just what she needed.

Asami managed to remove her blouse, bra, and skirt. Surprisingly, her panties were inside out. Had she put them on that way when she'd dressed for the party? She took them off and stepped into the shower. Lifting her face to the stream of hot water, she tried to awaken her body, awaken her mind. The latter blossomed. She was in Sam's shower. He had to have brought her to his home. He'd been a gentleman. He'd allowed her to decide whether she wanted to share his bed.

She cleansed herself with soap and chose one of the two shampoos on the ledge, an herbal scent. Her headache was beginning to dull. Her body's response was just the opposite. Driven by pent up yearnings, it had a mind of its own.

She quickly dried off, wrapped a towel around herself, and stepped out of the bathroom.

Fate had brought her to Sam's apartment.

She cautiously turned the handle to the adjacent door. From inside the dark room, she could hear slow, even breathing. The shades were drawn, but the faint light from behind enabled her to absorb Sam's riveting features: his tall frame resting on his left side, his bare butt peeking out from under the blanket, his hair tangled against the white pillowcase, his right hand's long slender fingers splayed toward the wrinkled bedding on the opposite side.

Asami took a deep breath, stepped inside the dark room, and closed the door behind her. She silently padded across the carpeted floor toward the invisible bed and let the towel fall. Her heart galloping, she climbed in, careful to leave space between her bare back and Sam's body.

His warm arm slid over her breasts and he pulled her close. "Mmm..." His voice was drowsy. "I'm glad you're still here."

Blood rushed into every molecule of Asami's body.

Sam wanted her too!

She knew how to please him. It was what Brad had taught her to do.

Asami gingerly turned toward Sam. She slid down under the sheet and found what she was looking for. Within moments, she heard Sam's muffled moans. She scooted back up and with ardor mounted him, her palms placed on his bare chest. Reveling in her love, she rode Sam like a sleek black steed until they exploded together in an exhilarating rush.

He breathed out, "Oh Etta!"

Asami jerked back. "What? What did you say?"

He gave an alarming cry and his hands pushed her away. A bedside lamp clicked on. "Christ, Asami!" A look of horror distorted Sam's face. "What the hell are you doing? I thought you were Etta!"

Bewildered, she covered herself with the sheet.

Sam's eyes were wild. "The two of us brought you home from the Pollards' apartment. What got into you! How could you be in my bed?"

Asami's fingers ravaged the sheet's stitched edge. She couldn't comprehend.

Sam placed his head in his hands. "What a goddamn mess!"

Still struggling to understand, Asami whimpered, "Are—are you saying Etta was here? She was here in your bed?"

His eyes closed. "Yes... I thought you were her. She spent the night, but I didn't hear her leave."

Mortified, Asami recalled the soft kiss on her forehead.

"Oh Sam! I thought she was seeing someone. How was I to know it was you?"

Asami's cheeks burned as she fled from Sam's room.

How could she have betrayed Etta?

How could she have basically raped Sam?

1988 - New York

Asami rode in a cab, sleet and snow assaulting its windows. The Central Park area known as Strawberry Fields was off to her left. Under the new fallen snow, the black-and-white mosaic circle encompassing the word "IMAGINE" would be hidden snug in the frozen ground. Like John Lennon's meditative song, she'd been doing that ever since she'd sat in Todai's auditorium. Stimulated by her Tripoint training, and her love for Sam, she'd finally believed her dreams were coming to fruition.

But they'd splattered on the sidewalk like rotten fruit.

Everything seemed beyond repair.

She closed her eyes. She'd never be able to erase that appalling picture from her mind: how she'd tried to cover her nakedness as she'd staggered out of Sam's bedroom; how she'd managed to dress in the bathroom while tears had streamed down her cheeks; how she'd cracked open the door, hoping to make a clean escape, but Sam had been on the other side, dressed in baggy sweats, a demoralized look on his face. He'd reached out and grabbed her arm. "Listen Asami, I promised Etta—"

"*Please*, Sam, don't talk!" She'd wrestled free. There was no way she could've conversed with him knowing what she'd done. Asami had picked up her heels, snagged her purse and coat, then sped out of Sam's brownstone. In bare feet, frozen snow between her toes, she'd waved down the cab she was in. As it had pulled away, she'd heard Sam yelling, "Wait, Asami, I promised Etta—" before the cab turned the corner, and his words drifted away.

As if that trauma wasn't bad enough, about five blocks from her apartment, the traffic came to a stop. Up ahead, she could see a three vehicle accident. She put on her shoes, paid the driver, and crawled out. Exhibiting a disgustingly miserable canter, she made her way home, her heels sliding on icy sidewalks, the sleet stinging her cheeks and bare legs.

Asami limped into her SoHo apartment. Thankfully, both her roommate and her roommate's wayward sister had traveled to Boston for the weekend.

Asami felt like one of the dust balls, chronically hiding in their cluttered front room, something that should be swept up and thrown out in the trash.

The answering machine was flashing with three calls. She listened to their playback, all from Etta, the panic rising in her friend's voice. The first two had been made from an O'Hare pay phone, soon after Etta had landed. The final call had come in from Etta's Evanston condo. "Please, Asami, please call! I tried Sam, but he hasn't answered. I need to know. Are you okay?"

Asami stared at the phone. When Etta had left those messages, she had yet to talk to Sam. She couldn't know about their humiliating bedroom encounter. So why was Etta so concerned? Sam had said he and Etta had brought her home from TJ's party. She'd figured she'd been drunk, a mortifying fact as well.

Asami squeezed her eyes shut, trying to remember, but all that surfaced was TJ's lecherous grin...

She sank down onto the rattan chair next to the phone. How could she talk to Etta? Yet if she didn't return her friend's call, Etta would keep trying to reach her. Asami groaned and finally dialed the Evanston number.

"Oh God, Asami, I'm so glad to hear your voice! I felt so guilty leaving you on Sam's couch."

"Etta, why didn't you tell me you two were a couple?" Asami wanted to place blame elsewhere. If Etta had told her, she certainly would've stayed clear of his bed.

"It's complicated. Just tell me, did Sam take you to a clinic?"

"I—I don't understand. For what reason?"

"What! He promised he'd convince you. Last night, the Dakota doorman said TJ's last party guests had departed about ten minutes before Sam and I arrived. Tom had asked Sam to pick up some papers for a client. Do you recall seeing us there?"

Asami shook her head. "No—no, I don't..."

"Sam had used the apartment key Tom had provided, but there was a security chain in place. We had to call out to TJ before he finally let us in. God! We were shocked to find you there. You were in a weird state, sitting on the couch, your clothes disheveled."

Her hands had turned clammy.

"TJ insisted you'd only had too much to drink, but I was afraid you'd been drugged or—or worse."

Asami's feet rapidly tapped the scratched hardwood floor. Why couldn't she remember?

"Right after Sam and I basically carried you to the cab, I wanted to take you to a clinic. But he convinced me we should let you sleep it off. That you should make that decision. After all, TJ *was* the CEO's son." There was rancor in her voice. "Sam didn't think we should create an issue if one hadn't occurred." Etta hesitated. "But, Asami, you must tell me. Did something happen?"

She cowered in the chair. Something *had* happened. But that mortifying "Sam situation" wasn't what her friend was drilling her about. "Etta, I'm fine. Nothing happened at that party."

But was that true?

She hung up, yet she felt no relief. Etta was furious with Sam, all because of her.

Little did Etta know Asami was the true culprit, the rapist. Forever, she'd push around that cartload of guilt.

Asami wanted to curl up in bed and erase the past dozen hours. But how could she?

In addition to her ordeal with Sam, Etta had escalated Asami's concern about her interaction with TJ.

Her pantyhose *had* disappeared. At the Pollards' apartment, had she removed them? Or, more likely, had he? And what about her panties? They'd been inside out? Her body had been achy. In Sam's shower, had she unknowingly washed away evidence?

She dashed into the bathroom and retched into the toilet. Through watery eyes, she peered up at the bedraggled philodendron, suspended in a macramé hanger.

What if Etta was right?

What if TJ had drugged her *and* raped her, as she'd raped Sam?

1976 - Chicago

Inside the murky depths of Baker's Tavern, hand clapping and shoe stomping accompanied an Irish fiddle and flute band. Odoriferous corned beef and cabbage scents spilled out from the kitchen and beer flowed from the taps. Rowdy patrons, mostly clothed in Irish gear, were effusively drunk. Etta envied their revelry. She'd like to partake in the festivities, but she had new responsibilities. A recent Washington University study had linked alcohol consumption, while pregnant, to possible birth defects. Recalling her pity party binge, she feared she might already have cast the die.

Moni grabbed Etta's arm. "Come on." She expedited Etta toward two vacated bar stools. Through shamrock frames, Moni's eyes shined. "Now, I'm ready for a drink!" She waved the bartender over. "We'll take two green beers."

"Wait!" Etta stopped him. "I'll take a Coke instead."

Moni's eyebrows disappeared beneath her bangs. "Since when are you abstaining on St. Patty's Day?"

"Since—since..." Etta started to cry—really cry—the gut-wrenching kind, nearly knocking her off the stool.

Moni slid an arm around her. "Honey, what's wrong?"

The bartender looked worried. He placed their drinks in front of them and scurried away.

Shit! How embarrassing. Etta swiped at her tears and her fingertips turned black, no doubt from her running mascara.

Moni stared at her and a sudden glint of realization unfolded. "Holy crap! You're pregnant, aren't you?"

Etta gazed down. "I—I wish you didn't know me so well."

Moni's arm flopped to her side. "Wow! Like, are you keeping it?"

Etta took in a deep gulp of air, as if it were her last, and blew it out. "Yes."

"Good girl!"

Etta peeked up at her friend's beaming face.

Moni clinked her beer mug against Etta's Coke glass. "That's some news! Tonight, I guess I'll be drinking for two *or* should I say three?" She leaned in, giving Etta a conspiratorial grin. "If you're up for it, I happen to have a joint inside my tampon case. As far as I know, Mary Jane usage, while pregnant, isn't taboo."

Etta managed a weak smile. "I think I'll pass."

"Honey, I know this is not the way you planned your life would go. But having met your mom and her crazy girlfriends, I'm certain they'll support your decision." Moni touched Etta's flat belly. "Wow! It's hard to believe you have a baby in the kiln. Just think! You'll be paving the road for other single *and* pregnant professional women."

"Oh Moni, I don't think so. I can't see myself waddling into work and cutting that path. Both my colleagues and clients would be snickering behind my back, wondering who knocked me up."

"Well who did? Tell me it wasn't your university heartthrob who happens to be your boss?"

Etta's guilty eyes met her friend's. Amid Moni's repeated head shaking, Etta's Miami Beach saga and its dismal aftermath tumbled out.

"God, Etta! You get into the damndest situations!"

"I do, don't I?" She ran her finger through her glass's condensation. "That's why I'm handing in my resignation."

Moni scowled. "There has to be another option."

"But what?"

Moni drained her beer and motioned for a refill. "You told me you chose yesterday's clinic because of its Northwestern affiliation. Think about it. Weren't your university years nurturing and liberating?"

"You know they were."

"Couldn't they be again? Couldn't you go back for your MBA? You know you wouldn't be alone. I'd be there too."

A sudden clarity took hold of Etta, her confusion evaporating like a Deering Meadows' rain puddle as the sun warmed that Northwestern green space. She could picture herself, her belly bulging, taking a break from her studies to picnic with Moni. On every step of her pregnancy journey, she knew her friend would be there to support her.

Etta clasped Moni into a bear hug. "You're the best."

"Hey!" She pulled back and shrugged. "What else would you expect from Auntie Moni?" She gently brushed a wayward strand of hair off Etta's cheek. "It has a nice ring doesn't it?"

Etta trapped her friend's hand and squeezed it tight. "It sure does."

* * *

Over the next two weeks, Etta spent her evenings studying for the Graduate Management Admission Test, and she passed it, just in the nick of time. Sam was due to leave for his New York branch management position at week's end.

Through his office window wall, she could see him working at his desk, his suit jacket off, his tie loosened, his face and hands still holding a bit of Miami tan. The latter evoked memories she'd never forget, the crashing surf, and the scent of him, as they'd made love on the moonlit beach.

Shit! She squeezed those heated thoughts into a tight little ball, swallowed them down, and peeked into his office. "Sam? Can we talk?"

Her unexpected request had caught him off guard. "Of course..." he said, his eyes those of a remorseful dog, asking for kindness when none was deserved.

Etta knew she had the upper hand as she shut the door and sat down. "I'm sorry for the way I've been treating you. I admit, I still love you, but I've come to realize, I need to let you go."

"Oh Etta, I—I…" He stopped, conflicted feelings marring his face.

Her heart was breaking once again. She watched his hands. She could tell they wanted to reach out and touch her. Although she'd given him her blessing, it was evident he still loved her. His eyes couldn't hide their sadness as he simply said, "Thank you."

Etta nodded and dusted off her emotions. That was crucial. She had to portray her most persuasive self. Her future, and her unborn child's, depended on it. Lips tight, she straightened up, her unwavering eyes meeting his. "Now, Sam, I need a favor."

"Anything…"

"I'd like a one year sabbatical."

He drew back, startled.

"Yesterday, I talked to Northwestern's admissions office. If I enroll by next week, I can begin their accelerated MBA program in the spring quarter."

"Advancing your degree is a great idea, but Tripoint employees normally attend evening graduate classes rather than taking a leave."

"I understand. But in Miami, a New York Technical Rep told me he'd taken an unpaid leave to get his MBA. That's what I'd like to do."

"Etta, are you certain?" He still looked perplexed.

She nodded, fearful he'd question her further.

He leaned back in his chair. "Okay, if that's what you really want, I'll make some calls and see what I can do."

From her desk, she had a clear view of Sam's office. He'd punch in a number and briefly talk, then choose another, and another. Each time he'd hang up, her heart would stutter. She'd search his face for any sort of positive clue. The stress was driving her crazy. To occupy her mind, Etta pulled out a client's project plan, but she couldn't concentrate.

Her phone finally rang. "Etta, this is Sam. Can you join me for a minute?"

She hurried into his office. His staid face greeted her and her heart sank.

"Okay, I tried to pull some strings—"

Shit! Her knees wobbled, performing a duet with her churning gut. It was bad news.

"I was working with someone in HR who wasn't being very helpful, so I went right to the top."

That notion made Etta even queasier. "What do you mean?"

"I called Tom Pollard."

"Oh no..." Eighteen months earlier, Tripoint's CEO had attempted to drive her out. He'd gotten a second chance.

"Just listen. Tom's wife had stopped into his office. I could hear Sylvia convincing Tom it would be a big mistake if he didn't approve your sabbatical. That Tripoint might lose a smart woman like you."

"Really? She said that? Did Tom agree?"

Sam's face was awestruck. "Yes... It's apparent Sylvia thinks a lot of you. And," he raised his brows, "she has more clout over Tom than you might know."

Etta was quite sure she did know. *God!* How lucky she'd been! By chance, Sylvia had been in Tom's office *and* she'd stood up for Etta.

Overwhelmed by her fantastic turn of events, her grateful eyes met Sam's. It was agonizing. She had such an urge to fold him into her arms, to press her lips to his, to run her hands through his hair, to rub her body against his, to...

Dammit! She had to scour away those thoughts. Although she was devastated by the way things had turned out between them, she knew Sam had gone out on a limb to secure her request.

Tears cropped up in her eyes. Little did he know, in addition to being granted a sabbatical, to earn her MBA, he'd given her the means to keep her job and, most importantly, have her baby.

Their baby.

Etta touched her belly. Intense joy exploded inside.

She was certain she was carrying a little girl—her daughter—her Chloe.

-17-

Tuesday - Tokyo

Fueled by renewed optimism, Asami strode between Jiro and Detective Hondo into the Roppongi nightlife. For once, she could almost keep up. She was still wearing Hana's workout shoes. Jiro had convinced Hondo it would be senseless to have another detective join them while they questioned employees at the district hotels containing indoor swimming pools. Their search would not be dangerous. Even if it was, for his films, Jiro had been trained by a Japanese martial arts master in the aikido self-defense style.

The three passed a group of male gaijin accompanied by two young Japanese females. Both women were dressed in seductive mini-skirts, black stiletto boots, and glittery evening jackets.

Jiro shook his head, his cigarette glowing in the dark. "Foreign men, from the embassies or a gaishikei like Tripoint, enjoy all the attention from our Japanese women." He leaned over and whispered into Asami's ear, "Not that I'm looking!"

She couldn't help but smile. Jiro's eyes certainly weren't focused on the women, just on Detective Hondo, who said, "I agree. Most gaijin don't respect our women. They rarely treat them as legitimate marital candidates. They just want to sleep with them." His gaze met Jiro's.

Asami let the two men flirt as she considered TJ Pollard and Sam's brother—both gaijin. TJ definitely fit Hondo's perception. Haruki did not. She often thought of him with regret. They'd always been civil when they'd bumped into each other inside their Tokyo building's elevator. Two months earlier, she'd given him her profound sympathy after his wife had died from an unexpected heart attack. The couple's twins had attended the same school as Hana. Unlike her daughter's other classmates, who'd bullied her child, Haruki's twins, only a year younger than Hana, had been kind to her.

Asami had first introduced Hana to Haruki when she'd been about four. Inside Inokashira Park, he and his wife had been pushing a double stroller while Asami and Hana had been picnicking—their traditional Sunday outing during good weather months. He'd squatted down to talk to Hana, asking about her preschool program, and pointing out the ducklings following their mama on the rippled pond. Over the years, it had seemed as if Haruki had made a point of being at that park at about the same time as Asami and Hana. He and her daughter had developed a special rapport.

If Haruki was mixed up in Hana's disappearance, Asami was certain he'd be doing his best to protect her daughter.

The eight-story Villa Fontaine Hotel was their first stop. Its lobby was attached to an atrium that featured a large swimming pool. At the check-in counter, the receptionist dipped her head toward Detective Hondo.

He did the same and showed his badge. "Were you on duty last Thursday night?"

"Yes? Why do you ask?"

"Between 10:00 p.m. and 1:00 a.m., do you recall any gatherings beside your pool?"

"No. To keep the noise down, it closes at 9:00 p.m. Each evening, I rope off that area, which I can view from here. I would've noticed if anyone had crossed those boundaries."

Asami's shoulders sagged. "I never considered the pools would've been closed."

Jiro slipped his arm around her. "My dear, don't give up hope. Guests don't always follow the rules."

The Intercontinental produced the same results, as did the Ritz-Carlton, Tokyo Prince, and Hotel Okura. Asami's earlier enthusiasm had waned. Her feet were weary, her heart heavy, her mind tangled with thoughts of Hana—her brave girl—waiting to be found.

Asami and the two men finally reached the Palace Hotel, the last one noted on Hondo's map. A few blocks earlier, they'd passed the seedy Casablanca Love Hotel, the deceased woman's last known whereabouts. Both hotels were located in the Roppongi Hills complex, just west of the central nightlife district. "The Palace," Jiro said, "is often the first choice for many visiting celebrities, VIPs, and American business travelers. My studio often puts people up here."

Asami slid her arm through the crook of Jiro's, her fingertips brushing his cashmere overcoat's sleeve. "I didn't ask Chloe where she was staying, but it could've been here."

The three entered the Palace's expansive lobby. A stone waterfall provided a backdrop for leather chairs and couches. All were grouped into intimate conversation areas and filled primarily with Western businessmen. Their voices generated a low hum like a swarm of docile bees.

Behind the reception desk was a Japanese woman, her hair secured in a knot. Hondo exchanged bows with her and showed his badge before asking the same question.

"Our pool and spa are open from 5:00 a.m. to 10:00 p.m.," she said.

Asami released a low moan. Their search had reached its end.

Jiro wasn't ready to give up. "Could there have been a private after-hours gathering in the pool area?"

"No. That would've been strictly prohibited, however," she hesitated, "there's an additional pool on our premises, one which would have no restrictions."

"Really?" Asami clutched Jiro's arm. "Can you tell us where it's located?"

"I'm sorry. My manager needs to discuss that with you." She glanced at a man who was checking in a guest. "It should only be a few minutes."

Patience had never been one of Asami's virtues. Her eyes zoned in on the manager, mentally commanding him to "Hurry up!" as her foot rapidly tapped the terrazzo floor.

Tuesday - New York

At a Bliss Café window table, Etta sipped strong coffee and waited for Sam. The daily specials' aromas filled the homey space, but neither the artichoke quiche nor the cinnamon coffee cake had enticed Etta. When the cheerful waitress had approached, her lips' downward slide had been proof Etta's grief was contagious.

Sam's flight had landed and Etta had suggested the Café for their talk. He'd known the place. He'd often met Chloe there when she'd needed his advice or insight.

Hopefully, Sam would provide Etta the latter. But the disturbing video footage, from Chloe's apartment building's lobby, continued to play inside Etta's head. She couldn't believe Sam was the person disguised as the Otis service man. Yet he'd been spinning his thumb on his ring finger as Sam always had.

Her worries weren't appeased when Sam's cab pulled up. Through its back window, Etta could see his tanned face, as if he'd recently returned from a Caribbean cruise. *Shit!* His hands would be tan as well. She steeled herself for their talk. Not revealing Chloe's death could be anything but a suicide would be a challenge. But if Sam was involved, as Tripoint's COO, he'd have full access to Pollard Property Group's security department. He'd know the authorities had requested that lobby video footage.

Etta wanted a private moment with Sam before he entered. She told the waitress, "I'll be right back." Chockfull of opposing emotions, Etta pushed open the Café's front door. Was Sam her enemy or her ally?

She prayed he was the latter.

Sam stepped onto the sidewalk. His silver hair framed his sturdy face lined in the proper places. He hadn't altered nature's course and neither had she. His lack of vanity attracted her to him all the more.

He saw her and murmured, "Oh Etta..."

She closed her eyes, tears squeezing out, and he gently enfolded her into his arms. "I don't understand." His voice was husky. "Why did Chloe do this to you—to me? I loved her too."

"I know..." She clung to him, to Chloe's father—to the man she still loved.

They pulled apart and she led him inside. Once the waitress had placed a mug of coffee in front of him, Etta carefully proceeded, per Detective Harper's instructions. "Chloe committed suicide, but I don't know why. At first, I believed Henri had been cheating on her, but he's sworn to me he's been faithful. So instead, I've been speculating about Chloe's time in Tokyo. Could something have happened to her there? Something bad enough to have caused her to take her own life? And could that same something *also* be connected to Hana's disappearance?"

Sam cupped his mug in both hands. "So in addition to Chloe's suicide, are you saying Hana's still missing? You left that in one of your voice messages."

"Yes."

He shook his head and frowned. "Neither situation makes sense. Let me step through the last two evenings I spent with Hana and Chloe and see what you think."

He took a swallow of coffee and began. On Wednesday, he said, the three had eaten dinner at the Hayashi restaurant where Sam had dined with Asami, more than twenty years before. "I told Chloe and Hana about the United Nations' *Decade for Women* initiative, how it had been in progress at that time, and we discussed the advances women had made since then. Etta, it was an honor to sit beside your daughter and Asami's, both of them such confident and beautiful young women, both of them such assets to our company."

Etta could picture that evening, Sam's face filled with pride as he'd unknowingly conversed with her daughter, not realizing his gene pool had contributed to the vibrant young woman she'd become.

But since that U.N. initiative, some things hadn't changed. Asami's daughter had recently been sexually harassed by Tripoint's CEO as Etta had been thirty-six years before. Etta had never told Sam and at that restaurant, even though Hana had had the opportunity to do so, it appeared as if she'd also kept silent.

God! It was hard to be a woman.

"Oh Etta!" Sam's voice hitched. "We had a wonderful time. "It's so hard to believe, just days later, Chloe took her life."

"I know..." Etta so wanted to tell Sam the truth, but she couldn't. "What about Thursday night? Asami said you three went to the British Pub for a drink."

"That's right. We only planned on having one, but then my brother called. Haruki had been in Osaka on business and he'd arrived back in Tokyo. He was going to have his cab drop him off at the Pub." Sam hesitated. "You may not know this, but his wife recently passed away."

"Asami told me. How tragic for him and their children."

"Yes." It was obvious Sam was suffering, not only for her daughter, but for his brother as well. "Anyway," he continued, "Hana wanted to stay to offer Haruki her condolences, so all three of us were still there when he arrived. But..." Sam scowled, "but he wasn't alone. His yakuza brother had tagged along. It's beyond me why my brother's on a constant mission to earn Kato's approval. Haruki's *never* treated me that way."

She reached across the table and touched his hand. "I'm sorry that hasn't changed."

Sam's emotional response and his words had both seemed sincere. She couldn't believe he was involved in Chloe's death. But then the waitress approached. As she refilled Sam's mug, his left thumb was busily performing that *damn* spinning motion on his bare ring finger. *Shit!* Maybe she was still treading in dangerous water.

Etta took a deep breath. "Asami told me the five of you left the pub at about ten. Where did you go after that?"

"To a party," Sam said without any hesitation. "It was being held inside the Palace Hotel's Presidential Suite. Kato had been invited, and he'd also been asked to provide a female companion for its registered guest. Unfortunately," Sam frowned, "that guest was Tom Pollard."

Tom Pollard! Even though Etta had speculated that Tripoint's CEO could've been involved, not until that moment had she actually confirmed he was indeed a potential player in her daughter's situation.

"Etta, I'm sure you know Tom's had issues in the past, so his involvement with that sort of sketchy female could only have meant trouble. I'm also sure you know Tripoint's IPO is scheduled for Thursday."

Unnerved, Etta shifted in her chair. He'd mentioned the IPO without her asking.

"If Tom's name had shown up in some sort of gossip rag, it would've been disastrous. For that reason, I decided to accompany Kato."

Etta stared at Sam. It was as if he and she were on different wavelengths. She was worrying about her daughter's death, trying to decipher how it could be tied to Tripoint's IPO. Sam had been worrying how to proactively manage Tom's behavior so the IPO would be successful.

"Tell me, Sam, did Hana and Chloe also go to that party?"

"Yes, and so did my brother."

Etta's stomach knotted. Maybe she'd been wrong about Hana. Rather than telling Sam about Tom Pollard's inappropriate behavior, had Hana wanted to confront Tom head on. At his Tokyo party, had Asami's daughter instigated the sort of situation Sam had feared? Etta had to find out. "Who else attended that party?"

"Other than that Japanese woman arranged by Kato, the rest were males, primarily retail executives and DPJ politicians. And, Etta, I was right to worry about that woman. Haruki didn't know her name, but he was certain she was a health shop worker, the type who provides services similar to a U.S. call girl."

Etta flinched. Things were falling into place.

"We followed her out to the pool where—"

"A pool?" Etta clutched her coffee cup.

"Yes, the suite had a private lap pool. That's where Tom Pollard was stationed. About an hour later, his son showed up."

"I talked to TJ this morning. He said he and a client had been at a karaoke bar."

"That's where TJ and Masato Ito had been prior to their arrival."

"Masato?" Etta frowned. "Does he still work for Yamada?"

Sam nodded. "He's now a vice president. I shouldn't be telling you this, but when he and TJ arrived, they were both quite high, probably on more than saké. Masato also took an instant liking to that health shop worker and the two disappeared for a while."

Etta huffed. "That sounds like the Masato I remember."

"Yes." Sam's lips formed a thin line. "And once he'd had his fun, he quickly took his leave."

"What about that woman?"

"She returned to the pool area. About then, Hana and Chloe were ready to go. But Hana realized she'd left her purse by the pool."

"Did she go back for it?"

"Yes, and it was taking her some time. I was about to check on her when Tom and TJ entered the front room." Sam shook his head, consternation lining his face. "Both of them were soaking wet."

Etta's breath caught in her throat.

"Tom said TJ had fallen into the pool and Tom had jumped in to retrieve him. Etta, it was embarrassing to see our future CEO in the condition he was in. At least, most of our clients had already departed. Anyway, Tom asked Haruki and me to take TJ back to my room for the night since my suite had a pull out couch."

"So did you?"

"Yes."

"You left Chloe and Hana at the party, all alone?"

A sudden look of distress settled on Sam's face. "I never thought about it. Maybe I shouldn't have, but Chloe told me she was going to locate Hana and they'd leave together."

Etta stared at Sam. It didn't appear as if he knew her daughter—and Asami's—had later been seen at the Roppongi train station where Hana's clothes and hair had been wet. "Henri said you didn't fly back to New York with Chloe. Why was that?"

"Well..." He gave her a guilty look. "Because of TJ. Tom asked me to keep track of him until he found someone else to do the same."

Sam had to see the reproach in her eyes. He'd always protected TJ. If he'd been as concerned about Chloe, as he'd been about the CEO's son, would her daughter be alive? Etta shook off those troubling thoughts. "What about your brother? Where did Haruki go after he left you and TJ in your hotel room?"

"He was returning to the suite to make sure Chloe and Hana had left."

"Did you talk to Haruki after that?"

"No..." Another culpable look appeared on Sam's face. "Oh God, Etta, in retrospect, I guess I should've followed up."

He looked remorseful, so much so that Etta wanted to forgive him.

She couldn't.

Instead, she muttered, "Yes," and she gave him a curt nod. "Did you know your brother was to be in New York on Saturday for business?"

"Really? He never mentioned that."

"He'd made reservations at the Plaza, but he never checked in."

"That's odd. I'll try his cell." He selected Haruki's number and listened. As Sam left a voice message, Etta stared at his left hand. Once again, his thumb was performing that *damn* spinning motion.

Unaware of her distress, he hung up and glanced at his watch. "I'm sorry, Etta, I hate to leave, but I've got a client meeting." He stood and placed a hand on her shoulder. "When I hear back from Haruki, I'll give you a call. And, if you're up for it, we can continue our talk over a quiet dinner." He released a heavy sigh. "I'm devastated by Chloe's death, and I can't imagine how you must feel. Even though we don't know all the details about her Thursday night activities, we both know she arrived safely back in New York. Are—are you certain Henri's being honest with you?"

She didn't know what to say. She believed Henri had been telling her the truth. Had Sam? Or was he caught up in Tripoint's IPO frenzy? Had he omitted detrimental facts, those which involved her daughter and Hana? Those which involved that health shop worker? That corpse Asami had discovered in the forest had to be hers. When Hana went back to the pool area, had she witnessed that woman's drowning? In turn, had Hana revealed that to Chloe? Both Pollards had been soaking wet.

One of them *could* be the guilty party.

It appeared as if the Japanese detective's assumptions could all be true. Her daughter and Asami's could indeed have become risks to Tripoint's IPO success.

TJ and Tom were Tripoint's major stockholders.

Sam was a close third.

Tuesday - Tokyo

Asami stepped onto the lap pool's redwood deck totally enclosed within a rectangular box of glass. She turned to Jiro. "Look at the view. Can't you picture Hana doing the same last Thursday night?" From the Palace Hotel's thirtieth floor Presidential Suite, Tokyo's twinkling landscape surrounded them.

While waiting to talk to the Palace Hotel manager, Asami had received a call from Etta. She'd provided Sam's side of the story. Shortly after, the manager had confirmed the Presidential Suite's Thursday night guest had indeed been Tripoint's CEO. The manager had also agreed to take Detective Hondo, Asami, and Jiro into that currently unoccupied suite.

The manager slid apart two fusuma panels depicting a Mount Fuji scene. “Please follow me. Our security technician has queued up this floor’s hallway video footage for the evening in question.”

Detective Hondo dipped his head in a bow. “We appreciate your assistance.”

Asami entered the luxurious living room infused with the scent of aromatic teas. A wet bar lined the wall adjacent to a cranberry felted billiard table. The elegant “Katsy,” Japan’s first professional female billiard player, had been one of Asami’s childhood idols. She’d often racked up her balls and those of the men she’d defeated. Asami had savored Katsy’s grit much like the sweet taste of black cod marinated in miso.

At the present moment, there was nothing to savor.

Leather chairs were arranged for theater viewing. Asami sat down on one, Jiro and the detective on either side of her. On a low table, within reach, a room service employee placed two bowls: one filled with fruit, the other, roasted gingko nuts. He served them each ice water or tea as if they were settling in for a full length movie.

The manager used a remote to turn on a gigantic wall mounted TV. He selected a channel, entered a passcode, and the floor’s three elevators came into view. The left lower corner was timestamped with 8 p.m. on the prior Thursday. “I’ll fast forward,” he said, “until someone either heads toward or returns from the Presidential Suite.”

Asami’s eyes blurred as the video sped by.

The manager first stopped on a 9:32 p.m. timestamped frame and Asami blushed. “That’s Tripoint’s CEO.” A silver haired Tom Pollard was centered on the screen, lust in his steely gray eyes. He was cupping the right buttock of a Japanese woman dressed in a low-cut flouncy blouse and a tight black skirt. It was humiliating to see Tripoint's top executive behaving so flagrantly, but those in Japan often acted far worse.

Hondo squinted critically at the woman. "Thomas Pollard's with Chika Himura, the deceased health shop worker, the one you located inside the forest."

Asami's feet tapped. From the fruit bowl, she selected a mandarin orange and began to peel it over a napkin. She could see why she'd initially believed Chika was her daughter. Both were tall and had catlike slenderness in their bones.

The manager fast-forwarded the video until three Japanese men stepped off the elevator.

Jiro pointed. "Notice the gentleman on the far right? That's Eiji Tanaka, an important DPJ politician, and also a friend of mine." He turned toward Asami. "Do you know the others?"

"They're Tripoint clients from Sido Electronics." She placed two citrus segments into her mouth.

Jiro gave her an approving nod as she chewed and swallowed the tangy fruit. It was the first sustenance she'd had all day.

The video clipped along until three men and two females appeared in the frame.

Asami released a soft moan and sprung to her feet. "That's my daughter." She approached the screen, her hand hovering over Hana's cheek. "Beside her is Chloe Martin, our American friend and co-worker. Just two days later, she was found dead in her New York bathtub."

Hondo frowned. "What about the American male?"

"That's Sam Madrid, Tripoint's Chief Operating Officer. His brother, Haruki, is to his left. Next to him must be Haruki's yakuza brother, Kato Endo. Am I right?" Asami turned back toward Hondo. "I haven't seen him since the eighties, but he and Haruki still look very much alike."

The detective nodded. "Yes, that's him."

Asami walked back and resettled on her chair. Over the next hour of recorded footage, while Jiro and Hondo identified eight more DPJ politicians, Asami identified ten retailers and nearly consumed the entire bowl of nuts.

Two staggering men eventually stepped off the elevator. She couldn't help but wince as she identified TJ Pollard and Masato Ito. Seeing the son of Tripoint's CEO with her old Yamada nemesis made perfect sense.

In the next forty minutes, almost all the male Japanese guests departed: DPJ politicians and retailers alike, including Masato. The party seemed to be coming to a close.

At 12:23 a.m., a soaking wet and seemingly belligerent TJ, sandwiched between Sam and Haruki, came into view.

Asami was relieved.

The video footage was matching Sam's story.

She maintained her composure until Hana and Chloe walked in front of the camera.

Her heart went out to her daughter. She looked like a drowned kitten, her hair dripping, her eye makeup running, and her black suit sticking to her body. Chloe's protective arm was around Hana while Jiro's politician friend was on her daughter's opposite side. He had a concerned fatherly-sort-of-look on his face as he hurried the two young women into the elevator. All the while, he kept glancing over his shoulder.

Asami's gaze met Jiro's. "Your friend seems to be looking out for Hana."

He nodded.

Moments later, Haruki arrived on the thirtieth floor and stepped toward the suite. As the video continued, no persons of interest arrived or departed.

Asami's hands squeezed her face. "I don't understand. Neither Haruki nor his yakuza brother left the suite."

"Neither has that health shop worker," Jiro said, "nor, for that matter, Tom Pollard."

The detective addressed the manager. "Is there another way to access this suite?"

The manager pointed toward the dining area. "Behind that door is an elevator used for room service deliveries."

"Is there a camera in the kitchen area?"

"Yes, there are two." The manager called down to security, talked, then said, "Let's start with the kitchen's back door receiving zone. I've had that footage queued up."

It sped by until 12:53 a.m. when a Japanese man in kitchen scrubs came into view. He darted toward the receiving door and propped it open. About three minutes later, a Japanese man entered that door, pulling a large roller bag.

A purple birthmark stood out on his right cheek.

Asami gripped her knees. "That's the man who's been following me!"

Detective Hondo nodded. "He's the Wada-kai gangster we discussed."

The hotel manager's face had paled. "Rest assured, the Palace employee who aided that man will be held accountable."

The video continued until the gangster reappeared, struggling to pull the same roller bag.

The detective grimaced. "Chika's body is probably inside."

A moment later, Sam's brother, Haruki, appeared, followed by his yakuza brother.

Asami's hand flew to her mouth. "Could Haruki be involved?"

"Freeze that frame," Hondo ordered as his cell rang, and he excused himself to answer it.

Asami's worried gaze met Jiro's. "Look at Haruki's face. He doesn't look upset, does he? He's always admired his yakuza brother. Could that admiration have been misdirected?"

Before Jiro could respond, the detective returned, an astonished look on his face. “That was Sergeant Mori. Customs pulled your daughter’s passport records. She arrived in New York two hours ago.”

Asami gasped.

“But listen to this,” Hondo continued, “a companion ticket was purchased with hers. She cleared U.S. customs with Haruki Madrid.”

“Oh, Jiro-kun...” Asami bent over, clasping her arms around her legs, bringing her knees tight to her core. “Haruki *is* involved...”

Tuesday - New York

Long stem yellow roses were arranged in two cut glass vases centered on the Pollards’ marble end tables. Amid the flowers’ heady scent, Etta waited in the drawing room on a navy striped chair. To stop her hands from shaking, she tightly held them in her lap. She was taking a risk, meeting with the wife of Tripoint’s CEO, especially after Asami’s hysterical call.

Her Japanese friend had said, because Hana had passed through U.S. customs with Sam’s brother, the Tokyo authorities were still considering her daughter could be responsible for Chika Himura’s drowning. That Hana had willfully left the country with Haruki to escape the authorities. “But, Etta-san, I’m certain they’re wrong!”

Etta was too. Either Tripoint’s top executive or his son had to have drowned that health shop worker. Hana and Haruki’s yakuza brother knew which Pollard was responsible. Tragically, Chloe had too. A lucrative corporate extortion scheme had indeed landed in Kato Endo’s lap, and he’d somehow convinced Haruki to join forces.

That premise had really disturbed Asami. She’d believed Haruki would’ve been protecting her daughter. But since he hadn’t contacted the authorities, it appeared as if he'd also been swayed by greed, swayed by his yakuza brother.

Was Sam involved too? Did he have similar motives? Could he have been the Otis guy?

Etta stared out Sylvia's window. A clink of china came from the kitchen as her friend prepared coffee. It was hard for Etta to believe the man she'd loved, for nearly her entire life, could've murdered her daughter—their daughter.

Asami's quivering voice had asked, "Where in New York could Hana be?"

They'd discussed Deon's Hiro House business cards, the ones the teen had dropped in the park. Knowing that establishment could have yakuza connections made it a viable option.

But Detective Harper was still attempting to uncover its location.

Etta couldn't wait.

Sylvia entered the drawing room, her scent of Chanel N°5 mingling with the roses. On the end table, she placed a tray holding two white porcelain coffee-filled mugs, sugar, and cream. "Please help yourself.

"Thanks." Etta selected a mug. "And also thanks for seeing me."

"You know I always have time for you." Sylvia took a seat in a matching chair. "I understand Sam and you talked this morning. Was he able to provide you any insight into your daughter's death?"

"Not really." Etta took a careful sip of steaming coffee, her hands still shaky. She'd decided to dive right in, to ignore the risk. "Sam last talked to Chloe at a Tokyo party hosted by your husband." Etta's unblinking eyes remained focused on her friend. "Did Tom mention that party?"

Sylvia's forehead furrowed. "No? Why do you ask?"

"Sam said a Japanese woman, similar to a U.S. call girl, had been invited, per Tom's request."

Sylvia sighed. "It's sad to say, but that sounds like the norm."

It wasn't the response Etta had expected. "Sylvia, please help me understand. How could a smart and assertive woman, like you, put up with your husband's indiscretions for so long?"

She met Etta's gaze. "Can I trust you with something?" She hesitated. "A secret I've only shared with a handful of friends?"

Etta was startled. "Of course you can."

"Okay..." She still seemed reticent. "Back—back at Radcliffe, in the sixties, I was involved in every sort of movement: free speech, civil rights, anti-war demonstrations, women's liberation..." She paused. "That's when I fell in love. But it wasn't with Tom. It was with Evelyn Bengston, another Cliffee who shared my passions."

Etta couldn't say she was shocked. That thought had crossed her mind. Sybil, Mom's woman libber best friend, had been a lesbian, living a double life in Carter, Illinois. Etta knew how hard that had been for her.

"My father was a staunch republican," Sylvia charged on. "Growing up in that era, I often heard him disparage the homosexual lifestyle. How he believed it was a sickness spreading across America."

"I'm so sorry."

"I appreciate your words, but it was... what it was. I knew my father would never have approved of my partner choice. That's why Tom came into the picture. He was a Harvard playboy, dirt poor, and on a scholarship. My family, conversely, had accumulated its wealth in New York's real estate market."

"How did you meet Tom?"

"Through Evelyn. Her first cousin is Dick Bengston, Tripoint's former COO. He, Tom, and Tripoint's current CFO had a joint vision to create the company. But to do so, they needed backing. Tom knew Evelyn and I were a couple. He also knew my father would disown me if I divulged that fact to him."

"So Tom agreed to marry you?"

"Yes, and I agreed to invest substantial funds in his startup endeavor, which I secured from my father. It was a win-win for both of us. Tom promised to keep Evelyn and my relationship private. I promised not to object to his extramarital affairs."

"I bet you never imagined they'd become public so often."

"You're right. But overall, our relationship has worked. Tom has had his flings, and I'm still with Evelyn, and, obviously, Tom and I have TJ."

"Is he Tom's?"

She nodded. "Through in vitro fertilization. But from early on, I could tell TJ was his father's son, passionate about women and work." Sylvia shook her head. "I dearly love my son, even with all his faults, just as I know you loved Chloe." She reached over and covered Etta's hand with hers.

Etta stared at her friend. Sylvia had been one of the supportive and caring people in her life. She'd just trusted Etta with an extremely personal confession. Maybe it was time for Etta to do the same. Not with everything related to Chloe's death—not the most likely theory—but one of the safest, one which might provide some needed answers. "Listen Sylvia, I—I don't believe my daughter committed suicide."

Sylvia released her hand. "What are you saying?"

"I believe Chloe could've been murdered by Deon Endo, the teen my daughter was mentoring." Etta rattled off her reasoning: Deon's accusatory note at Saturday's TFK event, his phone call to Henri from the Rusty Nail, his darting out of Washington Square Park, and his elevator panel entry route into Chloe's apartment.

At a loss for words, Sylvia's mouth hung slack.

"Right before I arrived, Detective Harper called me. She'd stopped over at Deon's apartment. Nobody answered the door and no family members have been seen since Sunday. He's also been absent from school for two days."

"My goodness! I can't believe Deon would've murdered your daughter."

Etta removed the teen's business card from her purse and showed it to Sylvia. "Deon dropped a number of these in the park. Has his mother ever mentioned this place called Hiro House? You said she cleans for you."

Sylvia looked uncomfortable. "Lorna never brings up her father-in-law's business, but Tom and I met her because of it."

"Really?" She was finally getting somewhere. "How did that come about?"

"It was back in the eighties, after Sam won the Yamada deal, and their executives were visiting Tripoint's headquarters. That's when one of them asked if there were any New York establishments for, what he'd called, overworked 'salarymen.'"

"Are you saying both Sam and Tom knew about Hiro House?"

"Not initially. Sam's brother, Haruki, was the one who talked to his Japanese brother, and he hooked them up with Deon's grandfather. He'd recently arrived from Tokyo to establish Hiro House."

Etta sat back. Haruki's yakuza brother and Hiro were *definitely* connected!

"Through him," Sylvia continued, "my husband was introduced to his daughter-in-law. Ever since, Lorna has cleaned for us."

"So you *must* know where Hiro House is located?" Etta held her breath.

"I'm afraid not."

"Shit!"

"But Sam should know."

Etta closed her eyes.

Everything kept circling back to Sam.

-18-

1988 - New York

Asami entered Midtown Manhattan's Public Library, her hair still damp from the shower she'd taken to scrub away Sam's scent. Ricocheting around inside her head were thoughts about that shameful encounter, but her concern about TJ's party was transcending them.

She had to have answers.

Arched windows and grand chandeliers provided light to the Rose Main Reading Room. The smell of musty leather bindings and old paper made Asami sneeze. The card catalog pointed her to a drug reference manual. She located it and took a seat in an armchair at a long wooden table lit by green shaded brass lamps.

Asami's feet tapped.

She recalled the British man from the Roco Club arriving at TJ's parents' door.

Soon after, she'd drunk TJ's special saké martini and everything had gone haywire.

Asami paged through the manual looking for any sort of drug which could've caused the symptoms she'd experienced. She eventually located Rohypnol, a tranquilizer only available in Europe. Her finger followed the text: *It can cause drowsiness, confusion, dizziness, disorientation, and impaired judgment; the individual might look and act like someone who was drunk; the person might be rendered completely unconscious; when crushed into an alcoholic drink Rohypnol has no smell or taste.*

Sweat droplets had formed on Asami's upper lip. She forced herself to read on: *One of the most disturbing effects is Rohypnol can cause complete or partial amnesia. While under the drug's influence, individuals may not remember what was done to them.*

She closed the manual. She couldn't remember. Her judgment had been impaired at the party and afterward with Sam. Asami's face flamed. She'd been unbelievably reckless in his bed.

When she and Brad had been in their relationship, she'd shied away from birth control pills, asking him to use a condom. Back in Tokyo, if a Japanese woman discussed birth control with her boyfriend, he'd assume she was playing around. It was far more acceptable to admit to having had an abortion.

America was different.

Brad had told her the responsible thing to do was to go on the pill and she'd finally agreed.

Asami pounded her head with her hands. How foolish she'd been. Once Brad had abandoned her, she'd stopped taking her daily dose.

* * *

On Monday morning, Asami couldn't face Sam or TJ. She called Tripoint's receptionist and croaked out, "I'm suffering from a bout of Salmonella poisoning from bad sushi." Co-workers had wrinkled their noses when she'd told them she loved the taste of raw fish; that the flavors reminded her of home; that a bar down the street from her apartment was one of New York's first to introduce that Japanese culinary custom. Once her lie got around, she knew her colleagues would be saying, "I told you so."

A week passed. Apprehension had been Asami's constant mate. She couldn't claim to be ill any longer. She had to return to work. But a bigger fear was pressing on her mind. She made a trip to a local pharmacy and returned to her apartment with a brown paper bag, a One Step pregnancy test hidden inside. Asami waited until both her roommate and her roommate's sister departed for a Sunday afternoon shopping excursion. Inside the bathroom, Asami sat down on the toilet and, with a trembling hand, collected urine at one end of the wand. The test supposedly could register the pregnancy hormone in a woman's body as early as seven days after conception.

Asami's pulse thundered in her ears. She washed her hands and waited for the results.

As the blue stripe materialized, she dropped her head into her hands.

She was pregnant.

Asami could picture her family's humiliated faces on the opposite side of the world. Only two percent of Japanese children were born out of wedlock. A parent's absence was considered to be the worst type of child abuse. That was why nearly two-thirds of all Japanese women had aborted at least once. That procedure had been legal in Japan since 1952, deemed a private decision between a woman and her physician.

Could Asami follow the norm?

She curled up on the couch. Through the leaded glass window, winter sunlight flooded the room. Asami squinted down and gently placed her hands on her belly. It was hard to grasp. A new life was growing inside.

But the awful fact remained. She didn't know whether the father was TJ or Sam.

She'd always envied Etta's relationship with Chloe.

If Asami kept her baby, could that same joy be hers?

But how could she continue to work in New York once her pregnancy showed? If TJ had raped her—as she'd raped Sam—the two men, unbeknownst to each other, might each suspect they were the papa. Nearly as bad would be the lies she'd have to tell Etta. Could Asami somehow blame her pregnancy on Brad, telling Etta he'd made a trip to New York City for a secret tryst?

No... Etta would see through that lie. She'd know Asami was covering up for that dreadful night, yet Etta wouldn't know how appalling it had actually been. She'd certainly believe TJ had raped her. In turn, Etta would never forgive Sam for not convincing Asami to go to a clinic in the first place.

Of course, there was always Jiro—dear Jiro. Once she told him about her pregnancy, without hesitation, he'd offer to marry her. Jiro's current lover was married and had sired children. No Japanese laws prohibited homosexuality, but it was rarely discussed. Gay men and lesbian women struggled because of Japan's strict family and gender roles. An agreement was often reached allowing the homosexual partner to carry on discretely with his or her same-sex partner while maintaining their heterosexual marriage.

In Asami's case, it would be unfair to Jiro. She couldn't share him with another man.

Those troubling thoughts assailed Asami as she padded into the kitchen to make a soothing cup of tea. As it seeped, the aroma transported her back to Tokyo, making her homesick.

Her girlfriend Mao had recently returned there after studying abroad. She'd been in Asami's same condition but had passed the legal abortion timeframe. Until Mao could find a husband, a difficult task indeed, her parents had refused to welcome her back into their family. Mao had accepted a date with one of her parents' recently widowed friends, an ugly man, even older than her papa. His rheumy eyes had narrowed when he'd told her he'd marry her on two conditions: she'd give up her outside career for a lifelong domestic obligation and, on the snap of his fingers, she'd cater to his every whim.

Asami returned to the couch, her cup of tea in hand. Mao had nearly jumped at that chance to become his live-in prostitute and maid. But when she'd come to her senses, and realized her happiness was as important as her parents', she'd forged back into the prejudicial Japanese society, all alone.

Asami's feet tapped, the rhythmic beat matching her breathing's cadence.

Could she do the same?

1988 - New York

Bundled up in a black swing coat, Etta stepped off the elevator into Tripoint's New York sales reception area. An undercurrent of excitement raced through her veins. Her life was about to change.

Almost four years had passed since she'd attended a New York client meeting where Sam Madrid had been present. It had been 1985, nine years after their marathon Miami Beach love-making session. Over those years, she'd had numerous flings with eligible men. Nothing had stuck. Then back in '85, Sam had stopped her in the hall and whispered, "I made the biggest mistake by leaving you."

The passion in his voice had time-warped her back to that tropical lust-filled week, the one she'd never forgotten. Etta had glanced down. There'd been an indentation on his ring finger where his wedding band had been.

Sam's shining eyes had met hers. "My divorce was final this week."

Although it had been stormy outside, the sky had seemed to blaze blue. They'd gone out for dinner and ended up in Sam's bed. Maybe Etta should've played harder to get, but she'd never stopped loving Sam. For the first time, their love-making had felt exceptionally right—and it still did.

Etta hung up her coat. In a conservative black suit, always the safest choice, she entered the reception area's restroom.

That winter of '85, she and Sam had juggled their schedules to discretely rendezvous. When he'd won the Yamada deal, it had had to go perfect. Three years prior, Etta had been promoted to the Chicago branch's Technical Rep Manager position. Etta, he'd decided, would be the best Tripoint employee to manage the project. "The international exposure will leapfrog your career," he'd enthusiastically said, his gray eyes meeting hers as he'd rolled on top of her in bed. "And you won't have to go into that assignment alone. I'll fly in for periodic status meetings and afterward," he'd given her his bedroom smile, "we'll head back to my hotel to confer." He'd told Etta about Asami, how she'd selflessly helped his brother unearth details about his Japanese mother and locate his yakuza brother; how she'd been instrumental in Sam winning the Yamada deal; how, within the turbulent sea of Yamada males who'd expect a similar project lead, Asami would be a welcoming island for Etta.

Sam's claims had all been true.

Etta applied lip gloss in the bathroom mirror as she recalled her final week in Tokyo. When Asami had nonchalantly asked Etta about Sam, it had been obvious that her Japanese friend had formed an emotional attachment to him.

Etta had so wanted to tell Asami about her relationship with Sam, but he and she'd agreed it would be best if their Tripoint colleagues and clients didn't know. They might think favoritism had been involved when Sam had selected Etta for her lucrative overseas assignment. And that could've been the case.

There was an old Japanese saying: *Seek shelter in the shade of a big tree.* Etta knew it hadn't hurt to have friends or, in her case, lovers in high places.

She fluffed her hair and readjusted her headband recalling how, after her return from abroad, that had also held true. She'd been promoted to the Chicago branch management position—the first Tripoint woman to achieve such heights. But that had also meant her long-distance interludes with Sam had to continue.

It had been difficult to keep her love life under wraps, especially from her daughter. Chloe had made no bones about it—she wanted a dad. But Etta had promised Sam she wouldn't reveal their secret until they'd executed their well thought out plan.

That day had arrived.

Sam was going to be announced as Tripoint's V.P. of Operations, and Etta was slotted to assume his New York branch management position. A month later, they'd announce their engagement. Chloe would be thrilled to gain a dad. When Etta revealed Chloe was Sam's biological daughter, he'd surely feel the same.

The previous summer, at the annual Chicago Tripoint Family Picnic, Sam had finally met Chloe. Outside the Lake Michigan pavilion, as seagulls had screeched overhead, her daughter's gaze had bounced between the two of them, trying to read between the lines.

Sam had definitely taken to Chloe asking her about her soccer team, her *Nutcracker* ballet performance, and her favorite pop singers. It hadn't appeared as if he'd seen any of himself in her. Like others, he believed Chloe had been fathered by a guy Etta had met at Northwestern, the one she'd lied about marrying and divorcing soon after.

Etta stepped out of the restroom and smiled at the New York receptionist who would soon be on a first name basis with her. Etta secured a temporary badge then buzzed herself into the noisy bullpen area. The near corner office was Sam's. Its door was shut, but through its window wall, Etta's eyes landed on Asami dressed in a stylish winter white suit. She was seated on a chair facing Sam, his face intent as he nodded and stood.

Asami opened the door. Her eyes looked puffy, as if she'd been crying.

It had been ten days since Etta had tiptoed out of Sam's apartment and left Asami sleeping on the couch. Etta's irritation, over that badly handled situation, still remained—a mosquito bite which continued to itch. She approached Asami. "Honey, it's good to see you, but what's wrong? There wasn't any fallout from TJ's party, was there?"

Asami looked down, her hair covering her face. "No, Etta, nothing like that. It's just difficult to work in the same office as him."

Etta's breath hitched. "You didn't resign, did you?"

Asami shook her head, her fingers fiddling with the buttons on her suit. "I assume you know Tripoint's Tokyo branch is due to open later this month. I convinced Sam, I'd be a great fit." She lifted her chin as if to convince Etta as well.

"I don't understand."

"It's what's best for me. You know TJ's the CEO's son."

Etta was furious. "Is that what Sam told you?"

"No. It was my request."

"But, Asami— "

"Please, listen." She touched Etta's hand. "I've made my decision. You must honor it." She bravely smiled and hurried away.

Steamed and seeing her own shade of red, Etta burst into Sam's office. "So Asami's being banished because of TJ?"

Stress lines cropped up around Sam's mouth and eyes. "You know I can't discuss personnel matters with you."

"Like hell you can't! This isn't right! If nothing happened at TJ's party why does Asami feel she has to leave?" Etta cocked her head. "Or... did something happen?"

"You know as much about that party as I do." Sam's eyes drifted down.

"Look at me! What aren't you telling me?"

His eyes still wouldn't meet hers.

Etta's heart hammered, a steady rhythm, filling her ears. "What's going on?"

He stood and walked around the desk. "We can't get into this now. The announcement meeting's due to start." He grabbed her hands. "Etta, this is the moment we've been planning for years."

She yanked her hands away. "Don't change the subject. What happened that night? What aren't you telling me?"

He gave a nervous sort of laugh and looked out toward the bullpen. "I saw you talking to Asami. What did she say?"

Etta's eyes widened. "Are you saying something happened between the two of you?"

He reached for her.

"Dammit!" She pushed him away. "What happened?"

"I can't tell you."

"Was it after I left?"

He averted his eyes.

Etta's hand covered her mouth. "Did you sleep with her?"

"It's not what you think."

She backed away. "My God! Did you two have sex in the sheets I'd just left?"

"Listen Etta, I honestly thought Asami was you. I didn't hear you leave. The bedroom was dark. She'd even washed her hair with your shampoo. Believe me, it was all a mistake, a—a dreadful mistake!"

"Mistake!" Tremors gripped Etta's body. "No way!"

"Christ! I shouldn't have told you. I promised Asami I wouldn't. She had no idea you and I were seeing each other. Once I told her, she was devastated. Of course, so was I. Please, Etta, I'm so—"

"Stop!" She held up her hand. "Nothing you can say will make me believe you weren't a party to what occurred." Tears filled her eyes. "We had such plans. How could you have destroyed them all?"

"Be rational. This is not what you think. I have no feelings for Asami."

"So that makes it okay?"

Bitter and heartbroken, Etta stumbled out of Sam's office.

-19-

Tuesday - Tokyo

The Roppongi playground disappeared behind Asami as she stepped inside the Kingo Club's lobby. Beside her were Jiro and Detective Hondo. Asami was nearing her meltdown level. She'd hardly slept, hardly eaten, hardly exercised, all triggers, often causing her to explode.

Jiro knew that as well. She'd admitted to him she'd skipped her med-check appointment. He squeezed her hand and whispered, "Take deep breaths, my dear. There's a good chance both Haruki's yakuza brother and my politician friend will be here. If I'm right about the latter, when he discovers you and I are friends, I'm certain he'll tell us everything he knows."

Asami clung onto Jiro's arm. "Years ago, you and I remained in this reception area while Haruki met his yakuza brother. I refuse to do the same. I need to hear firsthand any information about Hana."

Asami had called her daughter's friend Lucas before leaving the Presidential Suite. The fact that Hana was no longer in Japan had shocked him as well. "I'll change my focus, Fujioka-san. New York's my home town. My friends there will help me locate Hana's whereabouts—possibly at that place you called Hiro House. Until then, I'll make sure Satu is fed and watered."

His kind words, and his ongoing assistance, stirred Asami's heart. She could see what her daughter saw in him.

Asami was booked on the first flight into New York. Jiro had wanted to accompany her, but she'd refused his offer. "That makes no sense. As soon as I land, I'll join forces with Etta and the U.S. authorities. Also, with all your connections, you might be able to uncover Hiro House's location while I'm in the air. Even if Hana's not there, we can at least rule it out."

In the end, Jiro had reluctantly acquiesced to her wishes.

Asami's departure time was 8:50 a.m.—almost ten hours away. That added to her current frustration. Because the flight time *and* time change were nearly identical, she'd land at LaGuardia at about the same time as she'd taken off. Tripoint's IPO stock release would occur approximately twenty-four hours later. If that event was the carrot being used to extort money, she had very little wiggle room to locate Hana.

Asami followed the two men into the smoky club. From an ornate desk, the club's mama-san ruled. Her piercing eyes, within her pale-powdered face, lit up at seeing a famous man like Jiro.

He bowed then spoke to her.

Asami jiggled back and forth, from one foot to the other. The woman was frowning and shaking her head. *Oh no!* Maybe neither Haruki's yakuza brother nor Jiro's politician friend were inside! But that was not it. Apparently, Jiro's friend *was* at a table. The woman's negative attitude was due to Asami's presence. But when Sergeant Hondo also showed her his badge, she finally motioned to one of the females standing behind her. "Take these gentlemen and," she scowled, "this woman to booth twenty-six."

Asami was in! She and the two men followed the hostess across the soccer-field-sized room lit by flashing lights and glowing cigarettes. The Kingo Club was filled with men, each seated beside their designated hostess. The politician, coddled by his own, sat at a burgundy banquette, his dark hair parted in the center, his face thin, his chin pointed. Dark framed glasses were set low on his narrow nose.

Jiro stepped forward and bowed. "How are you my friend?"

The politician inclined his head down and lifted it. "Quite well, Kishima-san. And you?"

"Not so good. Please, I need a moment of your time." Jiro introduced Asami and the detective.

The politician's cheeks twitched. He motioned for his hostess to leave while the men slid onto the circular bench seat surrounding the glass table. Asami slid in last.

Sergeant Hondo tented his fingers. "I understand you recently attended a party at the Palace Hotel's Presidential Suite." His stern eyes zoned in on the politician.

Asami's feet tapped. Biting her tongue, she forced herself to listen.

Hondo reviewed what they'd seen on the hotel video footage, including the politician's arrival and departure times. "That night, a health shop worker by the name of Chika Himura drowned. Can you tell me how that occurred?"

Asami's hands gripped each other.

The politician's did the same to his cocktail tumbler.

Jiro implored, "My friend! You must talk."

Asami finally spoke up. "Please! My daughter's life is at stake."

He lifted his glass, drained it, and finally said, "First, you must understand, I had no part in that woman's death."

Jiro said, "I believe you. Just tell us what you know."

His friend gave a resigned nod and his words spilled out: how he and a number of other guests had been out by the Presidential Suite's pool. How among those had been Tripoint's CEO. "Thomas Pollard seemed to be a fine man, but he had an eye for the women—both that health shop worker and a young Japanese business woman."

Asami slid her cell toward him. Hana and Chloe's photo was on the display. "Is this the Japanese business woman? She's my daughter, the one on the left."

He squinted at the photo. "I believe so. That Western female was also there. They both left the pool area, but your daughter returned. She told Pollard she needed to talk to him in private and they stepped off to the side."

Asami teetered on the bench seat. "Could you hear what they were saying?"

"No, but the exchange seemed heated. That's when an obnoxious gaijin joined them. I later discovered he was Pollard's son. About then, I left to refresh my drink."

"So my daughter was still talking to both Pollards by the pool?"

He nodded.

Hondo interjected, "What about that health shop worker? Was she there as well?"

"Yes, although she was on the pool's opposite side. But when I returned, she was in it, floating face down. Pollard and his son were also in the water. Your daughter was too. She's the one who dragged that woman out of the pool and tried to revive her." His eyes closed. "It was no use."

Asami's feet stilled. Sergeant Mori had been right! Her daughter knew what had transpired in that pool.

Detective Hondo's brow furrowed. "Do you know whether that woman's death was accidental or intentional?"

"I don't know. Thomas Pollard told me not to worry. He said he'd call the authorities from the bedroom where he was heading to change his clothes." The politician's eyes lowered. "I'm ashamed to say, I didn't stay to make sure that was done."

Asami said, "Listen! That woman's death has to be intentional. Her body would not have been secretly removed from the hotel if it hadn't been. And Hana can't be in anyway responsible. She tried to revive that woman. One of the Pollards must be the guilty party."

The detective's gaze met hers. "You may be right." He refocused on the politician. "I assume, since you're at this Wada-kai owned club, you probably know the yakuza gangster Kato Endo?"

"Yes. He was at Pollard's party, also out by the pool. Unlike me, he probably witnessed that woman's drowning."

The politician turned toward Asami. "Your daughter was extremely upset. The Western woman had joined her. They were both trying to leave, but Endo had blocked their way. He told your daughter she had to stay to talk to the authorities. But she refused to do so without Tripoint's COO being present. Instead, your daughter told Endo she'd contact the police once she arrived back at her apartment."

The detective frowned. "I bet he didn't like that idea."

"No. That's when I intervened and managed to escort the two women out of the suite, and down to the lobby, where we parted ways." He gave the detective a pleading look. "I swear that's all I know."

A hostess approached and crouched down beside Asami. "Is that Jiro Kishima, the movie star and director?"

Asami nodded while giving her a questioning look.

"When you arrived, I overheard him asking about that yakuza gangster Kato Endo."

Asami's shoulders tensed. "Do you know where we might find him?"

"Yes. If your famous companion will give me his signature, I'll show you where Endo lives."

Tuesday - New York

Sam's assistant escorted Etta into his executive office. In a navy suit, he sat behind a mahogany desk, a potted ivy plant on its corner, the greenery creeping down. The freshly watered earthy aroma mixed with Sam's distinctive scent.

Etta had changed into the dress she'd packed for the theater, a belted red jersey with black buttons down its front. It had been a gift from Chloe. "Mom," she'd said, "the color looks fantastic on you. I know you can't tell, but trust me. You'll turn all sorts of gray heads."

How she'd miss her daughter's candor...

As Chloe had predicted, Sam's appreciative eyes zoned in on Etta. That should've made her happy, but how could she be when suspicion was muddling her brain? How could she trust Sam when his name kept spiraling back into Chloe and Hana's horrific equation?

Etta sat down on the padded chair across from him. She had to put Sam on the spot. "At the Bliss Café, you tried to reach your brother. Has Haruki returned your call?"

"No. I've also texted and emailed him. I've contacted his assistant as well. She has no idea where he is."

"Well I know."

Sam seemed genuinely surprised, yet in business negotiations, he'd often act the same, even when a client's response had been expected. Sam was adept at hiding his strategy, only revealing it at the opportune moment, to create the most impactful effect. He knew how to win a client over—just as he might be attempting to win Etta over.

Nevertheless, she plowed on. "Haruki's here in New York, but he's not alone. Just hours ago, he passed through customs with Hana Fujioka."

Sam's forehead creased. "I don't understand. Are you saying my brother located Hana?"

"No. I believe he's actually involved in her disappearance."

"What? What do you mean?"

Etta studied Sam's face again. His perplexed look rang true. "It appears as if Haruki stumbled into a terrible situation—one which his yakuza brother and he are now using to their advantage." Etta relayed the Japanese politician's information, secured from Asami's last call, how one of the Pollards could be responsible for that health shop worker's drowning.

"That can't be!"

"Well nothing else makes sense."

Sam kept shaking his head while Etta told him about Kato's current Wada-kai job. How he looked for dirt on high-profile corporate executives. How he used that information as blackmail fodder. How the Pollards' situation would've been right up his alley.

"Fuck!" Sam sprung to his feet and began to pace. He'd only used that sort of language, on rare occasions, when he'd lost control of a situation. Had his agitated state been caused by the Pollards' damaging news—or by the fact she'd uncovered it and placed Tripoint's IPO in jeopardy?

Sam strode past Etta. "Ever since my brother discovered he had a yakuza brother, Kato's been a fucking thorn in my side. And this tops it all! But Haruki can't be involved, at least not willingly."

Etta stared up at Sam. Although he was defending his brother, that could still be Sam's strategy, to earn her trust.

He collapsed back onto his chair. "Haruki's always tried to win Kato's approval, but on Thursday night, my brother and Hana had this special rapport. It was evident he cared for her."

"Then tell me, why would Haruki have arrived here in New York with Hana? If he's as innocent as you want me to believe, why hasn't he returned your calls or texts?"

"I don't know."

"Hana must be the bargaining chip. She knows which Pollard drowned that poor woman. That's why Hana's more valuable alive than dead. What's more, I'm quite certain Chloe was planning to report that drowning incident to Tripoint's HR department."

Etta had been unravelling the facts, but she'd saved her biggest reveal for last. "I also believe Haruki's connected to Chloe's death."

Sam's face screwed up. "I don't understand. How could Haruki's actions be related to Chloe's suicide? Unless—wait!" Suddenly the meaning behind her words took root in his face. "Are you saying her death was not a suicide?"

Etta stared into his troubled eyes. "I believe Chloe was murdered."

The shocked look on his face seemed authentic.

"Tell me Sam," she took a deep breath, "where were you the night Chloe died?"

It was agonizing to watch his face transform, the hurt and disappointment crushing his features. Yet that Otis guy's left hand was still branded inside Etta's head.

"Christ, Etta! How could you think I had anything to do with Chloe's death? You asked me to mentor her. But—but it turned into far more than that." His voice caught. "I'd grown to love her—like a daughter."

"I know Sam. She told me."

"Then how could you ask me that question?"

"Believe me, I didn't want to. Please, just tell me."

He gave her a bitter smile. "You know your former Chicago colleague, Neil Thompson, who now works in New York?"

She nodded.

"On Saturday night, he and his wife had a dinner party. The gathering broke up at about midnight. That's when I left with about five other guests. Of course, you can verify that."

She could, but she wouldn't. She knew he was telling the truth.

Etta reached for Sam's hand. "Please, forgive me. It was wrong for me to think you had anything to do with Chloe's death. But I've been so confused." She told him about the elevator panel, the Otis man, Chloe's laptop. "And right before I arrived, Neil's assistant called. She said he'd run into some snags. Even if Chloe's Friday backup existed, it'd take him a few days to provide it to me."

A stony expression sullied Sam's face. "Someone must've roadblocked Neil. If Chloe's laptop *was* backed up, I promise you, we'll get that image copy."

* * *

Sam placed the reloaded laptop loaner on his office's conference table. He'd been true to his word. He'd gone directly to the horn-rimmed-glassed technician. Chloe's laptop *had* been backed up on Friday night, and the tech had performed his magic.

Etta booted up the laptop, Sam seated beside her, and she entered Chloe's password, praying she was right. For that HR meeting, her daughter had to have created a word document, one to provide Etta some answers.

It was excruciating to wait until she could double click on the documents' folder. Inside were the same five folders. She clicked on the one titled "Memos" and her heart leapt into her throat. "Look! The first document was authored on Friday, the day Chloe flew back from Tokyo. It was missing from her Saturday laptop image."

Sam pushed back his chair. "Let me get my reading glasses."

She grabbed his arm. "No. I can't wait. I'll read it to you." Her voice raced through the first half of Chloe's memo until she reached that Thursday night's crucial events, the ones Hana had revealed to Chloe after leaving the party:

"Hana told me, when she returned to the pool area, in search of her purse, Tom Pollard was there. Just a few weeks earlier, he'd sexually harassed Hana in New York—"

"Fuck!" Sam's voice exploded.

"I know... it's disgusting. I just found out." Etta pulled the laptop closer and read on:

"Hana decided to confront Tom Pollard about that incident. But as she initiated that conversation, his intoxicated son joined them. That was when both Pollards started to physically hassle Hana..."

"Christ!" Sam shook his head.

"Poor Hana." Etta couldn't help but visualize that frightening situation as her voice continued:

"Hana said she slipped and fell into the pool, as did both men, but that didn't stop Tom Pollard's sexual advances. While his son clung onto the pool's edge, a Japanese female guest jumped in to help Hana. Tom Pollard turned his attention on that guest, and he drowned her in the process."

"Fuck!" Sam rubbed the back of his neck as if attempting to knead out that sordid revelation. "What a mess!"

Etta closed her eyes and nodded. They finally knew the truth. *God!* She also knew it was her fault. "If I'd only reported Tom Pollard, none of this might've happened."

Sam looked confused. "What do you mean? Reported Tom for what?"

She finally laid bare her ancient Plaza Hotel incident and Tom's retaliating punishment.

"Oh Etta, why didn't you tell me?"

"Maybe I should have. But that was the seventies. Sexual harassment laws didn't exist. Then you became my manager and everything changed." She hesitated. "However, in the eighties, we both should've reported our suspicions about TJ."

His body tensed. She knew she'd hit a nerve.

"Just think." Etta placed her hand over his. "If Tom or his son had been reported, and one or both had suffered some consequences, Chloe might still be alive."

-20-

1988 - Tokyo

Asami arrived at the Narita International Airport immigration counter. An uneasy feeling drifted inside her like soupy morning fog. Soon it would dissipate to reveal the fraud she'd become. Dressed in a soft heather belted tunic, leggings, and three inch heels, she handed her passport to the agent. In the prior two weeks, she'd aged five years, no longer the fresh-faced girl in the photo, the one who'd been eager to start her new life in America.

Not telling Etta the truthful reason behind her transfer request had been painful, like sticking bamboo slivers under her fingernails and letting them fester. But it had been the first phase of her shameful plan. How could she have admitted she was pregnant, and she didn't know whether the father was Sam or TJ?

In addition, she'd decided to keep the baby.

To steady herself, Asami grabbed the escalator's handrail and headed up to the second floor baggage claim area.

Once her decision had been made, it would've been impossible to hide her on-going pregnancy from her New York colleagues. She also hadn't had the luxury of handing in her resignation. Without Tripoint's sponsorship, she would've been sent back to Japan anyway. Her best option had been to stay gainfully employed at Tripoint's Tokyo branch.

By working for a gaishikei, Asami would ironically have the best chance to succeed in Japan. The foreign affiliate branches of Western companies, most often, adopted non-discriminatory hiring policies which mirrored their Western counterparts. Gaishikei were "the Messiah" for Japanese women who'd studied abroad. Asami had unwittingly fallen into that opportunity.

She noted her flight number on the overhead baggage claim monitor and approached the proper luggage carousel. After she loaded her two bags onto a luggage cart, she proceeded toward customs, her fingers tapping the cart's metal handle.

Tripoint had built a proprietary communication system for their employees and for those at Pollard Property Group. Back in New York, she'd carefully authored an electronic note, addressed it, taken a deep breath, and pressed send—executing phase two of her plan.

Asami reached Narita's arrival lobby and her eyes searched the crowded area. It took a second pass before she recognized Haruki, his goatee and thin mustache things of the past. Filled with a mixture of relief and guilt, Asami called out and waved. Her red lips curved into a bewitching smile and hives broke out on her neck.

His face expanded into a look of wonder, as if gazing at Tokyo's Disneyland Castle for the first time, his Cinderella within reach. Haruki had possibly perceived he'd revealed too much for by the time he reached her side, he'd assumed a casual expression. He bowed, even addressing her as Asami-san. "It's so good to see you," he said in Japanese. "I can't believe it's been nearly three years."

She wrapped her arms around him and breathed in his soap and sunshine scent. Humiliated by what she was about to do, she pulled away and gazed into his startled blue eyes. "Ever since that week, when we hunted for your Japanese mother and brother, I've thought about you, the kinship we formed."

He was at a loss for words so Asami charged on. "I recently had dinner with your American brother and all he did was talk about you."

At Sam's mention, the corners of Haruki's mouth had drifted down. It appeared as if that same friction existed between the two men.

"I understand you graduated from NYU, landed a job at PPG and, as I can see, are now fluent in Japanese." She smiled. "I knew you'd succeed if you put your mind to it."

He modestly shrugged. "Yes, but it took long enough."

She squeezed his arm. "Not that long. When you moved here, Sam said you'd hoped to reconnect with your Japanese brother and—and me." She gave him a shy smile. "I guess fate made this happen."

Once again, he was tongue-tied.

"I also understand, I'll be working in the same building as you."

His posture relaxed as if he'd landed on safer ground. "Yes, but I'm rarely there. Real estate prices keep increasing. Yet everyone is still buying due to Japan's credit expansion. If PPG doesn't act fast, we'll lose out."

Asami laughed. "Look at you! You've come a long way from your bartending jobs."

He grinned. "I have, haven't I?" He picked up her bags.

She looked sideways at him and flushed as they climbed onto the escalator to reach the lower train station level. She was tricking him. Haruki wasn't Sam, he wasn't Brad, but he was a kind and half Caucasian man. The latter was extremely important. Her goal was to make him love her. Chances were, he already did. Could she learn to love him back? Her parents' marriage had been arranged. It hadn't mattered whether they'd been attracted to each other, only that they'd come from families of equal standing.

Asami touched her belly. She couldn't wait for a love match either. There wasn't enough time.

She stepped off the escalator and peered up at the signage, attempting to keep her nails away from her neck. "When I last saw you, I was living with my aunt and uncle. Now I want my own apartment. The Kichijoji neighborhood, near Inokashira Park, is where I'd like to live. I'll find a hotel in that area and begin my search tomorrow."

He shook his head. "You helped me three years ago. I insist on repaying that favor. Until you find a suitable place, you can take my bedroom and I'll sleep on the couch. Believe me, it's no big deal."

Asami clasped her hands together and gave him a dazzling smile, her hives cooling. "That would be wonderful!"

Haruki's offer would make it far easier for her to execute the third and final phase of her plan. It shouldn't take more than a few days to get Haruki back into his bed—with her in it as well. Two weeks later, she'd feign the Japanese reluctance to use birth control as the excuse for her pregnancy. She'd explain how she'd never save face unless they got married.

Asami was certain he'd agree.

She'd fill out the paperwork and file it. No marriage ceremony was required. On her first day at work, she'd introduce her new husband to her new Tripoint colleagues. As her pregnancy showed, nobody would question whether the baby was his.

Especially, Haruki.

1989 - Tokyo

It was a perfect Indian summer day. An Inokashira Park attendant helped Etta and her thirteen-year-old daughter out of a rowboat. Last was Asami who grunted while holding her very pregnant belly. "I didn't realize how difficult that would be. Now I need a restroom." She waddled off dressed in a fashionable maternity jumper and, for once, sensible flats rather than heels.

Etta dug inside her purse and pulled out some yen handing it to Chloe. Under maple and zelkova trees, bursting with russet, gold, and green, the air was filled with a sweet and salty scent. "The shop where we rented our rowboat is known for its kettle corn. Why don't you get a few bags and Asami and I'll join you there."

Chloe readily took off, her eyes focused on a cute Japanese boy headed in that direction.

It had been three years since Etta and her daughter had spent those memorable years in Tokyo—and about nine months since that fateful night in New York City. On a nearby park bench, a young couple held hands, their intimacy drawing Etta back to that night in Sam's bed. Amid their love-making, and Asami's snores, Etta had worried about her friend. Etta had known that initial discussion with Asami, concerning TJ's party, would be Sam's responsibility, not hers. Etta's flight back to Chicago had been scheduled for 6:30 a.m. to enable her to attend her daughter's ballet recital.

If only Etta hadn't tiptoed out of Sam's bedroom.

If only she'd attempted to rouse Asami rather than simply planting a kiss on her forehead.

If only...

Ten days later, Dad's lifelong influence had controlled Etta's miserable encounter with Sam. She'd created an internal measurement system—disgustingly an off-shoot of Dad's—one which others needed to stack up to. In that moment, in Sam's office, in the heat of her anger, Sam hadn't met the high expectations she'd set for him. She knew she should've believed him, trusted the episode with Asami had been a mistake. Although, just days later, when Etta had calmed down and had thought things through, reconciling herself to that fact, it had been too late. Her window of opportunity had disappeared. Another Tripoint employee had been promoted to the New York branch management position.

A bicycle chime interrupted Etta's thoughts and she stepped aside to let two young girls on Little Kitty bikes pass. Etta smiled, recalling her daughter at that age. Asami had so much to look forward to. Her friend's life had certainly changed since Etta had last seen her.

Soon after Asami's Tokyo departure, Etta had received an email from Asami: *Sam's brother and I are getting married! Sam told me Haruki had taken a job here, and he'd hoped to reconnect with me—and reconnect we did!*

Then three weeks later, a second email had arrived. Asami's words had been bursting with excitement as she'd shared her pregnancy news, but the email had ended with a question, one Etta had been prepared for. Asami had discovered Sam and Etta had broken off their relationship. *Why, Etta-san? Why?*

It was too difficult, Etta had typed back, lying through her fingertips. *I was in Chicago. He was in New York.*

Asami's response of, *Etta-san, you can still make it work!* had sounded frantic, undoubtedly motivated by guilt. If Etta had been in Asami's shoes, she would've been feeling the same—especially if she'd believed the two people she truly cared about had split up—all because of her.

But that wasn't the main reason Etta couldn't be with Sam. A New York friend had told her, just days after Etta's blowup with him, he'd hooked up with a female lawyer friend and their relationship had turned serious overnight.

That news had brought Etta to her knees. It was as if he'd been getting even with her, purposely adding salt to her self-inflicted wound.

What a mess she'd made of her life!

As a grinning Asami waddled back to her side, Etta couldn't help but wonder whether her friend was carrying Haruki's child. But what did that matter? Etta was happy for Asami. Although it had taken months of internal turmoil for her to reach that point—to recognize she couldn't give up Asami as she'd given up Sam. Asami, who'd had sex with him, and possibly TJ, all within a few hours, seemed contented while Etta was filled with remorse.

She shook off her self-pity cloak and linked her arm with Asami's. "Let's go find Chloe and, on the way, you can tell me about your pregnancy." As they started off, Etta could vividly recall hers. At Northwestern, while she'd flashed her fake wedding band, her belly protruding, her MBA classmates had treated her with care, much like surrogate siblings. Only her pledge sister had known Etta had been living a lie. And after all those years—*shit!*—she still was.

"Well..." Asami's voice drew her back, "my pregnancy's been, as you would say, "a piece of cake,' but my work focus, without medication, has been difficult."

"I bet that's been hard, but the end is nearly in sight. It's so exciting! You'll have three months of maternity leave to enjoy your new baby. What are your plans after that? Will you be returning to work?"

"Yes, but most of our Tokyo clients will probably disapprove. They'll condemn me for not solely assuming the honored mother and rice cooking hag roles—just like their wives."

Etta burst into laughter and Asami joined in. It felt good, just like the old days, before Etta's high-handed righteousness had dashed away her future with Sam.

Up ahead, Etta's eyes located Chloe who was indeed talking to the teenage boy. Her daughter had learned far more Japanese than Etta had during their earlier stay. "So..." Etta's gaze returned to her friend. "What about Haruki? Does he support your return to work?"

"Yes. He knows I wouldn't be fulfilled if I didn't resume my career."

"How lucky for you. I only met him that one time, back in the seventies, at that New York disco, but he seemed to be very kind and," she elbowed Asami, "very sexy!"

Her friend laughed. "My co-workers say Haruki's an anomaly. He looks mostly Japanese and speaks Japanese, but he's still an American. Japanese men often call white men *ketō*—hairy barbarians—but Haruki isn't the standard white guy. He's a wonderful mixture of both cultures."

Etta stared into Asami's bright eyes. Her friend's marriage may have been one of convenience, but it had blossomed into one of true substance.

How Etta envied her.

Asami suddenly reached for her belly and cringed.

A gush of liquid ran down her legs and onto the brick path.

Astonished, Etta gazed at her friend.

Asami's eyes were wide and her lips parted in a look that could only be called fear.

Etta squeezed her hand. "Honey, you're having your baby! Don't worry. I know just what to do."

1989 - Tokyo

The light coming through the Kichijoji Minami Hospital room's windows glowed like a halo around Asami's daughter's head. "My sweet child." Asami touched her tiny nose. "Why won't you eat?"

A new mother and baby's hospital stay was normally five days. It had been three since Haruki and Asami had welcomed their precious *aka-chan*—little red one—into the world.

She traced her finger down her daughter's soft cheek, a blend of wonder and foreboding running through Asami's veins. After her painful delivery, she'd convinced herself everything would be perfect. She'd given birth to her dear little girl—not so little actually at seven pounds eleven ounces—far larger than Haruki had expected.

Asami had wanted him to be in attendance for the birth, yet she couldn't provide him her truthful due date. New properties were being developed in Yokohama, Nagoya, and Osaka. He'd been in the latter the day her water broke, a four-hour train ride from Tokyo. Etta had luckily been able to reach him, and he'd arrived for the final six hours of Asami's labor—the most difficult segment. At every contraction, Haruki had pressed on the small of her back and instructed, "Breathe, Asami-chan, breathe."

He'd been an amazing coach, but he'd also been worried. He'd kept murmuring, "Our baby's so early. I hope there won't be issues." Gratefully, he'd been speaking in English and the nurses hadn't known what he'd been saying.

Their child had eventually struggled out, her little fists swinging, her voice wailing. Even before she'd been cleaned, her stunning multi-cultural features had shown through: black tuffs of hair, pink skin, black eyes, and double lids. They'd chosen a name for her—Hana—just like the song which still found a home in Asami's head and heart. Back at university, she'd often imagined what her life might become.

She'd reached one of its pinnacles.

But for three days, Hana had refused to nurse. Asami had diligently been trying to coax her child's tiny puckered lips toward her breasts. Instead of latching on, she would fall asleep.

Asami placed her hand over her daughter's fast-beating heart. "Hana-chan, why won't you eat?" The door opened and Dr. Akimoto and Haruki entered, stress lines on her husband's unshaven face. Poor Haruki. He'd spent three nights in the hospital's waiting room refusing to leave until Hana took some nourishment.

The doctor looked up from his clipboard. "The latest bilirubin tests have come back. Initially your daughter had mild anemia, but it's reached a severe level. A transfusion would help."

An overwhelming fear for the small person whom Asami had already come to love, more than herself, made her feel utterly helpless. Her hand found Haruki's. "Is Hana's condition life-threatening?"

The doctor said, "No. She has hemolytic disease of the newborn. Right now, she doesn't have enough red blood cells to carry oxygen through her body. In a few weeks, she'll begin to make her own cells. Until then, a transfusion would ease the stress on her heart and other organs. That'll strengthen her and she should begin to eat."

Asami calmed her breathing as she looked down at her sleeping child. "Why did this happen?"

"Your daughter and you have incompatible blood types. Yours is A. Hers is B. Your body produced antibodies which attacked her developing red blood cells."

Haruki's hand continued to grip Asami's. "She's so little. How will the transfusion be given?"

The doctor explained how the nurse would be gentle. How she'd place a small catheter into Hana's umbilicus area and locate a vein. How the donor's blood would be slowly run through an IV line attached to the catheter. How Asami could even hold Hana during the process.

Dr. Akimoto turned to Haruki. "As the father, you can be the donor, if you so wish. Your blood type will be either B or AB, two of the three types compatible with your child's."

Confusion supplanted the worry on Haruki's face, and Asami froze.

"I—I don't understand." Haruki's puzzled eyes darted toward her. "If I'm Hana's papa, how can my blood type be O?"

Asami's chin sunk to her chest, her shameful lies crushing her. How had she stooped so low? All her life she'd had issues. She'd been anxious, disorganized, needy, and literally, as Etta would say, "a pain in the ass," but she'd never been cruel and manipulative. Her inbred Japanese mores had driven her that way. Rather than telling the truth, and dealing with her shame, she'd chosen a deceitful path. She should've realized Haruki would find out. How could she not have grasped he'd suffer for her lies?

* * *

Asami's mama often said, "Blossoms bring storms." Misfortune had indeed been looming. What should've been a joyous occasion, especially since Hana had started to nurse, had turned into a funeral-like atmosphere. Haruki had lost the daughter he'd believed was his. The child he'd already cherished had been devastatingly ripped from his arms.

In her pre-pregnancy jeans, Asami sat on the bed wringing her hands. "I never meant for this to happen."

Etta settled on the bed beside her. "Honey, I know you didn't."

Asami gazed at her friend, the one who'd taken charge as she usually did, packing Asami's bag and loading flower arrangements and potted plants into a box. They'd been gifts from well-meaning friends and delivered, as Etta had said, "Before the shit hit the fan!"

Etta tenderly tucked a strand of hair behind Asami's ear. "I saw Haruki out in the hall. I'm so sorry. He's leaving you, isn't he? But there must be something you can do."

Tears pooled in Asami's eyes. Etta could always read her like a mystery novel: the gnawing on her bottom lip, her busy fingers on whatever caught her fancy, her shoes' constant tap, tap, tap—all clues to her inner feelings. "Oh Etta-san, Haruki can usually let things go. But this, he said, was a very big deal. It couldn't be fixed and, based on the way I deceived him, I don't blame him. He said I only married him so Hana would have a papa. That I've never loved him and, now, he could never love me. But he's wrong! I have truly grown to love him."

"I know. I could tell. In the last few days, every time you talked about Haruki, your face would glow. You've never looked as radiant—not even with Brad."

"That's what makes it even worse. Haruki didn't believe me. But why should he?" Asami clasped her hands. "Oh Etta-san, I—I've got something I must confess. It all goes back to that dreadful night in New York, when you and Sam brought me home from TJ's party, when—"

"Listen Asami, you don't need to tell me." Etta hesitated. "Sam already did."

"He did!" Her cheeks burned.

"Yes. But don't blame him. I forced it out of him."

"Oh Etta-san, you must hate me."

"Don't say that. I admit I was angry and hurt, and I could've continued to churn over that situation, but that wouldn't have changed anything. In the end, I realized I was the one who'd handled it poorly. I never could hate you, but TJ's another story. He's the one who instigated that entire situation." Etta's eyes locked onto hers. "So can you tell me? Do you know whether Hana's father is TJ or Sam?"

Asami's stomach churned. Her toes tapped. She couldn't lie anymore. Even if the truth destroyed their friendship, it had to be said. "TJ's blood type is O—like Haruki's."

It took Etta a moment to absorb her words—to realize, by default, Sam had to be Hana's papa. Etta pulled Asami into a bear hug and whispered, "Thank God!"

It was as if the cart Asami had been pushing had sprung holes and her guilt was trickling out, being absorbed by the rocky path she and Etta had traveled. Instead of condemning her, for having had Sam's baby, Etta was forgiving her, actually rallying for her.

It was far more than she deserved.

Etta released her. "Did you tell Haruki?"

"No." She bit her lip. "I told him Hana was the result of a one night stand with TJ. It would've been far worse if I'd told him, you know, I'd slept with his brother."

Etta placed her cool hands on Asami's cheeks. "My friend, we are more alike than you know."

"What do you mean?"

Etta took a deep breath. "Both of us now have daughters because of one man."

Asami's head jerked back. "I—I don't understand. Are you saying Chloe's papa is also Sam? But that can't be. What about that guy from Northwestern?"

Etta sighed. "He never existed. You and I have both been living a lie."

Asami had been riding an emotional rollercoaster. Once again, it had flung her around the bend, catching her off guard. For thirteen years, Etta had kept the identity of her daughter's papa a secret.

Asami closed her eyes.

She'd be doing the same.

-21-

Tuesday - Tokyo

Asami paced below the Kingo Club's flashing marquee. The hostess with a signed napkin in hand had pointed out a locked door, which provided access to both the yakuza club's second floor business office and to Kato Endo's apartment. It had taken Hondo nearly an hour to secure a search warrant and backup had just arrived.

Asami watched as the two uniformed officers helped Detective Hondo kick down the door. He told the male officer to position himself by the fire escape stairs and for Asami and Jiro to "Stay put," then he and the female officer entered, both of them armed.

Asami's cell rang and she quickly answered it, the name "Etta Martin" on the display. As her friend told her about Chloe's memo, Asami's stomach flip-flopped, a sour taste filling her mouth. She pressed END and staggered back. How could Tripoint's CEO *and* his son have ganged up on Hana? It was inconceivable that the company she worked for, and took pride in, was being led by those men—one a murderer as well.

Jiro reached out to grab her. "What is it?"

Asami told him about Chloe's memo.

He put his arms around her. "Chika Himura's a hero, Asami-chan. She gave her life to save Hana's."

Asami had believed Tom Pollard could've been involved, but the truth was hard to swallow. He'd been the one who'd made that snap decision to do away with her daughter—and Etta's—to selfishly protect himself—as if their daughters' lives meant nothing.

In the shadows, near the fire escape stairs, a movement caught her eye. Someone was crawling out from the second floor window. "Maybe that's Kato!" She pointed at the person racing down the stairs who plowed into the officer hiding in the dark.

Before Jiro could respond, Detective Hondo emerged from the street level entrance. "Hurry!" He waved them in. "You must follow me. The medic van will be here soon."

Asami's eyes widened. "Why is it needed?"

Her question went unanswered. The detective was already charging up the stairs.

Asami bolted up after him, Jiro close behind. Ahead was a door marked "Office." Another led into what had to be Kato's apartment. Following Hondo, Asami dashed inside. She passed a toppled over chair, then entered a hallway and noted an empty bedroom to her left. The detective stepped through the next doorway, as did she, and Asami stopped short, her eyes riveted to the sight on the bed.

The seated female officer was cradling a man's head with one hand and using the other to tip a glass of water into his mouth.

Asami shook her head, utterly confused. "Why—why are you here? Why aren't you with Hana?"

Haruki Madrid shoved the glass away and squinted up at her. "Asami-san? Is that you?" His eyes tried to focus. Dirty plates were scattered on an end table. Scents of takeout food and body odor permeated the room.

She knelt in front of him. "Haruki-san, look at me. Where's my daughter? Where's Hana?"

"I don't know." His voice was weak. "My—my yakuza brother locked me up. But I heard her voice—Hana's voice—through there." He nodded toward the shared wall between his room and the empty bedroom.

"Detective," Jiro said, "what about that guy who escaped through the window. Was that Haruki's brother?"

"No. I'm betting Kato's in New York with Hana, that he used Haruki's passport. From the Palace Hotel video, the two men obviously looked alike."

Shivers cascaded down Asami's backbone and fanned out to her extremities. "If my daughter's with that gangster everything changes!"

Haruki leaned in toward her. "Hana's in danger. She witnessed a woman's drowning. She—"

"Oh Haruki-san, I know. Etta just called me. Her daughter's memo named Tom Pollard as the guilty party."

Haruki placed his head in his hands as the paramedics rushed in. One attached a bag of fluids to a portable IV pole. The other sterilized Haruki's arm and inserted a needle to start a drip.

Asami touched Haruki's hand. "When you returned to the Presidential Suite, after you and Sam took TJ to Sam's room, what did Kato say?"

"That Hana and Chloe had left, and that was a big problem. I didn't understand what he meant until I saw the dead woman beside the pool. I told him to call the police."

"Did he?"

"No, he just sneered at me and pulled out a gun." Haruki closed his eyes and rocked. "My brother, the one tied to me by blood, showed me his true colors. Why did I believe he cared for me? Sam's my true brother, the one who's always been there for me, even when I treated him so poorly. Why did I discredit him for so many years?"

"Listen Haruki-san, don't fret. Sam knows you love him. Please, you must focus. Open your eyes and look at me."

He did.

"Now, tell me. What else did Kato say? What was he going to do?"

"He was so smug. He said the person who'd hired him—to deal with Hana and Chloe—didn't know the Wada-kai followed an honorable creed."

Hope surged through Asami. She twisted her head and looked up at Jiro.

He squeezed her shoulder just as the street officer and the man who'd fled entered the room.

"This guy works for the Wada-kai." The officer pushed the handcuffed man toward Detective Hondo, the gangster's oily hair plastered to his head, tattoos exposed on his chest where his shirt had been ripped apart.

Through repeated threats, the gangster's story dribbled out. How he'd been stationed inside the Palace Hotel's lobby. "Endo called me and described two women: one Japanese, the other Western. Both had just left the Presidential Suite. He told me I had to make certain the Japanese woman didn't contact the authorities." The gangster said he'd identified Hana and Chloe as soon as they'd stepped off the elevator. He'd then tailed them from the hotel to the train station, and only Hana from there to her second floor Shimokitazawa apartment. Once there, he'd threatened her with a gun. "We entered her apartment together and waited until Endo arrived."

Asami was dismayed. Why hadn't Hana gone directly to the Roppongi police station? But given the circumstances, her daughter had probably wanted to distance herself from Tom Pollard and Kato before doing so. What a mistake!

"When Endo arrived," the gangster continued, "he noticed a framed hiking photo. That gave him the idea for the forest suicide scam." After he'd forced Hana to leave her neighbor a note, to text her mama, and to call her office, he'd collected Hana's hiking gear and they'd dragged her down to Kato's waiting vehicle. "The American woman was also a threat. She'd been staying at the Palace Hotel so we drove back there, but she'd already checked out."

Asami gazed directly into the gangster's shifty eyes. "Listen, I'm that Japanese woman's mama. I'm also that American woman's friend. Did Kato contact someone in New York to take care of her? Hiro Endo by chance?"

"How—how did you know?"

Haruki looked confused. "Asami-san, what are you talking about?"

She gripped his hands. "It's very bad news. Chloe—Chloe Martin's dead."

Haruki moaned, "Could Hana be too?"

Asami shook her head hard. "We *must* believe she's alive."

Tuesday - New York

Sam stared out from his office window into the South Street Seaport District below, his posture stiff straight, his hands in tight fists as if ready to pick a fight. "Christ!" He spun back toward Etta. "Haruki's fucking brother has kidnapped Hana, and they're somewhere in New York."

Etta had placed her cell on speaker so Sam had heard Asami's last call. While Etta had listened, she'd been twisting a strand of hair around her finger, so tight, she'd nearly pulled it out by the roots. Needless to say, the call had distressed her as well.

"Just think, Etta, what would've happened if Haruki hadn't been rescued from Kato's apartment? How could Tom Pollard, the man I've considered to be a brilliant colleague and supportive friend, be behind all this?"

Etta shook her head, her cheeks hot. "And all because of him, my child's dead. It's so wrong, so unjust, so—"

"Etta?" He sat down beside her, his sorrow-stricken eyes gazing into hers.

At that moment, at that very moment, she knew that Sam knew.

His hand groped for hers. "Don't you mean our child? The one we both lost? The one we both loved?"

Etta shrank back against the chair. The words she'd wanted to utter, ever since Chloe's birth, had finally been spoken. But rather than eliciting joy, agony's crippling weight was pressing against her chest, constricting her breathing. "When—when did you find out?" she managed to whisper.

"On her last birthday. I joined Chloe and Henri for a celebration drink. That's when I really examined her hair, her mouth, her freckles, all similar to yours, but her eyes and cheekbones had this uncanny resemblance to mine."

She couldn't hold back a sob.

"Oh Etta, I realized she had to have been conceived during that week in Miami—the one I've never been able to forget."

Sam pulled her into his arms, his hand stroking her hair, letting her cry. "Chloe was something, so full of energy and ideas. But, most importantly, she had this selfless compassion for others. She enriched my life far more than Tripoint ever has. I only wish I'd known she was mine as soon as you knew. Why didn't you tell me?"

She drew away, her eyes downcast. "Maybe I should've, but I was in an emotionally difficult spot. Remember? You'd already decided to move to New York—to work on your marriage."

He sighed. "I do remember."

"I couldn't wave my pregnancy in your face, to guilt you into choosing me over your wife. Maybe my decision was wrong, but you must understand, that's what I believed was right at the time."

"Etta, I do understand."

"I'm glad..." She raised her chin. "So now that Chloe's dead—our Chloe, Tom Pollard *must* pay."

A strange glow filled Sam's eyes. "You told me about that Otis guy. Tom must've provided him that detail about my ring finger habit. If Chloe's death hadn't been deemed a suicide, it was just like Tom to have had a contingency plan. That bastard was going to frame me!"

"I agree. So we've got to locate Hana. She's the only one who can corroborate Chloe's memo." Etta dug inside her purse. "This could be our best bet." She handed Sam the Hiro House business card. "On Asami's call, she confirmed Kato had contacted Hiro Endo. He runs this place. He or someone who works for him probably murdered Chloe."

"Where did you get this card?"

"From Hiro's grandson, Deon Endo."

Sam looked stunned. "Are you saying Deon's grandfather works for a yakuza clan affiliated with Kato's?"

Etta nodded. "Soon after the Yamada Department Stores win, Sylvia Pollard told me you and Tom had established a relationship with Hiro House for Tripoint's Japanese clients."

Sam's brows knitted together. "That's not true. I've never heard of the place. It must've been only Tom's doing."

"Well that's just great!" Etta tried to regroup. "Asami told us about that yakuza creed, the one Kato and Hiro's Wada-kai clans follow." She hesitated. "So why is our daughter dead?"

He frowned, his eyes hooded in thought.

"Sam, we know Kato went to extreme measures to stage Hana's forest suicide by using that woman's body."

He nodded. "But in Chloe's case, there was only Chloe."

"Yes. And if a Jane Doe's body would've been propped up in the bathtub, Henri and I would obviously have noticed."

"Etta, think about this. Could Chloe's body have been used to stage her own death?"

"What do you mean?"

"When you and Henri saw Chloe—was she possibly alive?"

An astounding feeling spurted through Etta. Could Chloe's death be a sham? Could her child actually be alive? But if she removed her emotions from the equation, and only considered the facts, she knew Sam's premise didn't make sense—and that incredible sensation nose-dived. "I so wish Chloe was alive, but the police and paramedics confirmed she had no pulse. An autopsy was performed."

He gave her a defeated look.

"Sam, listen. We must focus on what we can do. We have Chloe's memo. It proves Tom Pollard's responsible for that Japanese woman's death. We need to report that to the authorities." She located Detective Harper's business card and showed it to Sam. "I'll give her a call."

He abruptly stood. "No. This is too important. I'll print the memo and we'll take it to the station. If Harper's not available someone else will be."

* * *

The cab dropped Sam and Etta off at the Greenwich Village Sixth Precinct. Henri was waiting outside the red brick building, transom windows high across its façade. School had let out so he'd been able to join them.

Henri's dark curls were blowing around his gaunt face, his eyes hard and flinty, just like his voice as he said, "I can't wait to see Tom Pollard behind bars!"

Etta nodded and firmed up her shoulders, then led them inside.

They were all on the same mission.

At the front desk, she told the receptionist, "I have an urgent matter to discuss with Detective Harper."

The woman looked puzzled. "I'm sorry. No detective by that name works here."

"I'm certain she does." Etta pulled out Harper's card and showed it to her. "See, it says Sixth Precinct."

"Well," the woman backtracked. "I could be mistaken. Maybe she's a new hire or a recent transfer. Let me check."

Sam scowled. "Etta, you must've met with Harper inside this station. Can't you explain where her desk is located?"

His question disturbed her. "No, Sam, I can't. This is actually the first time I've been here. All our meetings were at the GV coffee shop or inside Chloe's apartment building."

"That seems strange. Henri, what about you? Did—"

"I'm sorry," the woman's voice interjected. "I've checked the NYPD employment database. There's no record of any Detective Harper in our system."

It was as if a wooden bat had slammed Etta in the gut, knocking the wind out of her. She grabbed onto Sam's arm for support. "What the hell is going on?"

-22-

Wednesday - Tokyo

A laundry cart rolled past Asami, its wheels squeaking in the dimly lit hospital hallway. She and Jiro stood outside Haruki's room at around 2 a.m.

Asami's mind was scattered, fragmented as they talked to Detective Hondo. She listened with one ear, while her mind was attempting to organize all she needed to accomplish before her 8:50 a.m. flight to New York. Haruki's twins had been contacted. Once they arrived, she and Jiro would take their leave.

"Kato Endo committed serious crimes by kidnapping his brother and your daughter," Hondo was saying. "He unlawfully transported and held them against their wills. I'll be able to secure a warrant for his arrest."

Jiro asked, "If he's in New York, how will that work?"

"We have an extradition treaty with the U.S. Its embassy will contact New York authorities. They will provide assistance to capture Kato and return him to Japan. That's if he can be located."

Asami's shoulders felt that "if's" heavy burden.

"Kato will be a fugitive from our government. His passport will be invalidated. If he tries to use his brother's, he will be stopped. His financial assets, here in Japan, will also be frozen."

"By the time I land in New York, will that warrant be in place?"

Hondo's gaze met hers. "I'll make certain it is." He shifted from one foot to the other. "But you must understand, Kato probably knows his brother's been located. The yakuza has lots of eyes and ears."

Asami nodded. "I do understand." She peered into Haruki's darkened room. He appeared to be dozing. During his ordeal, he'd been given food but little water, and he was still hooked up to an IV. His electrolytes had been out of balance causing muscle contractions. The doctor had been worried about kidney failure, but the initial signs were positive.

While Jiro and Hondo continued to converse in the hall, Asami tiptoed up to Haruki's bed.

His eyes opened and he smiled up at her. "It's my morning beauty."

She couldn't help but return the smile. That was what her given name, Asami, meant. Haruki's term of endearment conjured up those idyllic months, prior to Hana's birth, when their projected future as a family of three had still been intact—when nothing but a happy ending had been in sight.

He asked, "How are you doing?"

She touched his hand. "Me? How about you?"

"I'm fine, just fine. It's no big deal. But finding Hana is." He hesitated, his gaze holding hers. "I need to discuss something with you. I should've mentioned it years ago, but I never found the courage."

"That sounds ominous." Asami had kept her voice light, yet his words had made her uneasy.

"It was back in the nineties, at a combined Tripoint and PPG event. That's when I talked to TJ Pollard."

Oh no! Haruki's narrative was heading in a dangerous direction.

"As you know, the Japanese love to talk about their blood types and their related personality traits. That's what TJ and some Japanese colleagues were doing."

She dipped her head, dreading Haruki's next words.

He gently lifted her chin. "TJ's blood type was O. If I wasn't Hana's papa, how could TJ be?"

Her shameful past had reared its ugly head. What must Haruki think? During Hana's pregnancy, and for the past twenty-one years, she'd lied to him.

"That first time we met in Tokyo," he said, "when you helped me search for my mother, I realized you were enamored by my American brother."

Asami's cheeks flushed.

"Then you were hired by Tripoint's New York office and you worked with Sam. After you contacted me, everything happened so fast. I convinced myself it wasn't too good to be true."

Asami sank down onto a chair. It *had been* too good to be true—until those days following Hana's birth. Haruki was still a wonderful man, a compassionate man. If she'd only told him the truth, when she'd initially landed at Narita Airport, the odds were, he would've understood and married her anyway. Given that, her life and her daughter's would've been far different.

"Asami-san..." Haruki's determined voice continued. "It was at that Tokyo event when I put two and two together."

Her fingers frantically picked at the chair cushion's welt.

"I knew Etta had severed her relationship with my brother. I also knew that event had occurred shortly before your arrival in Japan. I figured there was a good chance they'd split up because of you. If that was so," he hesitated, "I realized Hana could be Sam's daughter."

Asami's eyes wouldn't meet his. She'd dug her own grave and deserved to be buried in it. But her selfish worries clawed themselves up to the surface. She had to ask, "Did you ever mention your assumption to Sam?"

"No. It wasn't my place. But I did tell him the reason for our divorce—what I believed was true at that time—that Hana was TJ's child rather than mine. I've never told Sam any different. But—but I'm right about Sam, aren't I?"

She closed her eyes and gave him a miserable nod. The past decades made sense. Sam's career assistance could've been his way of attempting to make amends. He'd believed TJ had indeed raped her and Etta's concerns about that night had been founded. Then there was Haruki. After he'd deduced Hana could be his niece, he'd intentionally worked at developing a lasting kinship with Hana, without revealing Asami's lie. That had been considerate of him, generous.

Why had she erased both men from Hana's life? The brothers were kind-hearted men. That double-dimension would've been a precious gift. Filled with remorse, Asami looked down at her busy hands. She'd pulled Etta and Sam apart, then she'd kept her secret from those who had deserved to know.

Haruki leaned over and touched her cheek. "Please, don't fret. The past is the past. We must focus on the present, on finding Hana. The detective told me you're leaving for New York to continue your search. I wish I could travel with you, but the doctor is against it. On top of that, I still have to figure out how to secure a new passport."

"Even if you could go, I would've refused your offer. Jiro's out in the hall." She glanced that way. "And I told him the same. As soon as I land, I'll join up with Etta and your brother."

"Asami-san... you must know, Sam deserves to know what I know."

She knew Haruki was right.

She gazed into his sincere eyes, those startling blue ones, those which had once gazed back at her from across their bedroom pillows, and she ached for what might've been.

Tuesday - New York

Etta paced inside the Sixth Precinct's lobby. New York's "Most Wanted" photos were on one wall, an American flag on the other. Her mind was speeding. What the hell was going on? How could Detective Harper not exist?

A Hispanic detective stepped into the lobby, a sheen on his pock-marked face. Sergeant Sanchez introduced himself then piloted Etta, Sam, and Henri back to his desk. Before they could even sit down, Etta blurted out the details surrounding Chloe's death. "If Detective Harper's an imposter, her information could be false as well!"

"Let's slow down. Please, take a seat. I'll find the incident report on your daughter's death and see what's going on."

Etta sat down, but she couldn't sit still. While Sanchez poked away at the keyboard, and Henri and Sam threw conjectures back and forth, Etta wiggled on the uncomfortable chair. Inside her head, the prior days' events were spinning out of control. Even if Harper was a fraud, how would that change anything? Her daughter was dead. Nothing could bring her back.

Across the aisle, a uniformed cop was talking to what looked and smelled like a hooker. Loosely sprawled on a chair, the woman seemed to be "high" with no cares in the world.

Etta hunched forward. Wouldn't that be nice?

Sanchez's head popped up, his forehead creased. "I don't know what to tell you, but I can't find any record of your daughter's death."

"What?" Etta straightened up. "That doesn't make sense. They did an autopsy. I saw the report. They—" A thought suddenly crawled into Etta's brain. She fell back in her chair, her palm striking her forehead. "But who is they?"

Sanchez nodded. "Precisely. Can you recall the first responders' names?"

Henri jumped in. "There were two male officers. One was black, the other Asian, but I can't remember their names."

Etta's hands clutched her face as if she could squeeze out that memory... It was no use. "But Henri, those men arrived after you called '911,' right?"

"I was going to, but the black cop was near the elevator. He said he'd overheard our cell conversation and he offered to help."

Sam's eyes narrowed. "He just happened to be on your floor?"

A dismayed look settled on Henri's face. "What a fool I was! The cop said he'd just handled a domestic call down the hall and I believed him!"

Etta laid her hand over his. "Don't beat yourself up. I was deceived as well, especially by Detective Harper."

Sanchez asked, "Can you describe her?"

Etta closed her eyes, picturing the woman. "She's about forty and black, but her skin tone is light and her hair's close-cropped in a pixie style."

The detective prompted, "Anything else? Think hard."

Etta's eyes blinked open. "Oh yes! There's a gap between her front teeth and—"

"Wait!" Sam grabbed Etta's arm. "Your description... it could fit Lorna Endo—Deon's mom."

"Merde!" Henri ran a hand through his curls. "Is this whole thing a scam?"

Etta's eyes sought out Sam's. "My God! Could Chloe be alive?"

Sam's excitement could not be contained. "Listen Etta! You think Hana's at Hiro House. Maybe Chloe is too? It makes sense, doesn't it? You said it's operated by Lorna Endo's father-in-law."

Etta frenziedly dug through her purse and pulled out the Hiro House business card. "Do you know anything about this place?" She slid it across the desk toward Sanchez.

He scrutinized it. "No, but I'll talk to our vice squad lieutenant." Sanchez stood and walked over to an office.

Etta's arms hugged her body. "It's unbelievable. Chloe could actually be alive!"

"I know!" Henri scooted in closer. "Think about this. It's a given that Deon called me from the Rusty Nail. Maybe he's at Hiro House too. He attends Stuyvesant High School. I know the principal. He can certainly find at least one student who has Deon's cell number and—"

"I wish I had better news." The detective frowned, rejoining them. "The lieutenant has no knowledge of Hiro House."

"Shit!" Etta expressed what they were all feeling.

Sanchez resettled in his chair. "Tell me, what were you saying about a cell number?"

Henri explained.

"If you can provide me Deon's number, I'll work with the cell companies. If his phone's powered on and *if* he's inside Hiro House, we'll find its approximate location."

Etta slumped in her chair. "That's a lot of ifs..." They were so close, but not close enough.

"Etta," Sam's brow furrowed as he loosened his tie. "You told me Tom Pollard knows Hiro House's location."

She caught her breath. "You're right, but what if Sylvia told Tom about my discussion with her?"

"Even if she did, remember? Tom's in Chicago. He won't be back until about 9:00 a.m. tomorrow. And also remember, he's the reason we came here in the first place." Sam handed Chloe's accusatory memo to the detective.

Sanchez read it, his cratered face stretched tight. "So Tripoint's CEO drowned that Japanese woman?"

Etta nodded. "When you arrest him, can't you encourage him to disclose Hiro House's location, hinting it might help his case?"

"I'm sorry, I can't arrest him. He's a U.S. citizen who possibly committed a crime in Japan. He's subject to Japan's laws not ours."

Etta pounded the desk. "God! This is so frustrating!"

Henri touched her arm. "Listen Etta. Right now, finding Chloe's our top priority. Forget about Tom Pollard for the moment. We know Detective Harper's a fraud. But think about it. She doesn't know we know. She claimed she knew nothing about Hiro House, yet she probably does. If you call her cell it might go into voicemail, but she'll get back to you."

Sanchez nodded. "Go ahead, Ms. Martin, make that call."

She did, but Harper didn't pick up. Etta took a deep breath. She had to keep her cool. She couldn't tip Harper off at this critical juncture. Etta forced a neutral tone into her voice and left a message, asking the so-called detective to return her call.

* * *

Outside the brightly lit Sixth Precinct Station, hope bloomed inside Etta, its invisible thread tying Henri, Sam, and her together.

Henri tilted his head toward the dark sky. "Instead of looking down on us, I believe Chloe, our Chloe," his voice broke, "is still among us."

Etta wrapped her arm into Henri's. "I believe that too, and—" she hesitated, cautiously gazing over at Sam, "and I believe her dad does as well."

Maybe prior to making that significant announcement, she should've gotten Sam's permission. But when his shining eyes met hers, she knew she'd made the right call. "Yes, Etta, I absolutely believe our daughter's alive."

Henri's shocked gaze volleyed between the two of them and landed back on Sam. "You're actually Chloe's dad?"

Sam nodded and slipped his arm around Etta. "I am."

"Mon Dieu! This is fantastic! Chloe will be doing pirouettes when she finds out... We *must* locate her! I'm going to dash home and try to reach Deon's principal tonight."

The street lamps gleamed like silver dots in the night sky as Henri headed west.

Etta peered up at Sam. "Everything's changed. Now we both share a daughter and we both believe she's alive."

His lips crushed hers. It was like that first passionate kiss in Miami Beach, the one that had led to Chloe's conception, the one Etta had relived literally thousands of times. A shudder slid down her spine. But how could she feel that way? How could she wrap her arms around Sam, feel his perfect fit, a friction of pleasure at every pressure point, when Chloe was out there waiting to be found?

She pushed Sam away. "I've wanted this for so long, but I can't do this now. We must keep looking. There must be another way to find Chloe."

"Etta, what else can we do? We have a good plan. Henri will get Deon's phone number. That Harper impersonator will call you. Detective Sanchez will stay on duty until we locate Hiro House." His hands squeezed her shoulders. "We have to get through these next few hours, and I want to spend them with you."

A few months earlier, she and Chloe had split an order of sesame chicken at the Village's China Bistro. The fortune cookies had arrived at meal's end and Chloe had cracked hers open. "*You cannot love life until you live the life you love*," her daughter had read, then placed that paper strip into Etta's hand. "Mom, this is meant for both of us."

Chloe had been living the life she loved—with the man she loved.

It was time for Etta to do the same.

* * *

The Bryant Hotel room was smaller than an Amtrak berth compartment, but neither Etta nor Sam cared. They'd chosen it over Sam's brownstone because it was within walking distance to the Sixth Precinct.

For days, Etta had been living in the shadows.

A slice of bright light had slipped in.

She gazed up at Sam and felt young again. "Can you handle a bunk bed?"

He laughed. "What do you think?" He kissed her hard, plowing his fingers through her hair, making her shiver.

From the sidelines, Etta imagined Chloe's rambunctious cheers giving her a heartfelt blessing and an absolution from guilt.

Sam pulled back. "God, I've missed you!" His gray eyes met hers. "I seem to remember a suit you had that was the same color as this dress."

She arched her brows and nodded. "My Little Red Riding Hood suit. Thinking back, I guess it attracted the wolves."

He gave her a wicked smile and Etta abandoned any sort of chaste thoughts.

He began to unbutton her dress.

Shit! She suddenly felt modest. When she'd last slept with Sam, she'd been a sleek thirty-five year old woman. Etta grabbed his hands. "I—I certainly don't look the same as I did back in the eighties."

He laughed. "Neither do I."

She grinned. It felt unbelievably good.

The pale moonlight seeped in from the room's tiny window as they slowly undressed each other. Sam directed her toward the lower bunk, taking care not to bump her head as he pushed her down. She felt the warmth of his hands, his urgent breath, his tongue—all intent on pleasing her...

Etta awakened to the sounds of Sam snoring, rain pounding the window, and her cell ringing. It was 7:02 a.m. Chinese takeout scents still hung in the room. On the windowsill were two empty containers. Both had been consumed prior to their second bout of love making.

She crawled off the narrow bed, barely big enough for the two of them, and picked up her cell. "Sam!" She kicked his leg hanging over the bedside.

His sleepy eyes opened.

"Get up! It's that imposter, Detective Harper!"

-23-

Wednesday - New York

Asami jerked awake as the plane jolted down. She reached out to touch her daughter's face, no longer there. On the thirteen hour flight, she'd spent most of it dreaming about the people she'd come in contact with over the past few days. They'd raced around, all jumbled together, until Hana's sweet face had emerged. "Mama," she'd smiled, "I'm okay."

Asami had to believe Hana's words were true—that her dreams were a good omen.

She pulled out her cell and texted both Jiro and Haruki, as promised, to tell them she'd safely landed. While the plane traversed La Guardia's complicated highways, she called Etta.

"Listen Asami!" Etta sounded giddy. "You won't believe this. Chloe could be alive!"

"Alive? Am I hearing you right?"

Amid Asami's elated exclamations, her friend explained what had occurred. "Sam and I are holding our breaths. He told me he recently discovered he was Chloe's dad. He only wished he'd known sooner. Maybe—maybe Sam deserves to know Hana's his daughter as well."

Ever since Asami had shamefully confirmed Haruki's assumption—that Sam was Hana's papa—she'd been turning that same idea over in her head. It would be difficult to tell Sam. But continuing to burden Haruki with her lie was wrong. "Etta-san, I—I think you're right, but first things first. We've got to find our daughters."

"I know. Sam and I are off to meet the woman I formerly believed was Detective Harper. She may have Hiro House's address. I pray to God it's where our daughters might be."

Instilled with newfound optimism, Asami's long flight's wear and tear seemed to vanish. With a bounce in her gait, she passed through immigration, U.S. customs, and located signs for ground transportation. Etta had told her to go to the Greenwich Village Sixth Precinct where Chloe's boyfriend would be. By the time Asami arrived, Etta might already know their daughters' location. The police would storm Hiro House and rescue them. Within hours, Hana would be safely within Asami's arms—Chloe in Etta's.

Asami stepped outside in her heels, quilted jacket, jeans, and a mint-green cashmere sweater, her roller bag trailing behind. The temperature was similar to Tokyo's and rain splashed down on vehicles inching along.

From seemingly out of nowhere, two Japanese men wrapped their arms through Asami's. Before she could even register what had transpired, she was shoved from behind and her body landed in the backseat of a car.

Asami finally screamed, her heart clubbing her chest, as the man seated beside her aimed a gun at her face.

She managed to sit up then jerked around. She had to escape! But another man had already slid in behind her and the door slammed shut.

Pinned in between the two men, Asami frantically thrashed about as the car took off.

What was she to do?

The man to her right gave her a shark-like smirk. "Fujioka-san, I noticed you slept well on our flight." He cocked his head, a purple birthmark exposed on his right cheek.

She gaped at him, at the man she'd repeatedly spotted in Tokyo, the one who worked for the Wada-kai, for Kato Endo. How foolish she'd been! She'd never considered he'd actually follow her to New York. Neither had Jiro.

"Hand over your cell!" he demanded, his eyes black and beady.

Her mind kept reeling. Why had she dissuaded Jiro from coming? If he'd been at her side, the men wouldn't have approached her. Even if they had, Jiro would've protected her. He would've kept her safe. He would've—

"I said, hand over your cell!" The gun moved in closer.

Asami fumbled for it.

"Hurry up!"

Her hands shaking, she did as he'd instructed.

He dropped it on the floor and ordered, "Place your hands behind your back!" He handed the man to her left a roll of masking tape.

Hives exploded on Asami's neck. "Where—where are you taking me?"

"Silence! I said place your hands behind your back!" He waggled the gun in her face.

She finally did and the man with the tape yanked them together before tightly wrapping her wrists.

A burlap hood was slipped over her head, the stench of rancid oil making her gag.

She cried out, her voice muffled, "Where are you taking me?" Tremors charged through her torso and down her bound arms.

There was no response.

What could she do?

What good was she to her daughter and Etta's? Unable to busy her hands, she rocked, the hood's scratchy fabric doing a job on her neck.

They had to be taking her to Hana.

To Chloe.

That was the only good thing.

She'd find her daughter and Etta's.

But not how she'd imagined.

Wednesday - New York

Etta and Sam shared an umbrella. It felt so right. She leaned against his shoulder, her frizzy hair's herbal scent filling their humid quarters. Sam had showered at the hotel and used her razor to shave—just like the old days.

They stood across from the GV Coffee Shop and waited for Detective Sanchez's arrival. Etta had talked to Henri about their change in plans. He'd agreed to wait for Asami at the Sixth Precinct. "If Detective Harper is Deon's mom, she'll be able to provide you his cell number making the Stuyvesant principal's hunt for it unnecessary. Let me know."

Etta watched the so-called Detective Harper jump out of a cab and dash inside.

Sam was dumbfounded. "Your description seemed to match Lorna Endo's, but it's still shocking to see it's actually her. While she cleans my apartment, she's been so forthcoming about her life, sharing personal concerns about her son and her brother. I never thought twice about leaving her alone in my home. Christ! I can't believe she's involved."

A black sedan parked and Detective Sanchez climbed out. He joined them, nodding toward the coffee shop. "Did she arrive?"

"Yeah." Sam frowned. "And she's definitely Lorna Endo."

Sanchez turned toward Etta, a resolute look on his face. "Okay. You and I'll go in first. Mr. Madrid, give us a few minutes, then you can follow. She may get spooked at seeing you."

Lorna Endo was seated in a corner booth, a good distance from the door. It would be hard for her to escape. Etta led the way and Sanchez followed.

"Detective Harper?" Etta said using her take charge voice.

Startled, Lorna looked up as Sanchez flashed his badge. "I understand you're a detective. Can I see your identification?"

Lorna sprang to her feet. She looked like a caged panther, panic in her immense eyes.

His hand clamped onto her wrist. "Not so fast. You're under arrest for impersonating an officer."

While Sanchez read Lorna her rights, Etta glared at the woman, the one who'd tricked her. She should've noticed the signs: Lorna's nervous demeanor, her reluctance to get Sam involved, her combative words when Etta had been overstepping her bounds, and her recommendation that Etta not view Chloe's body in the morgue. That would've been impossible. Her child had never been there.

Sam approached.

At seeing him, Lorna's body crumpled.

Sanchez helped her into the booth, sliding in behind her.

Across from them, Etta slipped in first and Sam followed.

When the waitress came over, the detective held up his badge and waved her away.

Etta's eyes drilled into Lorna's. She needed the truth. So did Sam.

"Help me understand." His voice was intense. "How could you be involved in all this?"

"Oh Mr. Madrid," Lorna started to cry. "I never should've been. It—it's all because of my brother." Tears ran down her cheeks.

"Your brother?" Sam had always been a softie. Lorna had played a major role in Chloe's staged suicide, yet Etta wasn't surprised when he located a clean handkerchief and handed it to her.

Lorna nodded her thanks, dabbing at her eyes. "One of my brother's many addictions is gambling. He owes huge debts to Hiro Endo, my—my father-in-law."

Etta scowled. "Forget about your brother. Just tell me! Where is my daughter?"

Lorna's hands covered her eyes and she sobbed louder.

Fear settled into Etta's belly. She grabbed Lorna's hands, wrenching them from her face. "Where's Chloe? Where's my daughter? She's alive, isn't she?"

It seemed as if Lorna had tuned her out, as if her only concern was to justify her actions. She insisted her brother's life had been at stake. That Hiro had called in his debt. If she and her brother assisted in Hiro's scheme, her brother's slate would be wiped clean. "I initially refused, but my brother got my son involved."

Although there was a motive behind Lorna's madness, Etta didn't care. She shook the woman's arm. "I asked about my daughter?"

"Hiro said you'd believe her death was a suicide."

Etta's breath caught. "So Chloe's alive?"

Lorna moaned and closed her eyes.

Behind Etta's rapid heartbeat was her daughter's. Chloe *had* to be alive. Etta jerked her eyes toward Sam, imploring him to make her talk.

Sam understood. "Listen Lorna," he soothed. "For days, you've told Etta lies. She deserves to know the truth and—and so do I." He hesitated. "Etta's daughter is also mine."

"Your daughter?" Lorna's face caved in. "What have I done?" Her sordid facts finally trickled out. How her brother had entered Chloe's apartment through the panel he'd installed earlier in the day. How he'd injected Chloe with a high-powered sedative and staged her bathtub suicide. How he'd pretended to be one of the cops the next morning. "When he broke in through the window, he kept Mr. Broussard out of the bathroom until he could inject your daughter again, but," Lorna sobbed, "but the drug dosage was too much. When I arrived, she had a slight pulse. By the time the men, dressed as paramedics, took her away, it was too late."

Etta pounded the table. "No! That can't be!"

Lorna reached out and grabbed Etta's hand. "I'm so sorry. She was supposed to live. That was the plan. You know I'm a mother too. I desperately wish your daughter wasn't dead."

Etta yanked her hand away. *Oh God!* Chloe couldn't be dead. For a brief spell, her hopes and Sam's had been resurrected. They'd been plunged into the darkness again. She turned toward Sam and his arms enfolded her.

"Oh Etta..." His anguished voice spoke into her hair.

She clung to him. It was so wrong. After all these years, they'd finally had the chance to love their child together, their Chloe, their compassionate free-spirited daughter who'd now been truly ripped from their arms and flung into the heavens.

Sam pulled away and touched her cheek. "Neither of us wants to believe Chloe's dead, but, Etta, she is. We must channel our grief into something—something that will make a difference. Something Chloe would've wanted us to do. She wrote her memo for a reason. We must locate Asami's daughter, not only for Hana's and her mother's sake but for Chloe's as well."

His words were true, yet everything seemed futile. She slumped against the booth. Through her fog of misery, she tried to follow the conversation. Lorna was claiming she knew nothing about Hana. The whole plan had solely been centered on Chloe. That due to Lorna's and her son's involvement, Hiro had told her they'd both become accessories in Chloe's death.

Detective Sanchez interjected, "So where is your son?"

"With—with my brother. At Hiro House. If I refused to keep up this miserable act, Hiro told me I'd never see Deon again."

At hearing that illusive establishment's name, Etta's mind had snapped back into focus. "So is my daughter's body there as well?"

Lorna grimaced. "I don't know. Maybe so? But you must believe me. That part of my father-in-law's life has always been kept separate from me. I don't know where Hiro House is located. I only know it's here in Manhattan. I'll give you Deon's cell number. You can try to reach him, but he hasn't been answering my calls."

Etta couldn't look at Lorna. She'd helped destroy her daughter. If her child's body *was* inside Hiro House, what state would Chloe be in?

Sam's cell rang, thankfully extracting Etta from her thoughts.

He glared at the display. "It's that bastard, Tom Pollard." Sam turned away to answer.

In addition to locating Hana, revenge for Chloe took hold of Etta. Her daughter was dead because of Tripoint's CEO. A familiar Bible passage came to mind: "an eye for an eye, a tooth for a tooth..." Etta was supposed to turn the other cheek.

That was not going to happen.

-24-

Wednesday - New York

Asami sat in semi-darkness, slowly breathing the burlap hood's rancid air in and out, to calm her racing heart. Her fingers were making no headway at loosening the tape securing her wrists. Japanese *shamisen* music played from the car's speakers: drums, flutes, and three-stringed lutes. She'd been counting the number of songs. Assuming they were each about three minutes long, they'd been driving for about a half hour. They had to be en route to where Hana and Chloe had been taken.

Asami kept picturing the last time she'd seen her daughter. Hana had been sitting beside Chloe at Kimura's, both young women, so full of life. Based on Etta's last call, that could still be the case. She had to hope they were together. That each was assuring the other their mamas would never stop searching until their daughters were found.

The car turned once, then twice, and pulled to a stop. Her ears picked up a text's incoming ding. The door locks clicked and the burlap hood was removed. Asami stole a downward glance at her cell. "No!" she cried out.

The purple-birthmarked gangster sneered at her.

On her cell's screen was Etta's text: *Chloe's dead, my baby's dead...*

Asami shuddered. How could Etta's belief—that Chloe was alive—have done a 360 degree turn in that short segment of time?

The man to her left yanked her out onto the gravel footing of what appeared to be a back alley. The late morning sunlight reflected off his gold front tooth.

Asami stumbled. If Chloe was dead could Hana be too?

No! She quashed that thought like a Japanese beetle.

That couldn't be so.

Her heart, though, went out to her friend. Dear Etta. She'd been given a warm blanket of hope and it had been snatched away, only to be replaced by a second serving of agony.

Would that do Etta in?

It couldn't!

She needed her friend more than she'd ever needed her before.

Directly in front of Asami was a weathered brick building. Two doors were spaced about thirty feet apart, both stenciled with kanji characters. One said "Employee," the other "Delivery."

The gold-toothed man typed a code into a silver keypad outside the "Employee" entrance. Two red lights flashed multiple times, then turned green, and the man pulled the door open.

The purple-birthmarked gangster joined them. He smashed Asami's cell against the adjacent trash can and pitched it in. The two men then pushed her into a short hallway. The heavy scent of incense made Asami's eyes water. She could hear her native tongue being spoken from behind the door to her left.

The gold-toothed man knocked and the conversation stopped. Kato Endo opened the door and stepped out, warmly welcoming the purple-birthmarked gangster.

For most of Asami's life, she'd depended on Jiro, on her daughter, on Etta, but she was all on her own. She couldn't give into fear. She put on a brave face. She had to be strong.

Kato's icy blue eyes gazed into hers. "Well, well, Fujioka-san. It's been far too long since we last met. My friend Hiro-san and I were expecting you at his fine establishment." He nodded toward a tall white-haired Asian male who had joined him, his cheeks a sickly yellow, a jagged scar below his left eye.

Asami knew it. She'd been right! She was indeed inside Hiro House. Most likely, Hiro was suffering from liver failure, a common occurrence, due to his full-body tattoos. She took some pleasure in that as she raised her chin. "Tell me! Where is my daughter?"

Kato snorted. "Back in the eighties, you lacked fear, but my brother and your movie star friend were beside you. Let's see how well you manage on your own."

Hiro turned to the gold-toothed man. "Tape her mouth shut until you lock her inside the Red Velvet room."

The man ripped off two pieces from the same roll he'd used for Asami's wrists. She struggled as he secured the tape over her mouth. The adjacent door was opened, and he pushed her into a hallway suffused in red light, jockeying her past a salon-type setting. Inside it, she could see three seductively dressed Japanese women being eyed up by a flashy Japanese man. Asami tried to get the women's attention, but her cries came out muffled.

She was drag-walked down another hallway, the tape chafing her wrists. Each closed door was marked with kanji characters: Cockpit, Operating Room, Classroom, and finally Red Velvet Room. Hana *had* to be inside.

A small table was positioned by the door. A biracial teen and a light-skinned black man, sporting an Afro, were playing cards. The teen looked up, his face distressed, and the older man stood and unlocked the door. Asami cringed as the gold-toothed man ripped the tape from her mouth. The black man then shoved her inside the room and the door closed behind her.

On a heart-shaped bed, covered in a cheap red velvet quilt, cowered a woman, her matted dark hair hiding her face. She was attired in a flouncy low-cut blouse and a short black skirt.

Asami's heart sank. Hana would never wear such tacky clothes, yet they looked vaguely familiar. Hand and leg restraints were attached to the bed for roleplay fantasies, but only the woman's left hand was locked in place.

She looked up, her vision muddled, her dazed eyes seeking out Asami's. Like a mosquito's cry, faint, nearly inaudible, yet with a sliver of hope, the word, "Mama?" escaped from her lips.

An outpouring of love swelled through Asami.

She rushed toward Hana, snuggled down beside her, and pressed her cheek to her child's. "Yes, Hana-chan, I'm here. Mama's here."

Her daughter had always mothered her.

It was time for Asami to assume her proper role.

Wednesday - New York

Cars and taxies splashed by. Rain pounded Etta's umbrella. She hurried down the sidewalk, her loafers squishing through wet leaves. She'd called a devastated Henri and told him they'd been tricked into believing Chloe was alive. The dismal truth was driving her forward, sparking her internal mantra: *Tom Pollard will pay, Tom Pollard will pay...*

A squad had picked up Lorna Endo. Detective Sanchez and Sam were en route to the Pollards' Dakota apartment. Tripoint's CEO's flight had landed. After Tom secured his luggage, he'd told Sam, he'd be heading to the Dakota to have breakfast with his wife and son. Tom had asked Sam to join them so they could go over the IPO briefing details one last time.

The detective and Sam had a different plan in mind. Their goal was to deliver Tom to the Sixth Precinct where Etta was to meet them.

Etta's cell rang. She dug inside her purse. Although an unfamiliar international number was displayed, she answered anyway.

"Etta-san?" The male voice sounded concerned. "This is Jiro Kishima, Asami's friend. She texted me she'd safely landed, but since then I've tried to reach her. My calls keep going into voicemail. Have you talked to her?"

"Yes. Don't worry. I'll see her soon."

He gave an immense sigh of relief, yet a niggling sense of unease was bothering Etta. Asami hadn't responded to her short text that Chloe was dead. That was not like her friend, but with all the Manhattan skyscrapers, maybe Asami's cell reception was nil. "Jiro, is there something you want me to tell her?"

"I have Hiro House's address."

At his startling words, Etta stutter-stepped and a male pedestrian almost ran into her.

Jiro explained how a Yamada vice president had been at Tom Pollard's Tokyo party. "In Masato Ito's position, I figured he might've traveled to New York on business. My politician friend told me, at Pollard's party, Masato had escorted that health shop worker into a bedroom to have some fun."

It was what Sam had told Etta as well.

"Since Masato had enjoyed her company, I thought he might've sought out the same sort of companionship in New York City. I called him and told him, if he didn't assist me, his bedroom antics might be of interest to his wife. He was more than willing to talk. He had indeed been to Hiro House for both gambling and girls. It's situated in the West Village behind an establishment called Endo Pawn Shop."

"Jiro! You're amazing!"

"Well, let's save the accolades until Hana's safe. I'll text you the address. Her friend Lucas contacted me as well. Through a friend of a friend, he also confirmed Hiro House's location, next to a Japanese restaurant called Biwa Ramen. Both Masato and Lucas's friend said a different phrase is required to gain entrance each day. The American authorities should be able to provide you another way to get inside."

Etta hung up and immediately called Sam. It was frustrating when he didn't answer, and she had to leave him a voice message containing Hiro House's address. She would've called Detective Sanchez, but Sam was the one who'd kept his business card.

Etta raced the last block to the precinct and entered the reception area. The woman at the desk should be able to reach Sanchez. Before speaking to her, Etta approached Henri. He was slouched over in a gray cargo jacket, a desolate expression on his face. At seeing her, he stood. "Mon Dieu! The fact that Chloe's dead seems even worse the second time around."

She pulled the man her daughter had loved into a hug. "So let's get the bastard who did this." Etta dropped her arms and looked around. "Where's Asami?"

"I don't know. She hasn't shown up."

Percolating inside Etta was that same disquiet as her cell rang, "Sam Madrid" on the display. Etta quickly answered with a question, "Did you listen to my message?"

"Not yet. I was talking to Tom Pollard. He's hung up at the airport. His luggage didn't arrive and he's standing in line to file a report."

"Shit! Maybe that's a ploy. What if he's already at Hiro House or on his way there? My voice message contained its address."

"You actually got it?"

"Yes, from Asami's friend Jiro."

"Nice job! Here, I'll let you talk to Detective Sanchez."

He came on and she recited the address for him. "Ms. Martin, even if Hana Fujioka's not there, Kato Endo might be. A warrant for his arrest was issued in Tokyo. Based on our extradition treaty, the NYPD has been asked to locate him. Requesting SWAT team assistance will not be questioned. Until those officers are positioned outside, I'll have an unmarked squad park on the pawn shop's street to keep tabs on any activity."

"What time span are you talking about for the SWAT team?"

"About fifty minutes."

"That long!"

"Yes. You must be patient."

That was fine for him to say.

Asami had often called them two halves of the same cucumber. Asami's lack of patience was understandable. Hers was not.

"Etta?" It was Sam's voice again. "We're only a few blocks from the Dakota. I'm going to have the detective drop me off there. I'll ask him to provide me backup while I wait inside. I can't afford not to be in the lobby if Tom does show up."

Etta agreed that made sense. She pressed END and quickly updated Henri. "If Tom Pollard's inside Hiro House, or headed that way, the SWAT team will be too late."

"But what can we do?"

"I don't know, but I'm not waiting here. Are you coming?"

"Merde! Let's go."

She tried to wave down a cab. It was exasperating. They were all occupied or another party would grab one before she and Henri could. One finally pulled up. On the ride, Etta texted both Asami and Sam, to relay their change in plans. She also called Asami multiple times but only got voicemail. Asami's initial call had come in at 9:12 a.m. It was close to 11:30. Even if her friend had poor cell reception, she would've found some way to contact Etta, to explain why she was going to be so late.

Something must've happened to Asami.

The driver announced, "Endo Pawn Shop is coming up on your left."

Henri sank down low in his seat.

Etta followed suit, her eyes peeking out. "Drive by slowly," she instructed, "but please don't stop."

Squashed between a shoe repair shop and Biwa Ramen was the pawn shop. All three were on the ground level of a string of older brick buildings. The pawn shop's signage read, *End-o High Prices*, and the barred windows were filled with all sorts of electronics, purses, watches, and jewelry.

But the window dressings weren't what had caught Etta's attention. Near the front stoop, amid the passing pedestrians, were two men, both smoking. One was black with an Afro, the other Japanese.

Rage hit Etta like a smack in the face. "Picture that black man in an NYPD cap. I'm certain he's the cop impersonator—Deon's uncle—the one who killed Chloe."

"Etta, you're right! What about the other guy?"

She felt the color drain from her face. The Japanese man had turned, exposing a purple birthmark on his right cheek. "My God! I bet he's the gangster who was following Asami in Tokyo. Maybe he was on her flight. Maybe he grabbed her at the airport. Maybe she and Hana are both inside."

-25-

Wednesday - New York

Asami huddled beside her daughter on the heart-shaped bed. It was disgusting to imagine the scuzzy men who patronized that brothel room, those who would gaze up at the ceiling mirror to admire themselves in action.

Hana had trouble sitting up, due to her overwhelming fatigue, but she'd managed to use her free hand to remove the tape securing Asami's wrists. All the while, with Asami's prompting, her daughter had tried to reconstruct her ordeal. "I was locked up in Kato Endo's apartment and he told me to put on my hiking clothes. After that, I was given food and water. From that point on, nothing makes sense. It was like my body wasn't there, yet it was."

Asami felt certain Hana had been drugged, as she'd been at TJ's party in the eighties. Asami placed her arm around her daughter's shoulders. "Do you remember going into a forest?"

Hana squeezed her eyes shut. "Was I actually there? I thought it was a dream, more like a nightmare. There were dense trees and this putrid scent." She shook her head. "That's all I can remember until I woke up on this sleazy bed, in these filthy clothes." She gazed down at the wrinkled flouncy blouse covered in stains.

Asami realized why Hana's clothes had looked familiar. They'd been that health shop worker's, the ones she'd worn in the Palace

Hotel video, and what her corpse, stuffed in the roller bag, had probably worn into the forest.

Hana's tormented eyes found hers. "I was drugged wasn't I? And it's all because of that Palace Hotel party. And now I've gotten you into this mess."

"Hana-chan, listen, there's nothing I want more than to be here with you. We're two bright women. We'll figure something out."

"What about Chloe? Didn't she report that woman's drowning? She'd already left for the airport when Kato's car arrived back at her hotel."

Asami's heart shifted. She didn't know what to say. Should she tell Hana the terrible truth or keep Chloe's death to herself. What good would it do if her daughter knew? But if Asami didn't tell her, and someone else did, it could be far worse. She took a deep breath and relayed the grisly details, from beginning to end, including Etta's last text message.

Hana sobbed, "I'm the one who wanted to attend that party. I'd decided to confront Tom Pollard about—"

"Oh Hana-chan, I know about your frightening Plaza Hotel incident."

"I—I should've told you, but I didn't want to worry you. Last Thursday night, I thought I was doing the right thing. But if I hadn't gone to that party, Chloe never would've come. I killed her, Mama. She's dead because of me."

"That's not true. She's dead because of Tom Pollard. If he hadn't drowned that poor woman, none of this would've happened."

A perplexed look appeared on Hana's blotchy face. "No? You've got it all wrong. His son drowned that woman."

Asami's backbone stiffened. Her toes tapped the shag carpeted floor. "That's not what Etta told me."

"I was challenging Tom Pollard when his drunken son arrived—and TJ came onto me. Somehow, all three of us ended up in the pool. That's when that woman came to my aid. That's when TJ turned his attention on her and she drowned in the process."

Hana's shoulders faltered. "I tried to save her, but I couldn't."

"I know you did. But how could Chloe have gotten the facts so wrong?" Asami told Hana about Chloe's memo, how it had accused Tom Pollard, not TJ.

"Well Chloe definitely knew the truth." Hana hesitated, her brow creased. "But you said the memo was a word document, not an email?"

"Yes?"

"Just think. If someone had access to Chloe's laptop, its system date and time could've been moved back to Chloe's return flight date. Modifications to the original document could've been made, to implicate Tom Pollard, before the laptop was changed back to its proper settings."

"You're so smart! Someone must be framing Tom for that woman's death. You know it, and I know it, but Etta doesn't." Asami mulled that over. "I know you don't remember your forest trek. But, I assume, someone took photos of that woman dressed in your clothes, to prove you were dead. Has anybody done something similar?"

Hana nodded, her cracked lips slightly parted. "Early this morning, a man brought in a *New York Times* and held it over my chest while Kato took photos."

"That's good!" Asami's fingers sped up and down the repulsive bed cover. "*Very* good! Kato's extortion scheme must still be in progress. But Tripoint's IPO is tomorrow morning. Kato doesn't have much time."

Hana grabbed Asami's busy hand. "Mama, neither do we."

Asami tried to think. "What about that teen guarding the door? Did you hear his name?"

"The older man called him Deon."

"Really! He must be the young man Chloe was mentoring. Etta said he was somehow involved." Asami hatched her plan. Could she step up? Without the crutch of her meds, could she take risks to protect her child? Without Jiro's support? Without Etta's?

Asami's feet stilled. She had to. "Tell me, are the two men always stationed outside the door?"

"I don't know. Every couple of hours, the older man checks on me. He opens that small trap door right there." Hana pointed to the spot on the brothel room door. "Then I speak to him. He's the one who takes me out to use the bathroom."

Asami had noticed a crushed bag on the floor stamped with Biwa Ramen. "What about food?"

"That same man provides me bento meals."

Asami checked her watch. "It's close to noon. The older man could be getting lunch right now." She stood. "I'm going to knock on the door. If they're both outside, I'll only ask to use the bathroom." Asami tapped once, twice, three times, her heart pummeling her ribcage. The small trap door finally opened and the teen glanced in, an anxious look on his face.

She asked, "Are you alone?"

He looked over his shoulder and nodded.

Asami settled her breathing. It was time for her to use her authoritative voice—the cry of the crane—the wise old bird of Japanese folklore. "You're Deon Endo, aren't you?"

His face tightened, but he didn't speak.

"I'm Chloe Martin's friend. I know she's dead." Asami stared into Deon's pain-stricken eyes, his lower lip quivering.

That gave her hope.

"She mentored you, didn't she?"

He looked away.

"She said you were bright—that you'd do great things if you were given a chance. Well, Deon, I'm giving that to you right now."

Wednesday - New York

Backlit shoji screens and Japanese shamisen music were gentling Etta's nerves. She and Henri sat in a Biwa Ramen booth next to its window wall. Her cell was on the table, her eyes on the lookout for any activity at the adjacent Endo Pawn Shop. Its seedy storefront provided the perfect camouflage for the lucrative Hiro House hidden behind.

Etta felt certain Asami and Hana were both inside that building.

Her daughter's body could be as well.

Was Tom Pollard there too?

Etta had heard from Sam again after Tom had contacted him a third time. Sylvia and TJ had picked Tom up at the airport and they were all headed back to the Dakota. He'd asked Sam if he could still make that breakfast meeting at their home. "As you said, Etta, that could be a ploy, but if it's not, a uniformed cop and I'll be inside the Dakota lobby to greet them."

A few tables down, a couple was enjoying noodle bowls topped with pork, egg, and dried seaweed. She and Henri had only ordered tea. Etta looked at her watch. It was maddening. The SWAT team's estimated arrival was still thirty-five minutes out. She peered through the window her eyes searching for the unmarked squad and her nose nearly smashed into the glass. "Shit, Henri! A limo pulled up and Tom Pollard and his son are climbing out. I knew it! Tom lied to Sam. What's more, Tom's carrying a metal briefcase, the sort that might contain money. Wait... Sylvia just slid out too!" Incredulous, Etta shook her head. "I can't believe she's going along with her husband's plan, but she's approaching the pawn shop with Tom and their son."

"Well, Etta, maybe Tom told her about that woman's drowning. Sylvia would have a vested interest in the IPO's success as well."

"Even so, I can't believe she'd engage in criminal activity to protect her husband. She doesn't love Tom. If I could only talk to Sylvia, I think I could reason with her." Etta's eyes refocused on Henri, but his were trained on a different target.

He cautioned, "Don't turn," and he dipped his head. "Deon's uncle just came into the restaurant."

"Oh no! Did he see you?"

"I don't think so. His back's to me. He and the man at the register are pointing at a menu. He must be ordering food."

"What should we do? What if he sees us?"

"I think we're okay. He's going outside for a smoke while he waits."

"That's good. I've got to call Sam and tell him about the Pollards." Etta reached for her cell, just as it rang, an unfamiliar number on the display.

Henri motioned. "You better answer that."

She did and a frantic "Etta-san" filled her ear, followed by a muffled male voice, its tone angry.

The caller *had* to be Asami!

"Hiro House," her friend's words sped out, "with Hana—TJ not Tom... Please! Please, don't take it away!"

Etta's cell went dead.

Fear bubbled up inside her. She tried the number and it went into Deon Endo's voicemail.

Henri's brows had forged together. "What's going on?"

"Oh God, Henri! It was Asami." Etta relayed her friend's cryptic message and the cellphone's source.

Henri wrapped his hands around his forehead, his eyes meeting hers. "So Hana's alive and Asami's with her?"

"Yes, and they're both inside Hiro House, as is Deon. I bet he let Asami use his cell—"

"Or she stole it from him."

"Either way, we must do something. The Pollards are inside. One of them could've stopped Asami from speaking to me. She used my name. That person knows I was on the other end."

"You said, Asami said, 'TJ not Tom.' Merde! What does that mean?"

"It must be important."

He rubbed his fingers into his forehead then abruptly stopped. "Do you think Asami meant TJ drowned that Japanese woman, not Tom?"

"No, Henri, that can't be. Chloe's memo specifically accused Tom."

"I know. But someone stole Chloe's laptop from her Tripoint desk, and you said you located her password inside her drawer. That same someone could've used it to log on—to doctor up her memo."

"You could be right! Maybe instead of Tom confessing to Sylvia, TJ did. God! Sylvia would do anything to protect her son."

But still, Etta had to grab at hope.

Her cell vibrated and she seized it, praying it was Asami.

"Ms. Martin, this is Detective Sanchez." His voice was strained. "There's an active terrorist threat at the Jefferson Market Library. I'm sorry. It takes precedence over yours."

"Shit!"

"I'm calling in additional resources, but you'll have to be patient."

"Listen, the Pollards—"

The line went dead.

"Dammit!" Etta repeated Sanchez's words for Henri's benefit. "We can't wait that long." She snuck a peek out the window. Deon's uncle was speaking on his cell. "I know that unmarked squad is nearby, but the street's lined with cars. If we go outside and try to find it, Deon's uncle might recognize us." She turned back. "What can we do? We know Kato's extortion scheme must include money. If the Pollards are handing it over, what will happen to Hana and Asami? We have to get inside."

Henri had been tapping a spoon on the table and he paused. "It's against my better judgment, but I have an idea." Their kimono dressed waitress started to pass and Henri stopped her. "Can I please speak to the manager?"

"Certainly." The tall Japanese woman disappeared behind Etta.

Henri's eyes followed her. "The manager's the guy behind the register."

A balding Japanese man, with wire-rimmed glasses, arrived at their table. "My daughter said you needed to see me?"

Henri quickly introduced Etta and himself. "Are you familiar with the place next door? Not the pawn shop but the establishment behind it?"

The manager looked uneasy. "Why do you ask?"

"Don't worry. We know it's operated by the yakuza. We believe a mother and her daughter are being kept there against their wills."

"Oh my!" The manager clearly looked distressed.

"Is there any way you could help us get inside?"

"Well..." he hesitated. "We often deliver meals there. The man out front," he jerked his head toward Deon's uncle, "is from that place. He's waiting for an order right now."

"But if he'd called it in," Henri was persistent, "how would you have delivered it?"

"Through a receiving door in the alley. We've been given an access code."

"Really!" Etta exchanged a look with Henri as he charged on and said, "This might be too much to ask, but could you possibly stall that man's order and provide us some takeout to deliver?"

"Please!" Etta pulled out her wallet. "We'll pay whatever you want."

The manager's gaze strayed to his daughter and landed back on Etta. "Don't worry about the money. I want to help. But if you two enter together, it will cause suspicion. My daughter has an extra kimono in a locker. If you wear it," he eyed Etta, "and carry in takeout food, nobody will question you. I employ a Caucasian waitress and both she and my daughter often make deliveries there." He gave a slight bow. "Let me know what you decide."

As the manager departed, Etta leaned in toward Henri. "You know his suggestion makes sense. When I enter, you could be inside the pawn shop trying to gain access from there."

"Forget it. I'm going in with you."

"Listen Henri, if you cause a ruckus, flash some money, say you've previously gambled at Hiro House, but you just don't have the silly phrase, Hiro's staff will come. That will distract them from me."

"Mon Dieu! This is crazy!"

"Maybe? But Chloe's already dead. If I don't attempt to reach out to Sylvia Pollard, Asami and Hana could soon be too.

-26-

Wednesday - New York

Asami lay face down on the filthy brothel room carpet, dust and dirt clogging her nostrils. Her daughter's gut-wrenching cries filled the dismal space.

Asami was devastated. Her call to Etta had failed.

Out of the corner of her eye, she watched as Hiro Endo glared at his grandson. "I'm disappointed in you. You could have compromised everything! You *never* should've let that woman use your cell."

At the same moment as Asami had been saying, "TJ not Tom," Hiro and TJ Pollard had entered the room. They'd both seen Deon's cell in her hand and TJ had grabbed it from her. Asami's begging had only seemed to heighten TJ's pleasure as he'd thrown her onto the ground. While he'd straddled her, Hiro had rewrapped her wrists with tape.

Hana's cries had never let up.

"Fuck!" TJ shouted, his eyes directed at her daughter, white residue below his nostrils. "I can't stand your whining." He ripped off four strips of tape from Hiro's dwindling roll and plastered them across Hana's mouth.

While TJ had been in Tokyo, Asami had believed he might've been using drugs as he'd done in New York. Why hadn't she reported him? If she had, he would've been sent back to the States in disgrace. If she had, she and Hana wouldn't be shackled up in their dire situation.

TJ pulled out his cell and selected a number. "They're both here," he reported. "You can go ahead." He ended his call and jerked Asami to her feet and onto the bed. Ignoring her pleas, he used the last of the tape to secure her wrists to the bedframe. She tried to focus on the positives: Etta knew where they were; she would find them; Etta wouldn't let her down; she never had.

Asami's eyes connected with her poor child's and she silently implored Hana to hold on.

The gold-toothed man entered, whispered into Hiro's ear, and departed. Hiro looked pleased. "It appears as if everything's in order. The Wada-kai's work is done." He handed TJ a key. "This opens the locks to this room and the bed restraints. Whatever you do to these women is a choice you and your family will own."

Asami's lips and chin trembled. "Wait! You can't leave us here with this man!"

Hiro brushed off her words and pushed his distressed grandson out of the room.

Asami was frantic. She had to stall TJ, to gain some extra time. "Listen, you must let us go! TJ, this isn't you. You're not thinking straight." But he continued to tune her out as he overpowered her daughter. While her brave child kicked and scratched, he locked Hana's remaining wrist and ankles into the bed restraints.

Sweating profusely, TJ stepped back and sneered. "Look at you! The mama-san who's come to her daughter's aid and all for naught."

Asami forced herself to slowly breathe in and breathe out, to calm her speeding heart—to think. As Hana thrashed about on the bed, it took all of Asami's willpower to do so. "Listen TJ." Her voice rallied for her daughter's sake. "You've got too much to lose. If you release us, I promise we won't press charges. I promise Hana will keep silent about that woman's drowning. I—"

"Nice try!" TJ scowled. "If you were a meek-mannered Japanese woman, like so many others, I might consider your proposition. But you're an uppity bitch. You've always looked down on me." His dilated pupils drifted over toward Hana. "But your daughter's different. Ever since that Tokyo party, I've been thinking about her." An evil smile crossed his lips. "And what the hell! While I'm waiting, I may as well take advantage of what this room's designed for."

He squinted up at the bright track lighting, framing the ceiling mirror, and he winced. "Fuck!" He fumbled with the dimmer switch, bringing the lights down low. Elongated shadows joined the horrific tableau.

Asami's anxiety was like a living thing, thrumming in the air. Hana had always been her Samurai warrior, ready to face adversity head on. But as TJ slowly ran his hand up her daughter's leg, and under her skirt, fear stretched Hana's face tight, her tears darkening the red spread like a festering sore.

Asami couldn't let him rape her child! She started to scream, her jarring voice reverberating off the brothel room's walls. Surely one of those young women from down the hall would come to their aid. Or what about Hiro's grandson? He'd helped them before. He'd do so again. He'd...

"Shut up you fucking bitch!" TJ peeled off his suit jacket. "Or I'll ride your precious daughter even harder!" He unzipped his pants.

Asami's wild eyes focused on the brothel room door, willing it to open, but no employees were coming to their rescue. She'd been counting on Etta, but time had run out. Defeated, Asami quieted her voice. She had to protect Hana from further harm.

"Good girl!" TJ patted Asami's head, his sour breath filling her nostrils. "Now you can watch me fuck your daughter—and I'm betting it'll be better than the fuck I had with you."

Asami couldn't move, couldn't breathe.

TJ *had* raped her.

He'd confessed to that vile act, the one she'd secretly dreaded had taken place decades before.

How could she not respond to his taunt? Her eyes burned into his smug face as she spat out, "What a pathetic man you are!"

TJ's eyes gleamed. "Bitch, I knew you'd slip up!" He slapped her cheek hard, jerking her head painfully to the left.

From his pants pocket, he removed a handkerchief. As he stuffed it into her mouth and secured it with the piece of tape he'd ripped from Hana's lips, Asami realized her grave mistake.

She pinched her eyes shut. How stupid she'd been! She'd lost the use of her voice, her only weapon to stop TJ's assault on her daughter.

She and Hana were like carp on the cutting board. There had to be something she could do.

She couldn't give up.

She couldn't allow TJ to rape her daughter as he'd raped her.

Wednesday – New York

Tokyo scents escaped from the take-out bag Etta held in one hand, her cell in the other. She stepped into the damp alley behind Biwa Ramen, the borrowed silk kimono swishing around her ankles.

She'd called Sam and told him about the Pollards' arrival, Asami's call, and the SWAT team's delay. "Christ, Etta! What a mess! I'll be there as soon as I can. Please, don't do anything rash. I've lost Chloe. I can't lose you too."

His words had struck deep, but Etta had made her decision. She wasn't about to back down. She'd simply said, "Don't worry. I won't do anything you wouldn't do."

And that was the truth.

Along with four bento boxes, the manager had provided Etta the code to Hiro House's receiving door. "Once you enter the code, wait until the two flashing middle lights change from red to green, then pull the door handle." He'd given her a bow. "Good luck. I'll stall the man's order as long as I can."

Etta hurried toward the "Delivery" door. She couldn't think about the risk involved. As mom would've said, she was probably walking into a hornets' nest with a short stick. In addition, the owner's instructions worried Etta. The LED lights were reminiscent of her initial incident with Tom Pollard.

She reached the proper door, situated by a large puddle, and, just as planned, Henri called, his voice low: "Etta, I managed to slip by Deon's uncle and I'm inside the pawn shop. There's a Japanese man stationed beside a rear door which probably provides access to Hiro House. Are you certain you want me to make a commotion?"

"Yes, but give me five minutes. I'm going to enter the access code right now." She pressed END then fumbled, trying to slide her cell into the kimono's side pocket, but as she did she heard a splash. *Dammit!* She looked down. Her cell had landed in the puddle. She grabbed for it and repeatedly pressed the "home button." When the display remained blank, she knew it was too late. Etta tucked her cell away. She'd deal with that later.

Mounted next to the door was a keypad. Etta typed in the passcode, her eyes focused on the four LED lights. They flickered once, then again. *Shit!* Were they red or green? To her colorblind eyes she couldn't tell. She pulled on the door handle, but it was locked. She tried the code again, then again, *and* again, growing exceedingly worried. She took a calming breath and carefully entered the code, being extra precise. She waited one, two, three seconds then pulled.

Thank God! She was in!

The manager had told her, "Once you enter the storage room, there's a buzzer to alert those inside. Speak into the intercom and tell them you're from Biwa Ramen."

In the dimly lit room, Etta did as instructed and the door leading into the gambling den clicked open.

Another hurdle crossed.

Etta peeked inside. The light was low and hazy from tobacco smoke. Men were seated on tatami mats and grouped around dealers, all shirtless, their intricate tattoos exposed. The dealers sat in the formal *seiza* position—knees on the floor, buttocks resting on their heels. Two women, also wearing kimonos, were shuffling around and providing cocktails.

The gambling den was about a mini-mart size. On the far wall was an entry vestibule. It had to provide access to the pawn shop where Henri was stationed. The wall to Etta's left contained two openings, the first, a small hallway at about the midpoint; the second, a large archway about six feet farther down. A stern-looking Japanese woman sat at a desk below it, negotiating with a man. A tall white-haired Asian male in a black suit and red tie interrupted them. The woman listened, abruptly stood, and rapidly spoke to three seductively costumed women standing behind her.

Etta had to stay focused. Biwa Ramen's manager had said, "Down the first hall to your left is the canteen where the woman who accepts deliveries is located. Beyond that is the business office." Etta's goal was to locate Sylvia Pollard. Somehow, Etta had to convince her Asami's and Hana's lives mattered. Those of Sylvia's son and her husband did too, but Sylvia couldn't continue to enable their destructive behavior. Sylvia was a smart woman.

She'd had a loving partner since her Radcliffe years. Sylvia had to realize what she must do.

Nerves on edge, Etta removed her shoes and padded across the tatami, trying not to attract attention. The tall Asian man had stepped into the den to converse with the dealers. Each clapped their hands and stood. The players grumbled and lumbered to their feet.

Maybe that tall man was Hiro Endo? Maybe he'd been informed about the SWAT team's imminent arrival? If so, the Pollards might've been informed as well. Unless Etta did something, and fast, Hana and Asami would not be walking out of Hiro House.

Neither might she.

Henri's voice riddled in from the front vestibule. *Oh God!* Maybe their actions were a mistake. What if Hana and Asami were being whisked out through the "Employee Entrance" while she and Henri were both inside? As Etta questioned what she should do, two men stepped out of the small hallway and headed toward the front vestibule. She had to quiet her nerves. She had to believe everything was going as planned.

She dashed toward the hall from where the men had exited, and she took note of the stern-looking Japanese woman. She was rummaging through her desk and, luckily, didn't even lift her head.

Something was definitely going on.

Etta darted into the incense-scented hallway. It came to a four way intersection. What appeared to be a brothel salon was to Etta's right. But rather than waiting for a client, the scantily dressed Japanese women were chaotically rushing around. Straight ahead was a short hallway with two doors. The first would lead into the canteen, the second into the business office where the Pollards and possibly Asami and her daughter would be.

Etta glanced down the dimly lit hallway to her left. Each side contained four evenly spaced doors.

She drew in a breath.

At the hall's end, dressed in a New York Giants' hoody and baggy jeans was Deon Endo, the same teen her daughter had cared about.

What should she do? Should she locate Sylvia as planned? Or should she alter her course? Asami and Hana could be behind one of those doors.

Etta made her decision.

She rushed toward Deon and held up the Biwa Ramen take-out bag. "Your uncle was detained and he asked me to deliver his order." From under the door to Etta's left, muted screams seeped out. *Oh God!* Could those be Hana's or Asami's cries for help? Were they in there alone? Or was someone inside with them?

Etta had to remain calm, to focus on the teen, to not imagine what was happening behind that door. "Deon, do you remember me? Two nights ago, Henri Broussard and I saw you at Washington Square Park."

His eyes widened.

"I'm Chloe—Chloe Martin's mom."

A look of pain rutted the teen's youthful face, the heartfelt sort that had probably been swelling up inside him ever since her daughter's death. He couldn't look at Etta as his voice broke, "Believe me, when I called Henri from the Rusty Nail, I had no idea Chloe would end up dead."

She squeezed his arm. "I do believe you." And she did.

Although the chilling sounds had never let up, Etta couldn't rush things. She had to move slowly, to leverage Deon's obvious attachment to her daughter, to convince him it was in his best interest to switch sides.

He lifted his chin, tears in his eyes. "Chloe really looked out for me."

"I know she did. But she can't help you now—and neither can your mom. She was arrested a few hours ago."

"No!" He slammed his fist against the back wall.

"Listen... The police will be here soon. They may already be out front. If you help me, I'll let them know." She could tell he was a sensitive kid. He'd lost Chloe and now his mom. Etta could also tell she'd won him over. "I'm looking for two Japanese women, a mother and her daughter. Are they behind that door?" She motioned toward it.

"Yeah..." His desolate eyes met hers. "I let the mom use my cell. I'd help you too, but the door's locked, and my grandfather took my key."

"Shit! There must be another."

"My uncle has one, and—and so does the man inside the room."

Oh God! So there *was* someone inside. "Do you know the man's name?"

"The mom called him TJ."

Etta closed her eyes. Henri's conjecture had to be right: TJ was the one who'd drowned that woman and he had nothing to lose.

-27-

Wednesday - New York

Asami's overactive brain kept searching for a way to stall TJ's ultimate attack on her daughter. Mercifully, he'd been taking his time. While still secured to the brothel room's bedpost, Asami had been rubbing her cheek against her shoulder, attempting to catch the tape's edge, frantically trying to release it and the handkerchief gag.

To watch TJ rip Hana's blouse apart and paw her lace covered breasts had been agonizing. Hana had continued to thrash against the restraints, her muffled cries never letting up.

The Shinto religion was an optimistic faith. Humans were supposed to be fundamentally good. But evil had found a vessel inside TJ. Could Asami's mama's spirit be intervening on Hana's behalf? It seemed possible since TJ was having issues moving forward.

That was especially evident when, from his trouser pocket, he removed a small plastic bag and shook out a white substance onto the adjacent end table. Using a credit card and a rolled up dollar bill, TJ shaped the drug into two thin lines and snorted them into his nostrils. "Fuck!" he breathed out, arousal returning to his voice. "Japanese girls take my breath away."

Asami froze. He'd used that same phrase just days before he'd raped her. On how many other occasions had he used those exact words, on other unsuspecting Japanese females, *and* achieved the same sordid results? TJ had to be stopped! Asami thrust her tongue into the gag and simultaneously rubbed her cheek against her shoulder.

Miraculously, the tape released!

She coughed out the handkerchief and he looked up, startled.

TJ's sick confession had given Asami a last-ditch idea. Laced with adrenalin, she cleared her throat, priming it for her assault. "What a pitiful man you are! I remember that night at your parents' apartment. You said we fucked, but did you consider the consequences?"

His hands paused.

His shoulders tensed.

TJ was actually listening.

"Why do you think I left New York?"

Hana's body had quieted as well.

"I had a six-year work visa. Why would I give that up?"

Drawn into Asami's narrative, TJ seemed eager to wrench her down. "You were a fucking embarrassment! At that party, everyone saw how you came onto me." TJ twisted closer to Asami. "Everyone saw how drunk you were—how you couldn't even get off the couch. Sam Madrid arrived and he had to nearly carry you out. He couldn't lose face once he'd hired you, so he banished you to Tokyo."

She was stupefied by his response. "How wrong you are! I asked Sam for that transfer." She raised her head high, her cheeks burning, tangled hair hindering her vision. "But, TJ, it did involve you."

"What the fuck do you mean?"

"Do you know when my daughter was born?"

Confusion drained the lust from his face.

"I assume you noticed Hana's hāfu?"

"What are you saying?"

"My daughter, the one on this squalid bed, the one you've been trying to rape, is your child too!"

TJ bucked back and Hana whimpered. To see her daughter's tormented face crushed Asami—but her lie was necessary. It might be the only way to save them both.

Asami leveled her eyes on TJ. "Hana's twenty-first birthday was three days ago. You claim to be so smart. Figure it out. What a wonderful present she's getting from her papa."

"Fuck!" He floundered, his superior demeanor evaporating. "I'm not that kind of man."

"Well, TJ, prove you're not."

His coked-up eyes filled with tears and Asami held her breath.

Had she gotten to him?

Had she uncovered some humanity in that beastly man?

Wednesday - New York

Sweat trickled down Etta's back, the silky kimono sticking to her skin. Heart thudding, she paced back and forth outside the brothel room's door while Deon Endo rubbed his sore fist, the one he'd punched into the hallway wall. The situation was grim. Etta's cell still wouldn't power on and the teen's grandfather had taken his. Asami and Hana were locked inside with TJ Pollard and there was no way to gain access.

Should she attempt to kick in the door? Or should she wait for Deon's uncle? He had a key, but he was also the man responsible for Chloe's death. If he returned, what would he do to her? And where was Henri? Where was the SWAT team? And what about Sylvia and Tom Pollard? Should Etta still locate her friend and try to convince her to let Asami and Hana go?

A nostalgic fragrance mingled with the incense and Japanese take-out scents, and Etta spun around. Like Sunday morning eggs, her thoughts were scrambled.

Sylvia stood beside her husband, and *she* was the one pointing a gun at Etta's chest.

That didn't make sense.

Tom was in charge, wasn't he?

But could she be wrong?

God! She took a step back.

Maybe she was.

"Sylvia, what—what's going on? You can't be behind all this!"

"Of course, I am! Dammit Etta! Why couldn't you leave well enough alone? I've always had to clean up for my son, for my husband."

Etta gaped at the woman she thought she knew—the one she'd so admired throughout her career. The one who'd supported her sabbatical request decades before, allowing Etta to have her child, her Chloe, the young woman Sylvia had personally known, the young woman Sylvia had even called "special." How could she have destroyed Etta's only child?

But Sylvia had.

She'd done the unthinkable—to protect her son—and she was prepared to do it again.

Etta took another step back and joined Deon, both of them blocking the brothel room's door.

Suddenly, without warning, TJ's burly body burst out, knocking Etta off to the side.

Etta's hands covered her mouth as Asami followed, Hana close behind. *Thank God!* Her friends were alive! But it appeared as if they'd been in a war zone. Asami's cheeks were raw, her feet bare, her filthy sweater unraveled at the neck. Hana's blouse was ripped and torn, her skirt off kilter, her hair in knots, and below her humiliated eyes, dark rings marred her flawless skin.

TJ's feral eyes had found his mother's. "What have we done?" He shoved Hana toward Sylvia. "Just look at her. Can't you see yourself in her?"

Sylvia stared blankly at him. "I don't understand."

He grabbed Hana's shoulders and shook them. "Look closely. This is the young woman we've come to murder—this is Hana—this is my daughter—your granddaughter."

Sylvia's posture went rigid as Tom shouted, "What the fuck!"

TJ's words had stunned Etta as well. They could only mean he *had* raped her friend in the eighties, otherwise he never would've believed the lie Asami had to have told him.

Etta tried to catch her friend's attention, to silently mouth, "Don't do anything rash. Help is on the way." But it seemed as if Asami was in her own world, hyper-focused on Sylvia and her son.

TJ threw up his hands. "Mother, where will this end? Look around. They all know. Do we murder my daughter and the rest of them too?"

Sylvia glared at her son. "How ungrateful you are! I engaged the yakuza to protect you! That's what *good* mothers do." Incredibly, Sylvia's gaze sought out Etta's then Asami's. "You both know what I've sacrificed for my child, don't you?"

Asami breathed out, "Your child! What about Etta's and mine?"

Etta watched in horror as her friend lunged. In Asami's hand was a shoe, its slender heel aimed directly at Sylvia's face.

TJ grabbed Asami's wrist and their bodies rammed into Sylvia's.

Two gunshots exploded.

Etta screamed as Asami crumpled to the floor.

TJ's large frame followed, landing on top of his mother.

Oh God! Etta rushed toward her friend as loud shouts filled the hall, "Police, go, go, go."

Etta used her palm to apply pressure to the blood-soaked spot on Asami's sweater while black helmeted men raced in, assault rifles drawn. Among them was Detective Sanchez who zoned in on Sylvia and knocked the gun from her hand. Another SWAT team member backed Tom and Deon into a corner.

Etta kept murmuring, "Asami, hold on. You must hold on."

Hana knelt on the opposite side. "Mama, I'm here. Please open your eyes. Please look at me." Her soft voice continued in Japanese.

Asami's face was bleached, her breathing strained. Etta's bloody hand continued to press on her friend's abdomen as four paramedics rushed in with two rolling gurneys.

One paramedic checked Asami's vitals, another checked TJ's. An oxygen mask was placed over Asami's face. Her sweater was pushed up to expose the wound and a temporary dressing was applied.

Etta wiped her hand on the kimono then grabbed the paramedic's arm. "She's going to live, isn't she?"

"I can't promise that, but the bullet entered just below her breastbone. Most likely, it missed her heart and lungs."

Two men carefully lifted Asami onto the gurney, covered her with a blanket, then quickly rolled her out.

Hana followed, Sanchez and Etta keeping pace. They all passed through a doorway and into another hall, hazy like morning fog. The over-powering scent of incense was so thick Etta could taste it.

Sylvia's screams of "No! My son can't be dead! No!" pierced through the door.

Etta felt numb. Sylvia had joined her ranks. She deserved to suffer, but Etta couldn't wish a child's death on any mother.

A SWAT team member allowed the gurney and Hana to pass before he stopped Sanchez. Etta also halted to listen.

"Every other room as been checked and cleared," the officer said, "but we're still looking for a key to a locked door inside this office." He motioned toward it.

Etta looked inside. It had to be Hiro's. Beyond a desk was a three-tiered wooden shrine, a marble Buddha sculpture on top. The lower levels held burning incense sticks.

Another SWAT team member held up a single key he'd located inside the desk's top drawer. "This could be it." He turned and successfully unlocked the door, which provided access to another room rather than a closet.

Etta grabbed Sanchez's arm, her hand trembling. "In Japan, incense is used to purify the surroundings and to honor the dead. Lorna Endo told us Chloe's body could be inside Hiro House."

"I know. That's why you need to wait here."

"No, I'm coming with you. She's my daughter."

He sighed and gave a resigned nod.

Her legs unsteady, Etta followed Sanchez across the office then into the room. Glowing incense coils were placed on a tiled floor and a transom window was cracked open to provide fresh air and light. In addition to a toilet and sink, behind the rising smoke was an opaque shower curtain, pulled shut.

Etta couldn't open it, but Sanchez did, the shower clips making a metallic sound as they slid across the bar.

Propped up in the bathtub, clothed in a white kimono, was her dear child, her eyes closed, her hands placed crosswise on her chest, her face mottled. The incense couldn't hide the horrific scent.

Etta fell to her knees. Her shaky fingers reached out and gently touched her daughter's cheek.

Totally confused, Etta's hand jerked back.

She stared at it. "How could my daughter's skin be warm?"

The detective placed two fingers on Chloe's neck. "Sweet Jesus! I've got a pulse!"

* * *

Breathing through her mouth, Etta rode in the emergency vehicle, her hand stroking her daughter's filthy hair. The stench was appalling. For days, feces and urine had been saturating the back of Chloe's kimono.

Etta's thoughts and prayers were only focused on her child. She knew Asami was in safe hands. Yes, her friend's breathing had been strained, but the paramedic's words had sounded reassuring.

Yet, there *had* been a lot of blood.

Etta kept coaxing her daughter to open her eyes, to let her know she was going to be fine.

And it seemed as if that could be possible.

Chloe had obviously been heavily sedated, but when the paramedics had removed her from the bathtub, a tube had snaked out from Chloe's left sleeve. It had been attached to a portable IV pole hidden behind the shower curtain. A clear bag of fluids had been dripping into Chloe's arm, keeping her hydrated, keeping her alive.

The emergency vehicle pulled to a stop. The rear doors opened and sunlight poured in. Like fragile butterfly wings about to take flight, Chloe's lashes fluttered.

Etta gasped.

Her daughter's eyelids barely opened, but it was enough. Chloe whimpered, "Mom?"

"Yes, honey! I'm here."

Etta drew her daughter to her breast.

God! All of life's possibilities were spinning inside her head.

-28-

Friday - New York

Etta scuttled across the street, a white spray rose bouquet clutched in her hand. She followed a group of children linked together with rope, their teachers leading and trailing the pack. Amid the sounds of youthful chatter and the carriage horses' rhythmic walk, she entered Central Park through the Women's Gate. That name seemed disturbingly suitable. Over the past few days, four women had been on parallel journeys—desperate journeys.

Lines had become blurred.

As mothers, Etta, Asami, Sylvia Pollard, and Lorna Endo had each done whatever had been necessary to save their children. Two mothers had succeeded, two had failed.

Following the leaf carpeted pavement path, Etta approached the black-and-white mosaic circle strewn with flowers. She tried to "IMAGINE" a world without greed, without pain, without sorrow. She and Asami should be dancing, kicking up their heels, reveling in their strokes of good luck, in their blessings.

Both of their daughters were alive!

Etta sat down on one of the metal benches and pictured Asami beside her, Etta reaching over to calm her friend's busy hands. The two should be settling back into their comfortable groove, each handling the other's quirks, each reading the other's heart.

Etta smiled. And in a few days, that should certainly be the case. The bullet had passed through Asami's abdomen muscles, not touching any internal organs. She'd lost quite a bit of blood, which had sent her system into shock. But other than controlling her pain, she'd be back on her feet in no time, just—just like Chloe already was!

A tour director strolled past, her Asian entourage in tow, each member vying for the best listening spot. Etta couldn't help but laugh. One of them reminded her of Asami.

Their friendship had shifted. On Wednesday, after Etta, Sam, and Henri had spent time in Chloe's hospital room, Etta had walked down the hall to Asami's. Her friend had been propped up in bed, her fingers fiddling with the straw inside her water glass.

Asami had given her a loopy smile, the pain medication obviously doing the trick. "Oh Etta-san, I understand we have some major celebrating to do!"

"Yes, honey." Etta had kissed Asami's cheek. "How lucky we are. But what you've been through! I know you've always believed Hana mothered you more than you did her. But look at what you accomplished. How you located her. How your quick thinking kept her safe. Asami, you're something else!"

She'd laughed. "I am, aren't I? But, Etta-san, so are you."

That was the truth. They both were "something else."

Asami had demonstrated she could carry her own weight. Her admission to Sam—that Hana was his child—had been additional proof. Etta's sweet responsibility to her friend had been lightened. But that wasn't the major change in Etta's life. She'd finally be living the life she'd always imagined with Sam at her side.

Beneath the American elms, still bursting with yellow and golden hues, Etta watched in awe as Sam and his two daughters approached. A collection of shy and delighted glances danced between the three.

In the aftermath of the Pollards' arrest, Tripoint's Board of Directors had called an emergency meeting. Sam had unanimously been voted in as Tripoint's CEO. Sam's former COO position had been filled by Tripoint's VP of Operations, and Etta had readily accepted that VP's vacated New York position. A press release had announced those executive level changes, and Tripoint's IPO had fared much better than projected.

Both yakuza gangsters had fared much better as well. Kato and Hiro, along with the majority of their employees, had managed to elude the authorities by using a basement escape route. In a convoluted sense, Asami had pointed out that the two gangsters had actually honored their ancient Wada-kai creed.

Maybe that would provide some solace to Haruki.

Across the street, Etta could see the Dakota Apartments' high gables peeking through the trees. A new owner, most likely, would soon be occupying the Pollards' residence. Tom and Sylvia were awaiting arraignment on multiple charges as were Lorna Endo, her brother, and Deon. If Etta had her say, she'd have Deon's charges dropped entirely.

Hana had also decided to initiate a sexual harassment suit against Tom Pollard. She had the courage to do what Etta should've done decades before.

But it might not be too late for Etta.

With Hana leading the way, she and so many others were bound to come forward to add credence to Hana's claims.

Etta stood, the rose bouquet in hand, and she stepped toward the mosaic circle. Sam and his daughters joined her, and a swell of joy filled Etta's chest. She gazed over at Sam. "Your brother just arrived."

He smiled. "I know. Haruki called me as soon as he landed. I can't get over how he's actually initiating calls to me *and* talking about subjects that matter."

Etta touched Sam's arm. She knew how important that was to him. "And I bet among those is Asami." Etta tipped her head toward Hana. "These roses were delivered to your mama's hospital room while I was visiting. That's when Haruki entered with his own bouquet. He seemed flustered until your mama showed him the card inserted in the roses."

Hana grinned. "So they're from Jiro?"

"Yes. Your mama felt it was fitting for me to bring them to this spot." Etta carefully placed the bouquet on the mosaic. "For more than two decades, your mama and I have been sisters. As she would say, we've eaten from the same rice bowl, most of it tasty, some of it bitter, but we've always supported each other."

Chloe linked her arm into Hana's. "That will be the same for us, won't it, little sis?"

Hana laughed. "How cool is that!"

A shaft of sunlight pierced through the trees and spread across the "IMAGINE" mosaic.

Etta leaned against Sam and smiled, not just a little smile, but the contagious sort.

Their futures were waiting—every last one of them.

READING GROUP GUIDE

1. Have you or anyone you've known experienced sexual harassment in the workplace as Etta did? Any date rape like Asami's? If so, how was it handled? Were the issues reported? Why or why not?

2. Are there any pivotal events in your life where, if you'd taken a different path, you believe your life or your children's may have been far different?

3. Do you feel it was right for Etta and Asami to hide the fact that Sam was their daughters' father from Sam? Why or why not?

4. How are today's ideologies different from those Etta and Asami experienced in the '70s and '80s?

5. Could you relate to the four mothers (Etta, Asami, Sylvia Pollard, and Lorna Endo)? Would you do whatever it took to protect your children? Why or why not?

6. What surprised you most about the book?

7. How did Asami and Etta's cultural and gender factors affect their lives? Do you think they were realistically portrayed?

8. Did any of the book characters remind you of yourself or someone you know? In what way?

9. What past influences shaped the actions of the book's characters?

10. Did you think the ending was appropriate? If not, how would you have changed it?

11. Was the book title DESPRATE PARALLELS appropriate? If not, what would your title be?

ABOUT THE AUTHOR

Lynda Drews, a Wisconsin native, gave the commencement speech at her University of Wisconsin-La Crosse alma mater. She encouraged students to journal their lives as she had. In 2009, *Run at Destruction: A True Fatal Love Triangle* was the outcome. Publisher's Weekly said: "the author and victim's shared moments... are remarkable." The Investigation Discovery Channel filmed a segment based on that book, and it was endorsed by Ann Rule, the best-selling true crime author.

Lynda's Door County, Wisconsin mystery novel, *Circle of Innocence*, was published in 2014. Midwest Book Review said it "excels in psychological depth," and Brian Freeman, the best-selling author of *The Bone House*, endorsed it.

Desperate Parallels was inspired by Lynda's IBM global executive career. While working in America and Japan, she learned first-hand the issues women faced, and continue to face, in the corporate business world.

When Lynda's not writing, she teaches classes for WRITE ON DOOR COUNTY, reads, runs, knits, plays bridge, and drinks coffee. The latter is a necessity, even at bedtime.

www.lyndadrews.com

Made in the USA
Columbia, SC
06 December 2018